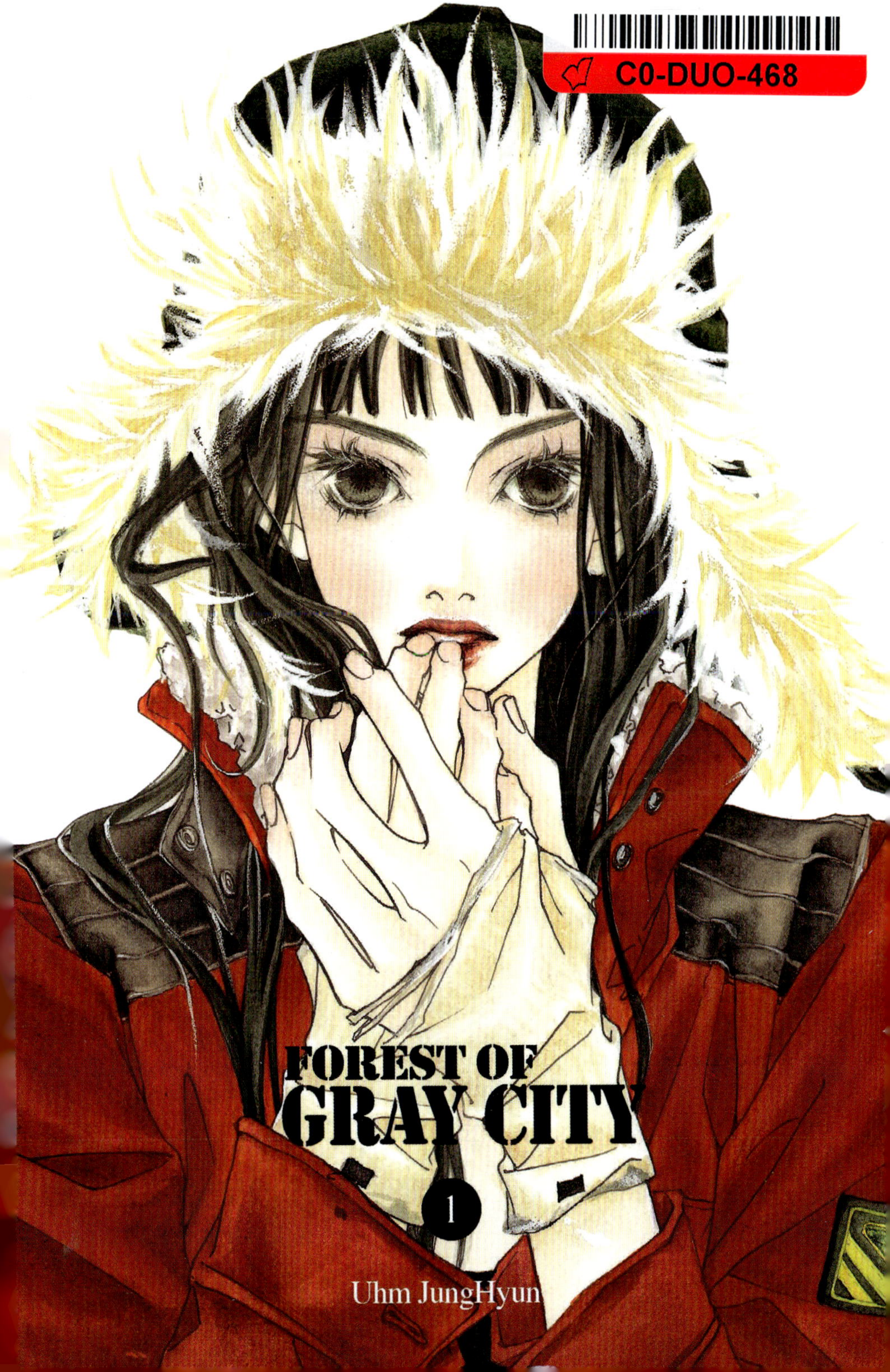
FOREST OF
GRAY CITY
1
Uhm JungHyun

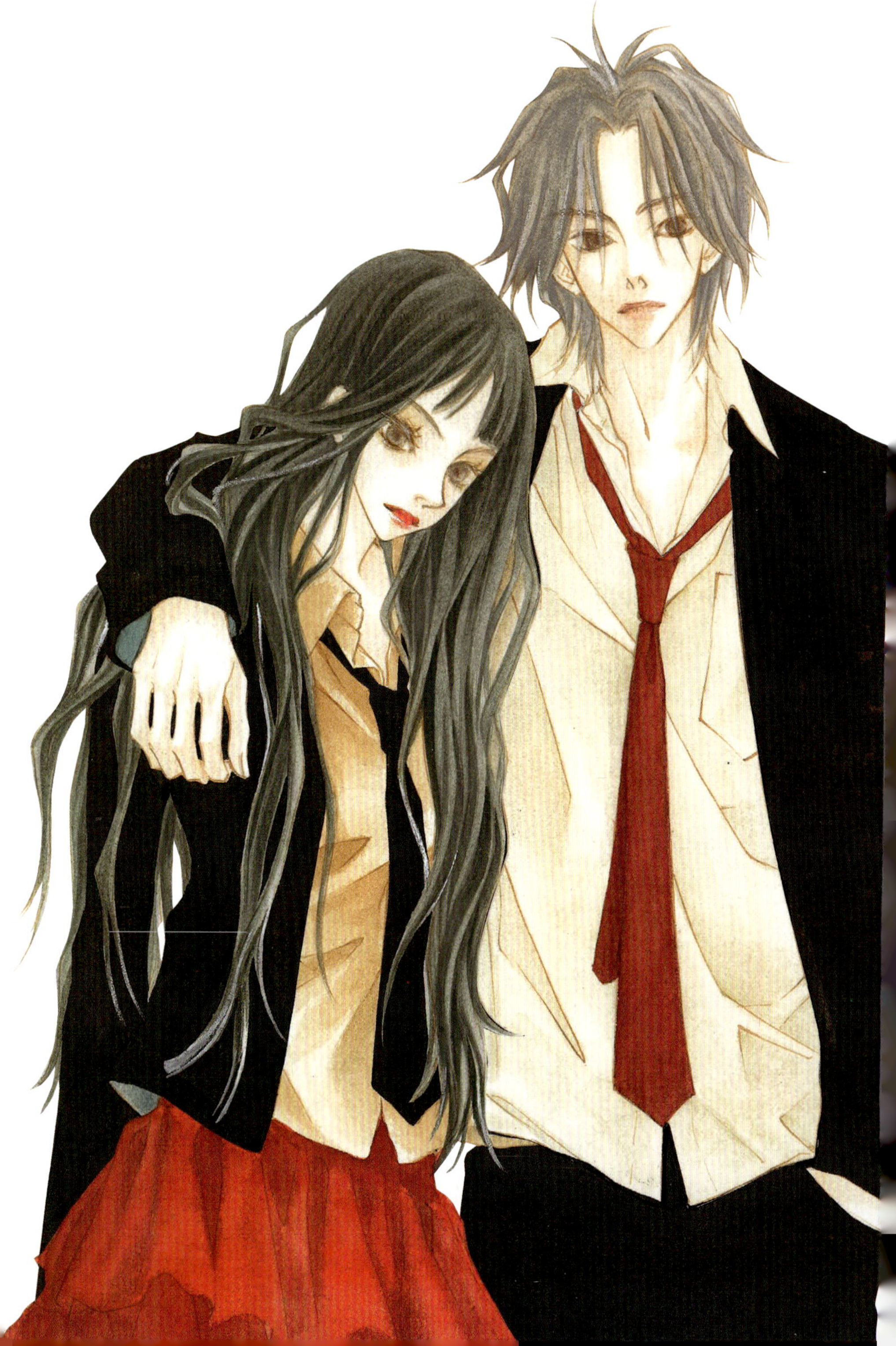

About the Creator

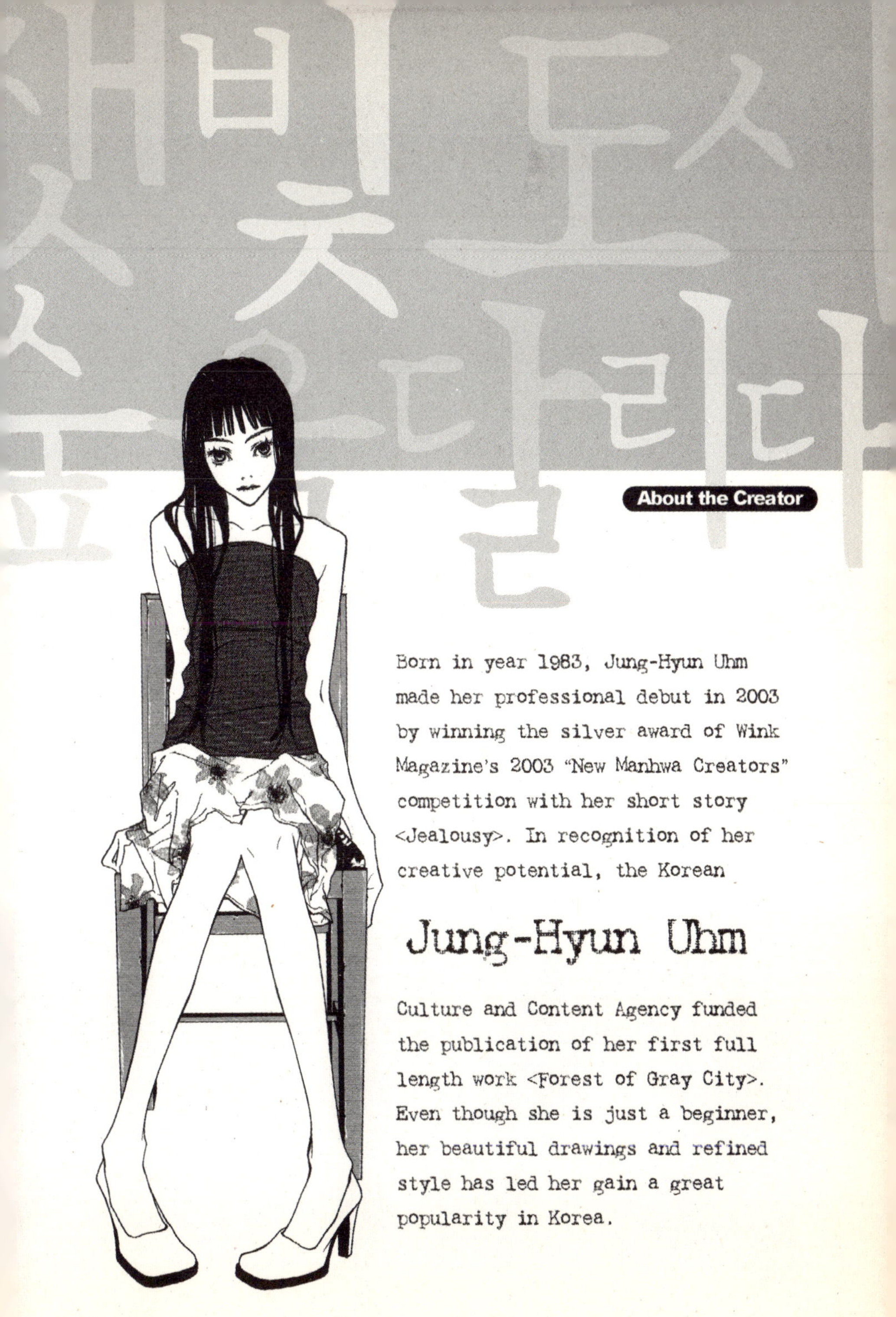

Born in year 1983, Jung-Hyun Uhm made her professional debut in 2003 by winning the silver award of Wink Magazine's 2003 "New Manhwa Creators" competition with her short story <Jealousy>. In recognition of her creative potential, the Korean

Jung-Hyun Uhm

Culture and Content Agency funded the publication of her first full length work <Forest of Gray City>. Even though she is just a beginner, her beautiful drawings and refined style has led her gain a great popularity in Korea.

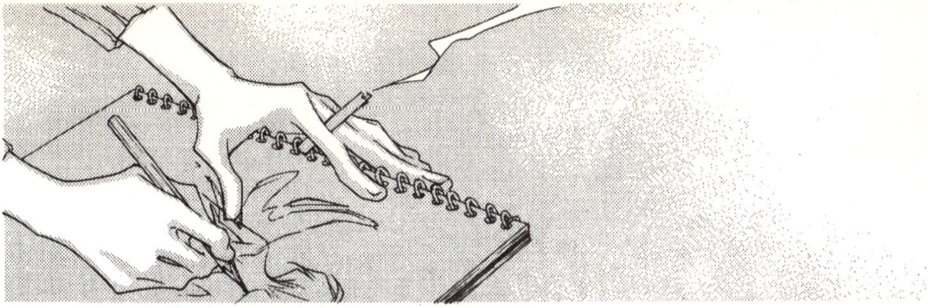

HE APPEARS BEFORE DAWN AND
STANDS THERE FOR A WHILE.

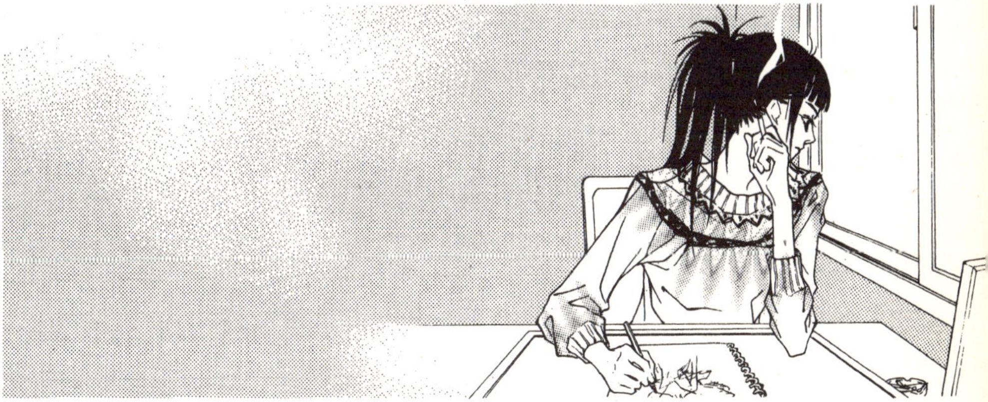

HE DISAPPEARS SOMETIME AFTER
THE SUN RISES.

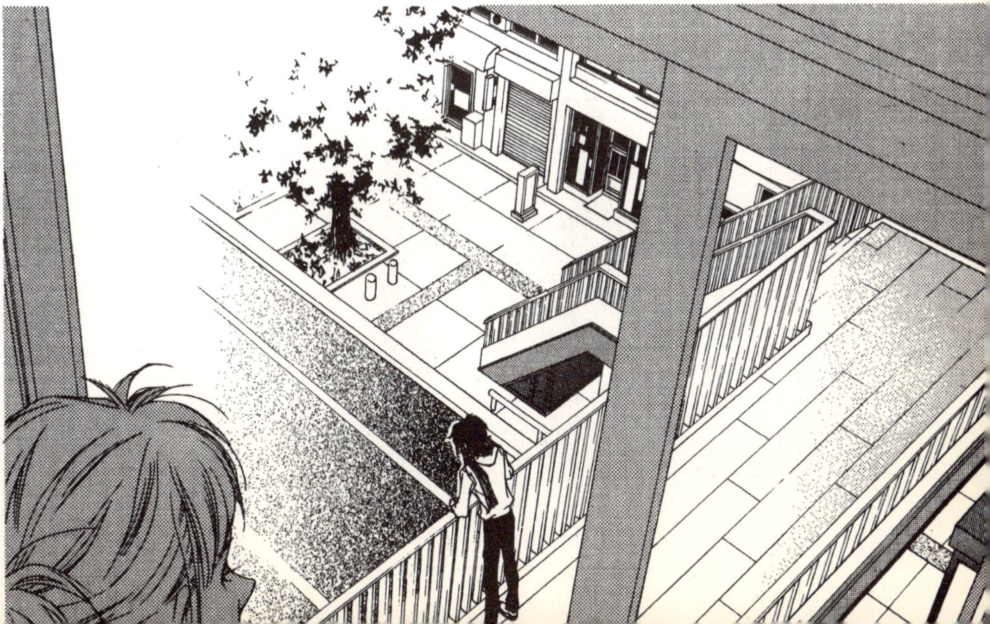

WHAT IS HE LOOKING AT?

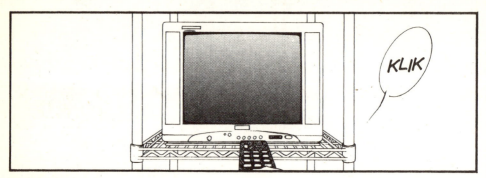

KLIK

NOTHING ON TV.

I SHOULDN'T LOAF AROUND ANYWAY...

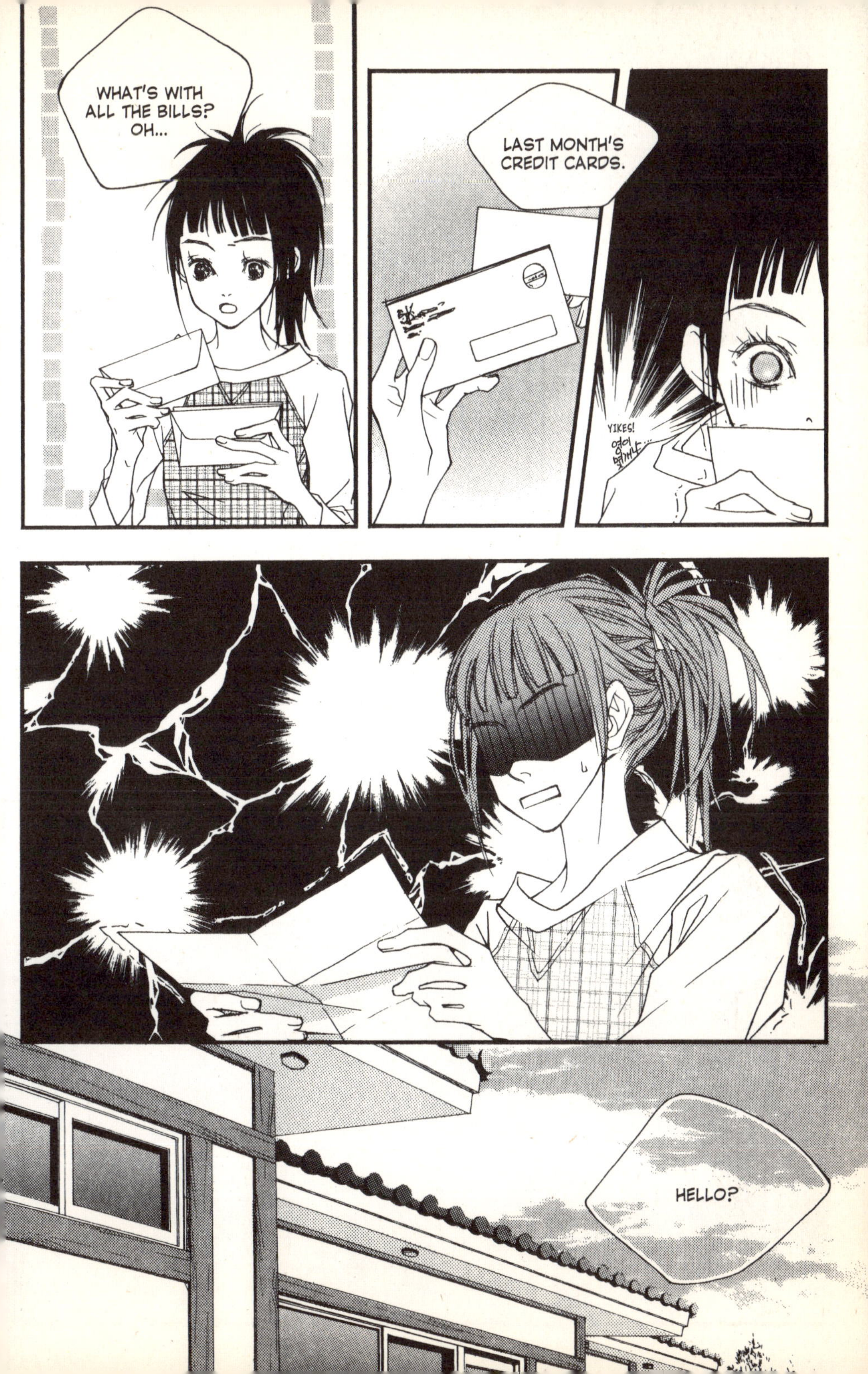
WHAT'S WITH ALL THE BILLS? OH...
LAST MONTH'S CREDIT CARDS.
YIKES!
영이 몇개냐...
HELLO?

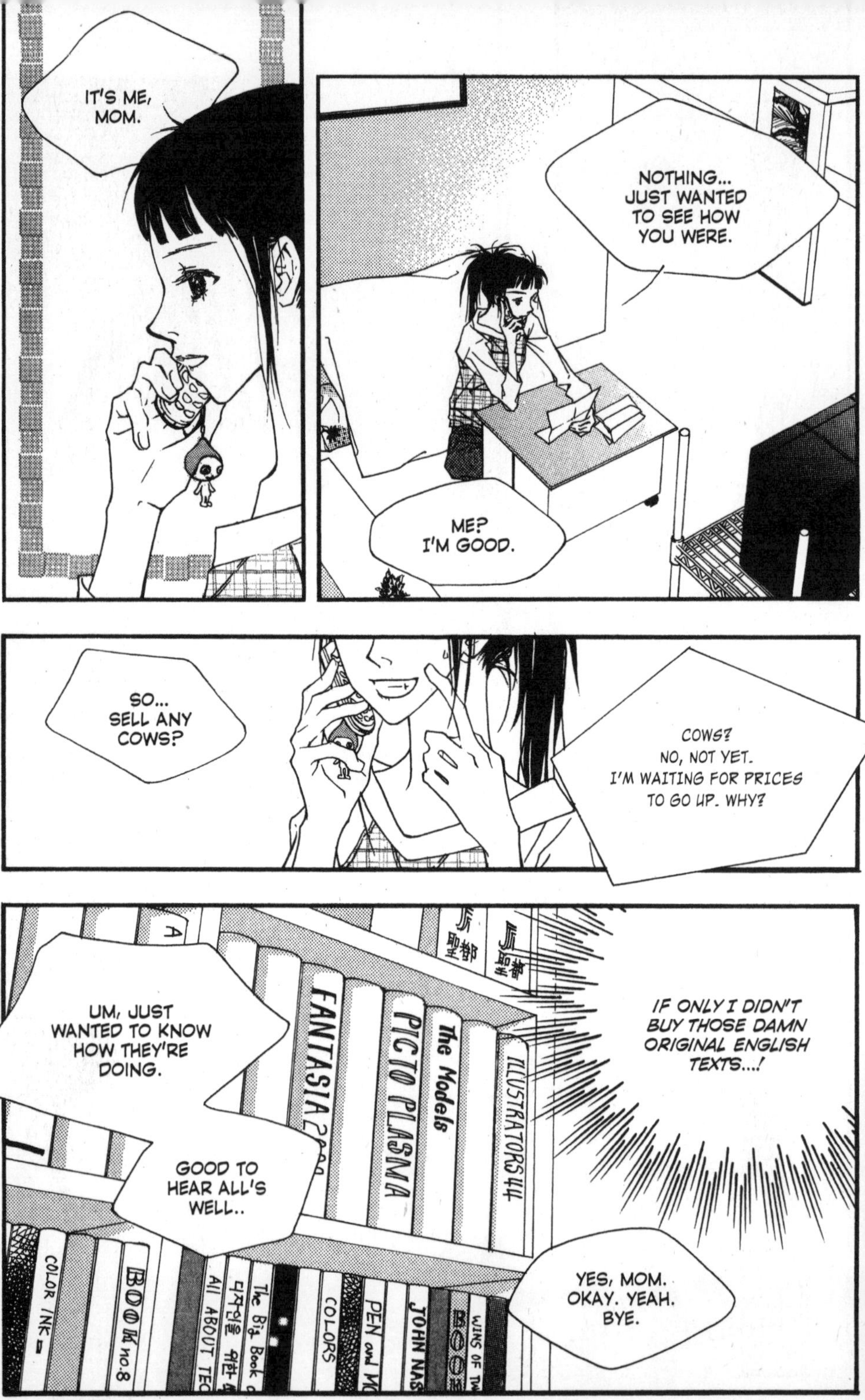
IT'S ME, MOM.
NOTHING... JUST WANTED TO SEE HOW YOU WERE.
ME? I'M GOOD.
SO... SELL ANY COWS?
COWS? NO, NOT YET. I'M WAITING FOR PRICES TO GO UP. WHY?
UM, JUST WANTED TO KNOW HOW THEY'RE DOING.
GOOD TO HEAR ALL'S WELL..
IF ONLY I DIDN'T BUY THOSE DAMN ORIGINAL ENGLISH TEXTS...!
YES, MOM. OKAY. YEAH. BYE.
FANTASIA
PICTO PLASMA
The Models
ILLUSTRATORS 44
COLOR INK
COLORS

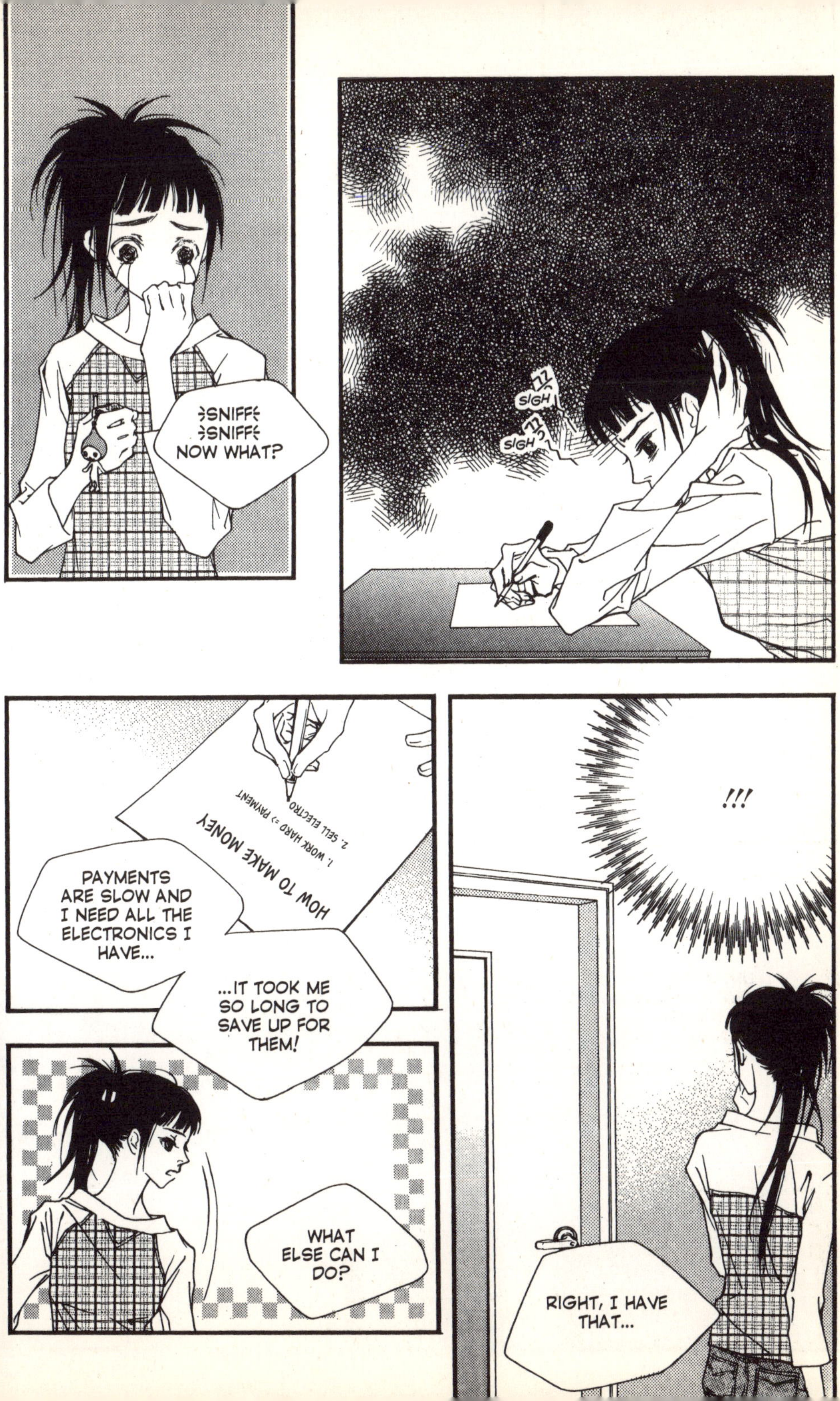

SNIFF
SNIFF
NOW WHAT?
SIGH
SIGH
HOW TO MAKE MONEY
1. WORK HARD => PAYMENT
2. SELL ELECTRO
PAYMENTS ARE SLOW AND I NEED ALL THE ELECTRONICS I HAVE...
...IT TOOK ME SO LONG TO SAVE UP FOR THEM!
WHAT ELSE CAN I DO?
!!!
RIGHT, I HAVE THAT...

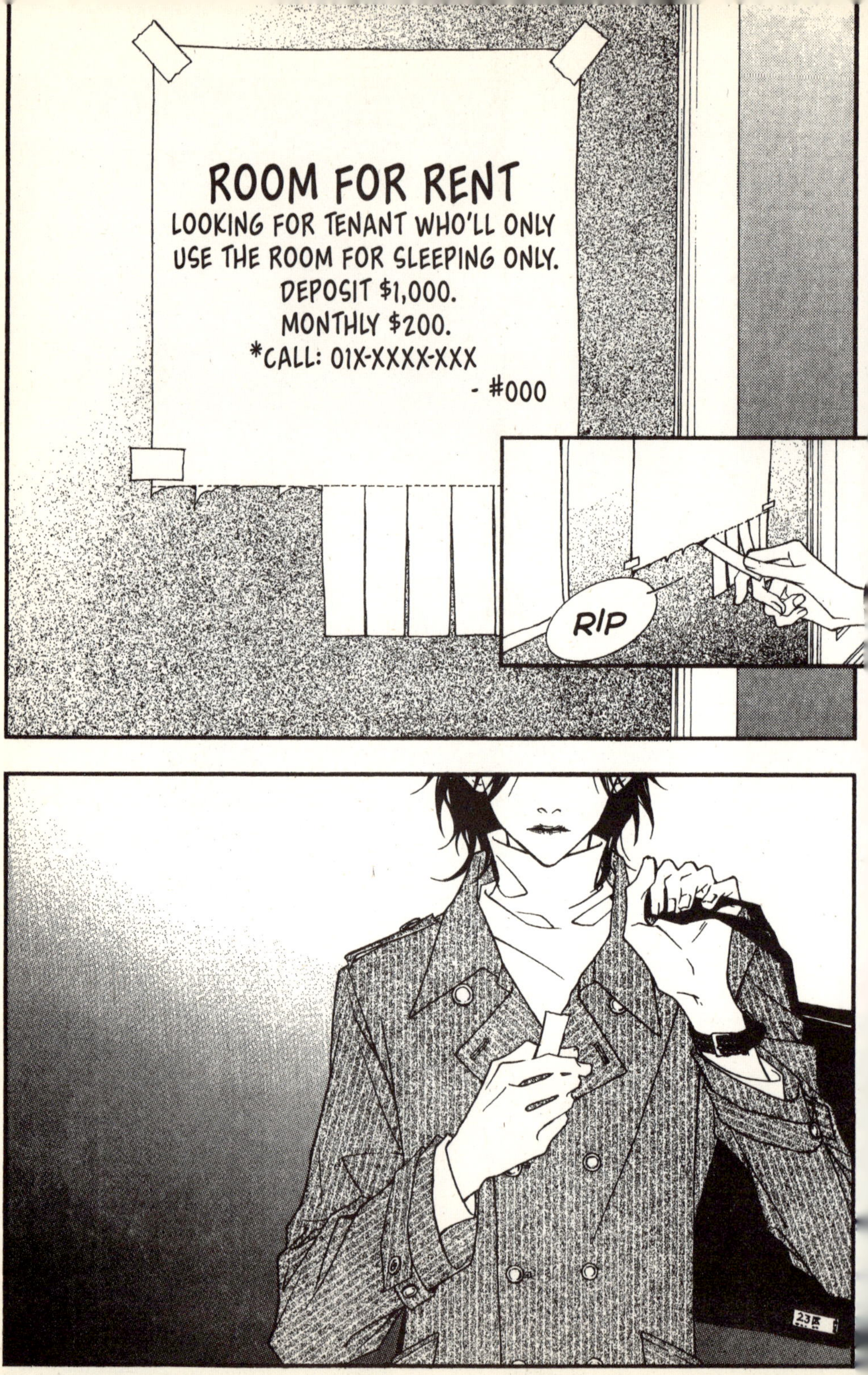
ROOM FOR RENT
LOOKING FOR TENANT WHO'LL ONLY
USE THE ROOM FOR SLEEPING ONLY.
DEPOSIT $1,000.
MONTHLY $200.
*CALL: 01X-XXXX-XXX
- #000
RIP

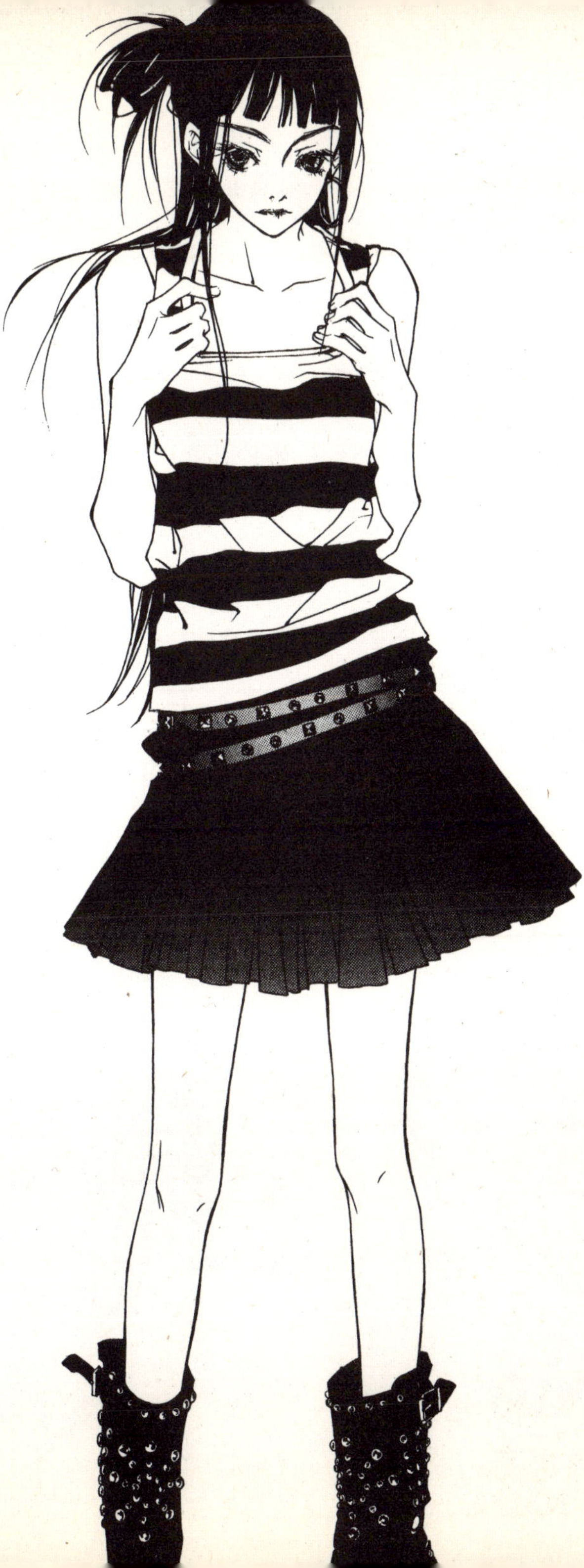

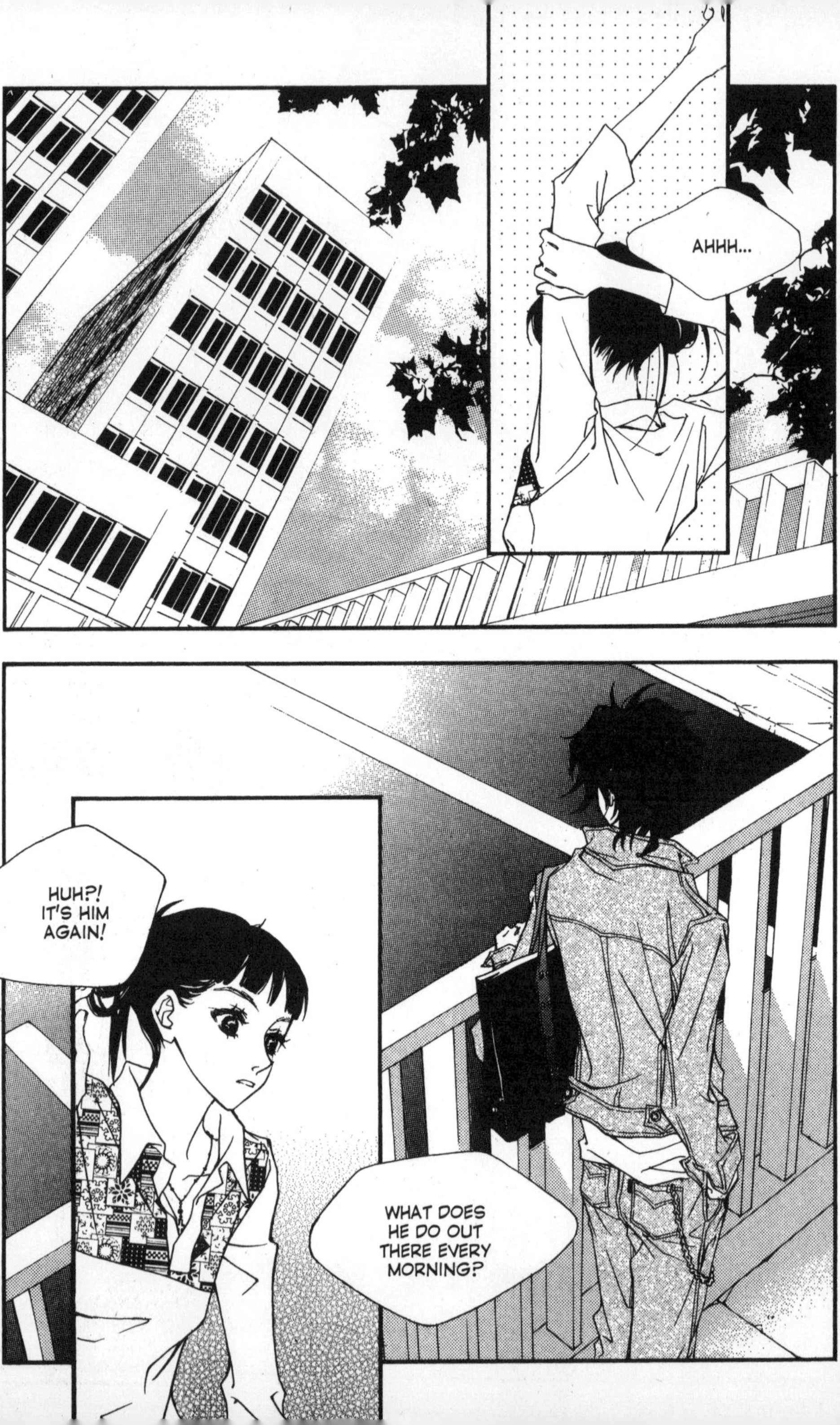
AHHH...
HUH?! IT'S HIM AGAIN!
WHAT DOES HE DO OUT THERE EVERY MORNING?

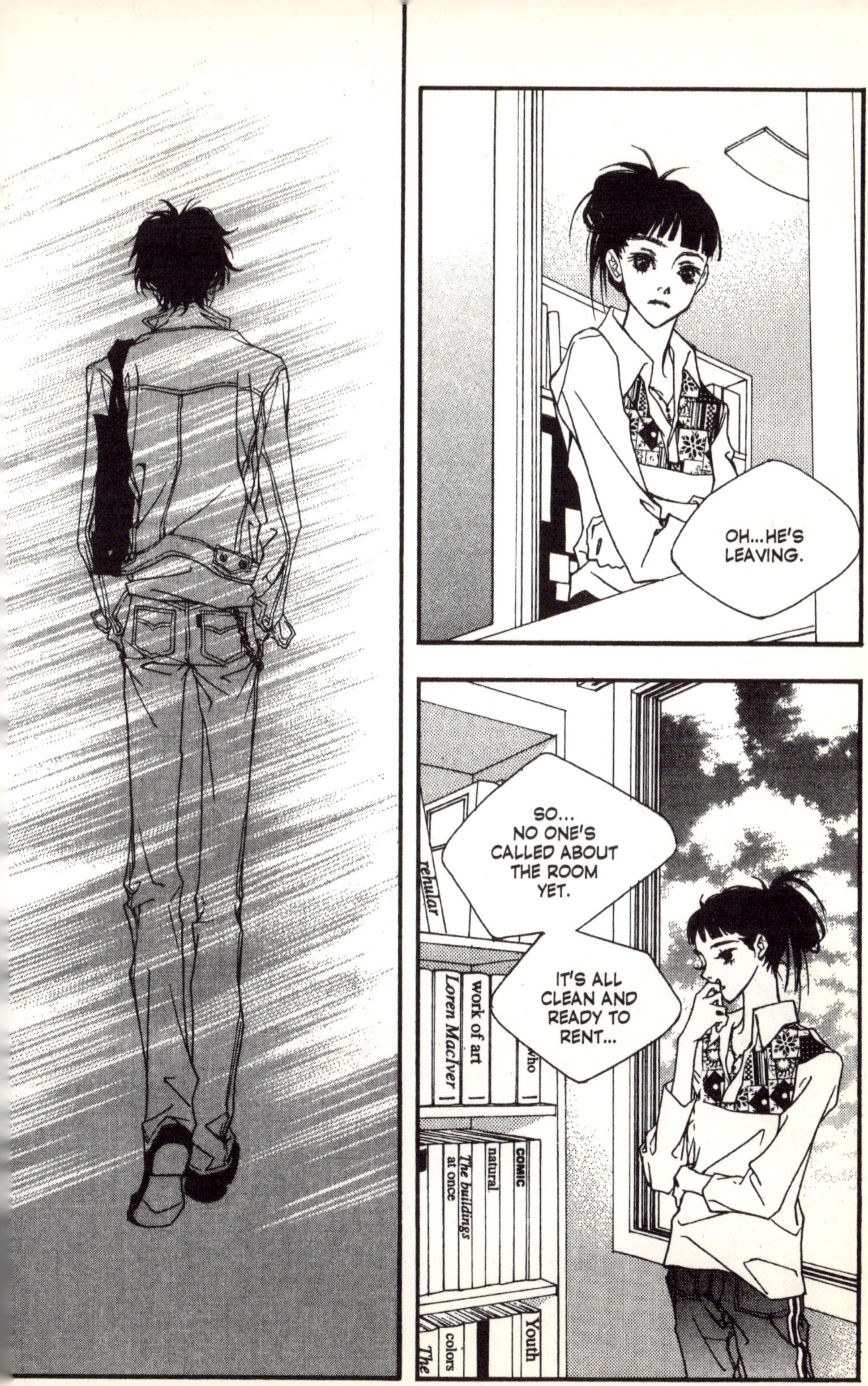
OH...HE'S LEAVING.
SO... NO ONE'S CALLED ABOUT THE ROOM YET.
IT'S ALL CLEAN AND READY TO RENT...
rehular
Loren MacIver
work of art
who
The buildings at once
natural
COMIC
colors
Youth
The

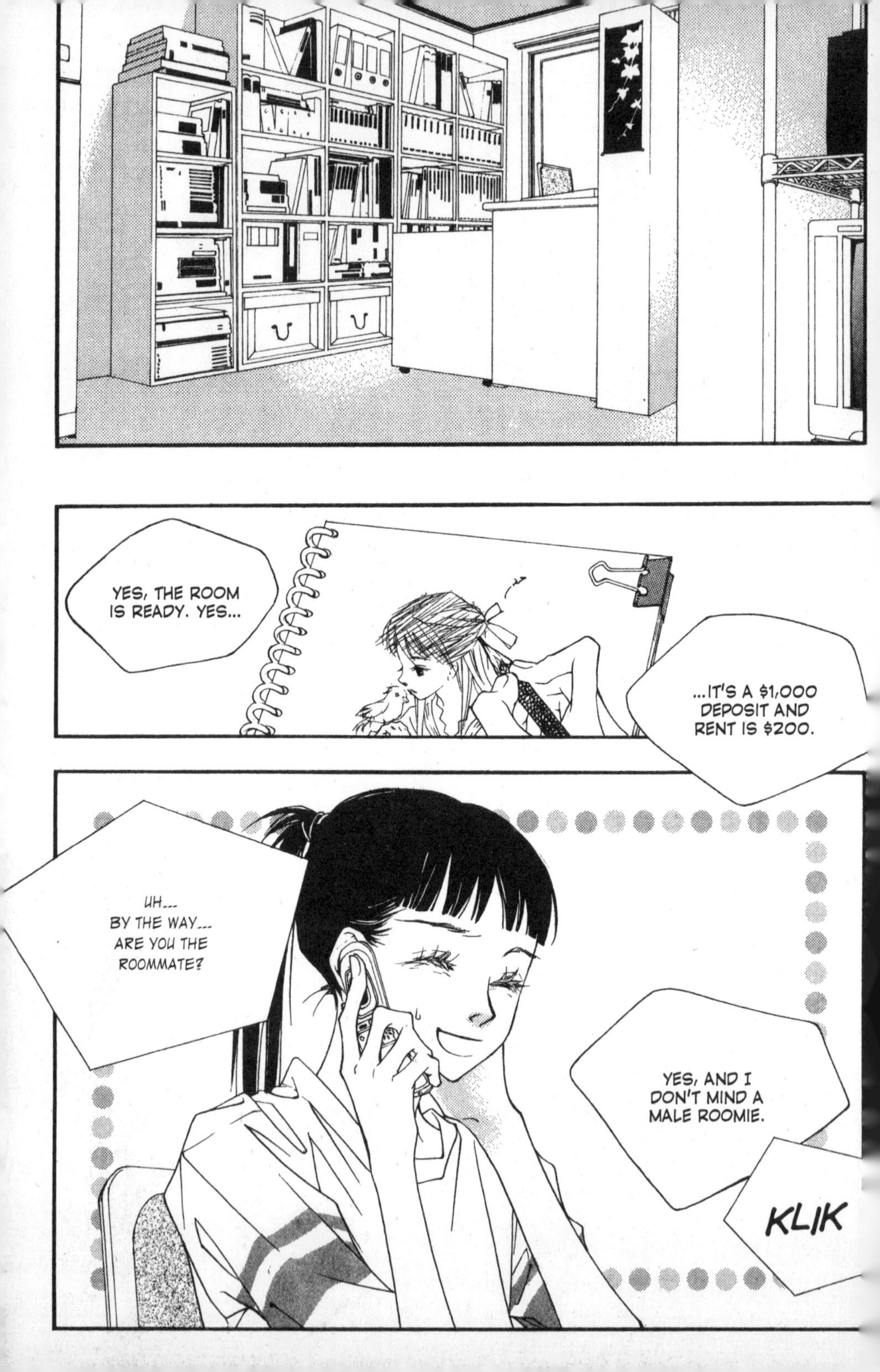
YES, THE ROOM IS READY. YES...
...IT'S A $1,000 DEPOSIT AND RENT IS $200.
UH... BY THE WAY... ARE YOU THE ROOMMATE?
YES, AND I DON'T MIND A MALE ROOMIE.
KLIK

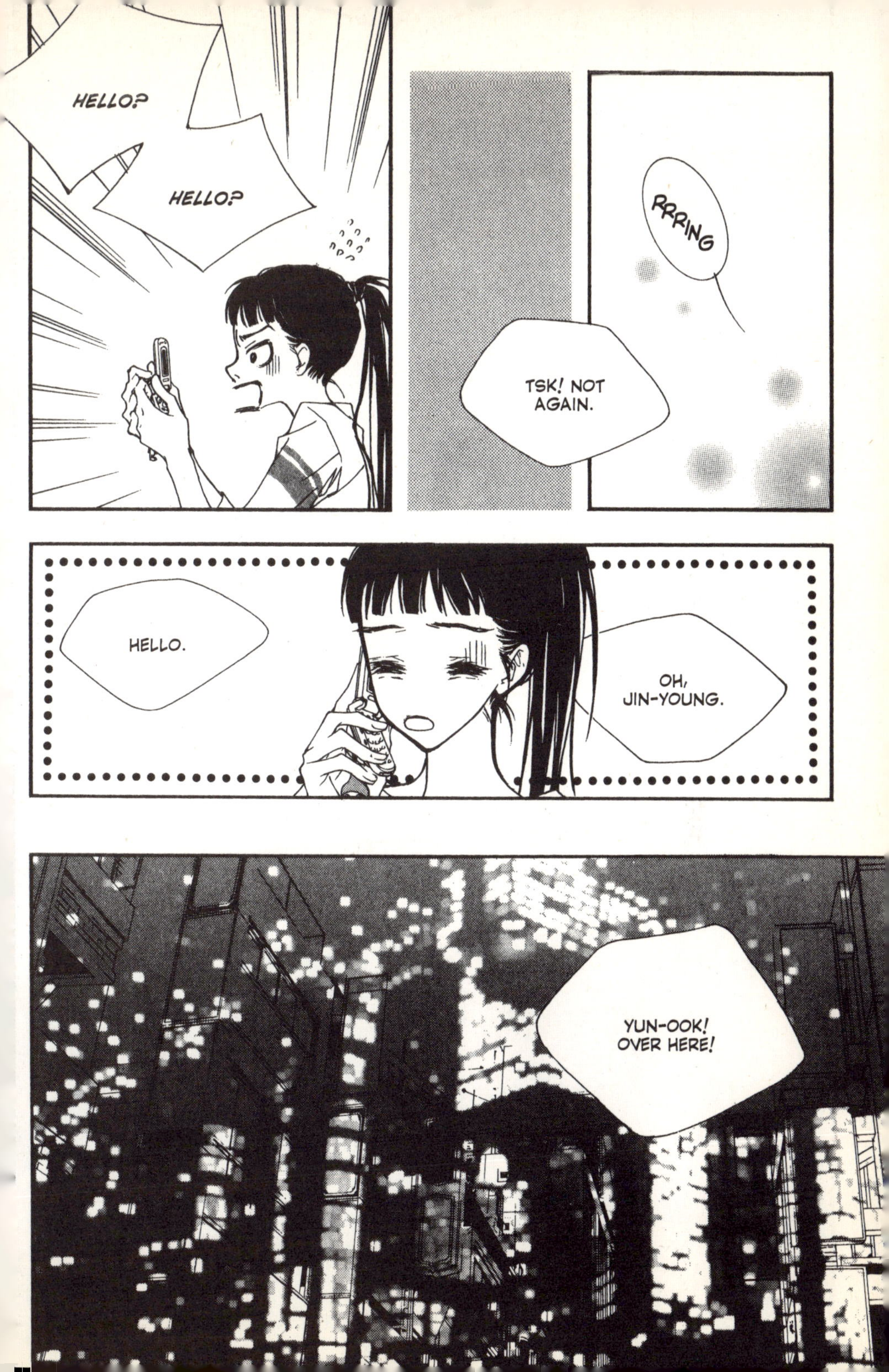
HELLO?
HELLO?
RRRING
TSK! NOT AGAIN.
HELLO.
OH, JIN-YOUNG.
YUN-OOK! OVER HERE!

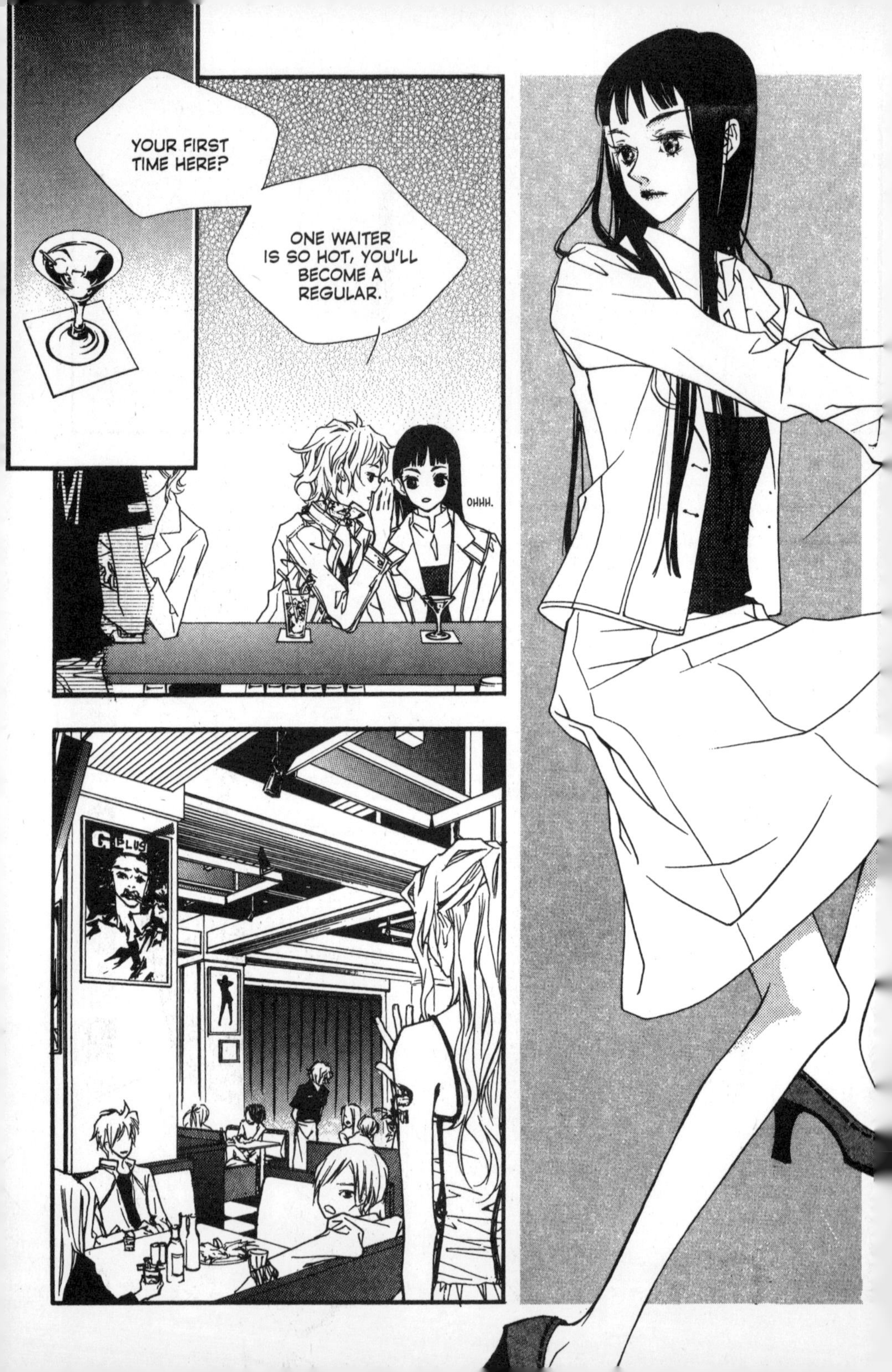
YOUR FIRST TIME HERE?
ONE WAITER IS SO HOT, YOU'LL BECOME A REGULAR.
OHHH.

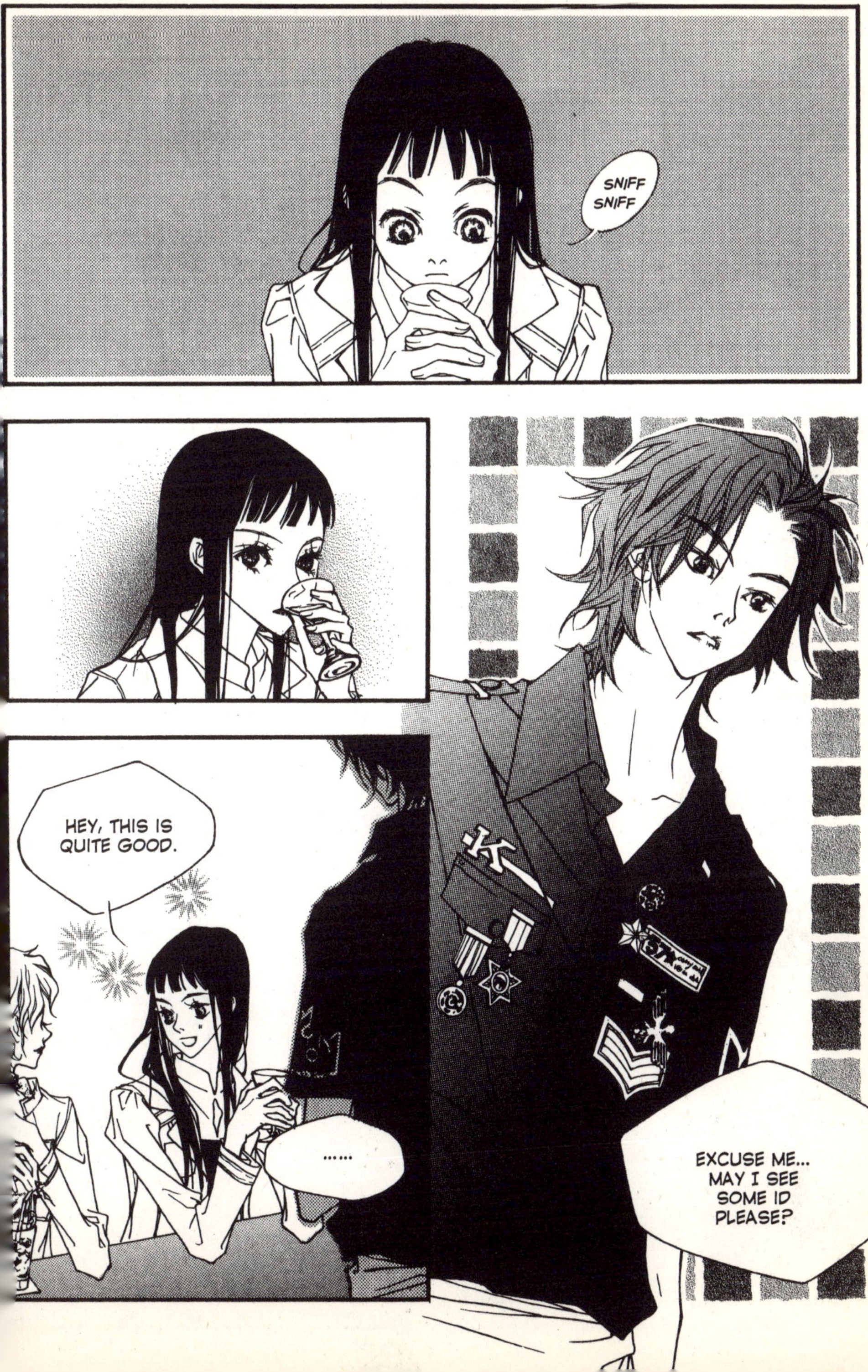
SNIFF SNIFF
HEY, THIS IS QUITE GOOD.
......
EXCUSE ME... MAY I SEE SOME ID PLEASE?

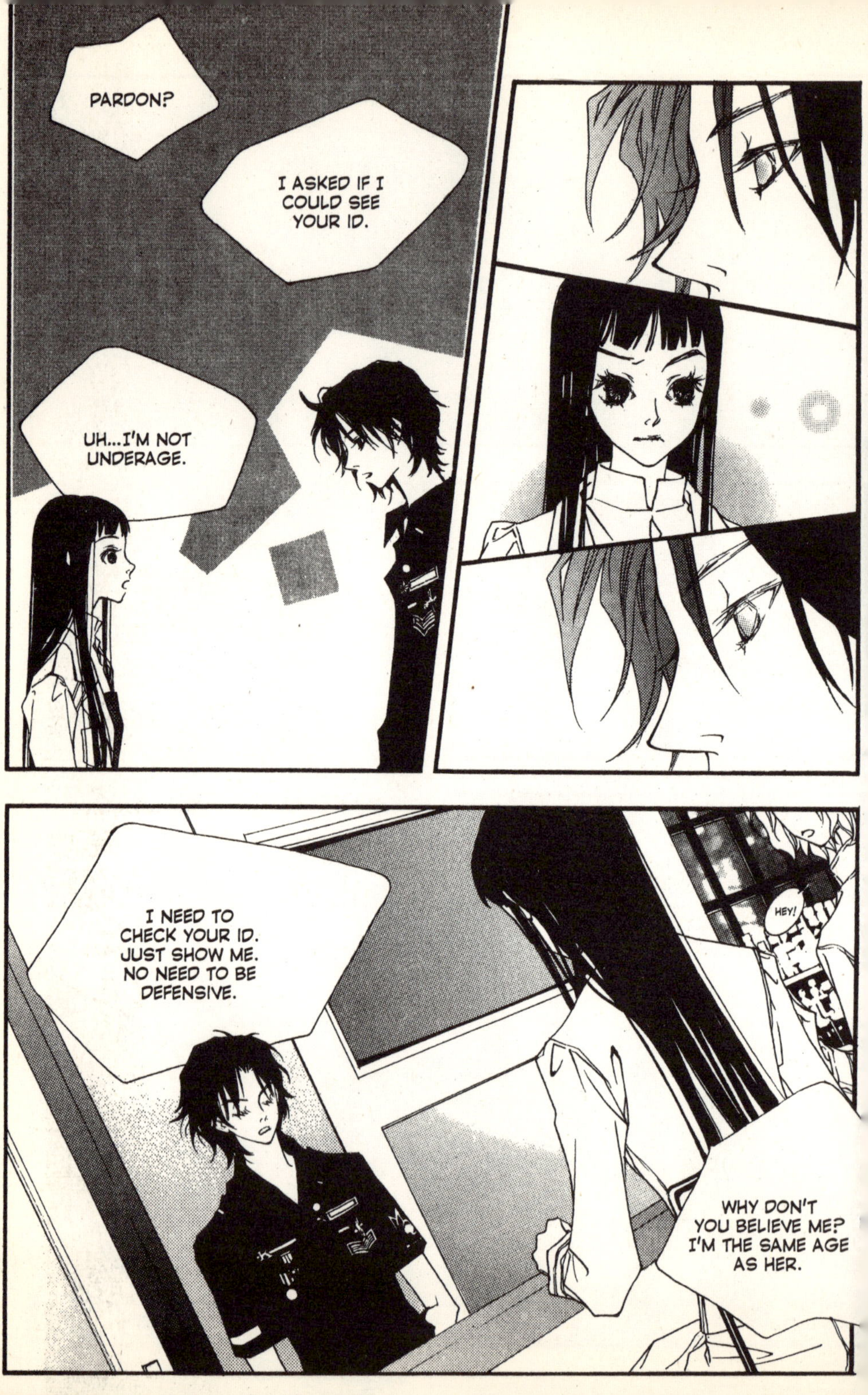
PARDON?
I ASKED IF I COULD SEE YOUR ID.
UH...I'M NOT UNDERAGE.
I NEED TO CHECK YOUR ID. JUST SHOW ME. NO NEED TO BE DEFENSIVE.
HEY!
WHY DON'T YOU BELIEVE ME? I'M THE SAME AGE AS HER.

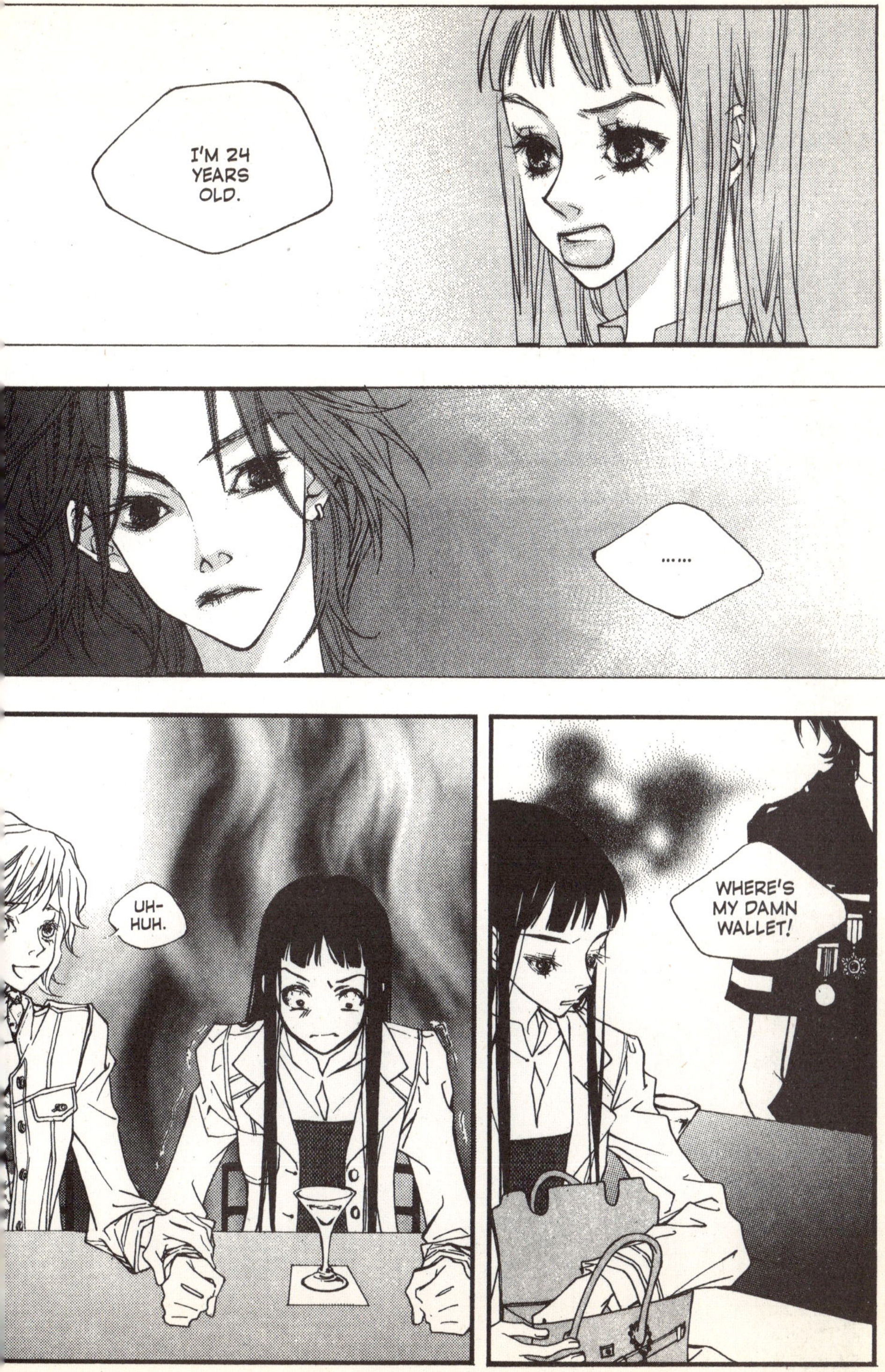
I'M 24 YEARS OLD.
……
WHERE'S MY DAMN WALLET!
UH-HUH.

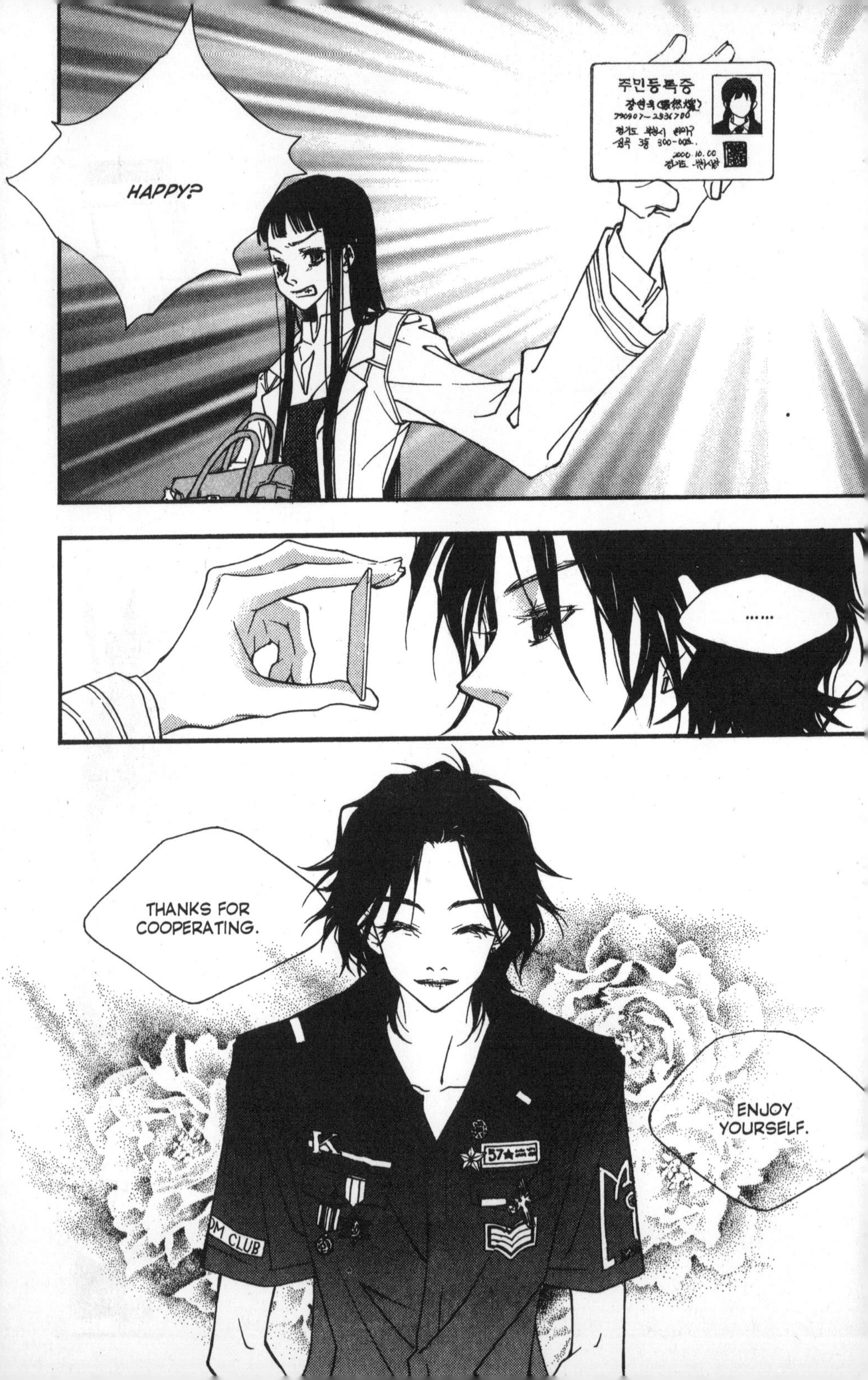

주민등록증
HAPPY?
......
THANKS FOR COOPERATING.
ENJOY YOURSELF.

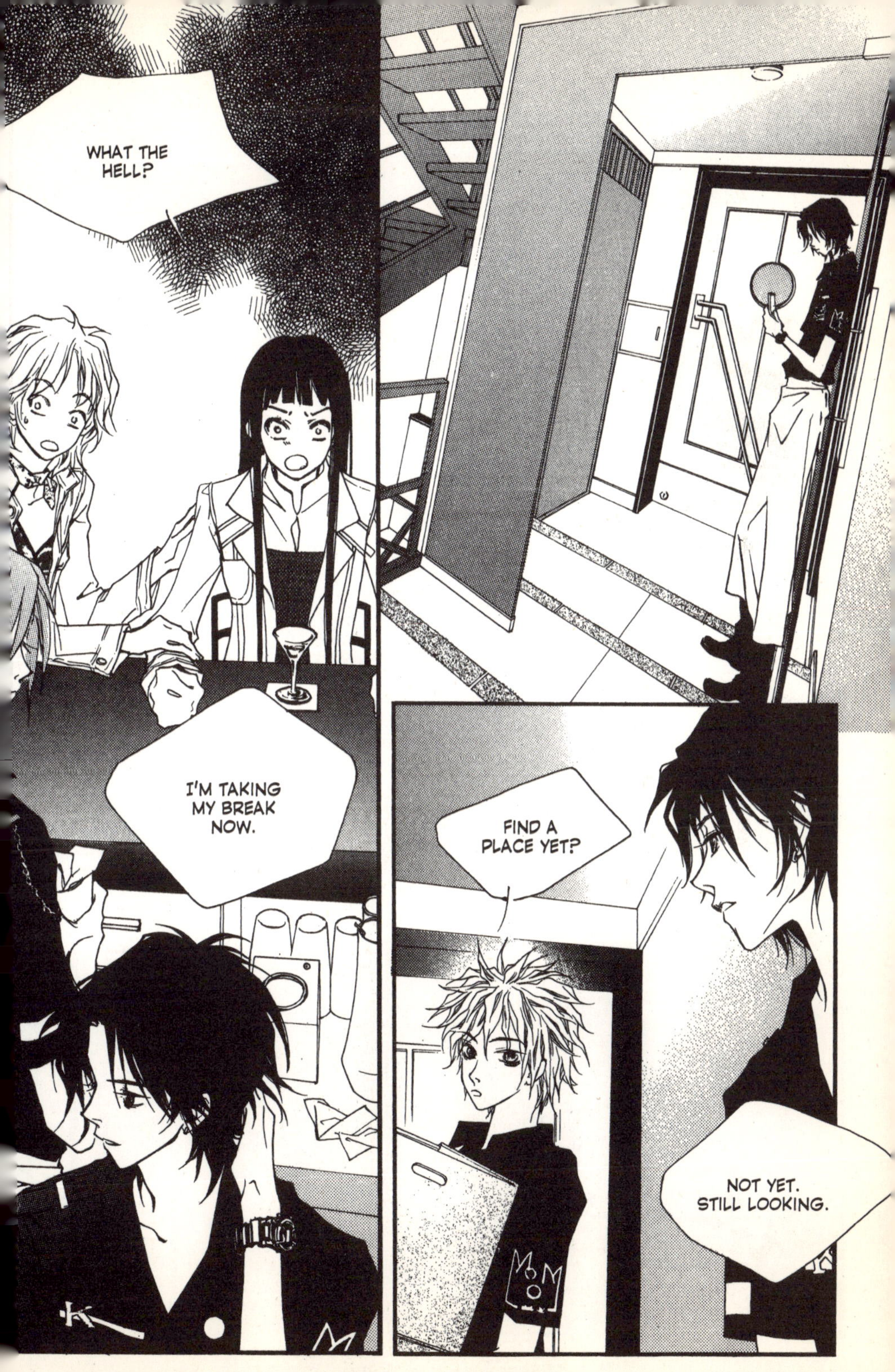
WHAT THE HELL?
I'M TAKING MY BREAK NOW.
FIND A PLACE YET?
NOT YET. STILL LOOKING.

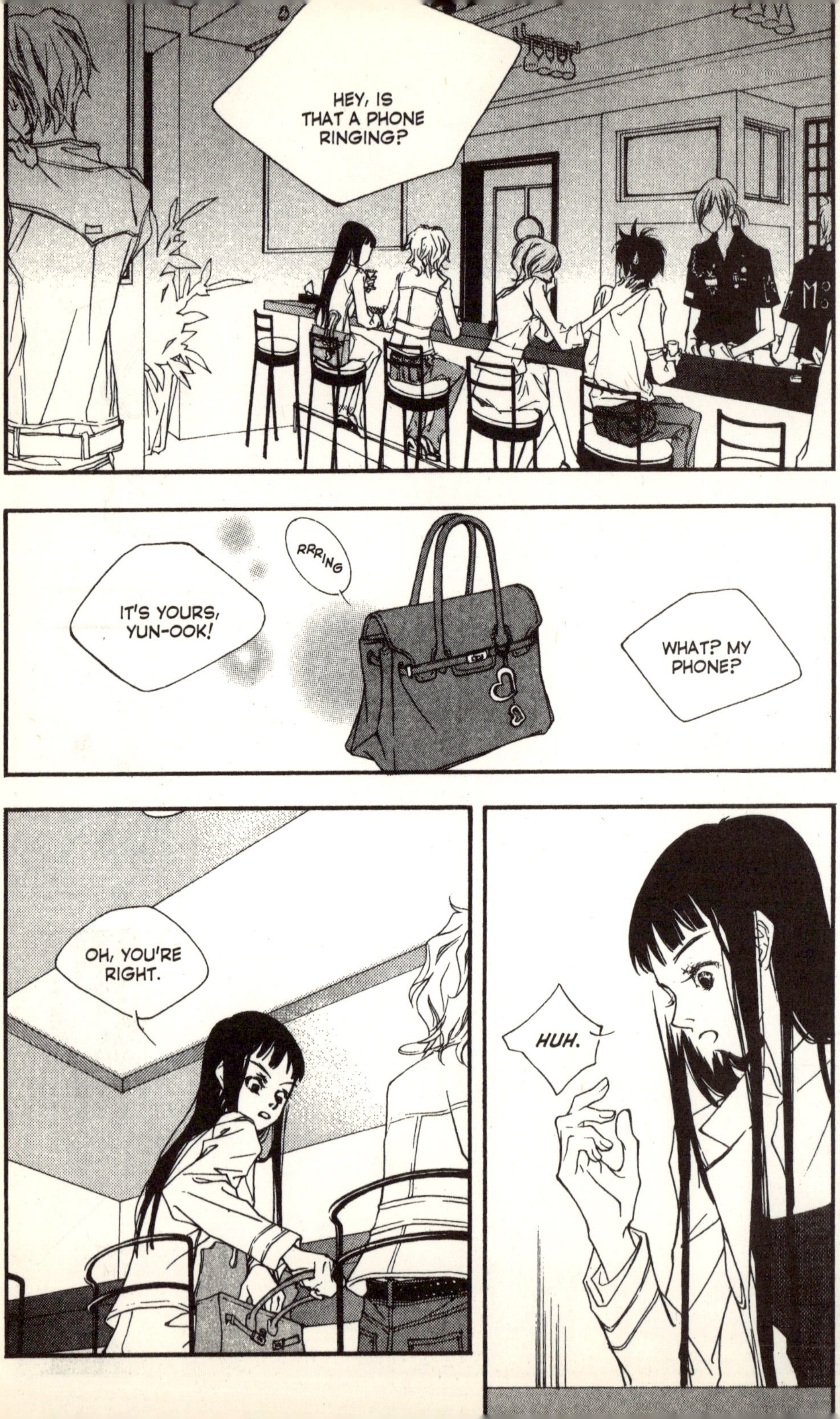
HEY, IS THAT A PHONE RINGING?
IT'S YOURS, YUN-OOK!
RRRING
WHAT? MY PHONE?
OH, YOU'RE RIGHT.
HUH.

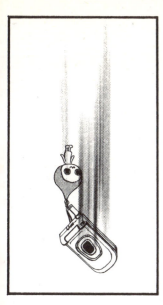

ARGH!

THE CUSTOMER YOU ARE TRYING TO REACH IS UNAVAILABLE. PLEASE LEAVE--.

OH, NO...

HE OR SHE'LL CALL BACK.

HOPE IT'S NOT BUSTED. I'M BROKE...

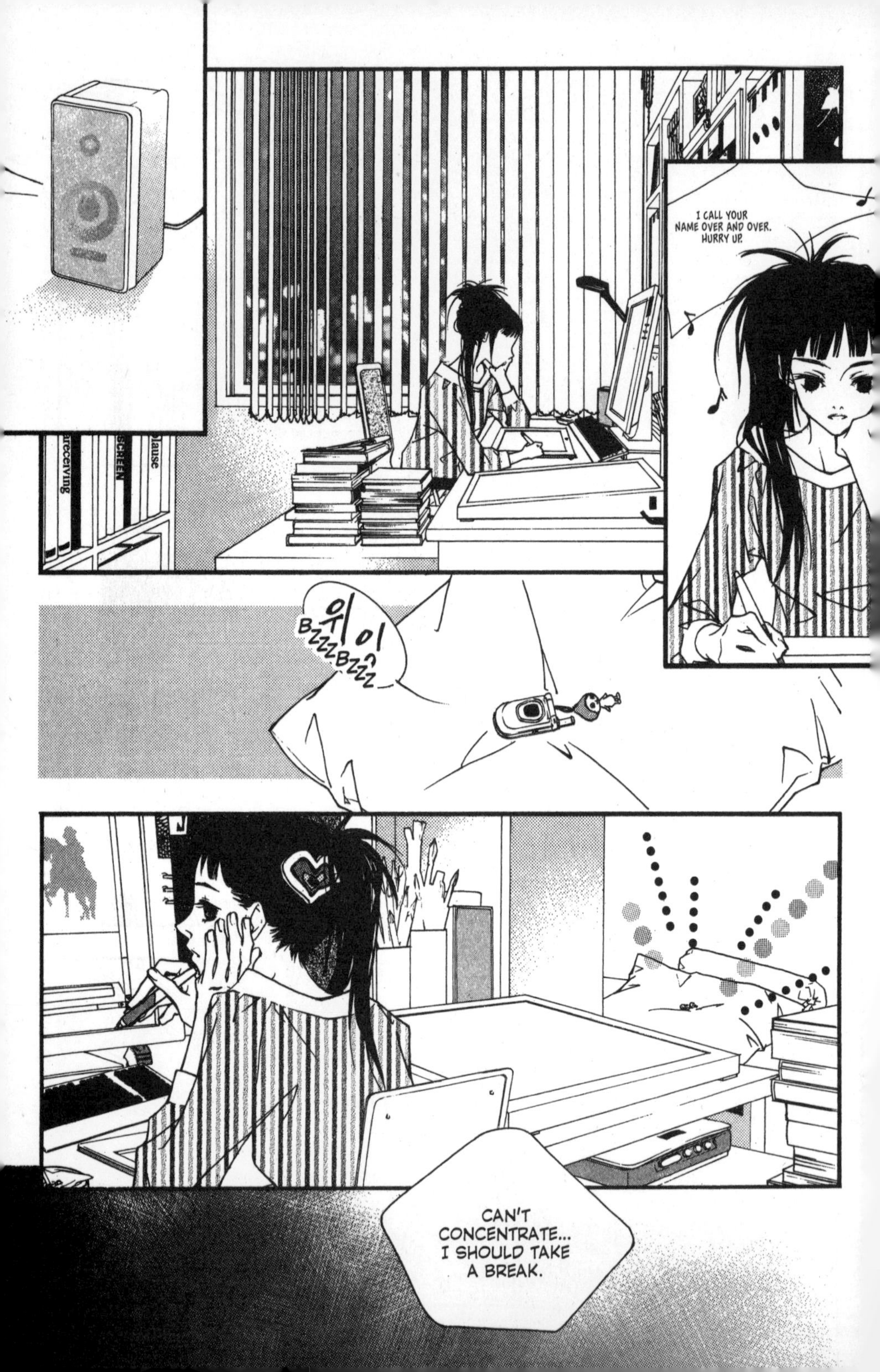
I CALL YOUR NAME OVER AND OVER. HURRY UP.
위이잉
BZZZ BZZZ
CAN'T CONCENTRATE... I SHOULD TAKE A BREAK.

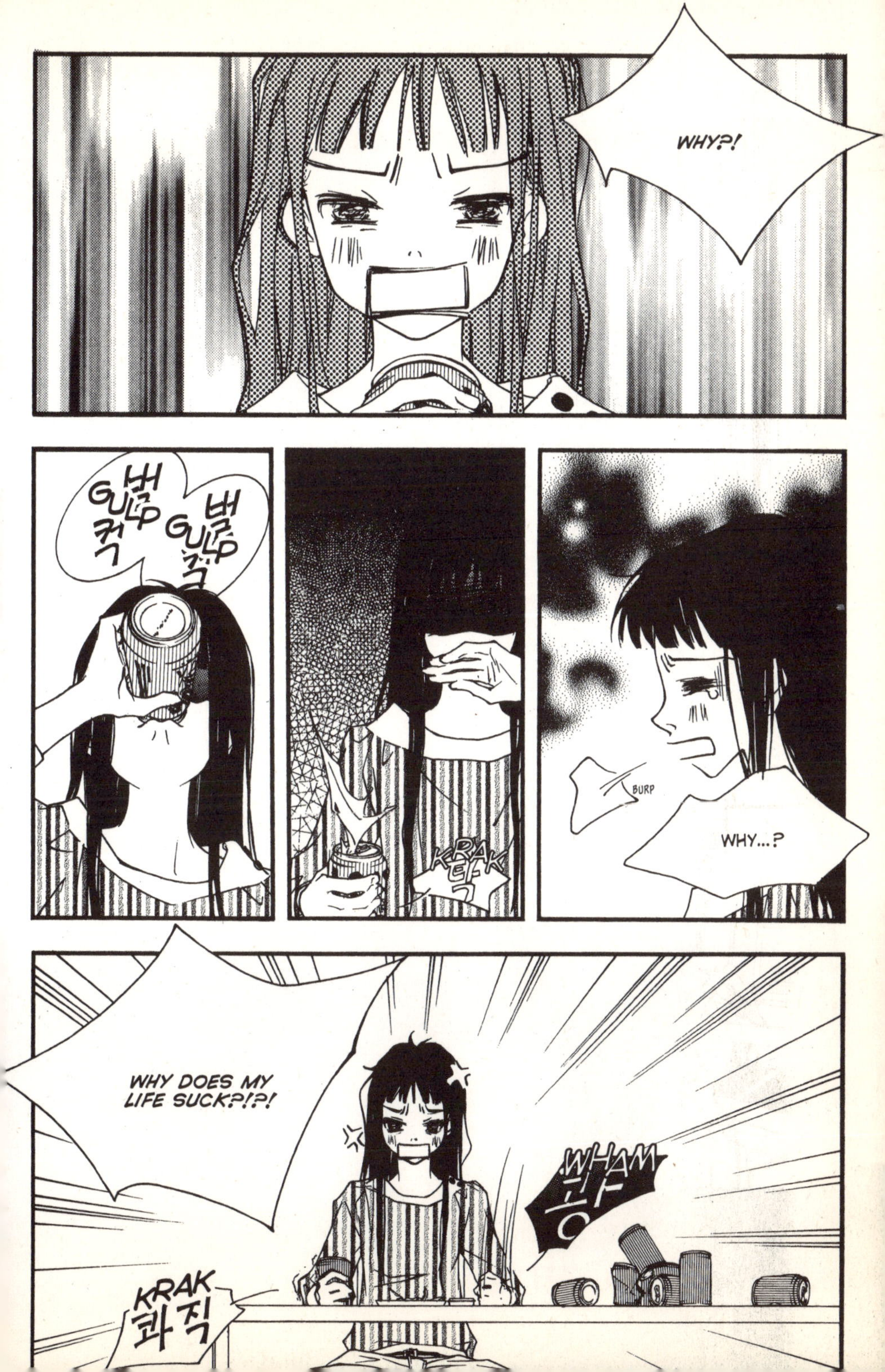
WHY?!
GULP
벌컥
GULP
벌컥
KRAK
탁
BURP
WHY...?
WHY DOES MY LIFE SUCK?!?!
WHAM
쾅
KRAK
콰직

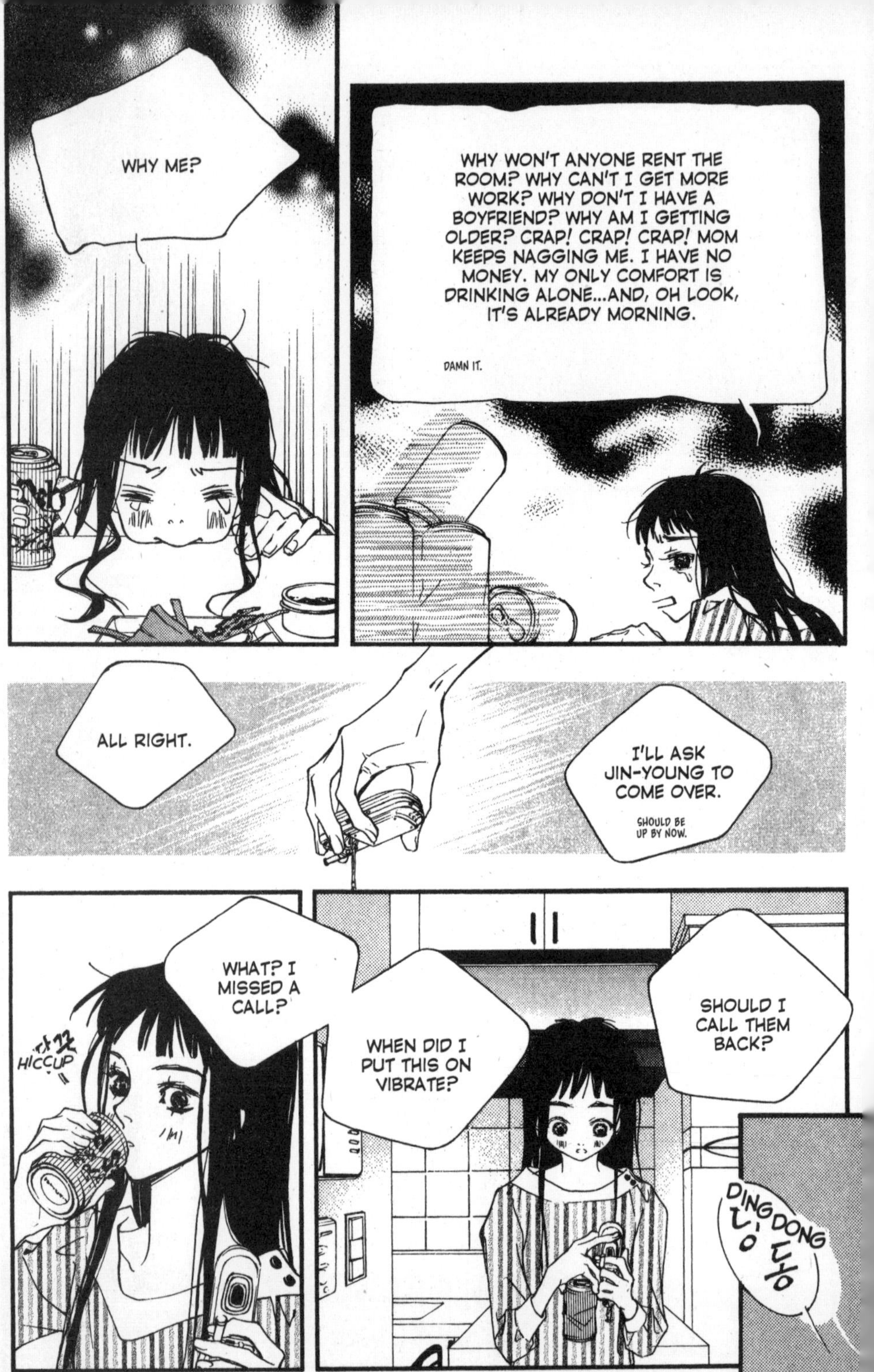

WHY ME?
WHY WON'T ANYONE RENT THE ROOM? WHY CAN'T I GET MORE WORK? WHY DON'T I HAVE A BOYFRIEND? WHY AM I GETTING OLDER? CRAP! CRAP! CRAP! MOM KEEPS NAGGING ME. I HAVE NO MONEY. MY ONLY COMFORT IS DRINKING ALONE...AND, OH LOOK, IT'S ALREADY MORNING.
DAMN IT.
ALL RIGHT.
I'LL ASK JIN-YOUNG TO COME OVER.
SHOULD BE UP BY NOW.
WHAT? I MISSED A CALL?
HICCUP
WHEN DID I PUT THIS ON VIBRATE?
SHOULD I CALL THEM BACK?
DING DONG

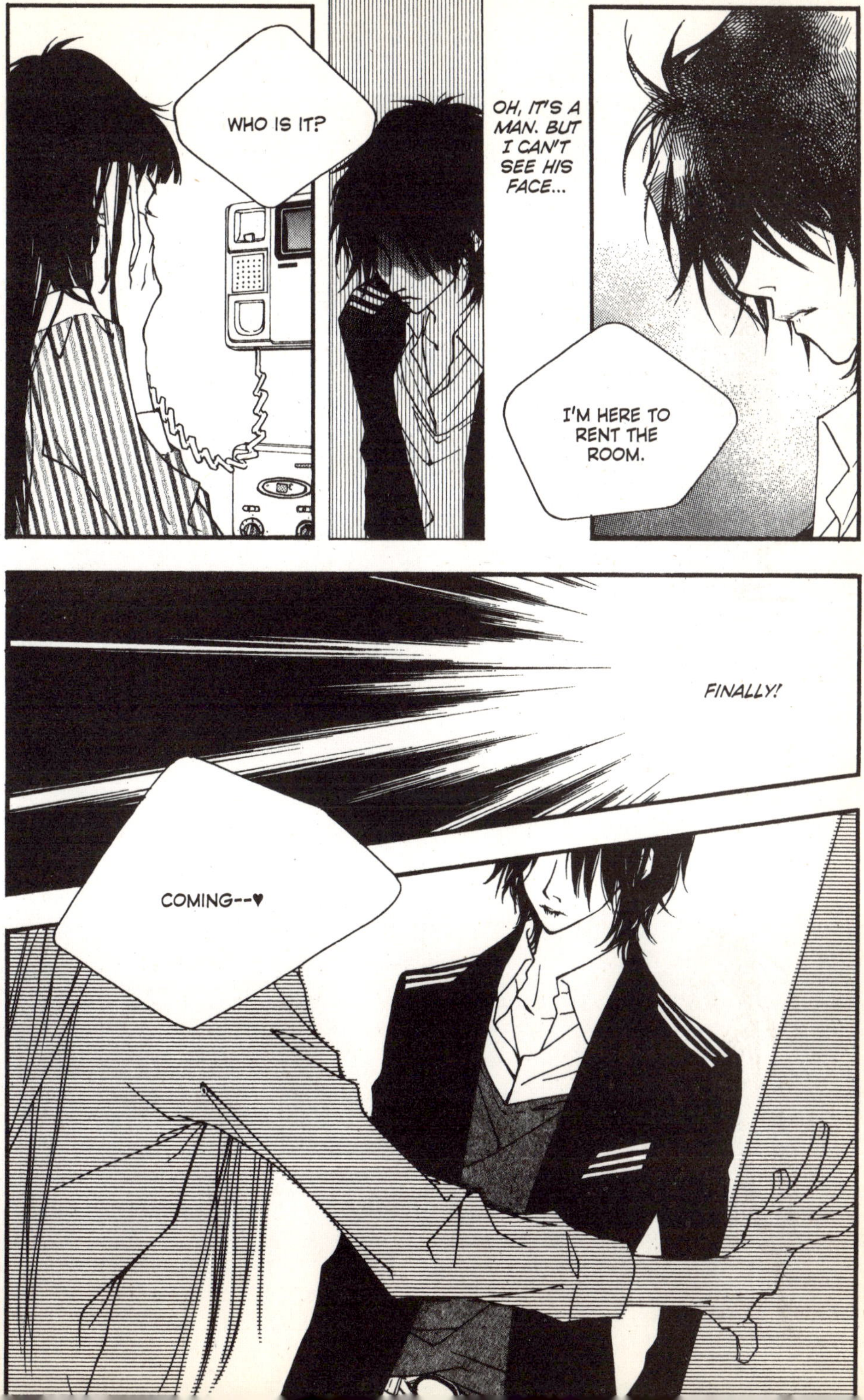
WHO IS IT?
OH, IT'S A MAN. BUT I CAN'T SEE HIS FACE...
I'M HERE TO RENT THE ROOM.
FINALLY!
COMING--♥

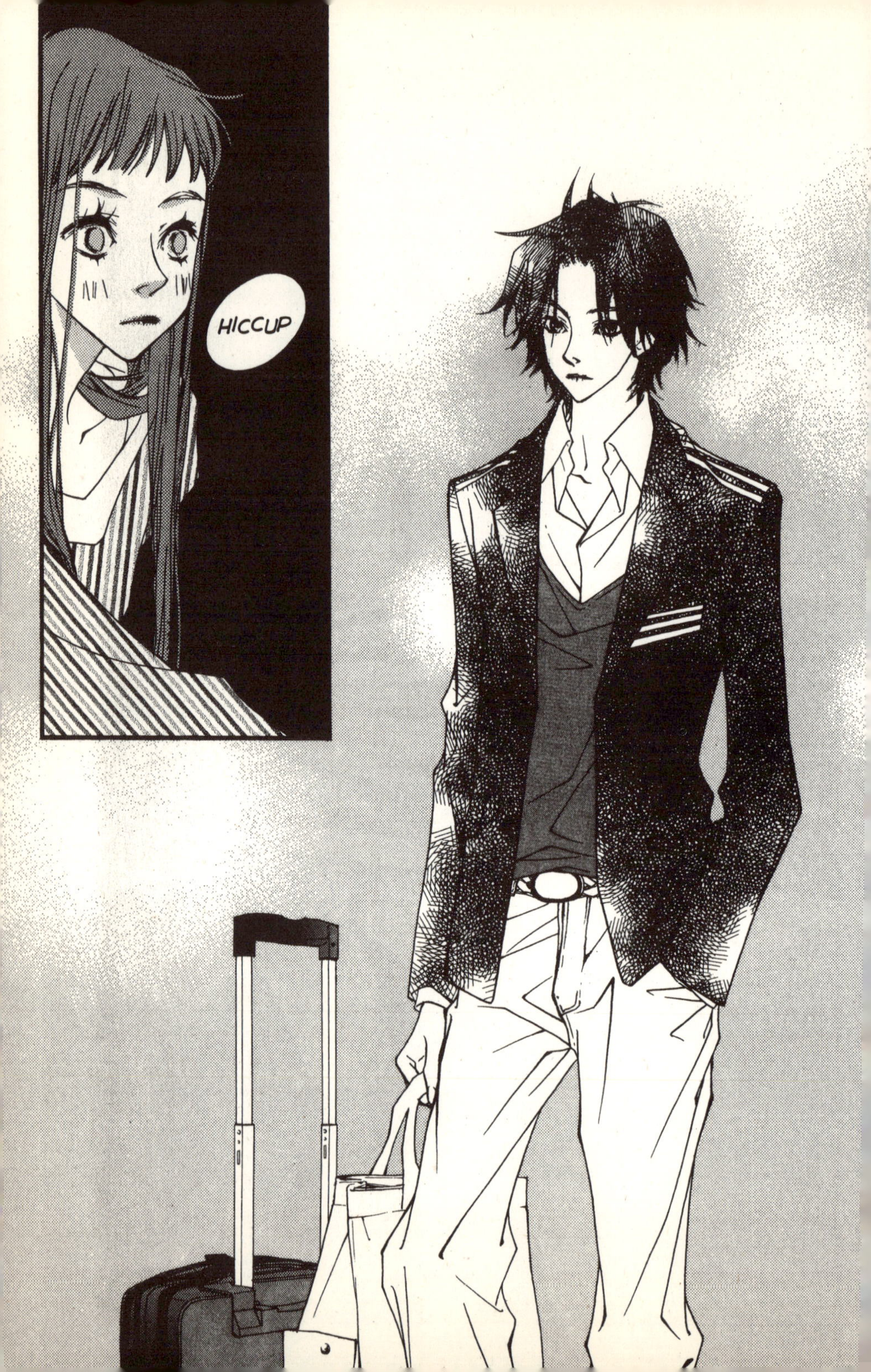
HICCUP

Forest of Gray City

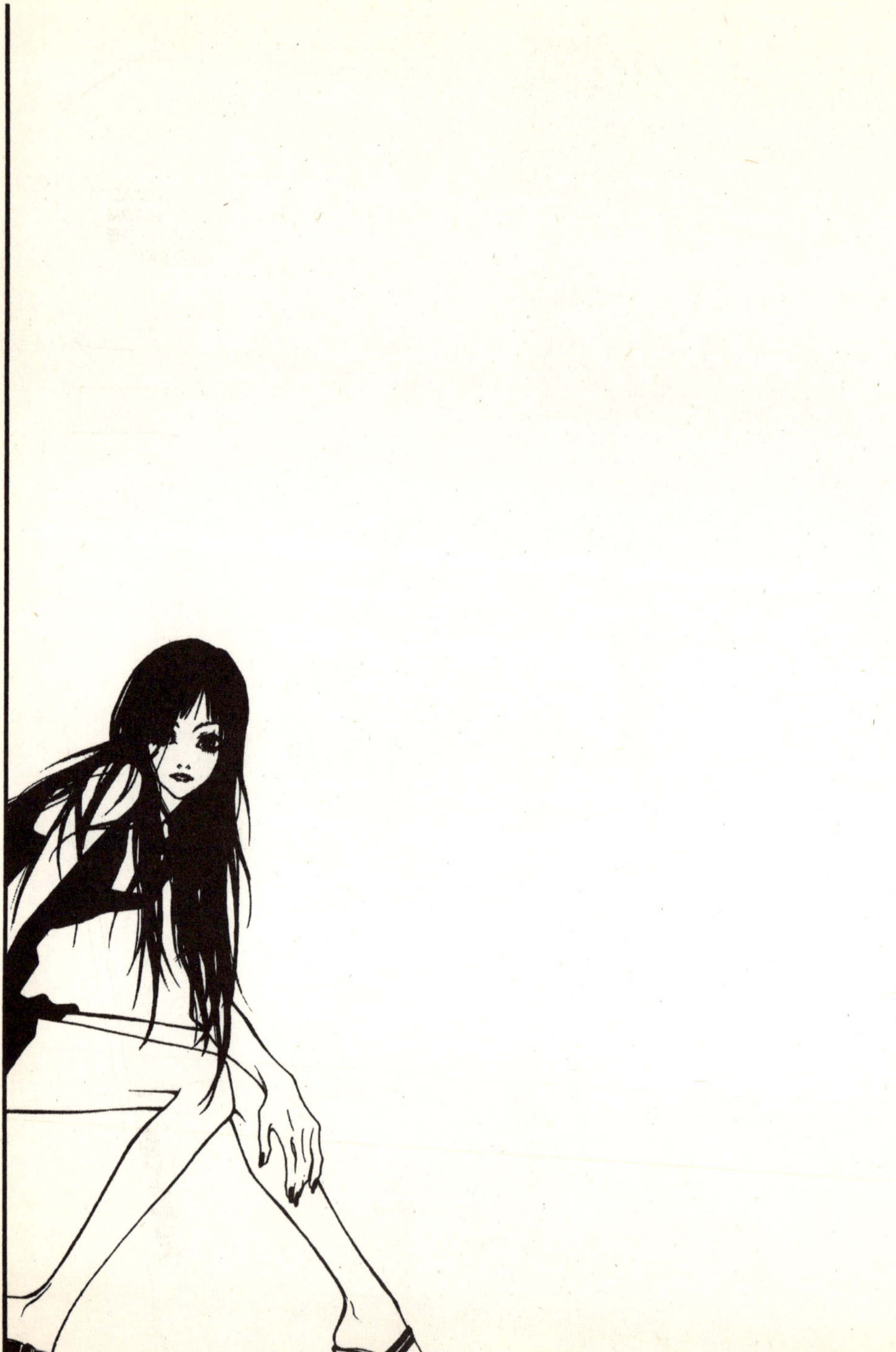

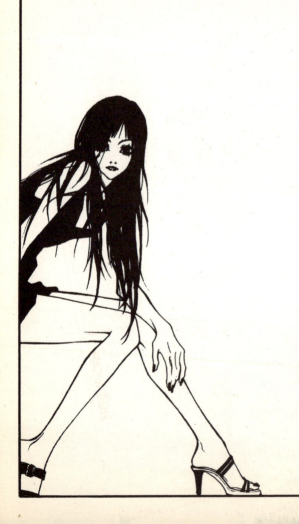

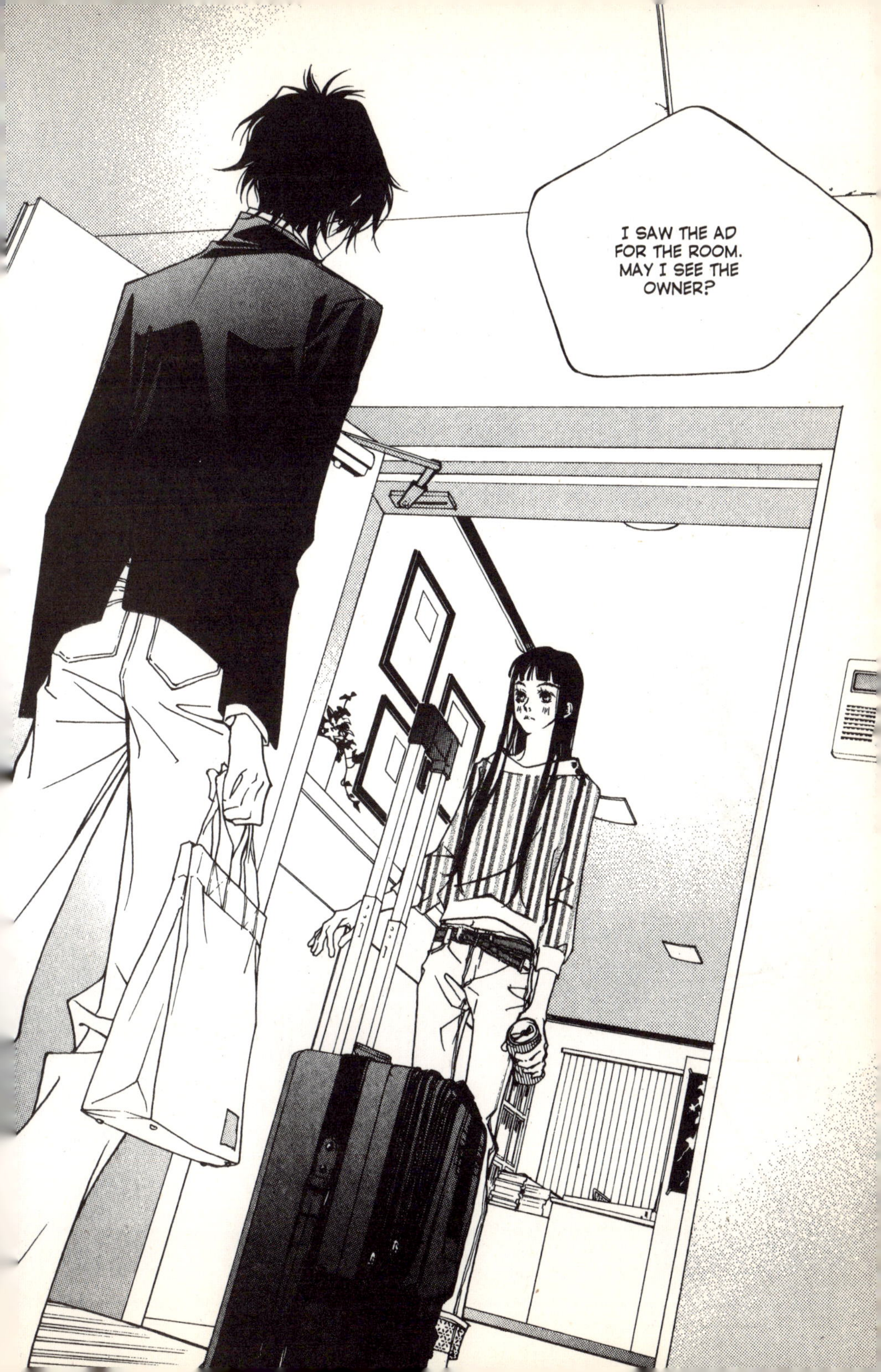
I SAW THE AD FOR THE ROOM. MAY I SEE THE OWNER?

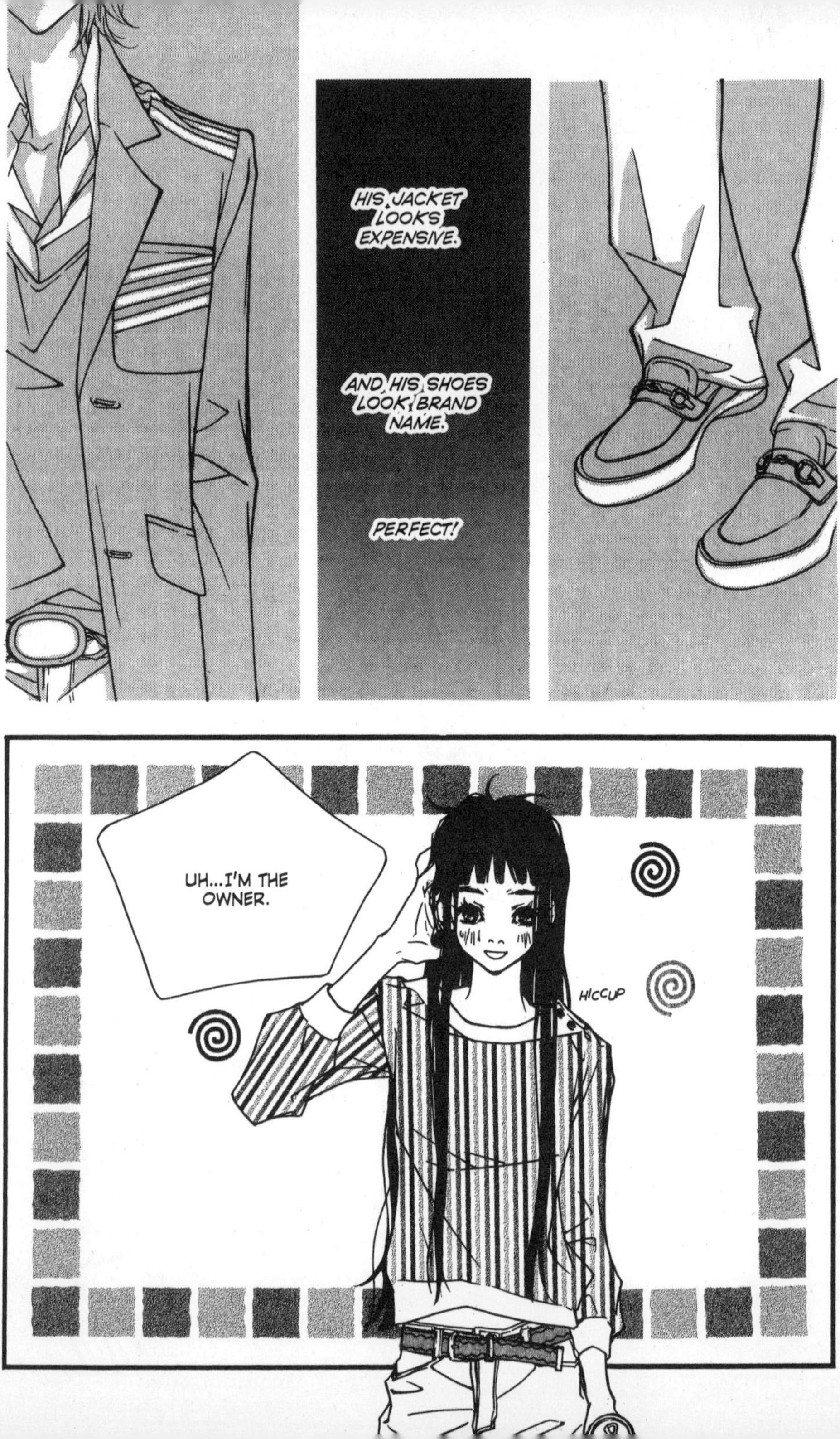
HIS JACKET LOOKS EXPENSIVE.
AND HIS SHOES LOOK BRAND NAME.
PERFECT!
UH...I'M THE OWNER.
HICCUP

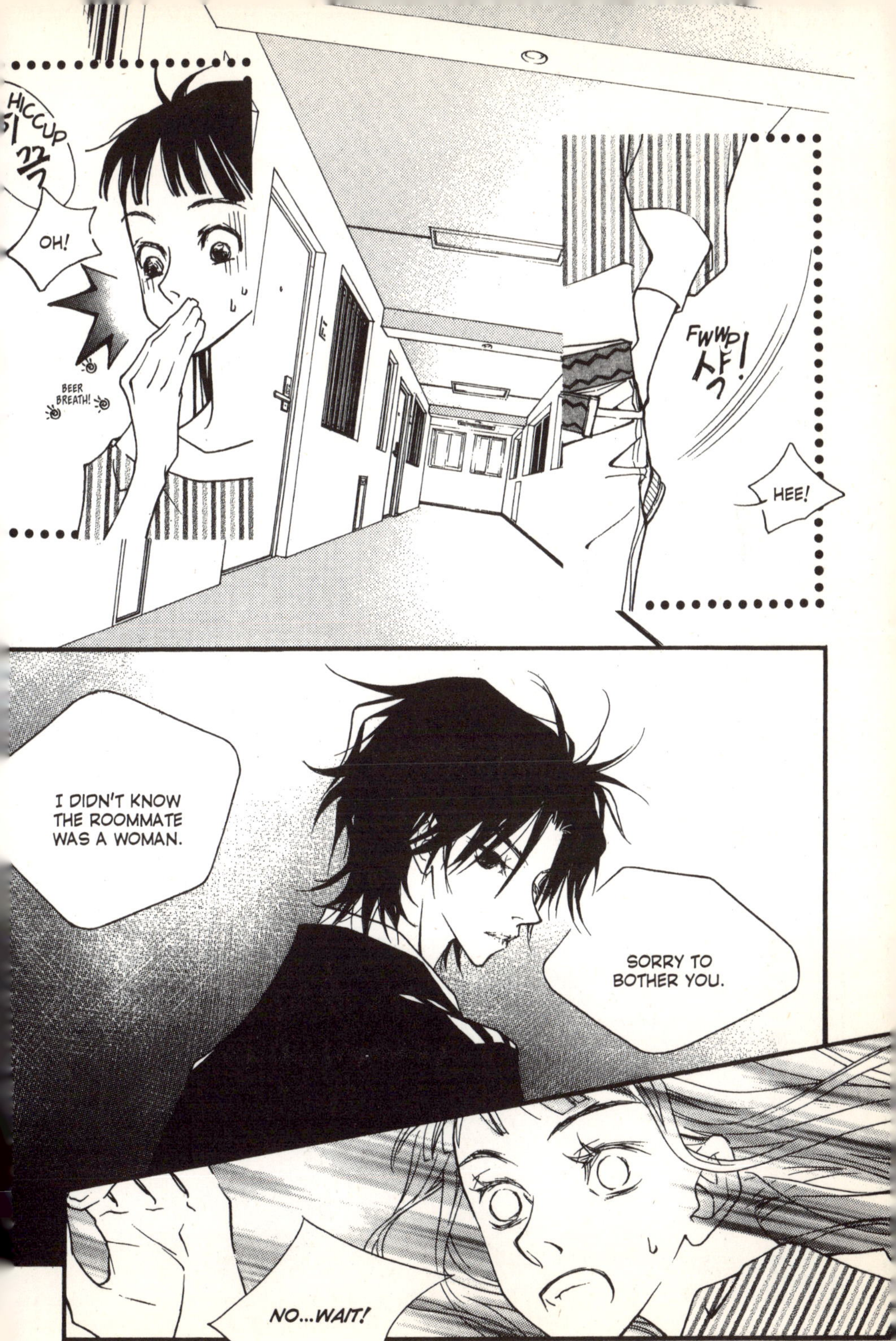
HICCUP
OH!
BEER BREATH!
FWWP!
HEE!
I DIDN'T KNOW THE ROOMMATE WAS A WOMAN.
SORRY TO BOTHER YOU.
NO...WAIT!

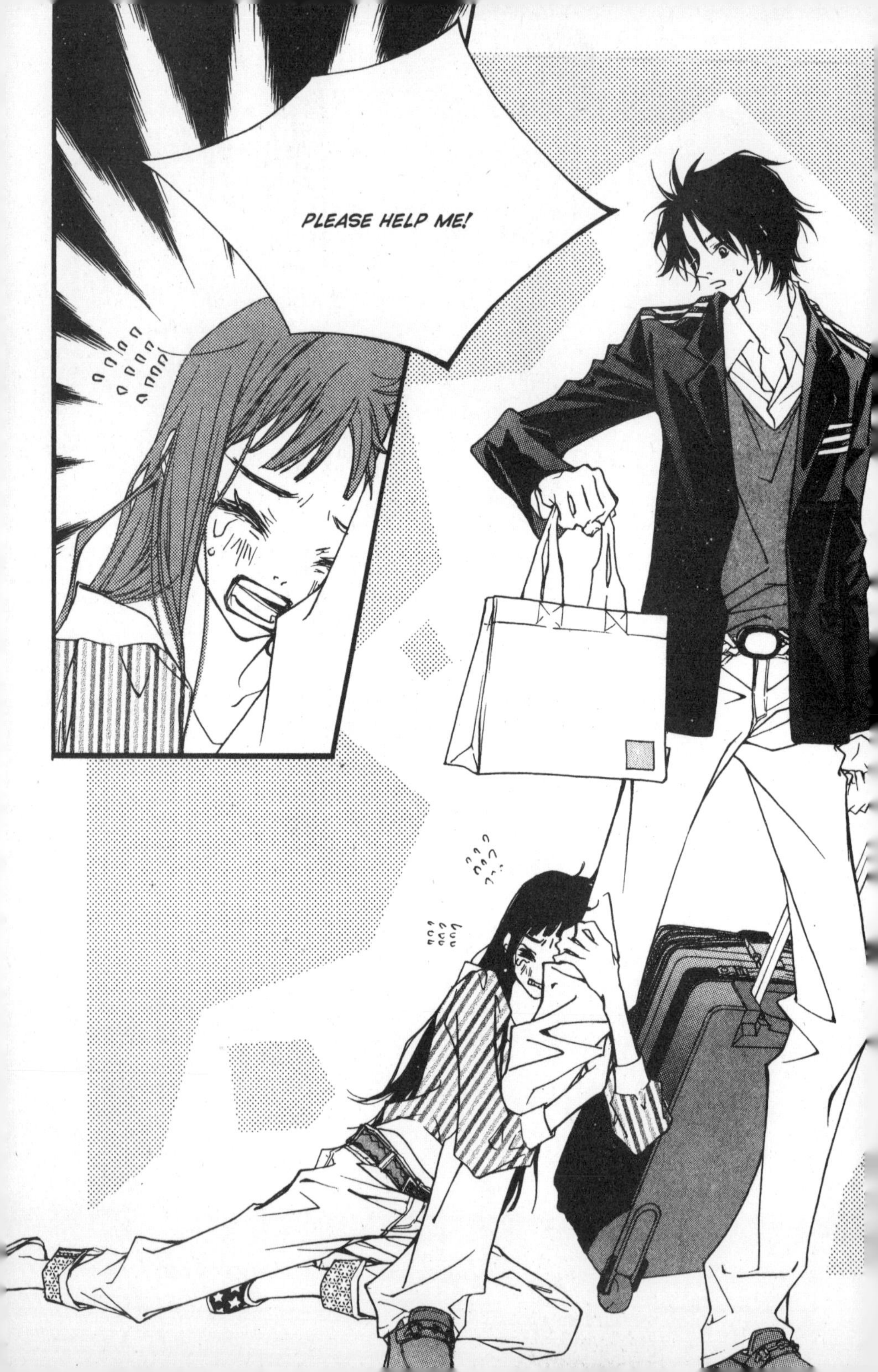
PLEASE HELP ME!

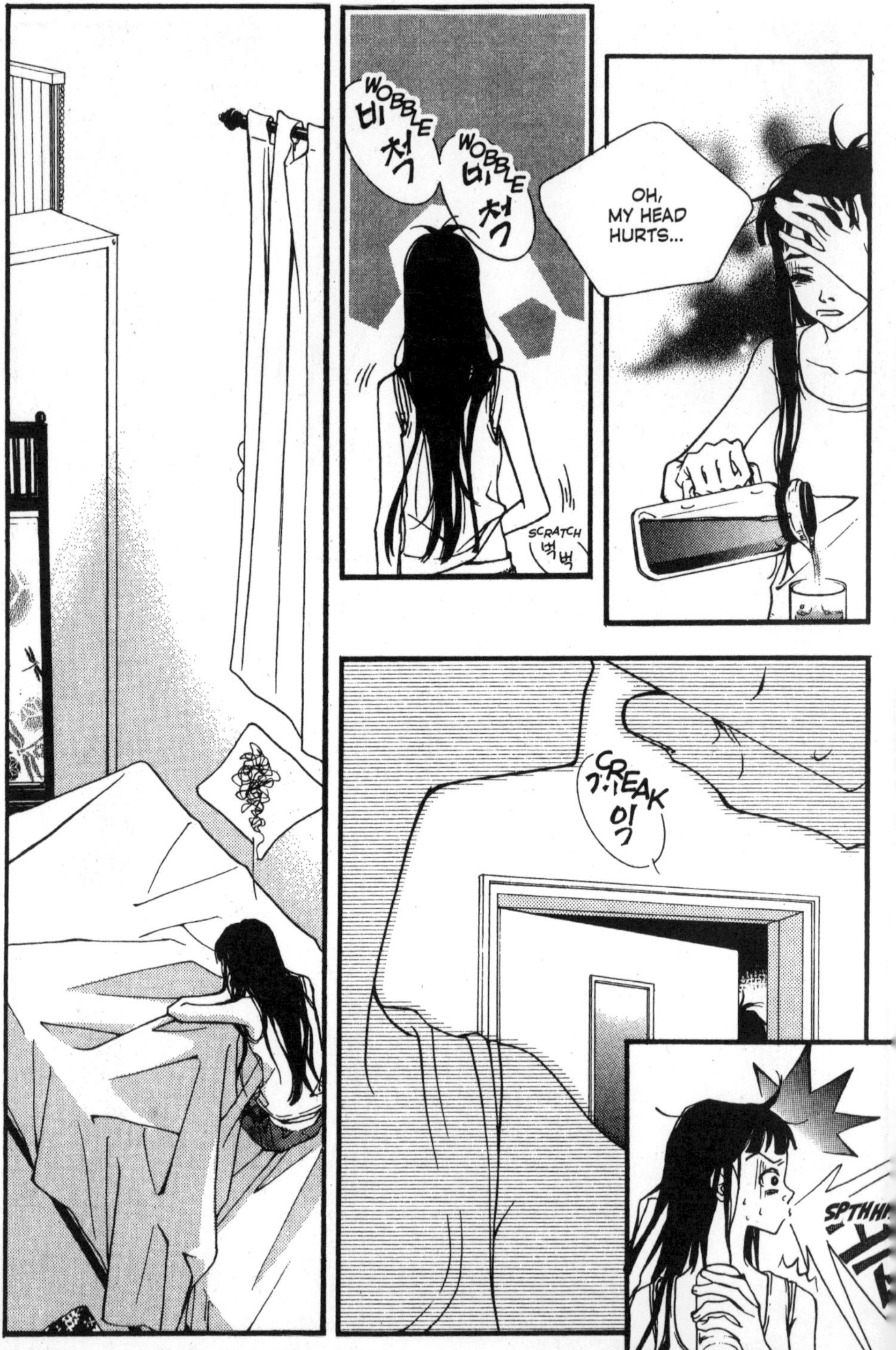

WOBBLE
비척
WOBBLE
비척
SCRATCH
벅벅
OH, MY HEAD HURTS...
CREAK
끼익
SPTHH

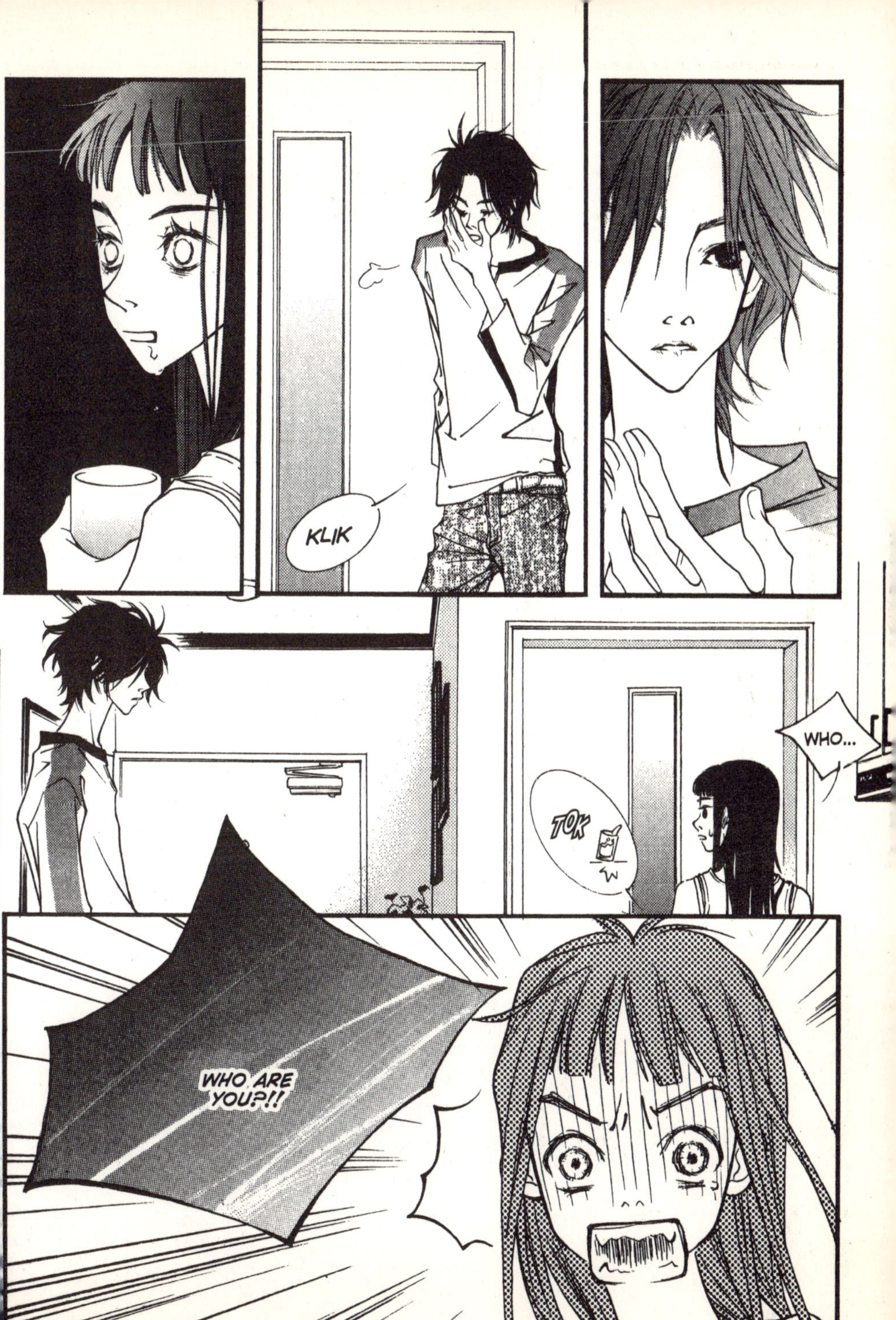
KLIK
TOK
WHO...
WHO ARE YOU?!!

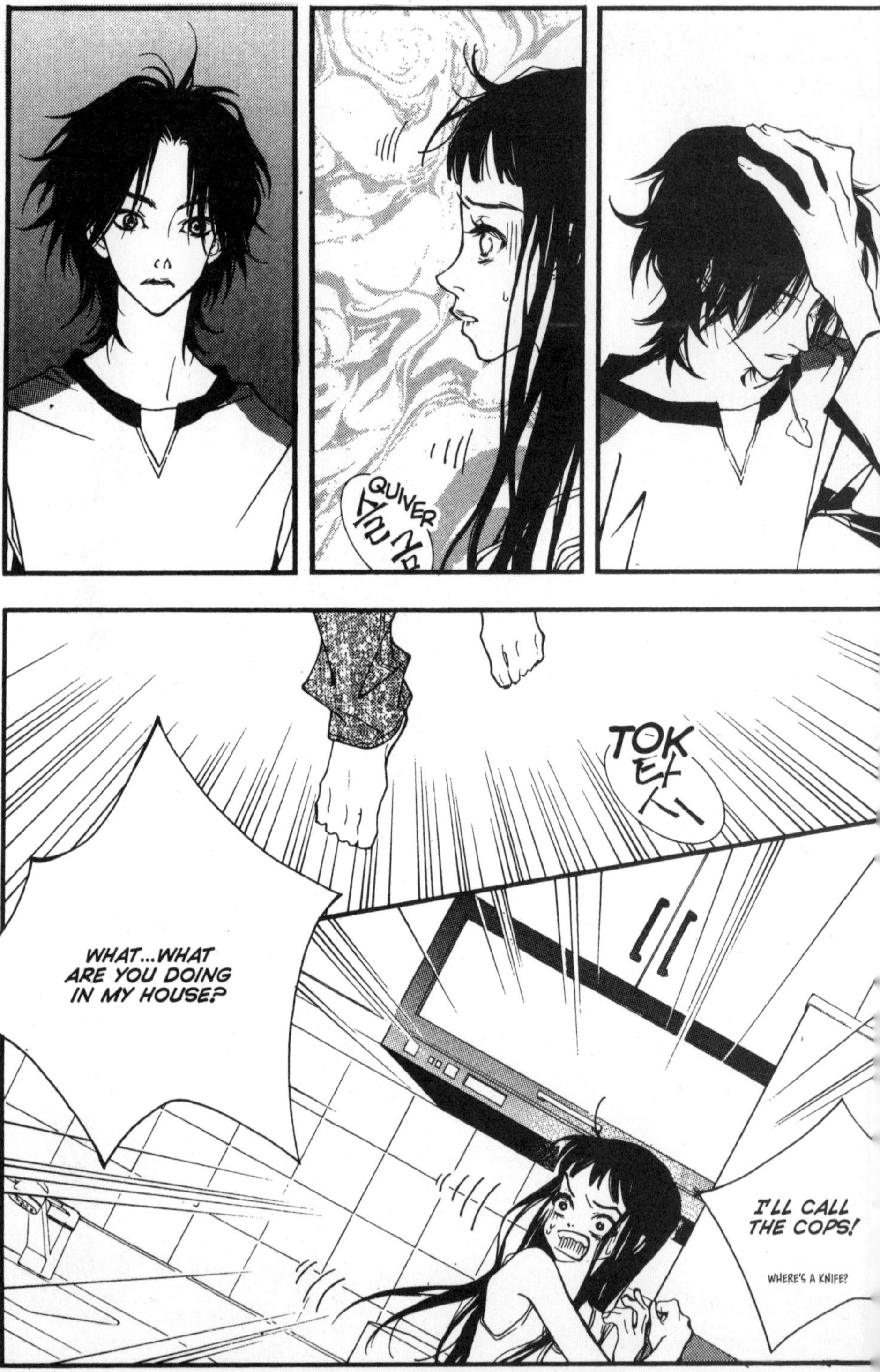
QUIVER
TOK
WHAT...WHAT ARE YOU DOING IN MY HOUSE?
I'LL CALL THE COPS!
WHERE'S A KNIFE?

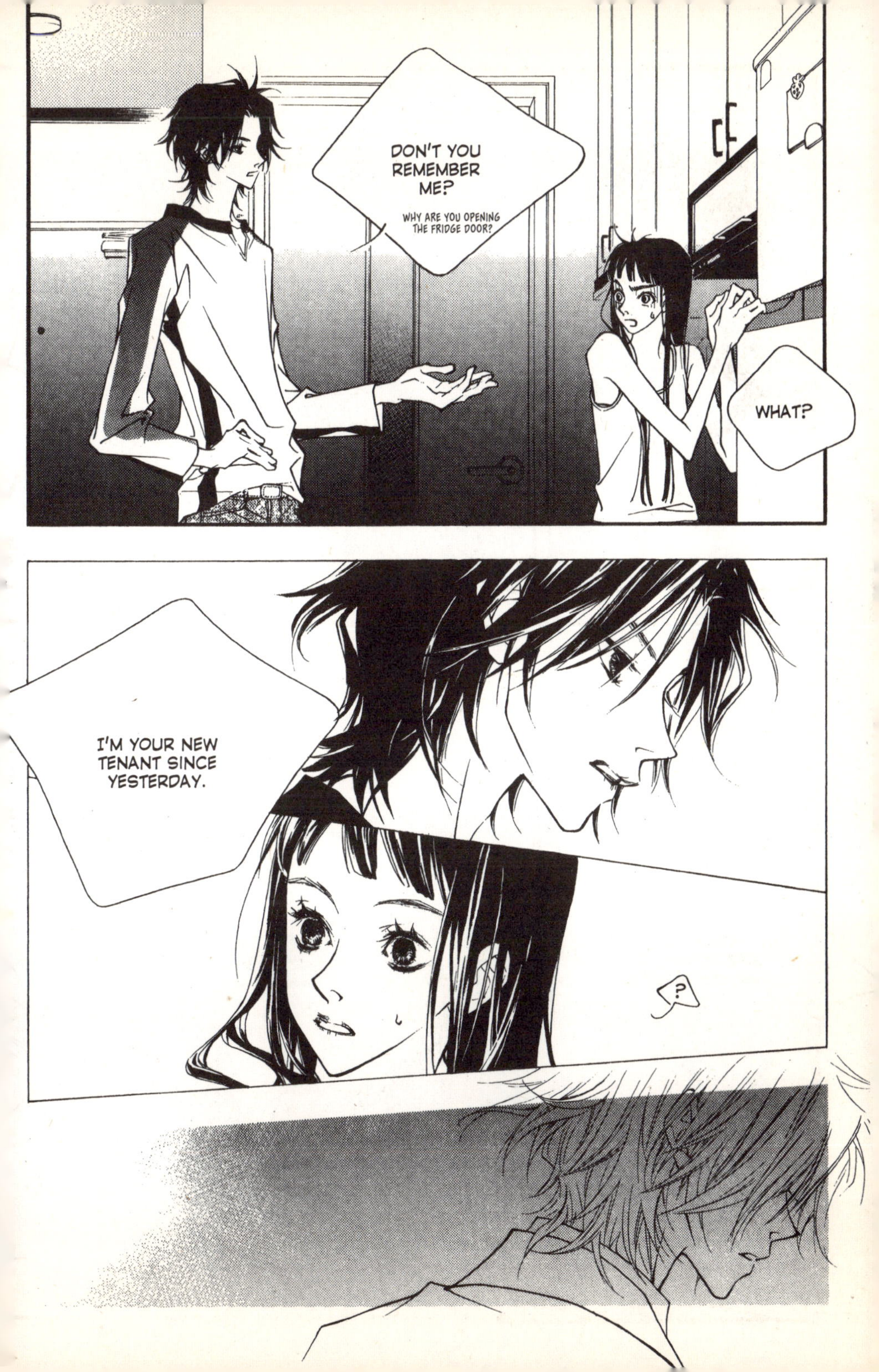
DON'T YOU REMEMBER ME?
WHY ARE YOU OPENING THE FRIDGE DOOR?
WHAT?
I'M YOUR NEW TENANT SINCE YESTERDAY.
?

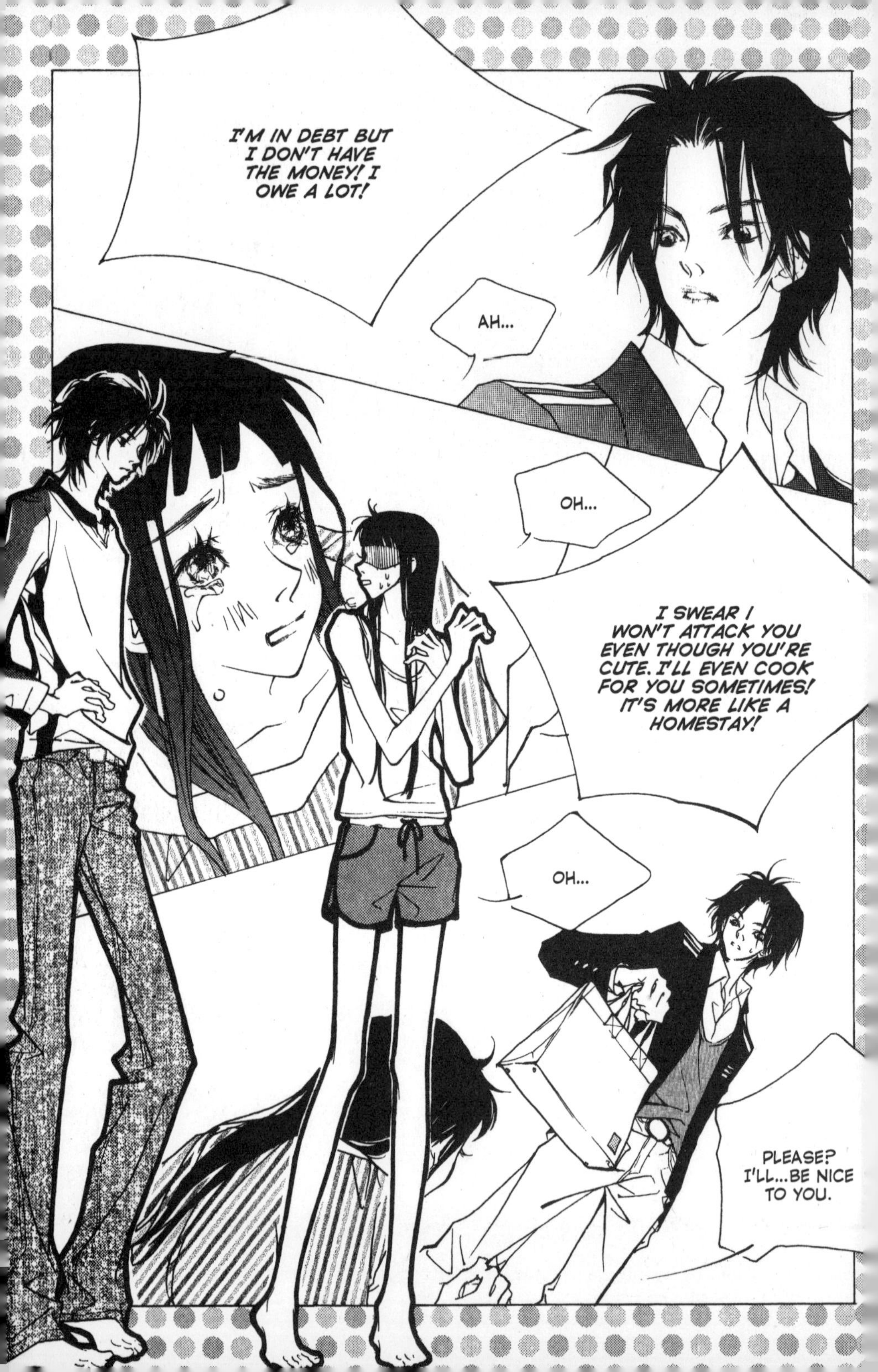
I'M IN DEBT BUT I DON'T HAVE THE MONEY! I OWE A LOT!
AH...
OH...
I SWEAR I WON'T ATTACK YOU EVEN THOUGH YOU'RE CUTE. I'LL EVEN COOK FOR YOU SOMETIMES! IT'S MORE LIKE A HOMESTAY!
OH...
PLEASE? I'LL...BE NICE TO YOU.

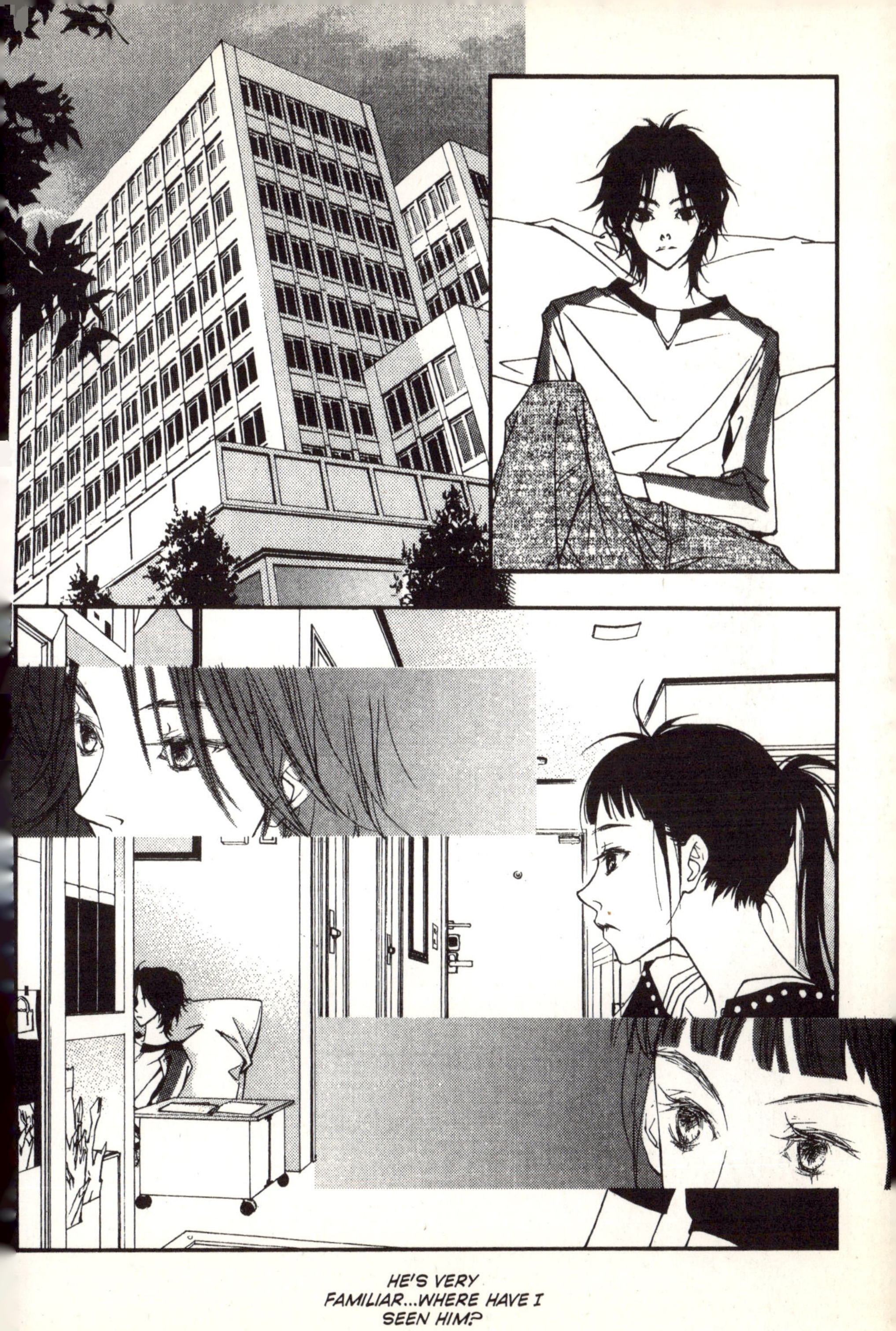

HE'S VERY
FAMILIAR...WHERE HAVE I
SEEN HIM?

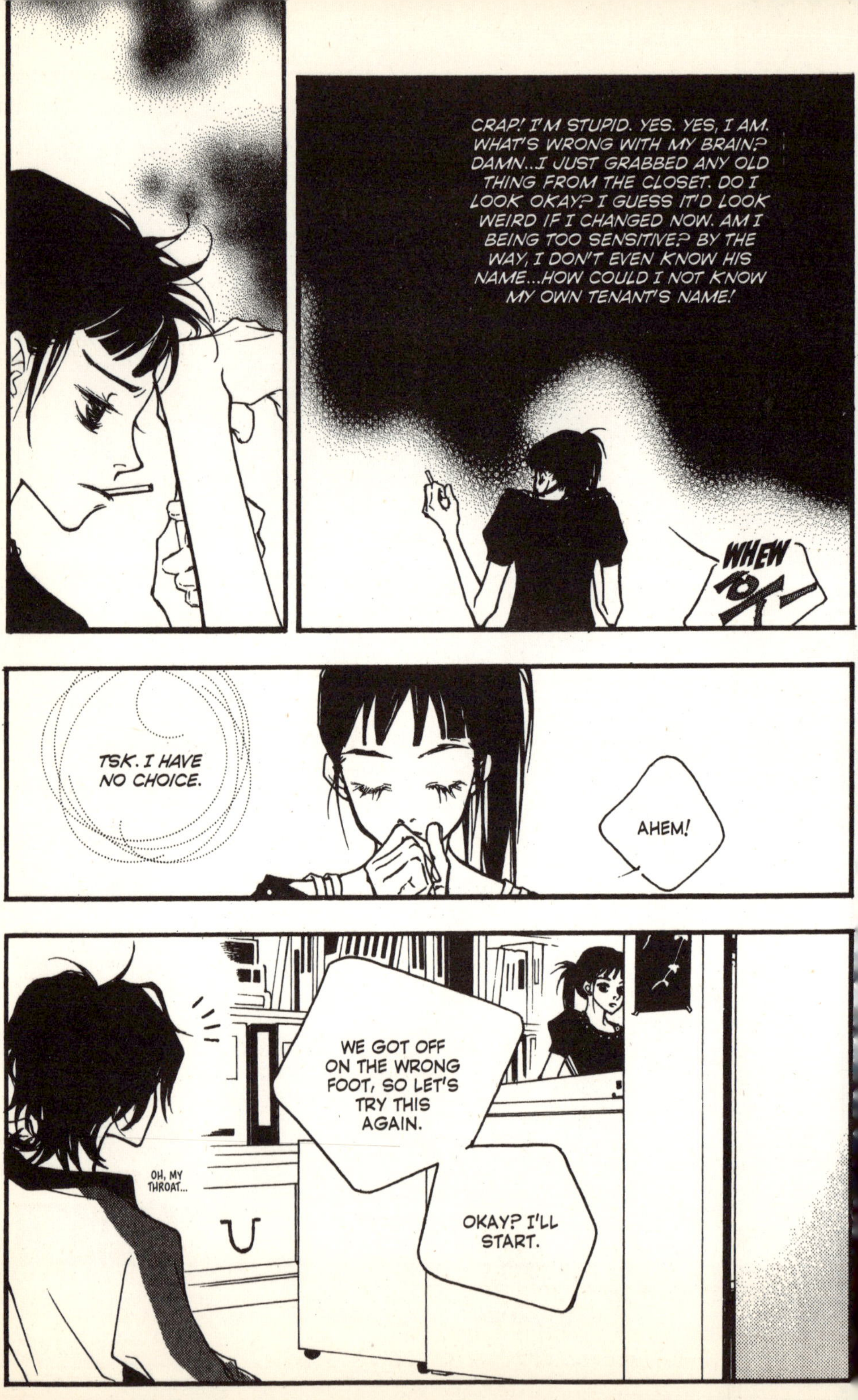
CRAP! I'M STUPID. YES. YES, I AM. WHAT'S WRONG WITH MY BRAIN? DAMN...I JUST GRABBED ANY OLD THING FROM THE CLOSET. DO I LOOK OKAY? I GUESS IT'D LOOK WEIRD IF I CHANGED NOW. AM I BEING TOO SENSITIVE? BY THE WAY, I DON'T EVEN KNOW HIS NAME...HOW COULD I NOT KNOW MY OWN TENANT'S NAME!
WHEW
AHEM!
TSK. I HAVE NO CHOICE.
WE GOT OFF ON THE WRONG FOOT, SO LET'S TRY THIS AGAIN.
OKAY? I'LL START.
OH, MY THROAT...

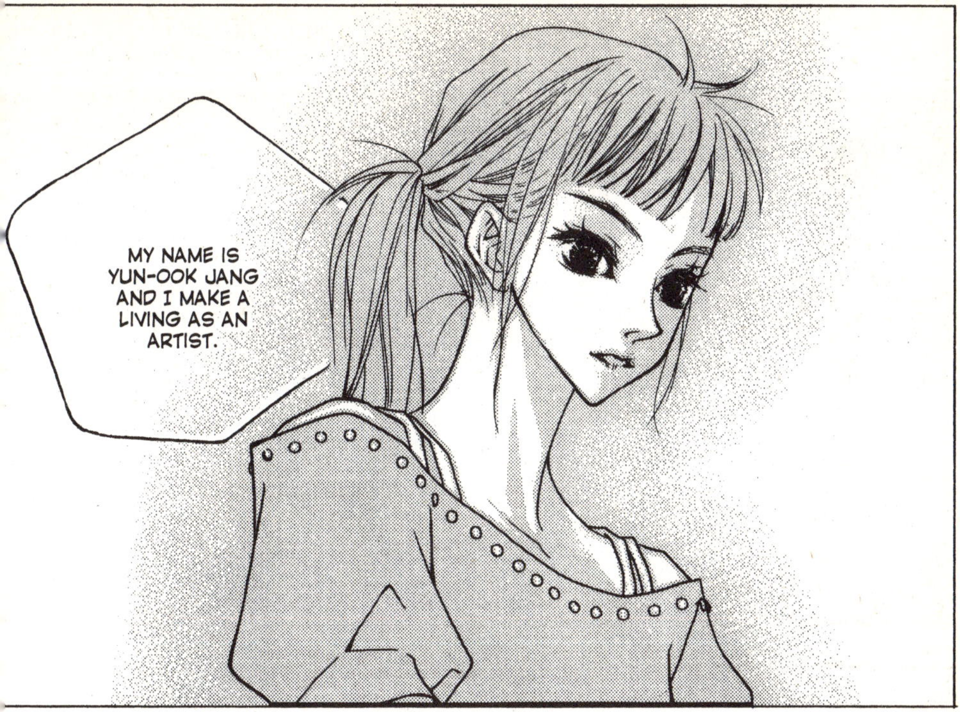
MY NAME IS YUN-OOK JANG AND I MAKE A LIVING AS AN ARTIST.

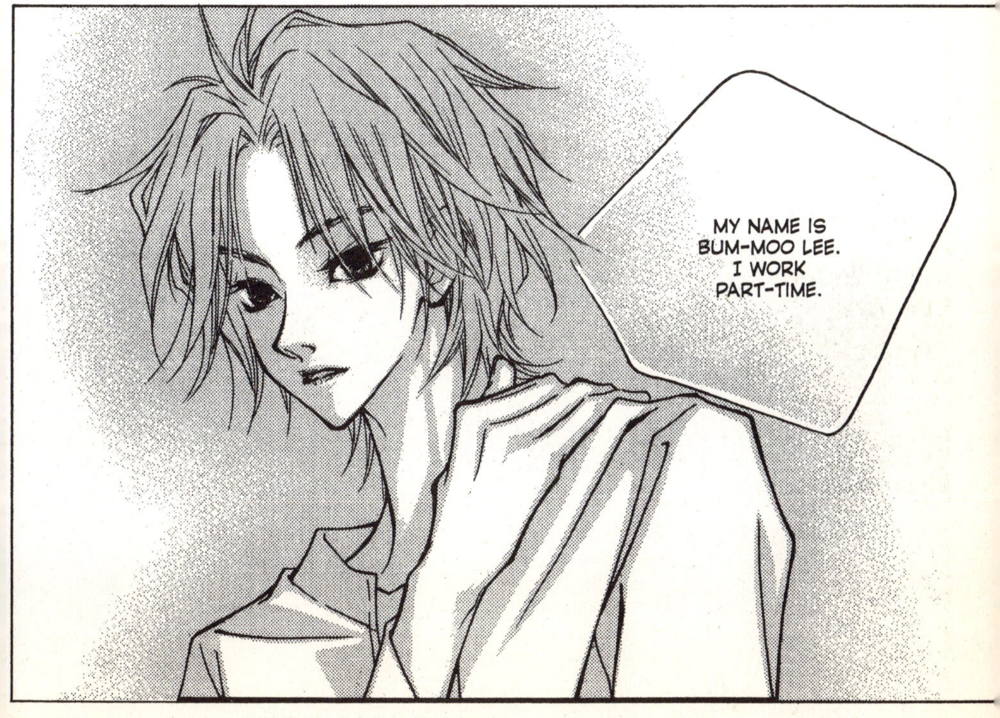
MY NAME IS BUM-MOO LEE. I WORK PART-TIME.

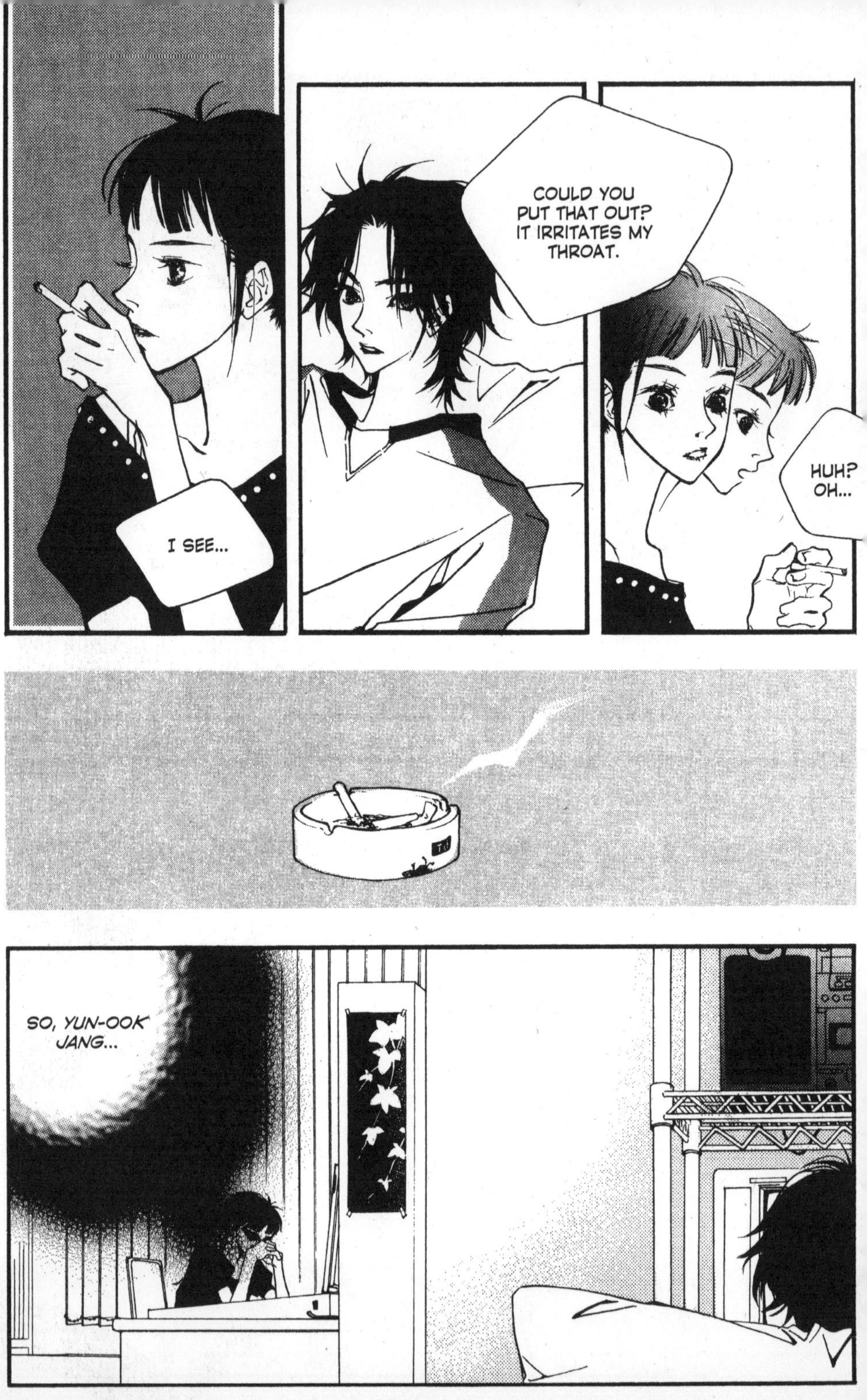
I SEE...
COULD YOU PUT THAT OUT? IT IRRITATES MY THROAT.
HUH? OH...
SO, YUN-OOK JANG...

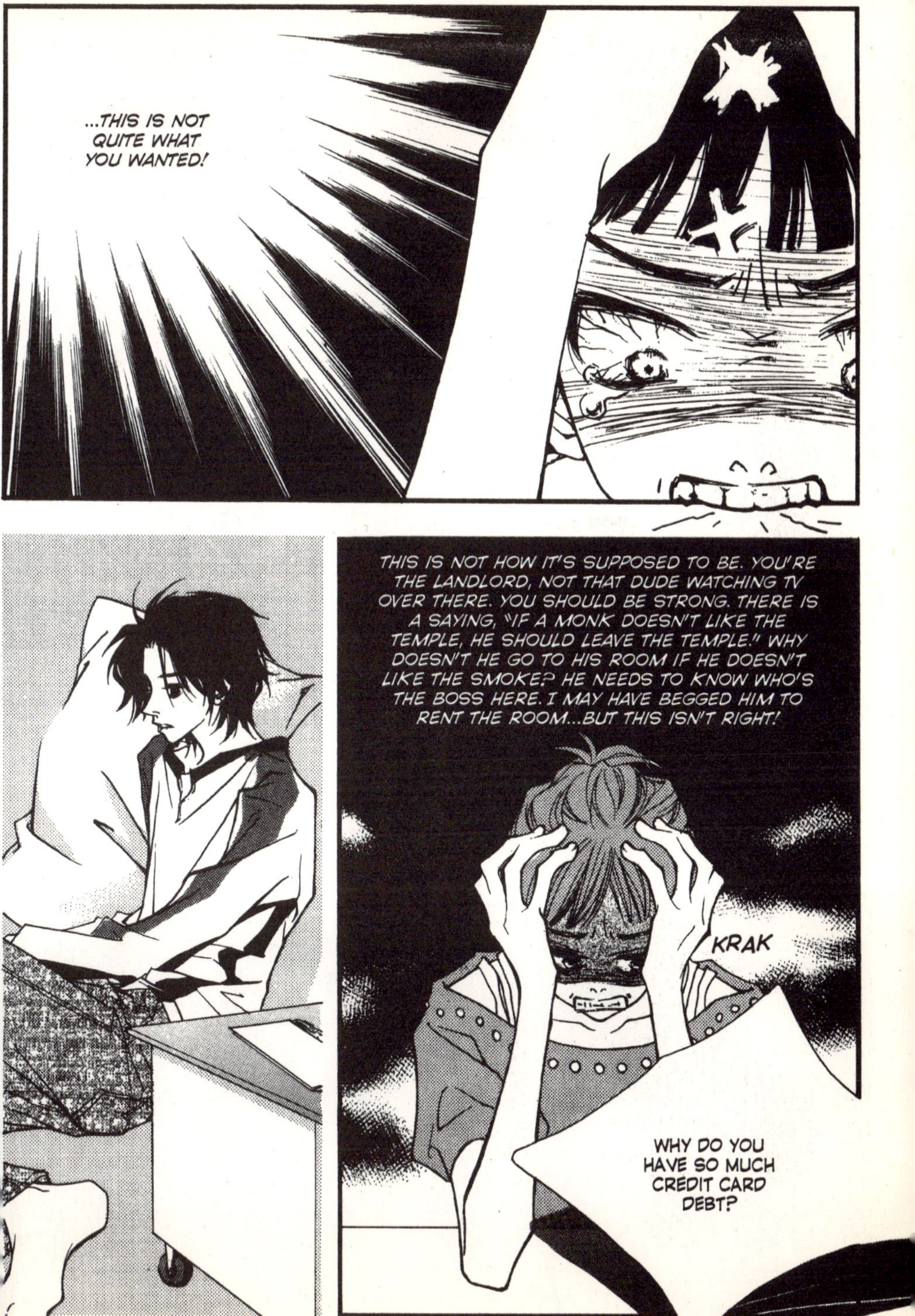
...THIS IS NOT QUITE WHAT YOU WANTED!
THIS IS NOT HOW IT'S SUPPOSED TO BE. YOU'RE THE LANDLORD, NOT THAT DUDE WATCHING TV OVER THERE. YOU SHOULD BE STRONG. THERE IS A SAYING, "IF A MONK DOESN'T LIKE THE TEMPLE, HE SHOULD LEAVE THE TEMPLE." WHY DOESN'T HE GO TO HIS ROOM IF HE DOESN'T LIKE THE SMOKE? HE NEEDS TO KNOW WHO'S THE BOSS HERE. I MAY HAVE BEGGED HIM TO RENT THE ROOM...BUT THIS ISN'T RIGHT!
KRAK
WHY DO YOU HAVE SO MUCH CREDIT CARD DEBT?

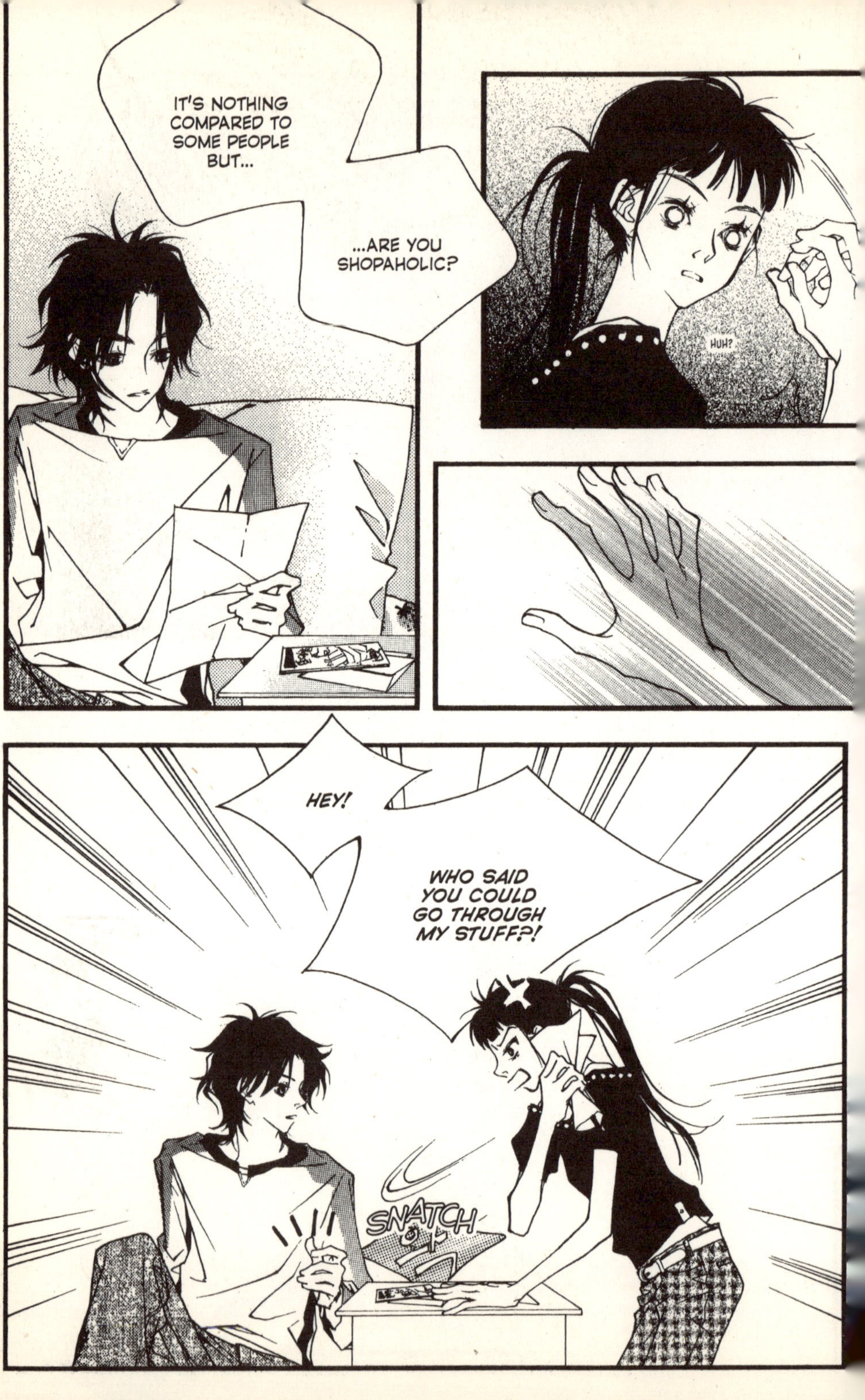
IT'S NOTHING COMPARED TO SOME PEOPLE BUT...
...ARE YOU SHOPAHOLIC?
HUH?
HEY!
WHO SAID YOU COULD GO THROUGH MY STUFF?!
SNATCH

OH, SORRY.

THIS ISN'T WHAT I
WANTED...

I HAVE TO
GO TO WORK
NOW.

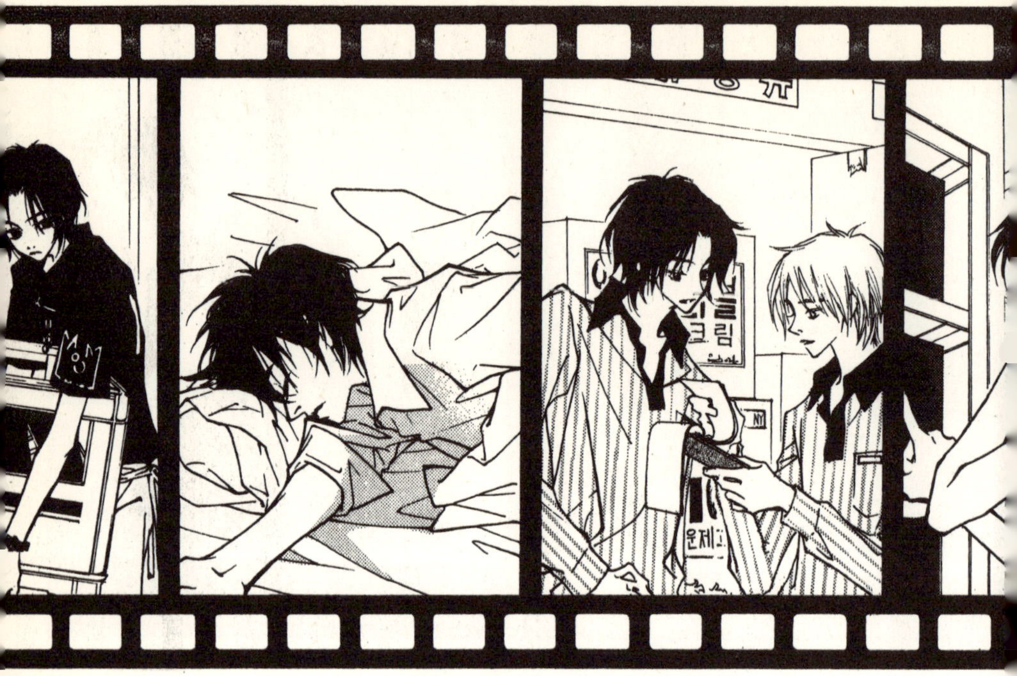

OTHER THAN HAVING TO CHANGE
MY BEDTIME AND BE CAREFUL ABOUT
HANGING MY DELICATES OUT TO DRY, IT
WASN'T SO BAD LIVING WITH HIM.

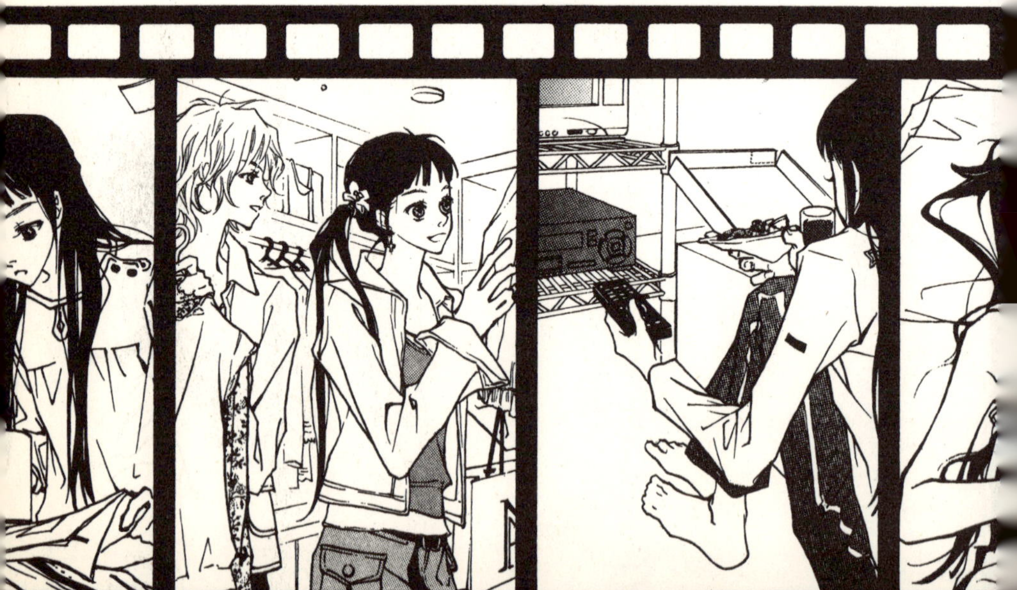

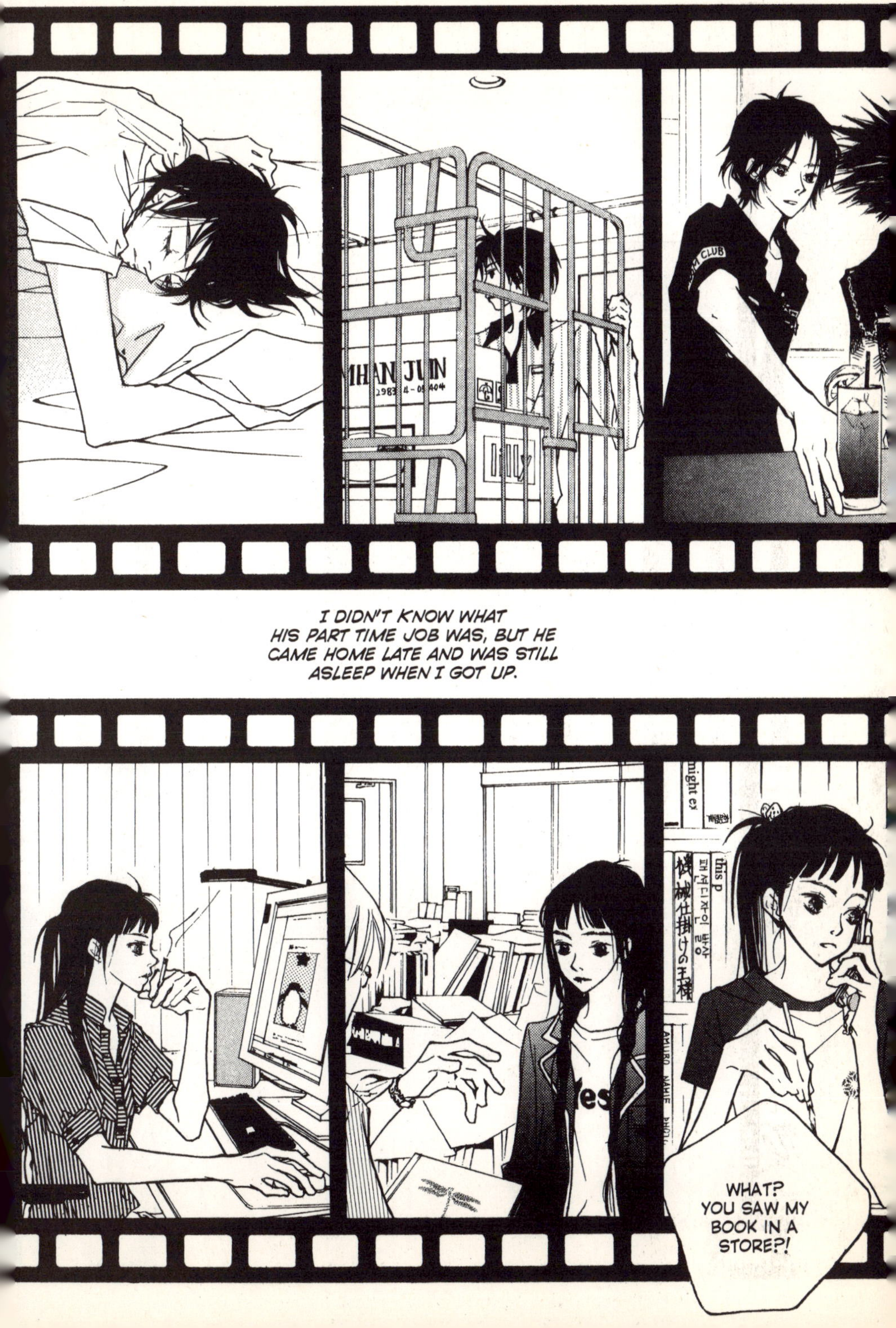
I DIDN'T KNOW WHAT HIS PART TIME JOB WAS, BUT HE CAME HOME LATE AND WAS STILL ASLEEP WHEN I GOT UP.
WHAT? YOU SAW MY BOOK IN A STORE?!

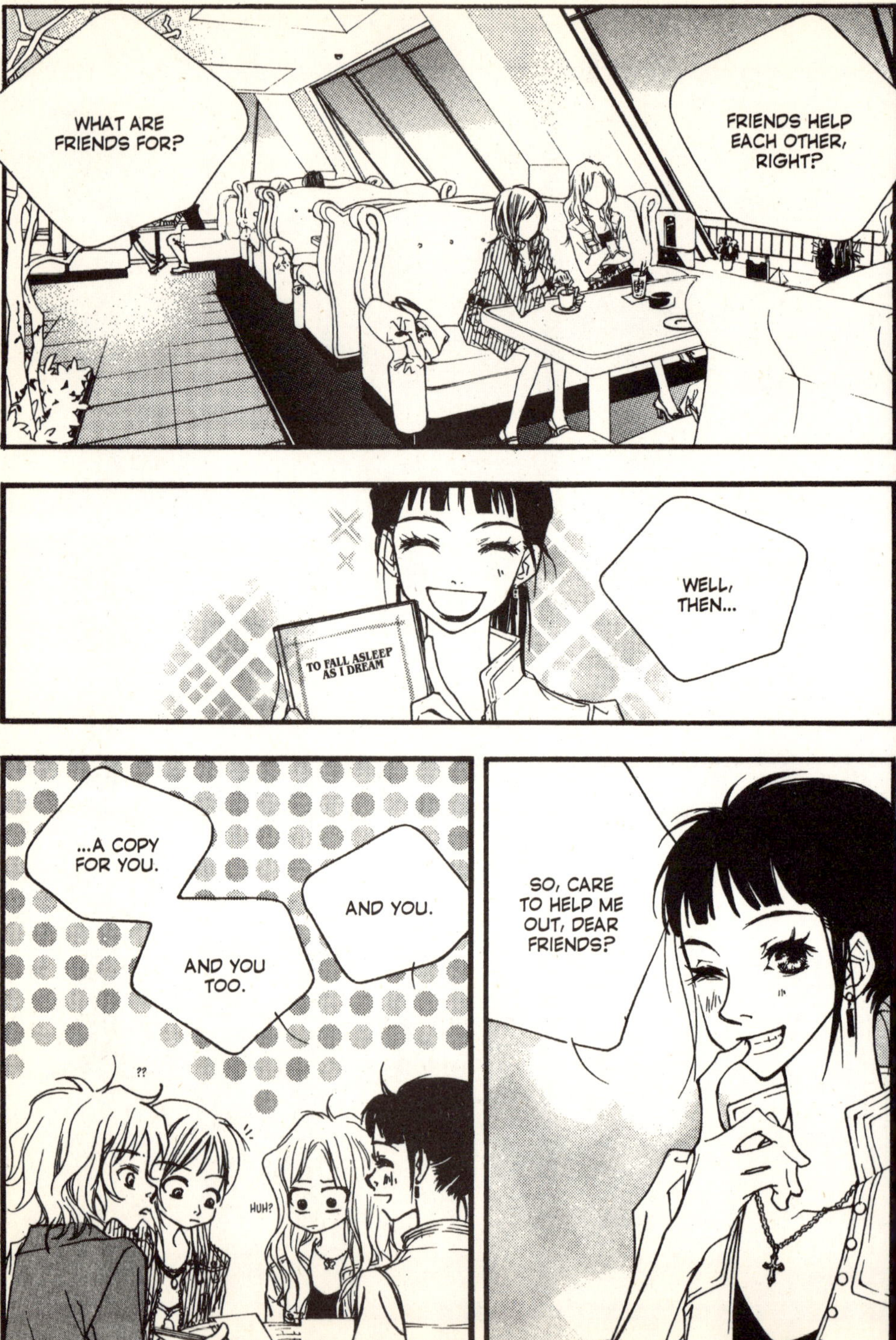
WHAT ARE FRIENDS FOR?
FRIENDS HELP EACH OTHER, RIGHT?
WELL, THEN...
TO FALL ASLEEP AS I DREAM
SO, CARE TO HELP ME OUT, DEAR FRIENDS?
...A COPY FOR YOU.
AND YOU.
AND YOU TOO.
??
HUH?

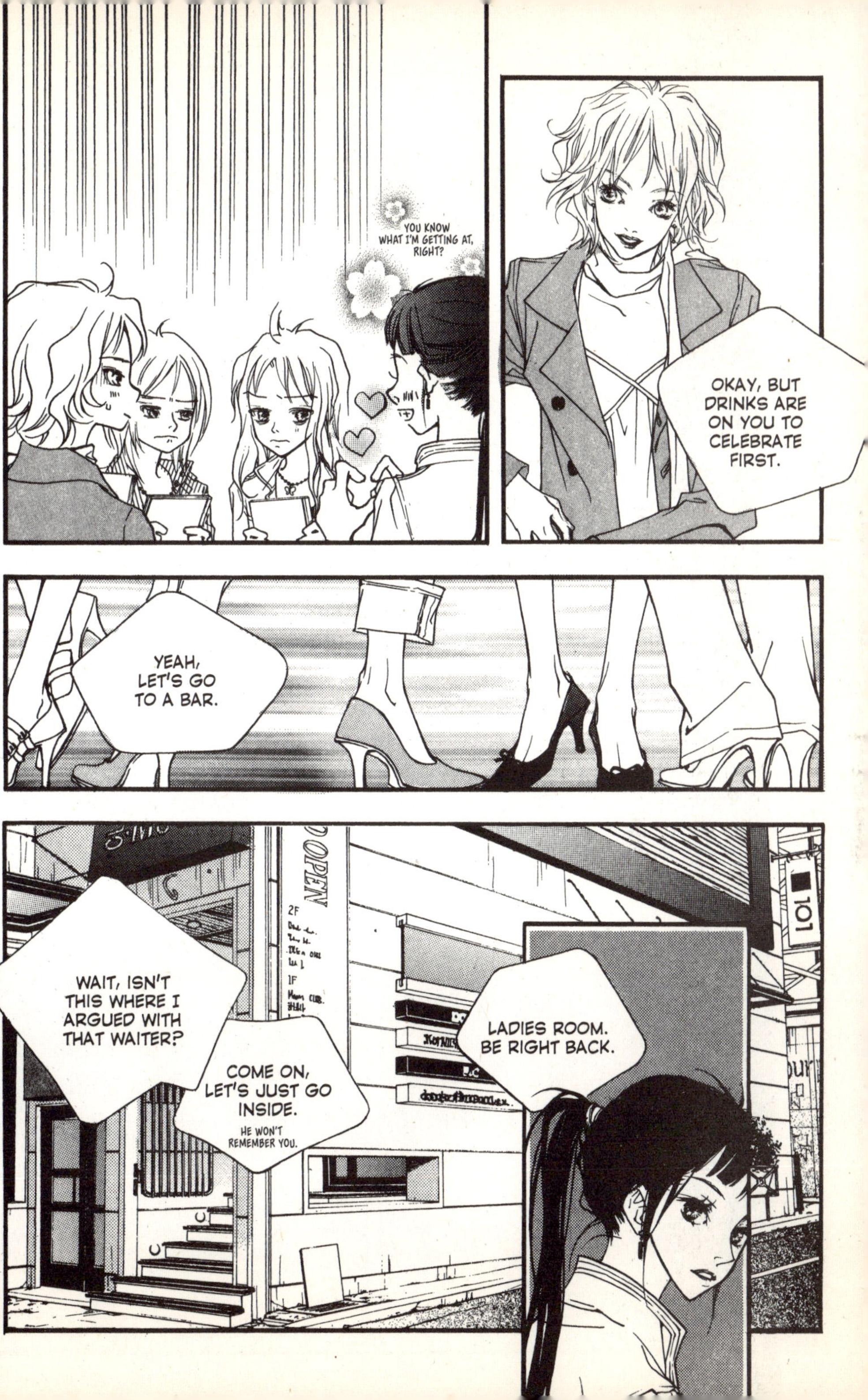
YOU KNOW WHAT I'M GETTING AT, RIGHT?
OKAY, BUT DRINKS ARE ON YOU TO CELEBRATE FIRST.
YEAH, LET'S GO TO A BAR.
WAIT, ISN'T THIS WHERE I ARGUED WITH THAT WAITER?
COME ON, LET'S JUST GO INSIDE.
HE WON'T REMEMBER YOU.
LADIES ROOM. BE RIGHT BACK.
OPEN
101

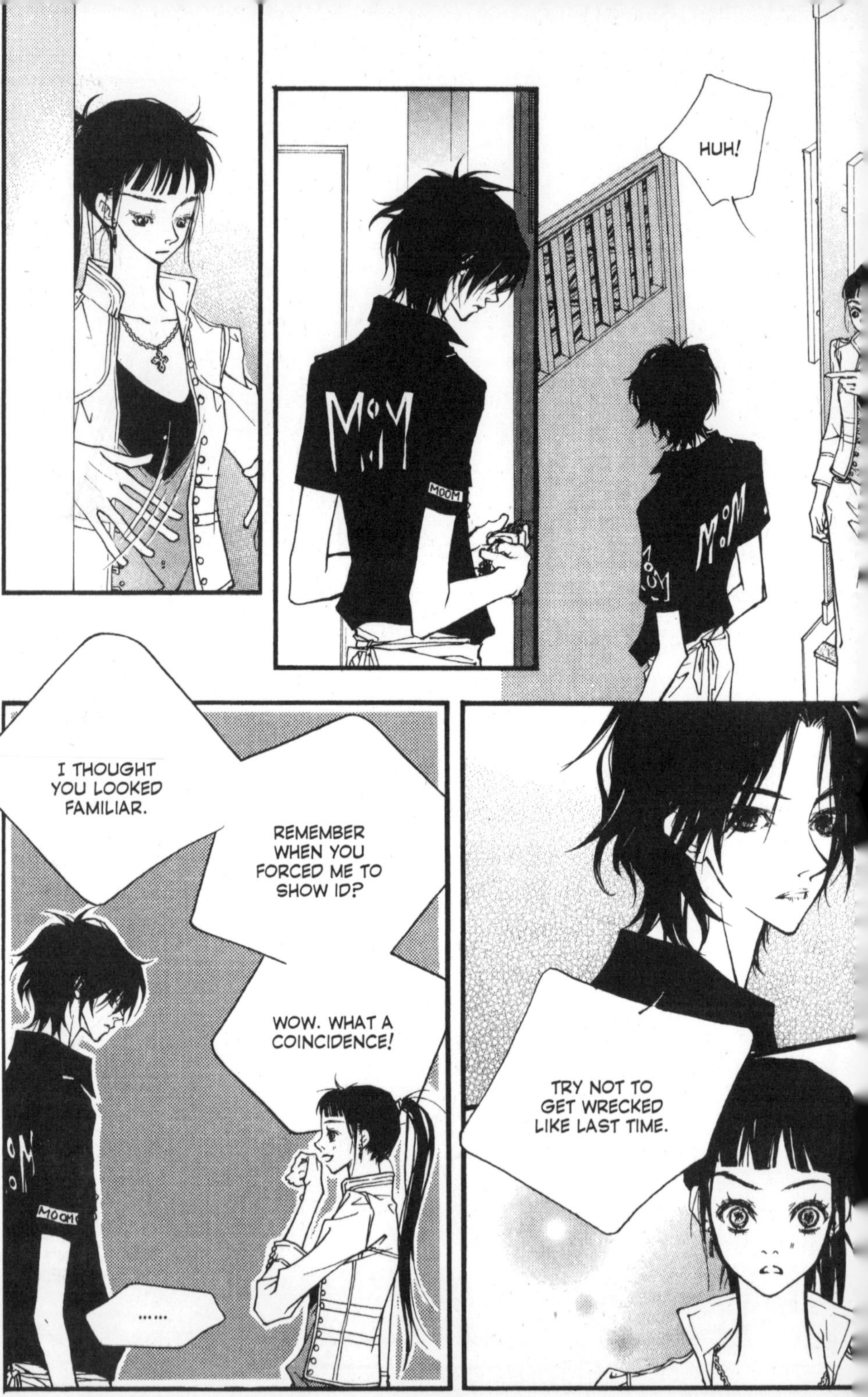
HUH!
MOOM
I THOUGHT YOU LOOKED FAMILIAR.
REMEMBER WHEN YOU FORCED ME TO SHOW ID?
WOW. WHAT A COINCIDENCE!
......
TRY NOT TO GET WRECKED LIKE LAST TIME.

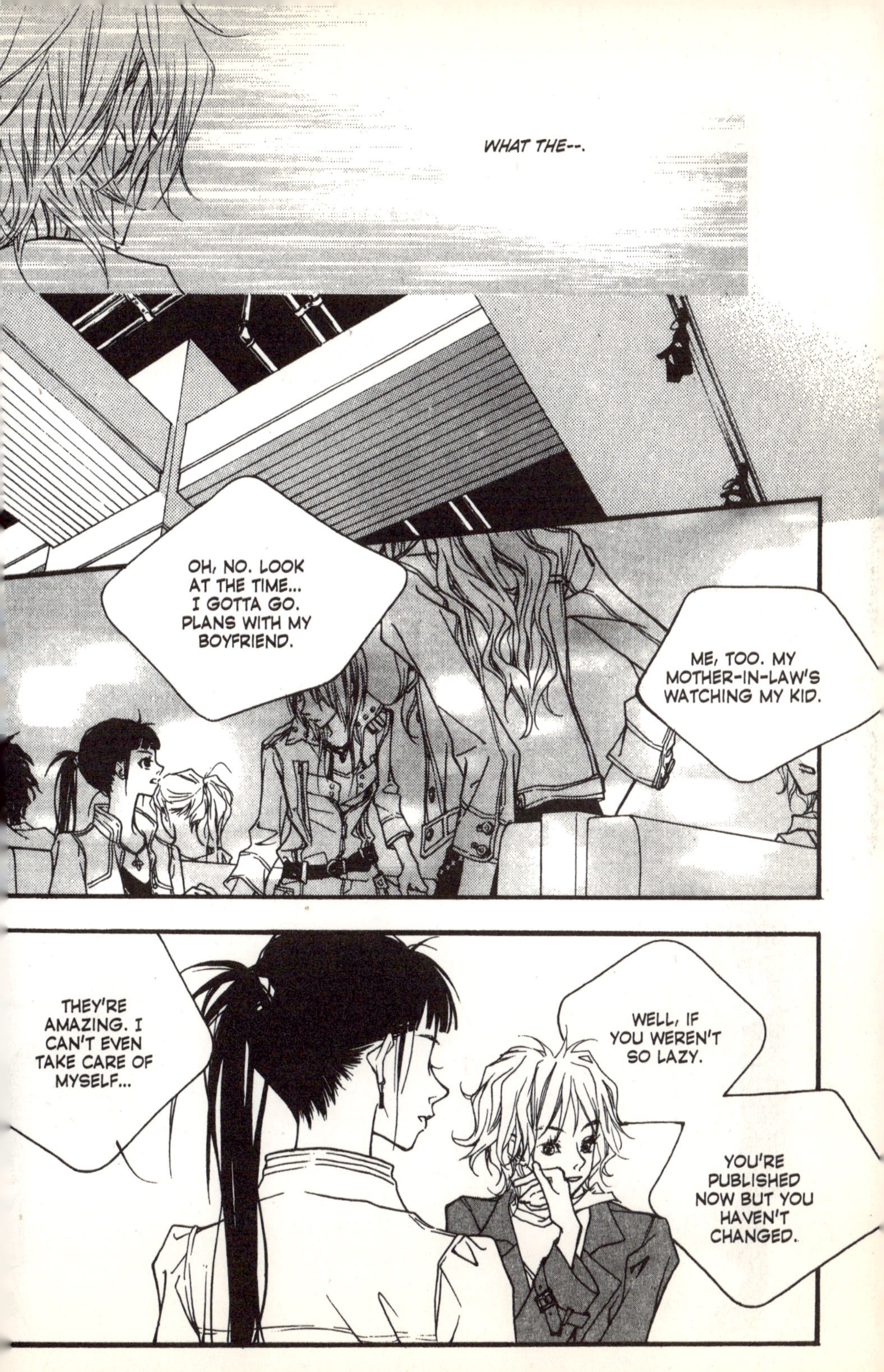

WHAT THE--.
OH, NO. LOOK AT THE TIME... I GOTTA GO. PLANS WITH MY BOYFRIEND.
ME, TOO. MY MOTHER-IN-LAW'S WATCHING MY KID.
THEY'RE AMAZING. I CAN'T EVEN TAKE CARE OF MYSELF...
WELL, IF YOU WEREN'T SO LAZY.
YOU'RE PUBLISHED NOW BUT YOU HAVEN'T CHANGED.

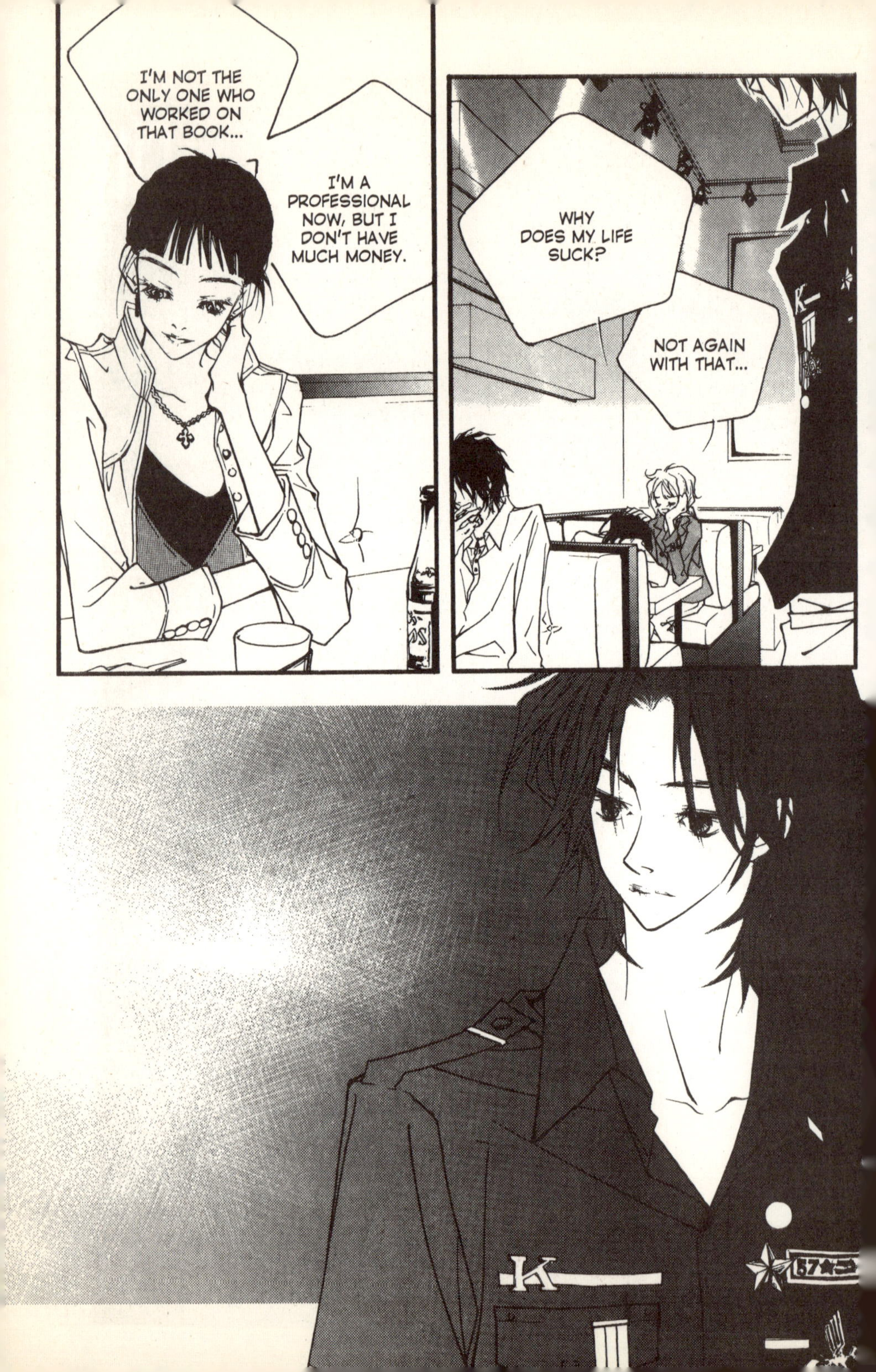
WHY DOES MY LIFE SUCK?
NOT AGAIN WITH THAT...
I'M NOT THE ONLY ONE WHO WORKED ON THAT BOOK...
I'M A PROFESSIONAL NOW, BUT I DON'T HAVE MUCH MONEY.

Forest of Gray City

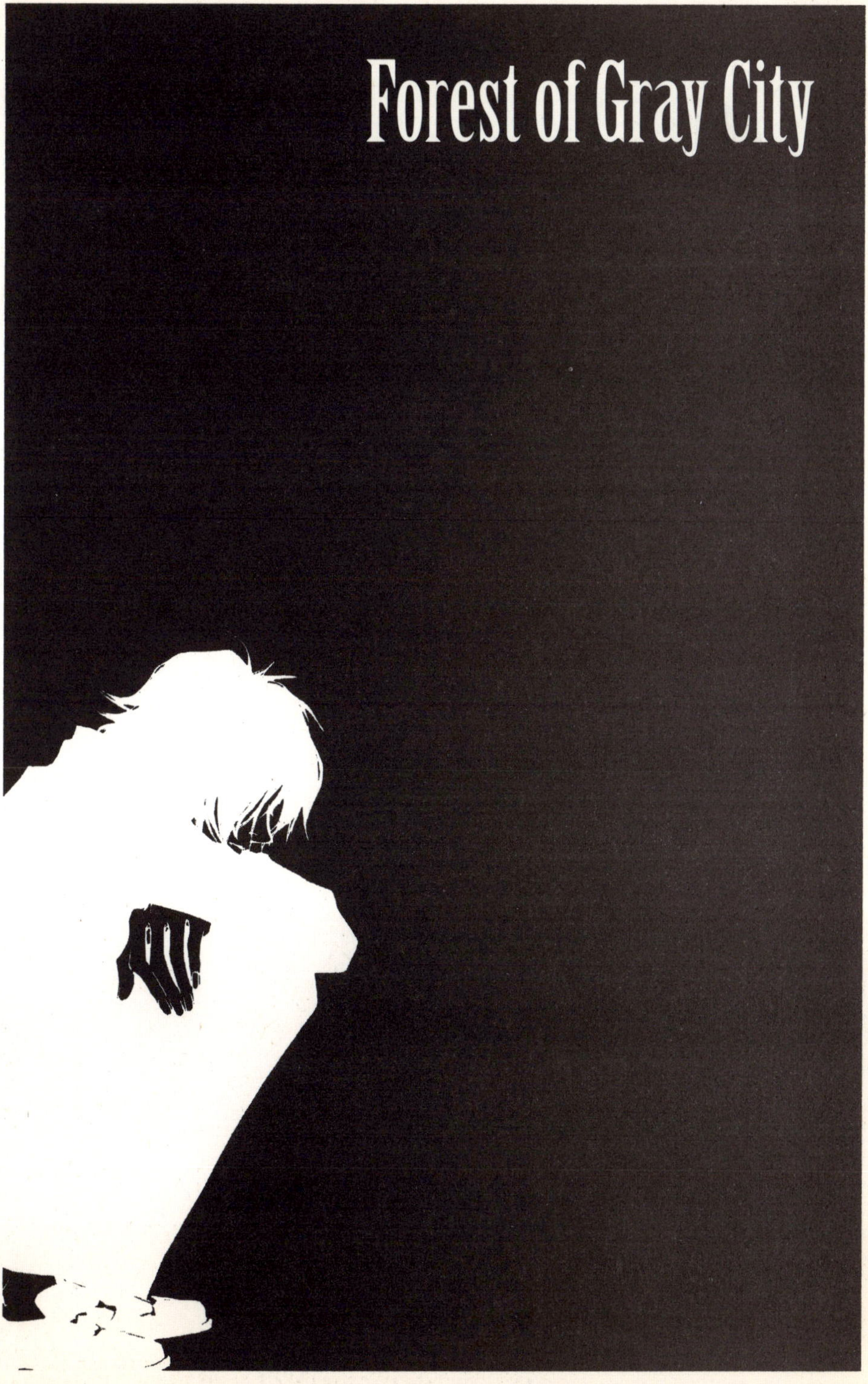

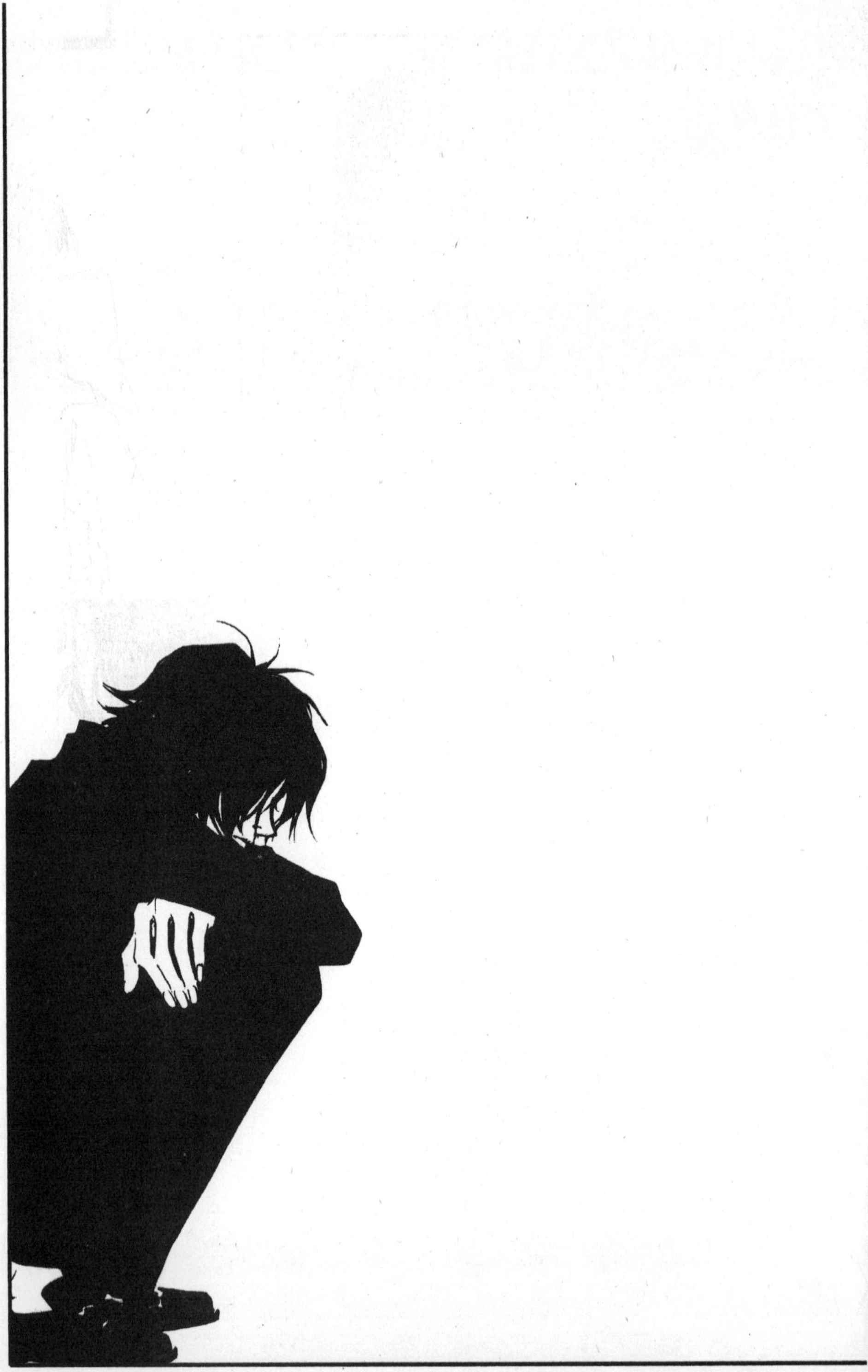

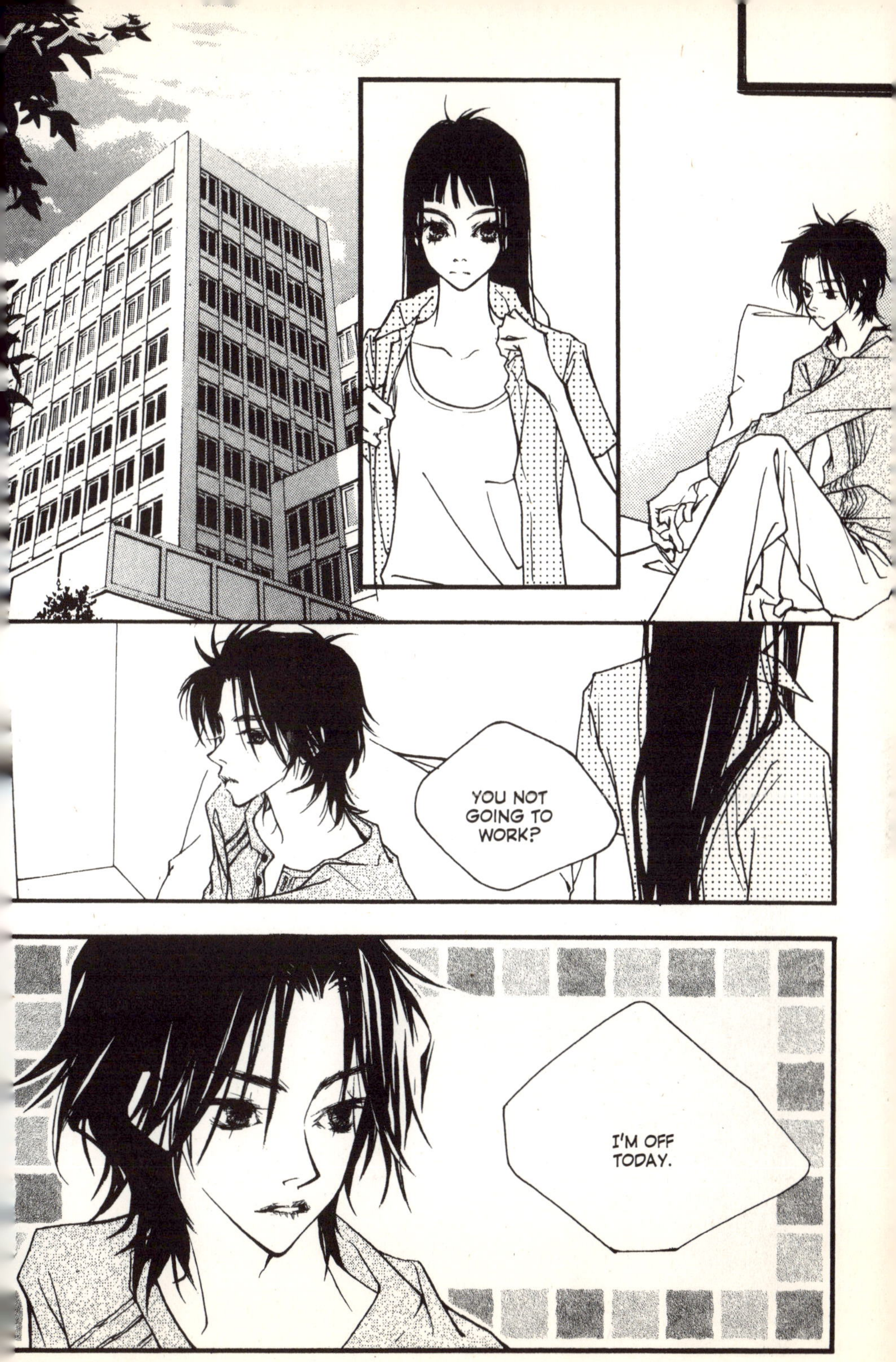
YOU NOT GOING TO WORK?
I'M OFF TODAY.

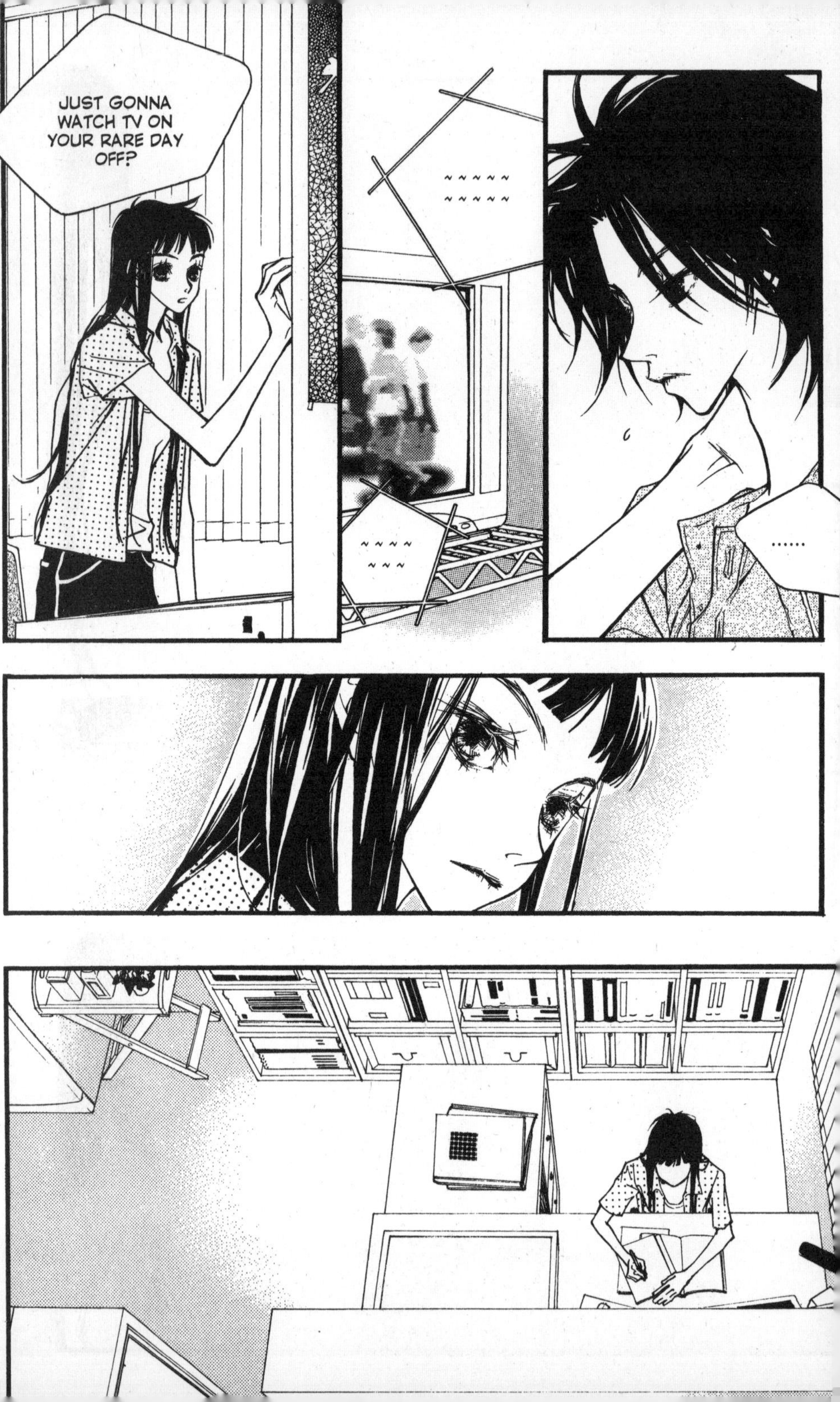
JUST GONNA WATCH TV ON YOUR RARE DAY OFF?
~~~~~
~~~~~
~~~~
~~~
......

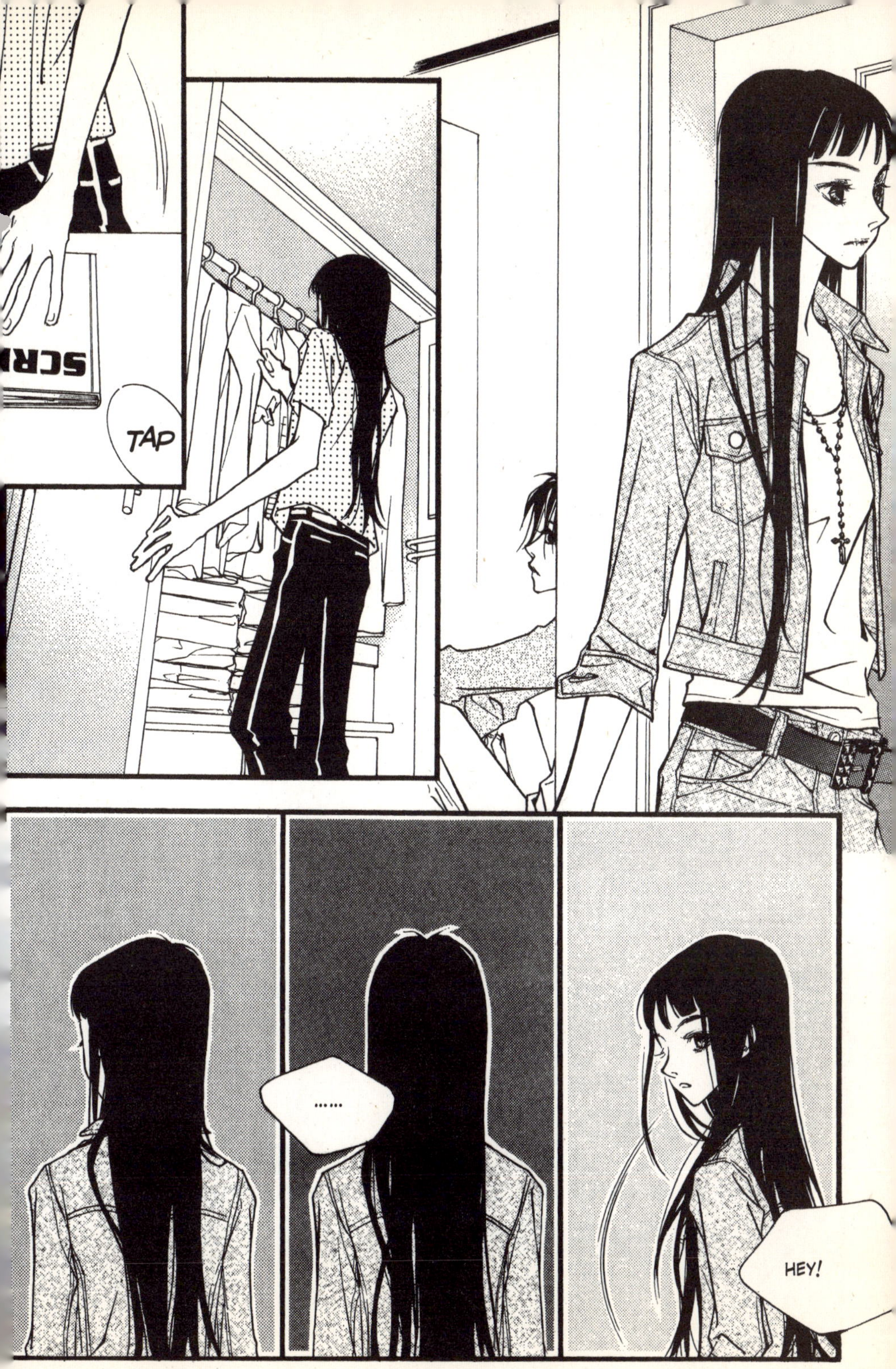
TAP
……
HEY!

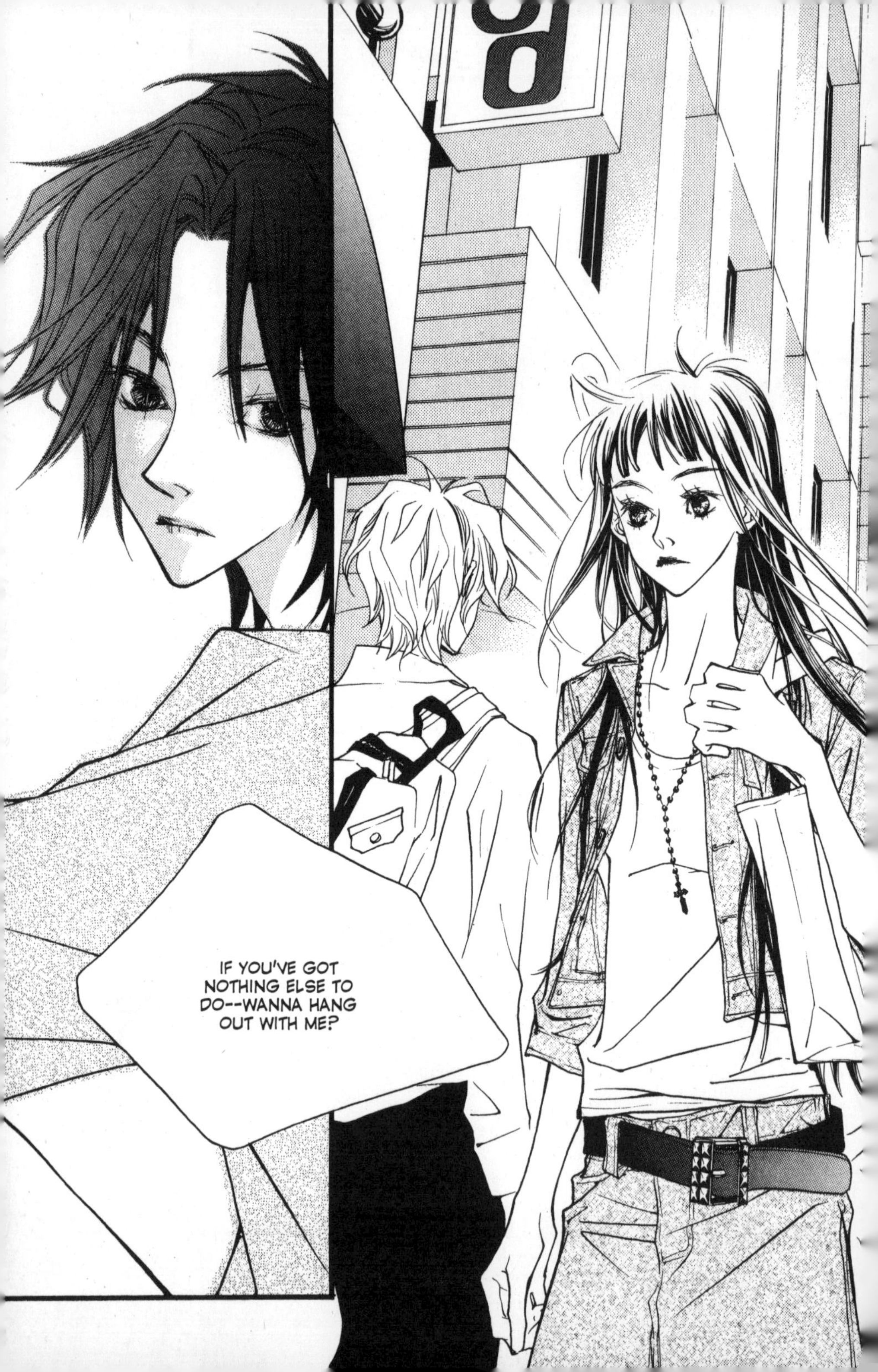
IF YOU'VE GOT NOTHING ELSE TO DO--WANNA HANG OUT WITH ME?

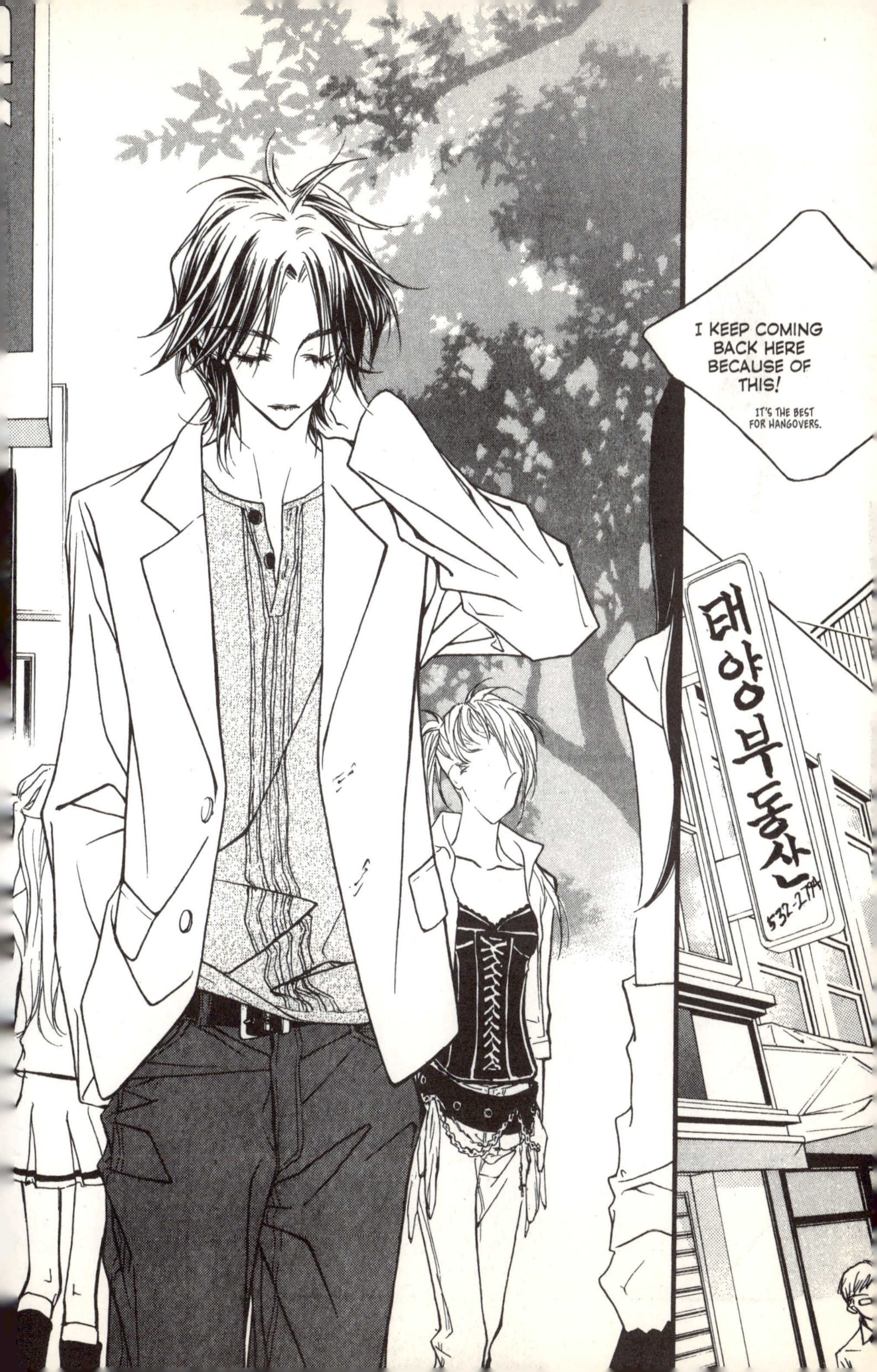
I KEEP COMING BACK HERE BECAUSE OF THIS!
IT'S THE BEST FOR HANGOVERS.
태양부동산
532-2794

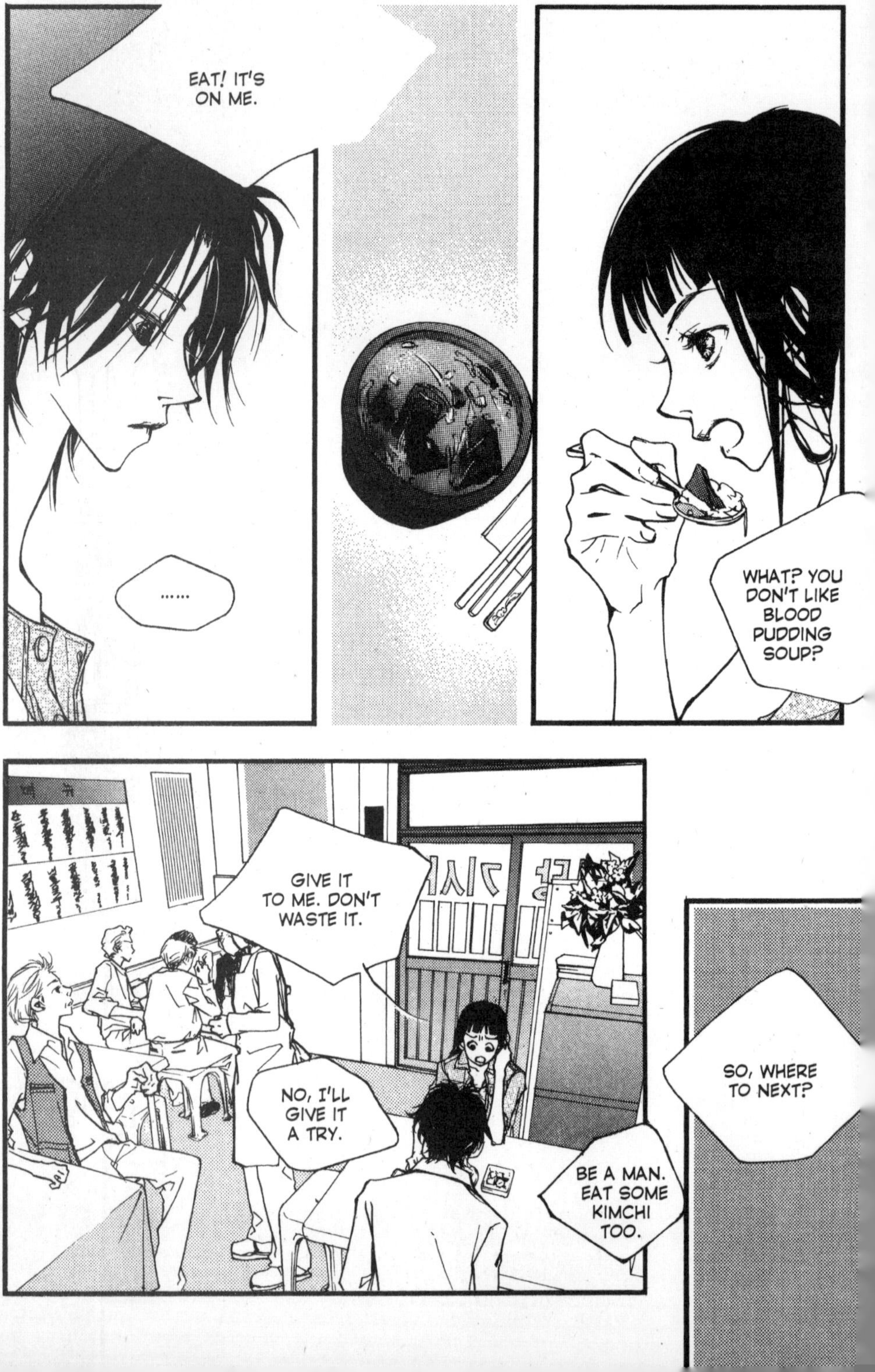
EAT! IT'S ON ME.
......
WHAT? YOU DON'T LIKE BLOOD PUDDING SOUP?
GIVE IT TO ME. DON'T WASTE IT.
NO, I'LL GIVE IT A TRY.
BE A MAN. EAT SOME KIMCHI TOO.
SO, WHERE TO NEXT?

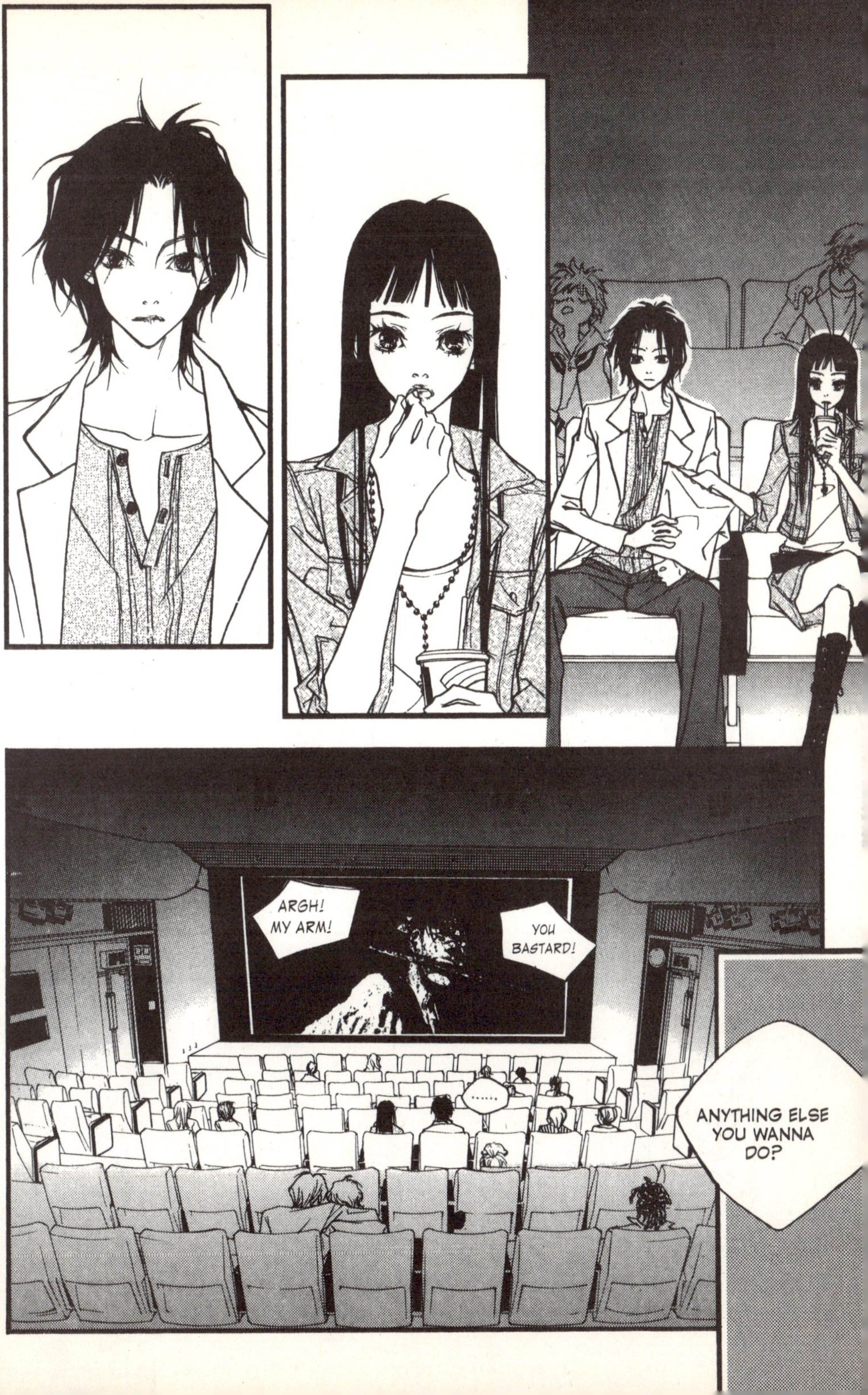
ARGH! MY ARM!
YOU BASTARD!
......
ANYTHING ELSE YOU WANNA DO?

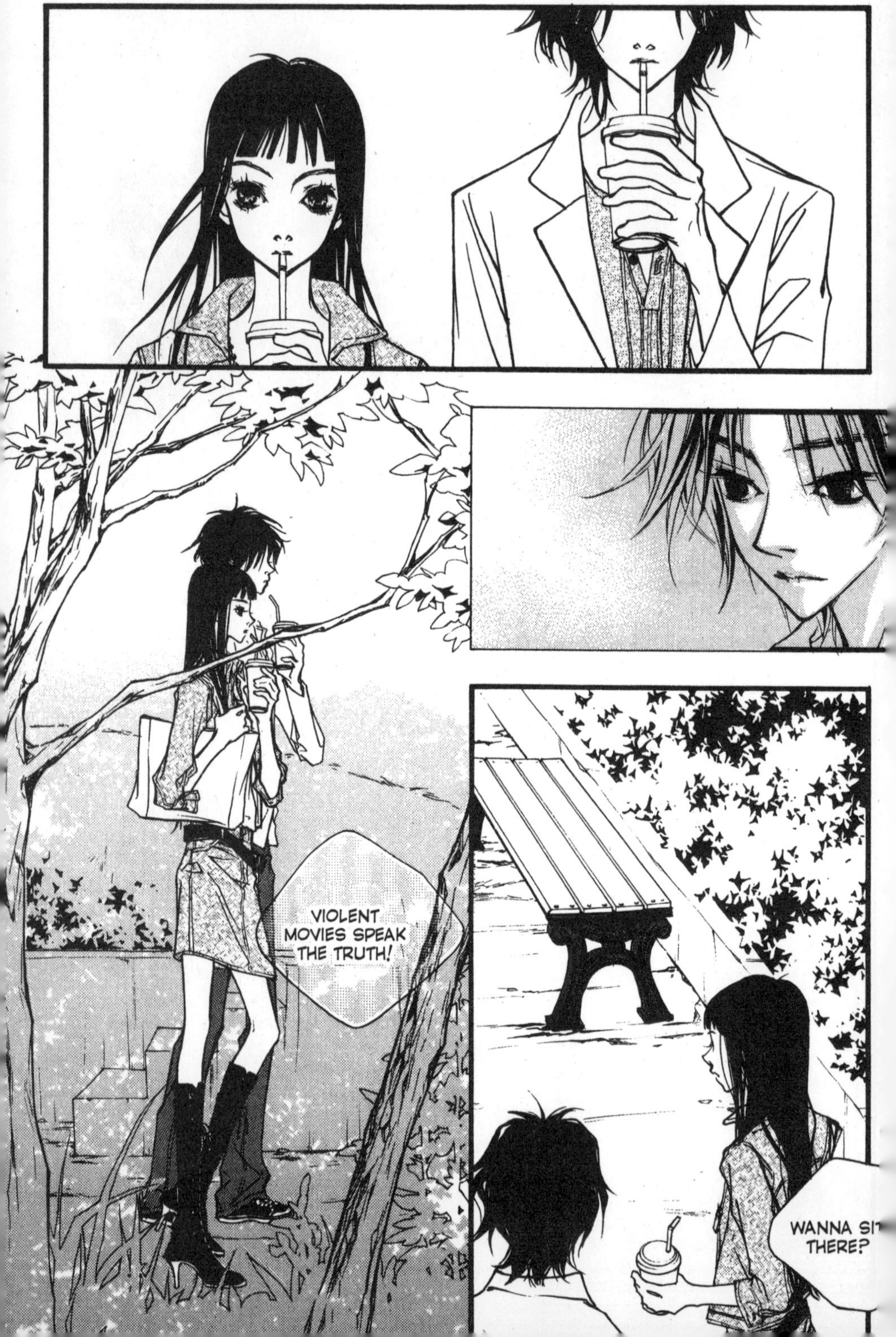
VIOLENT MOVIES SPEAK THE TRUTH!
WANNA SIT THERE?

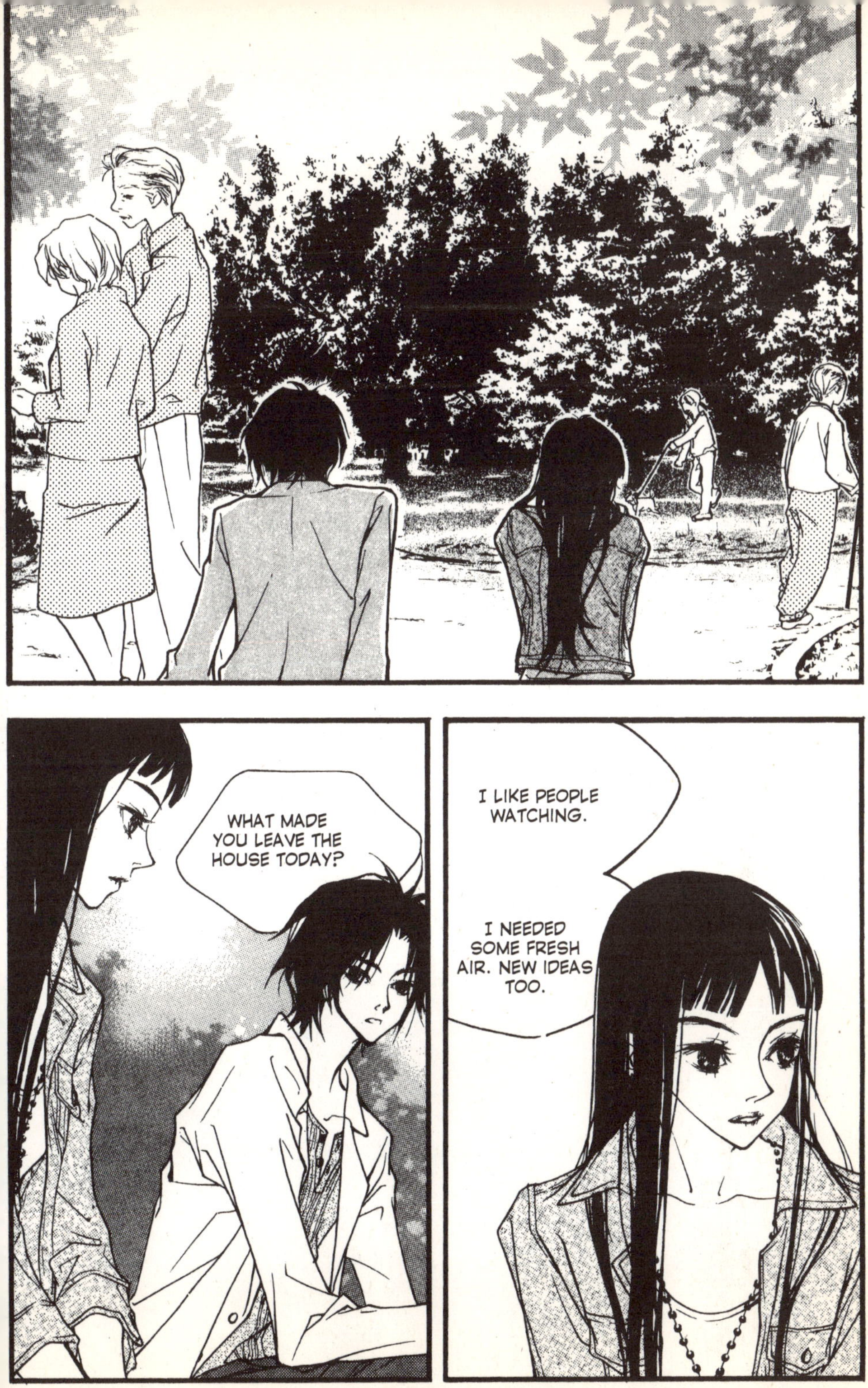
WHAT MADE YOU LEAVE THE HOUSE TODAY?
I LIKE PEOPLE WATCHING.
I NEEDED SOME FRESH AIR. NEW IDEAS TOO.

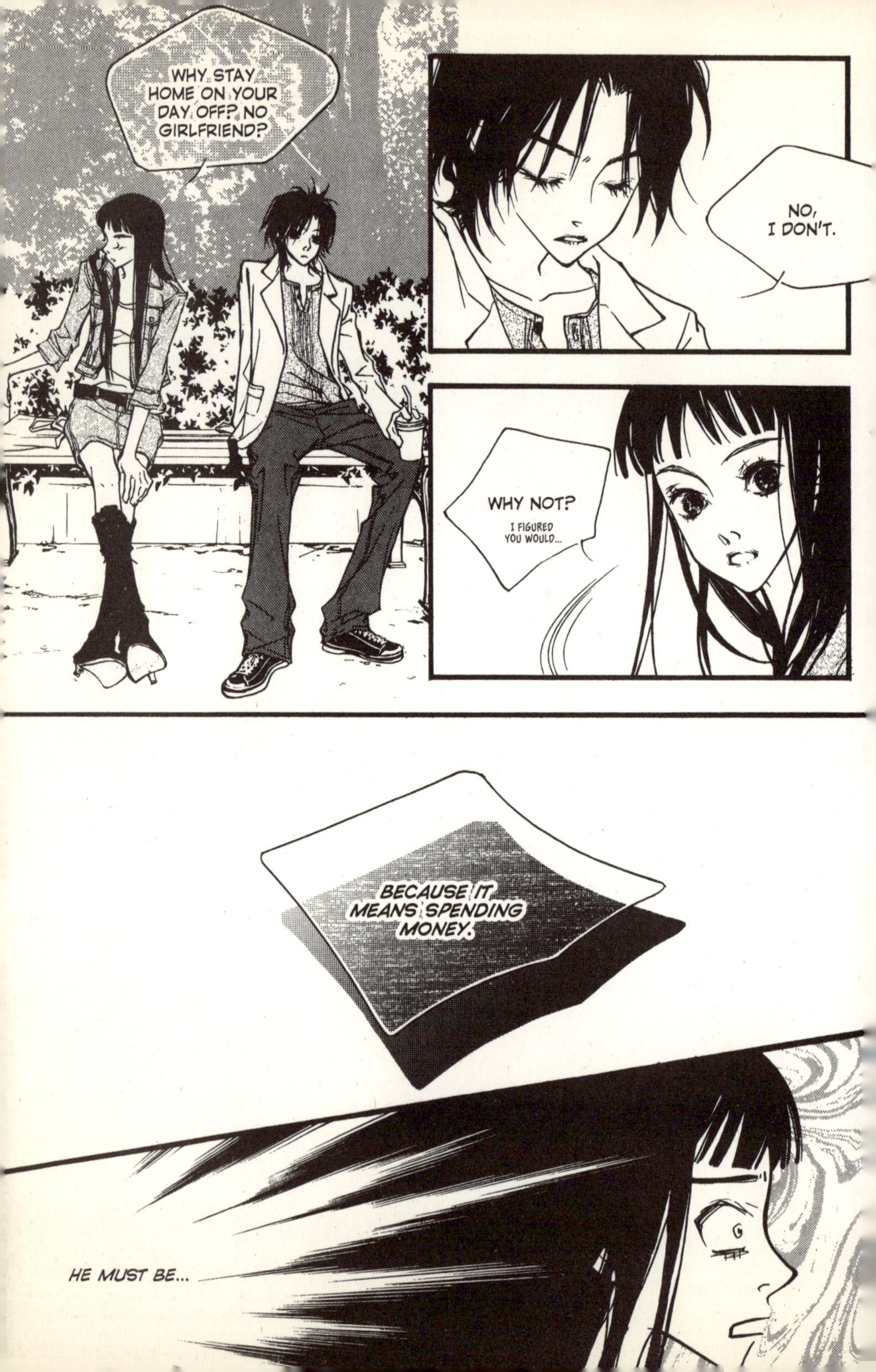
WHY STAY HOME ON YOUR DAY OFF? NO GIRLFRIEND?
NO, I DON'T.
WHY NOT?
I FIGURED YOU WOULD...
BECAUSE IT MEANS SPENDING MONEY.
HE MUST BE...

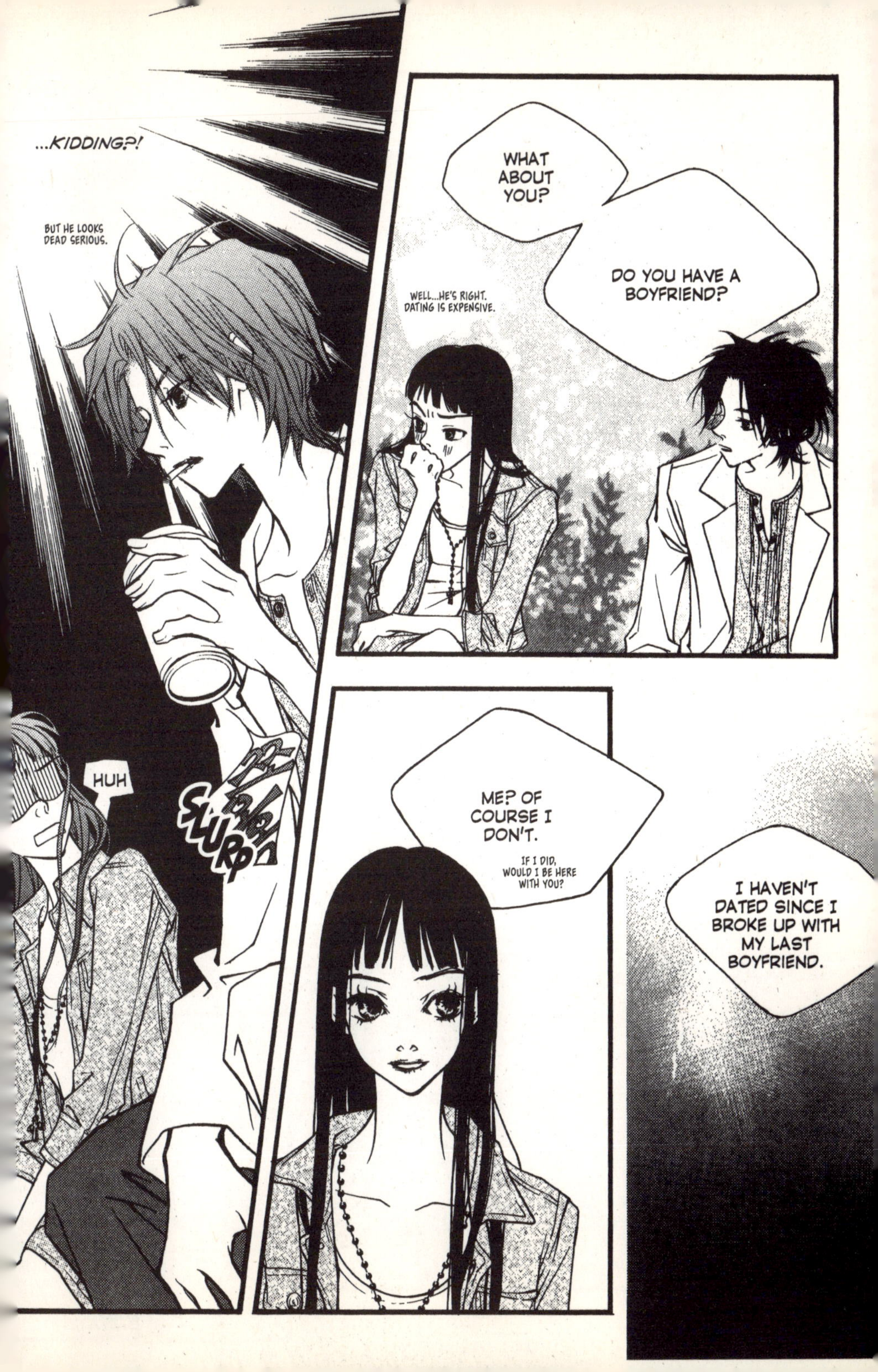
...KIDDING?!
BUT HE LOOKS DEAD SERIOUS.
HUH
SLURP
WELL...HE'S RIGHT. DATING IS EXPENSIVE.
WHAT ABOUT YOU?
DO YOU HAVE A BOYFRIEND?
ME? OF COURSE I DON'T.
IF I DID, WOULD I BE HERE WITH YOU?
I HAVEN'T DATED SINCE I BROKE UP WITH MY LAST BOYFRIEND.

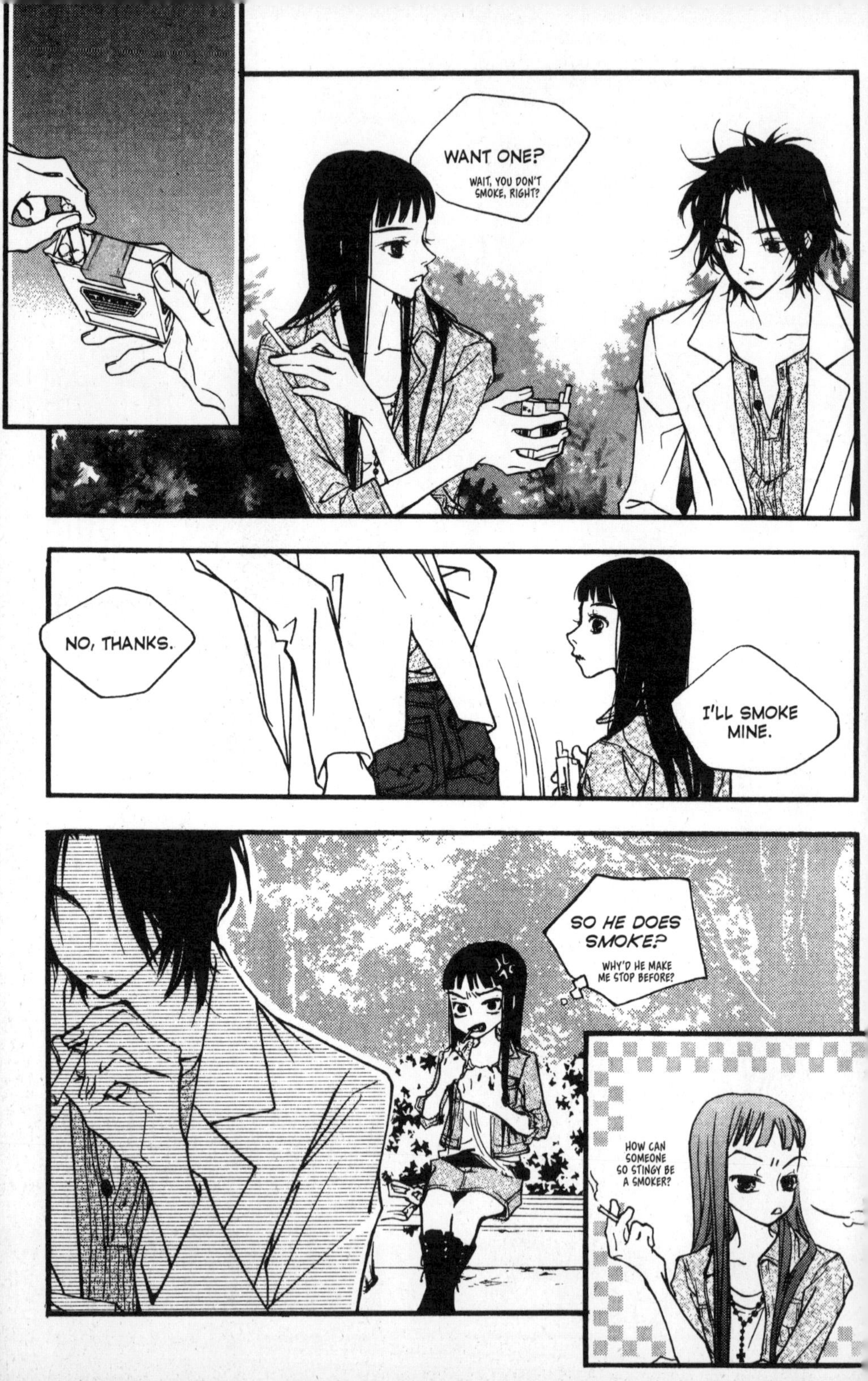

WANT ONE?
WAIT, YOU DON'T SMOKE, RIGHT?
NO, THANKS.
I'LL SMOKE MINE.
SO HE DOES SMOKE?
WHY'D HE MAKE ME STOP BEFORE?
HOW CAN SOMEONE SO STINGY BE A SMOKER?

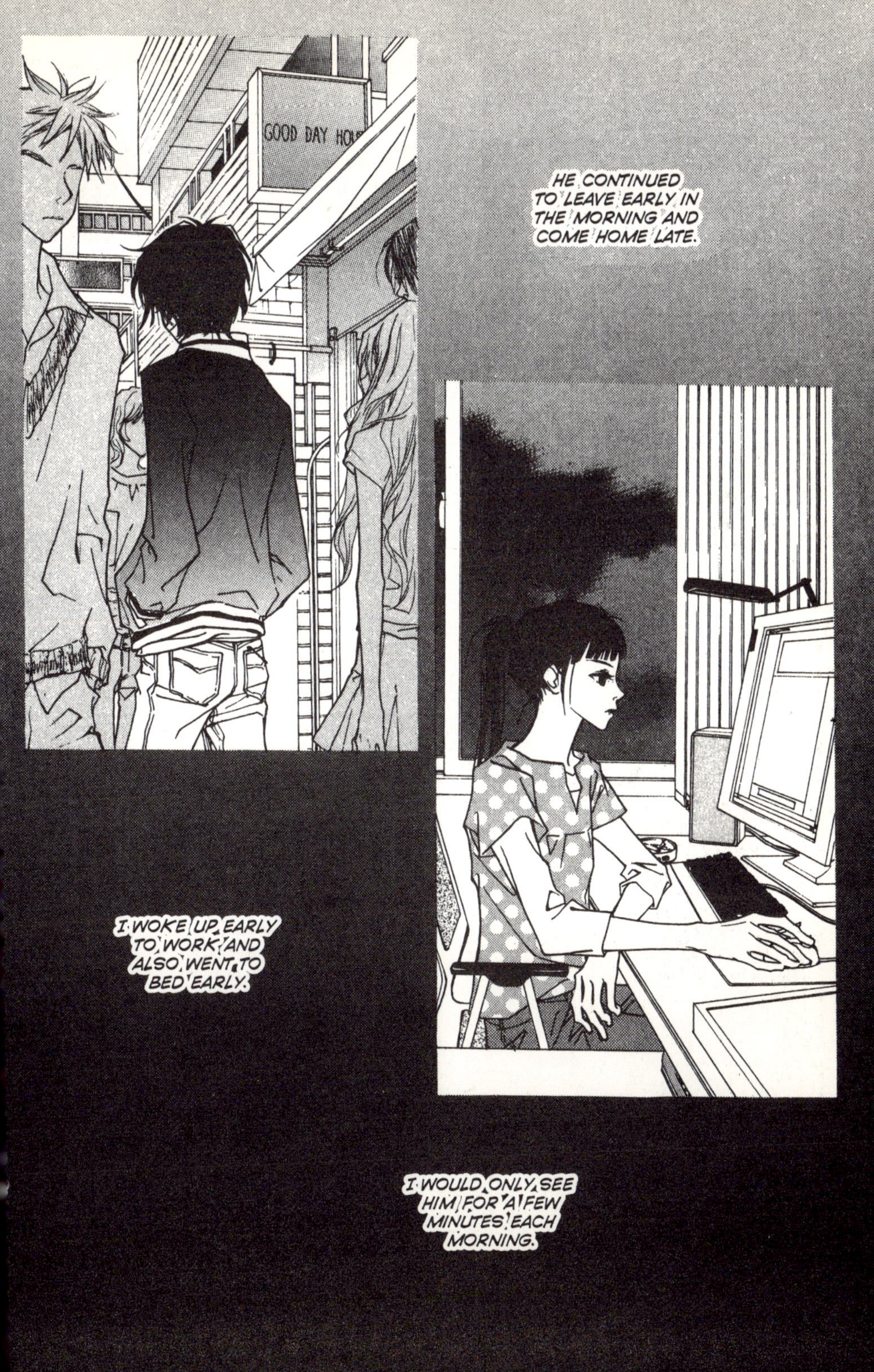
HE CONTINUED TO LEAVE EARLY IN THE MORNING AND COME HOME LATE.
I WOKE UP EARLY TO WORK AND ALSO WENT TO BED EARLY.
I WOULD ONLY SEE HIM FOR A FEW MINUTES EACH MORNING.

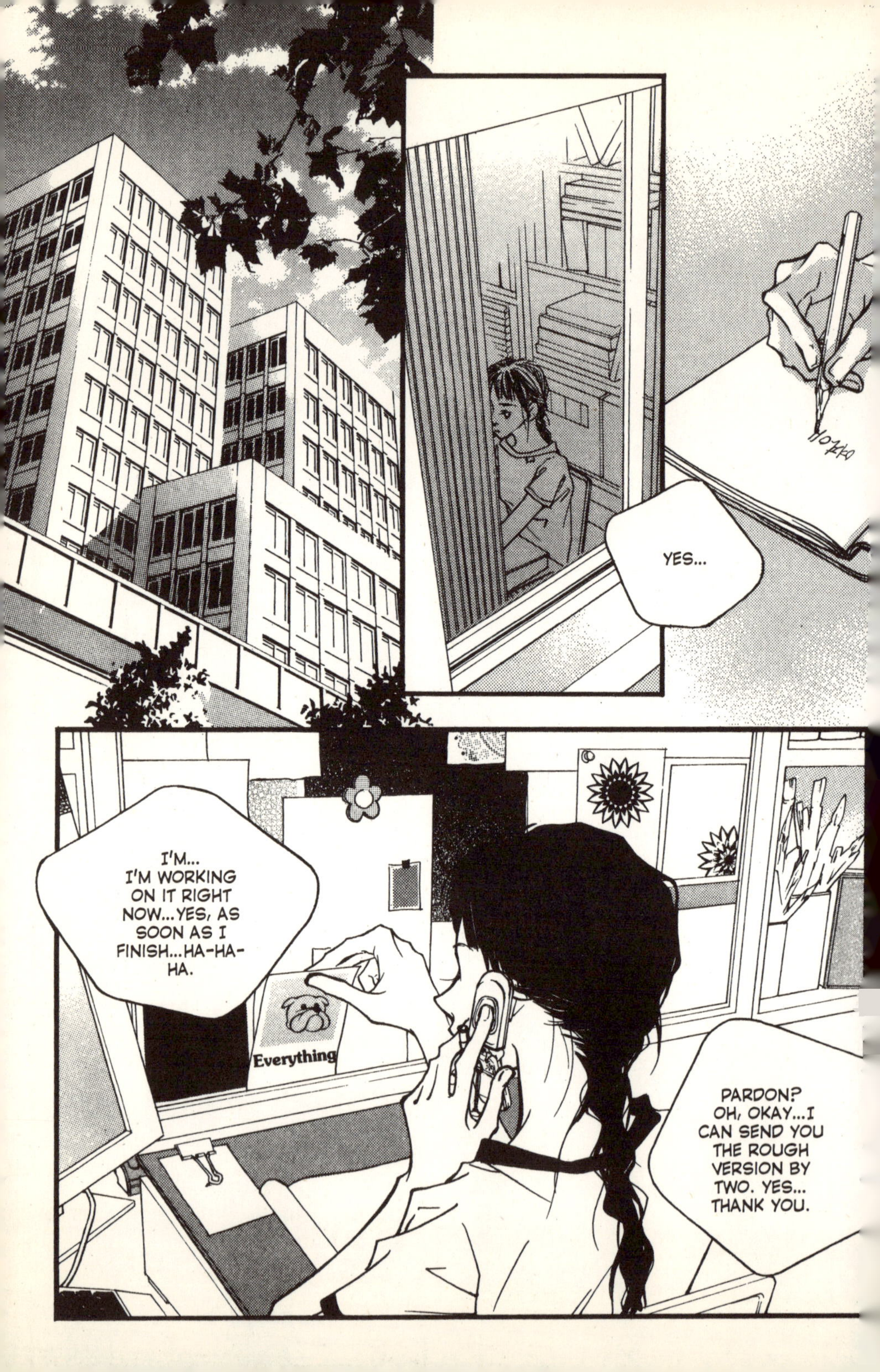
YES...
I'M... I'M WORKING ON IT RIGHT NOW...YES, AS SOON AS I FINISH...HA-HA-HA.
Everything
PARDON? OH, OKAY...I CAN SEND YOU THE ROUGH VERSION BY TWO. YES... THANK YOU.

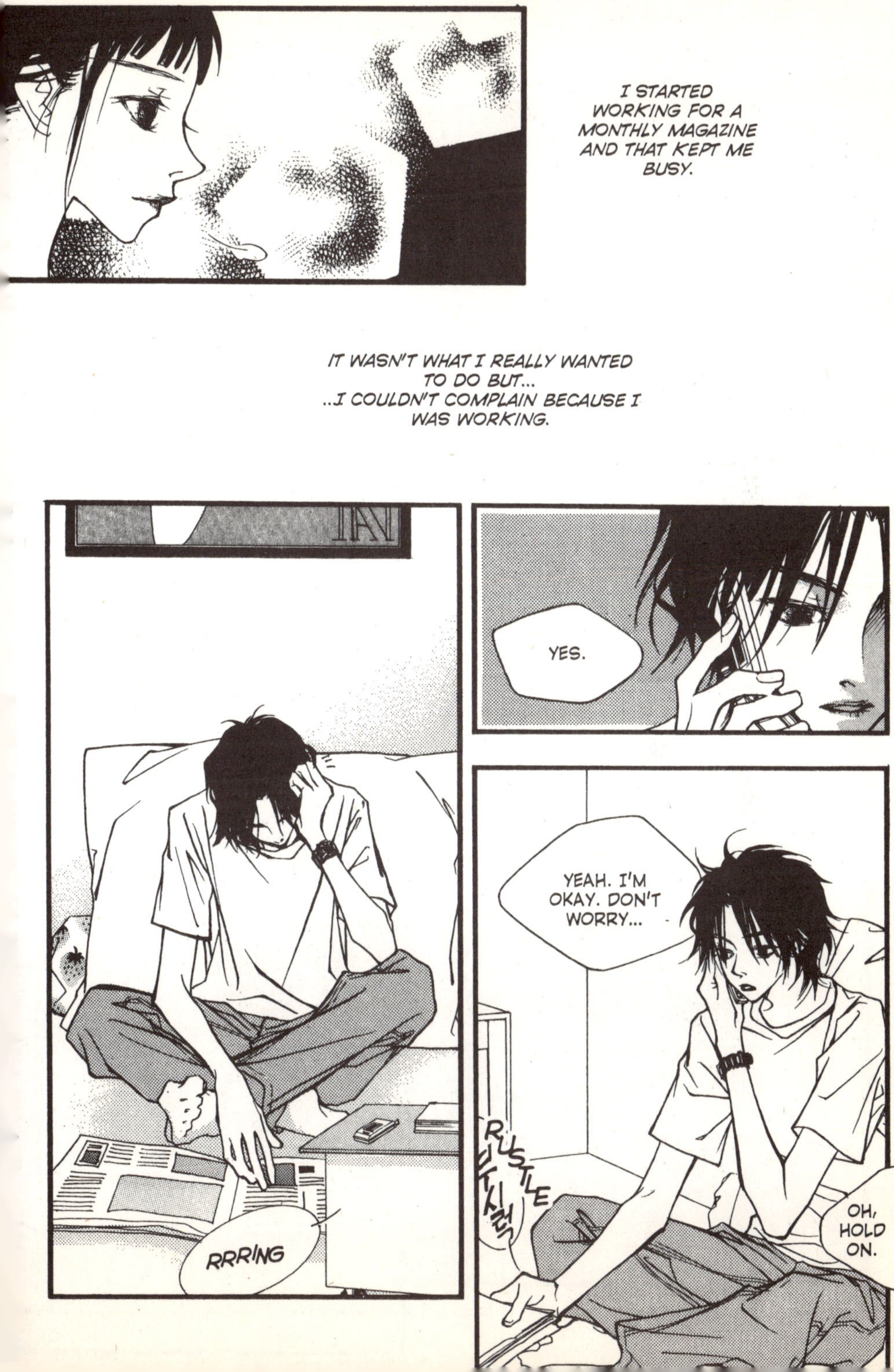
I STARTED WORKING FOR A MONTHLY MAGAZINE AND THAT KEPT ME BUSY.
IT WASN'T WHAT I REALLY WANTED TO DO BUT...
...I COULDN'T COMPLAIN BECAUSE I WAS WORKING.
RRRING
YES.
YEAH. I'M OKAY. DON'T WORRY...
RUSTLE
OH, HOLD ON.

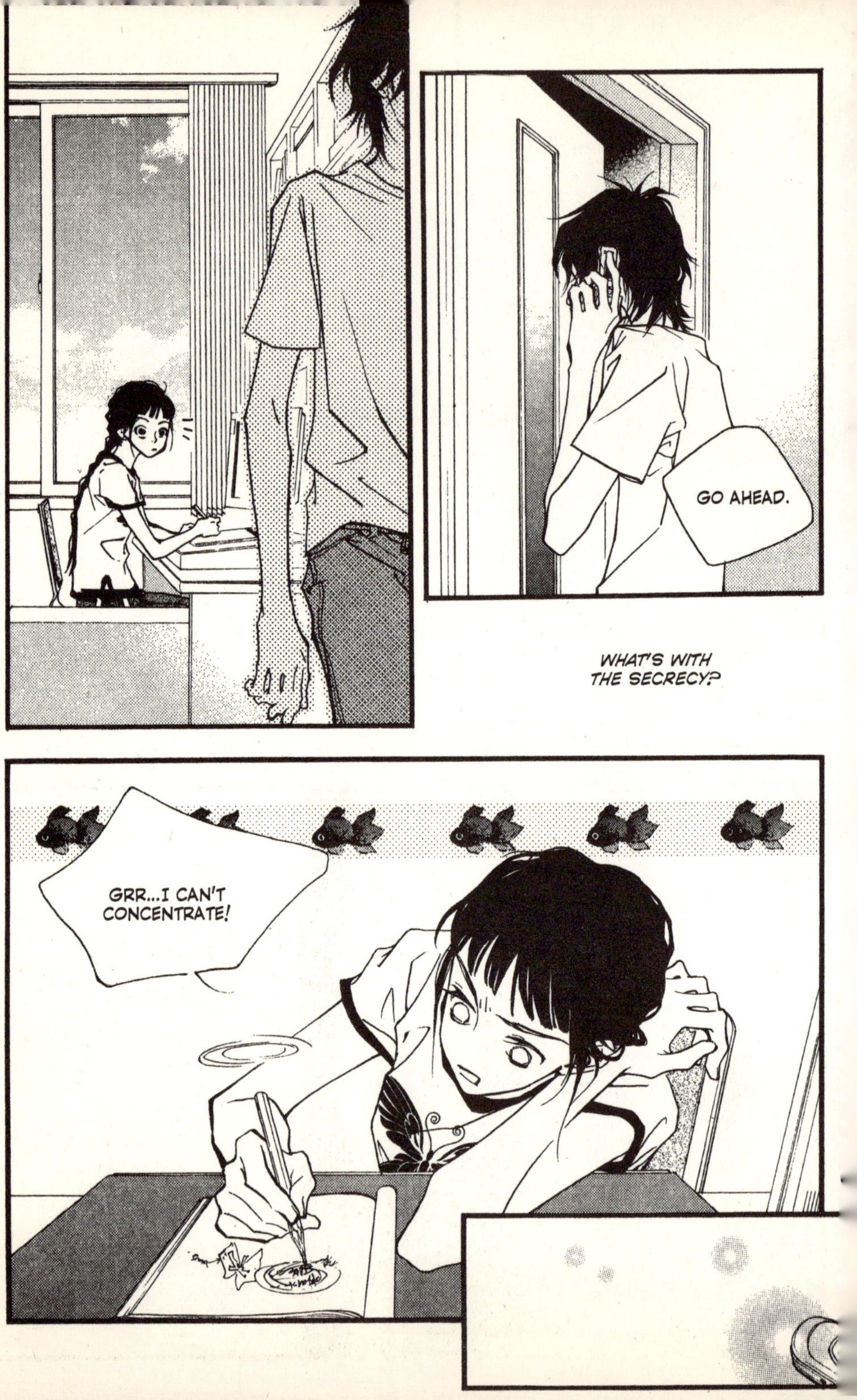
GO AHEAD.
WHAT'S WITH THE SECRECY?
GRR...I CAN'T CONCENTRATE!

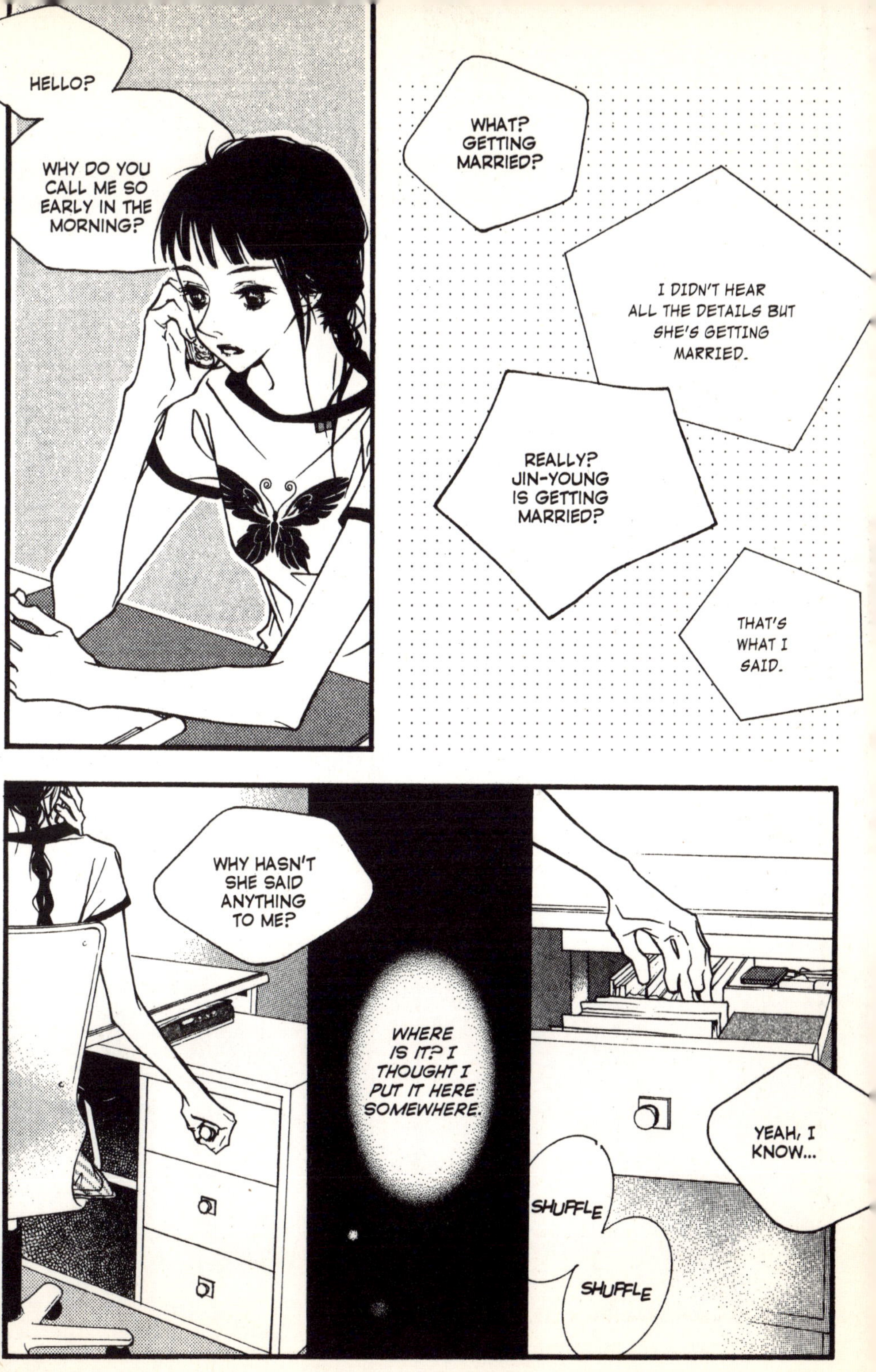
HELLO?
WHY DO YOU CALL ME SO EARLY IN THE MORNING?
WHAT? GETTING MARRIED?
I DIDN'T HEAR ALL THE DETAILS BUT SHE'S GETTING MARRIED.
REALLY? JIN-YOUNG IS GETTING MARRIED?
THAT'S WHAT I SAID.
WHY HASN'T SHE SAID ANYTHING TO ME?
WHERE IS IT? I THOUGHT I PUT IT HERE SOMEWHERE.
YEAH, I KNOW...
SHUFFLE
SHUFFLE

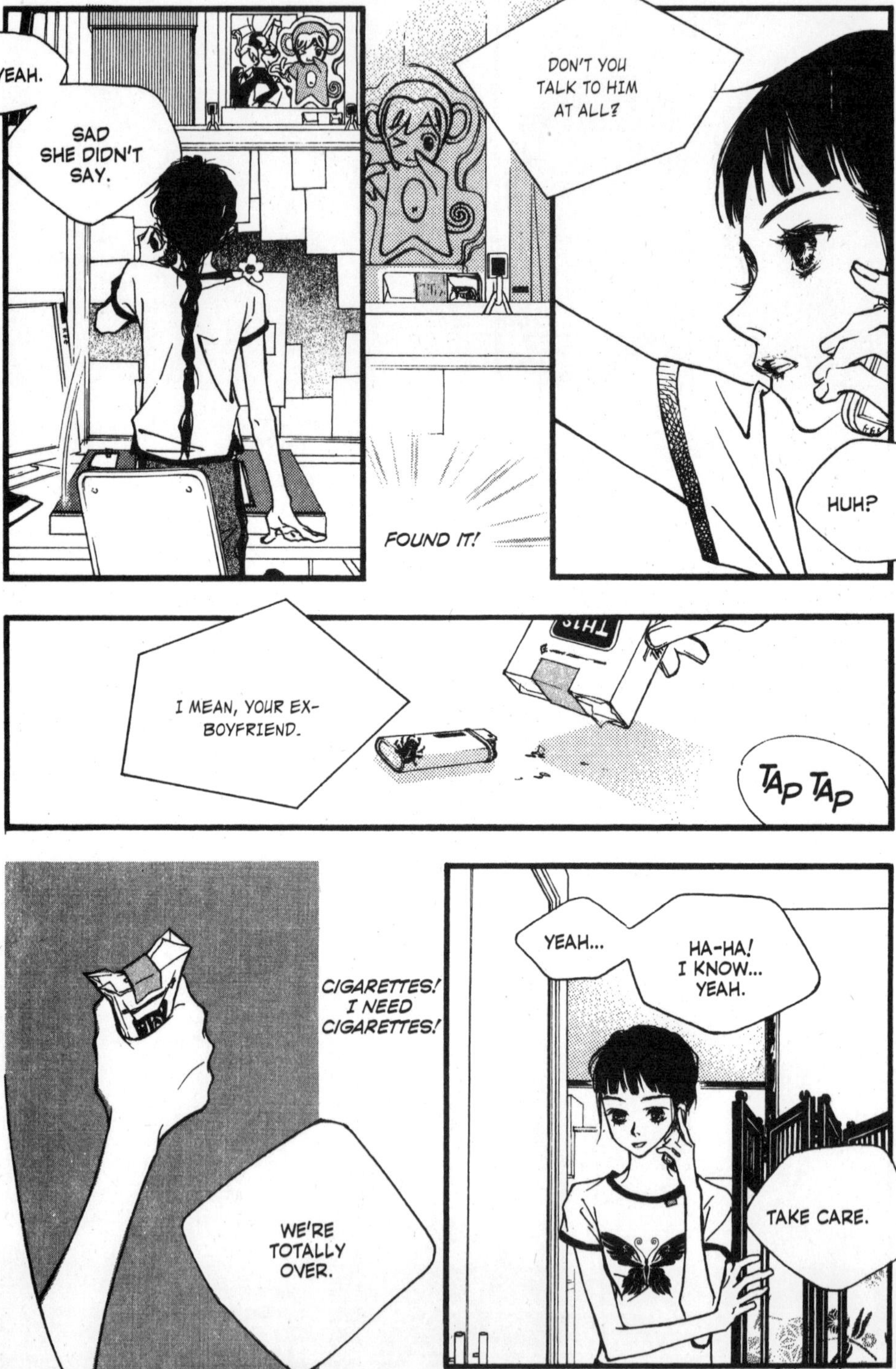
YEAH.
SAD SHE DIDN'T SAY.
FOUND IT!
DON'T YOU TALK TO HIM AT ALL?
HUH?
THIS
I MEAN, YOUR EX-BOYFRIEND.
TAP TAP
CIGARETTES! I NEED CIGARETTES!
WE'RE TOTALLY OVER.
YEAH...
HA-HA! I KNOW... YEAH.
TAKE CARE.

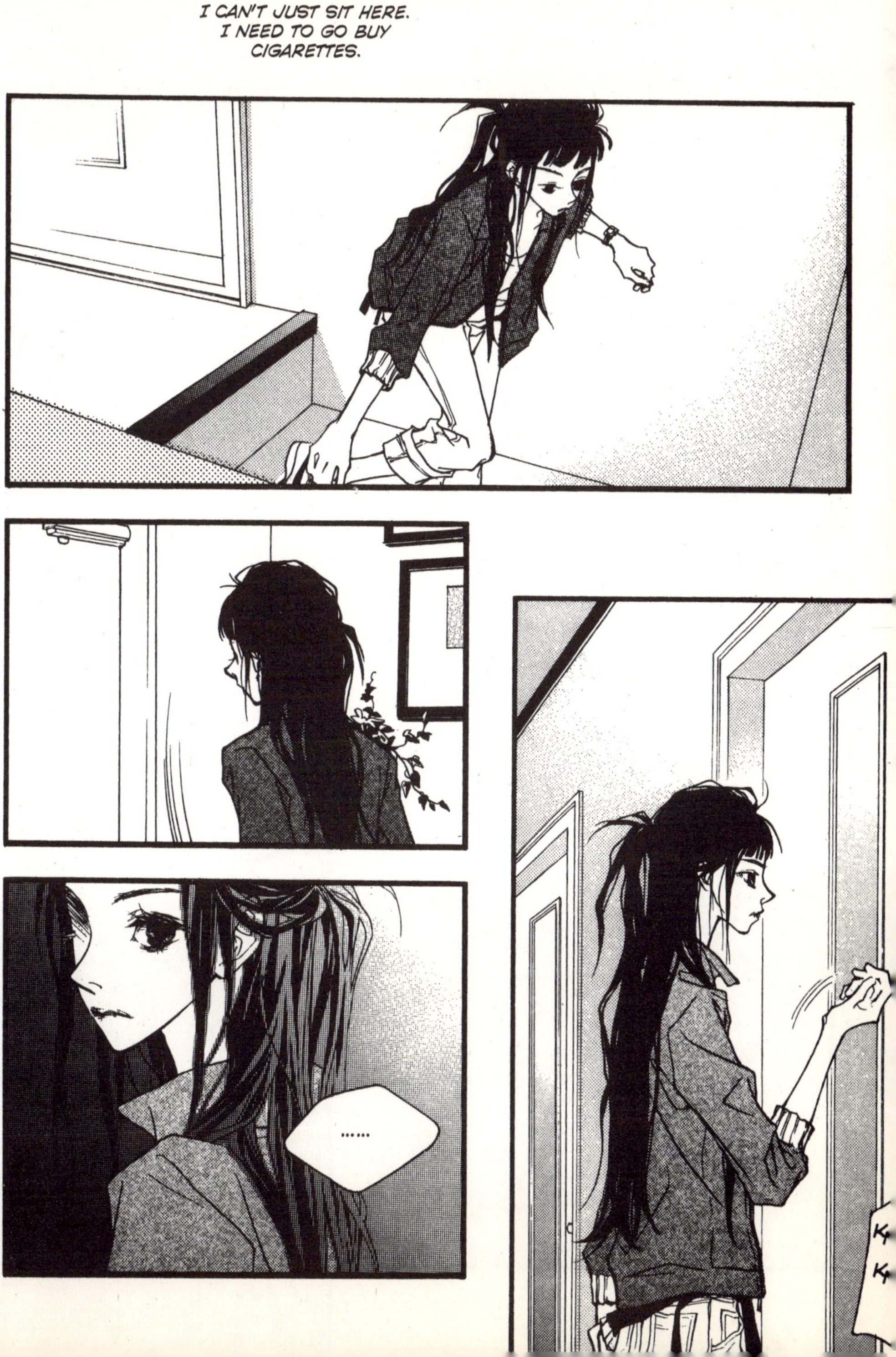
I CAN'T JUST SIT HERE. I NEED TO GO BUY CIGARETTES.
……

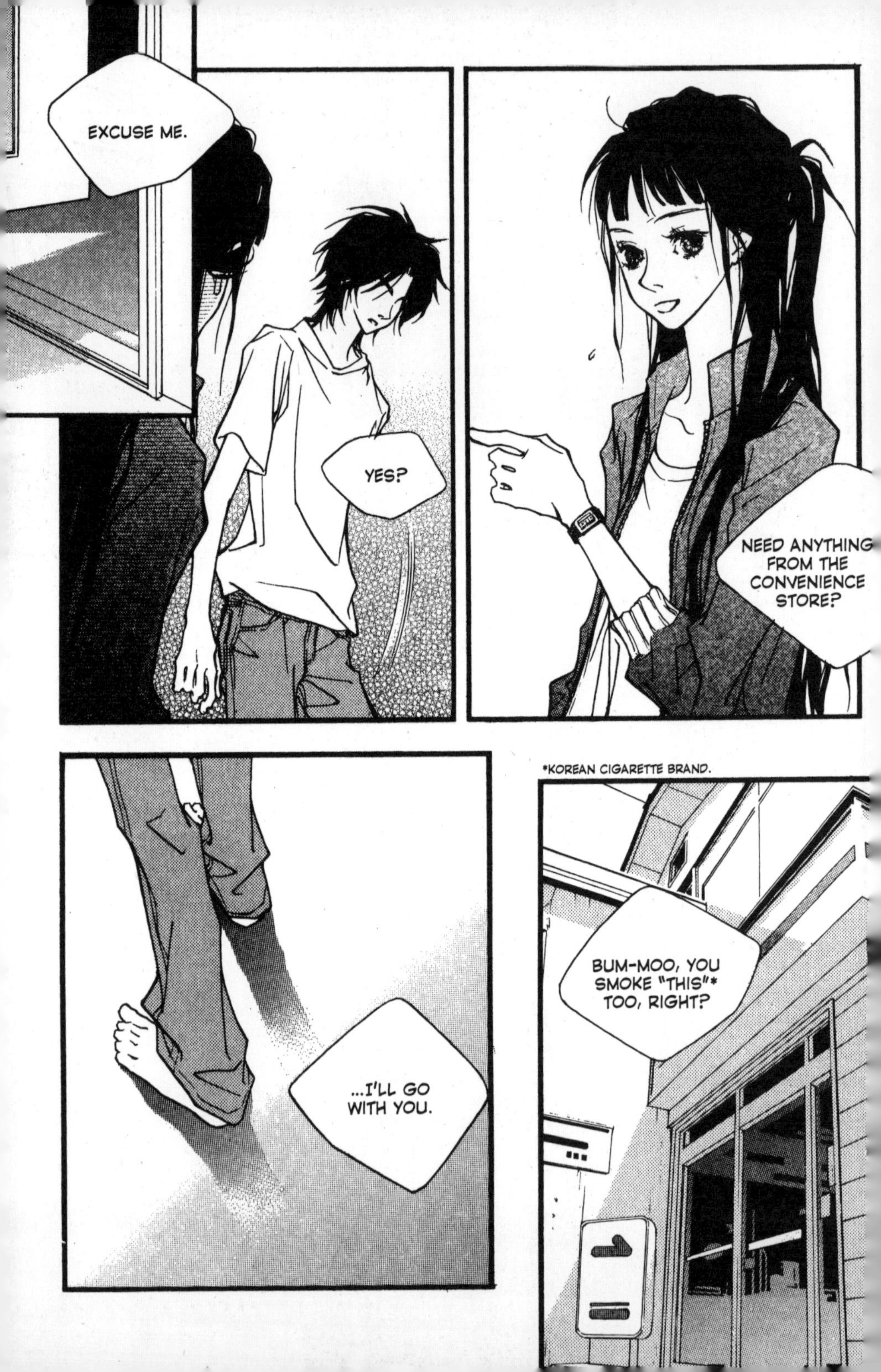
EXCUSE ME.
YES?
NEED ANYTHING FROM THE CONVENIENCE STORE?
...I'LL GO WITH YOU.
BUM-MOO, YOU SMOKE "THIS"* TOO, RIGHT?

*KOREAN CIGARETTE BRAND.

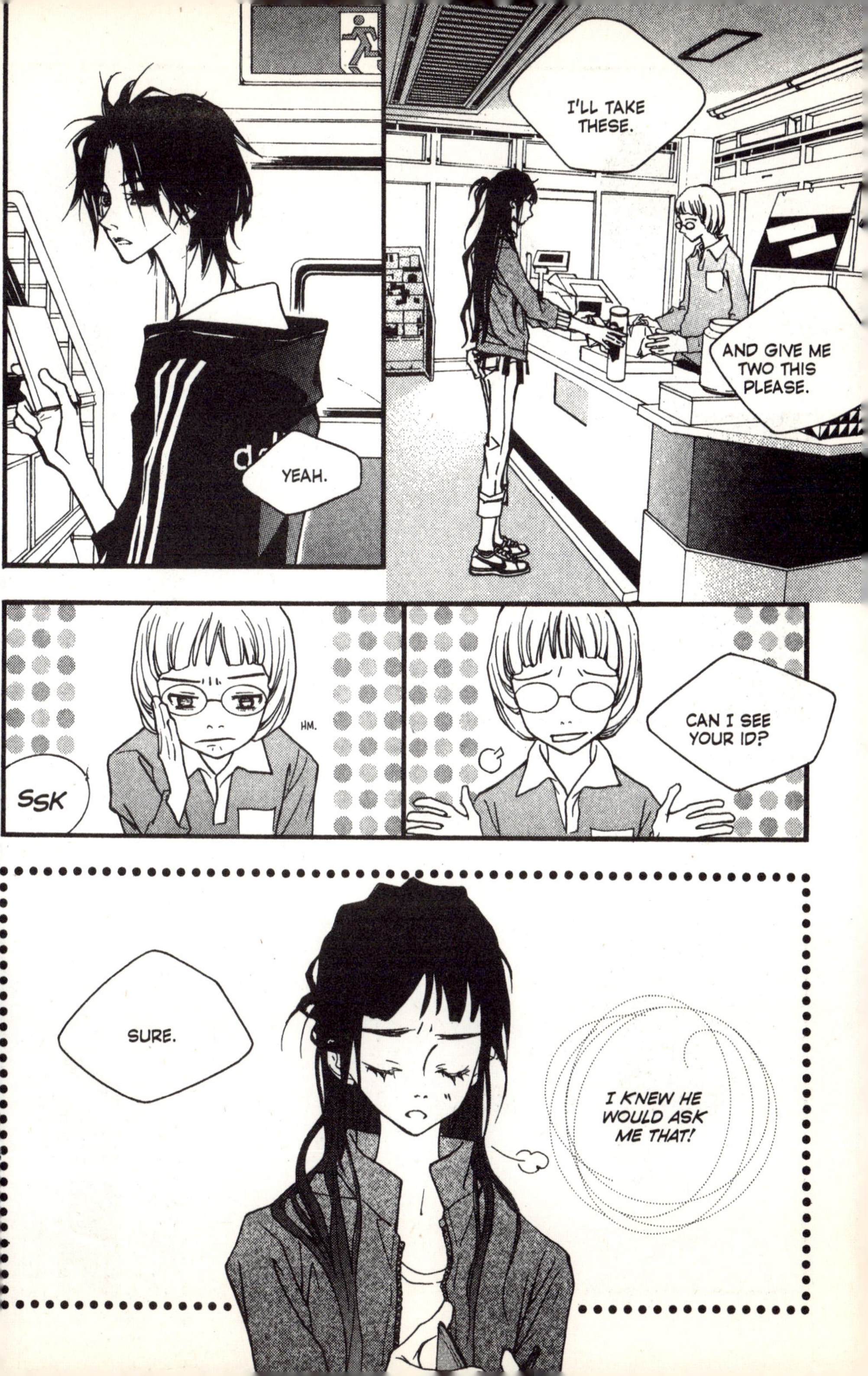
I'LL TAKE THESE.
AND GIVE ME TWO THIS PLEASE.
YEAH.
CAN I SEE YOUR ID?
HM.
SSK
I KNEW HE WOULD ASK ME THAT!
SURE.

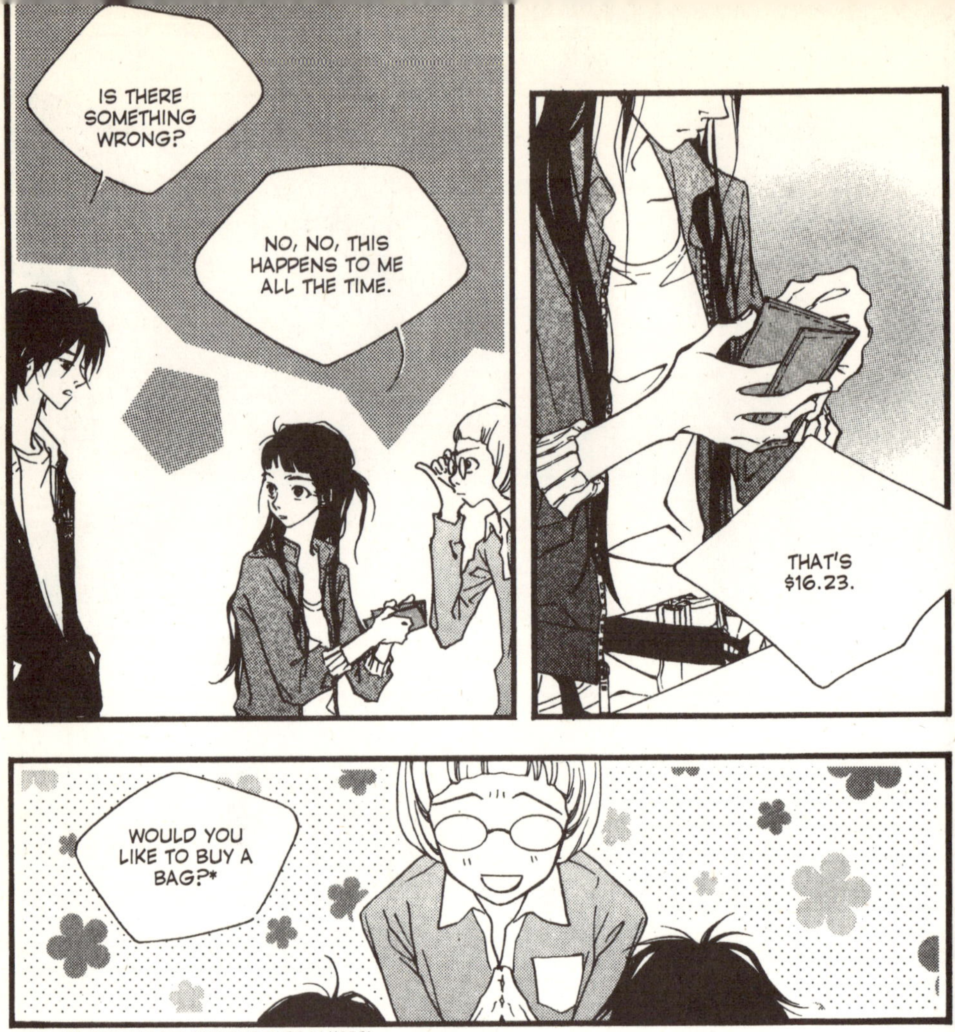
IS THERE SOMETHING WRONG?
NO, NO, THIS HAPPENS TO ME ALL THE TIME.
THAT'S $16.23.
WOULD YOU LIKE TO BUY A BAG?*

*YOU HAVE TO PAY FOR SHOPPING BAGS IN KOREA.

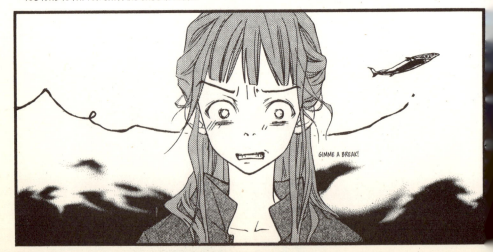

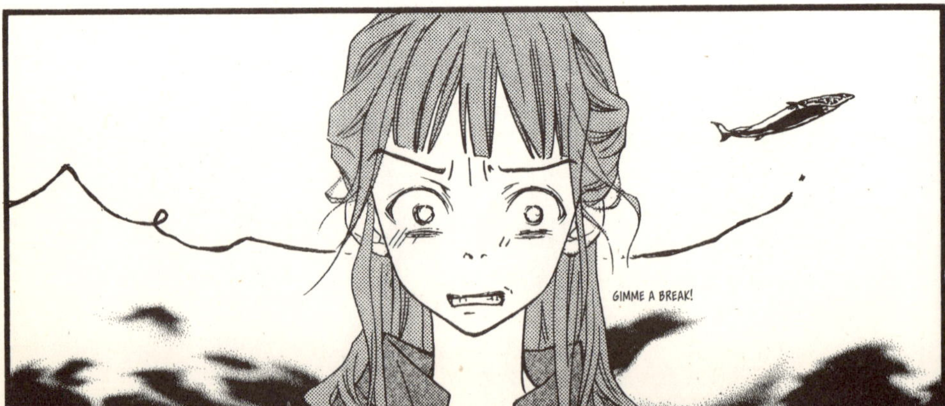
GIMME A BREAK!

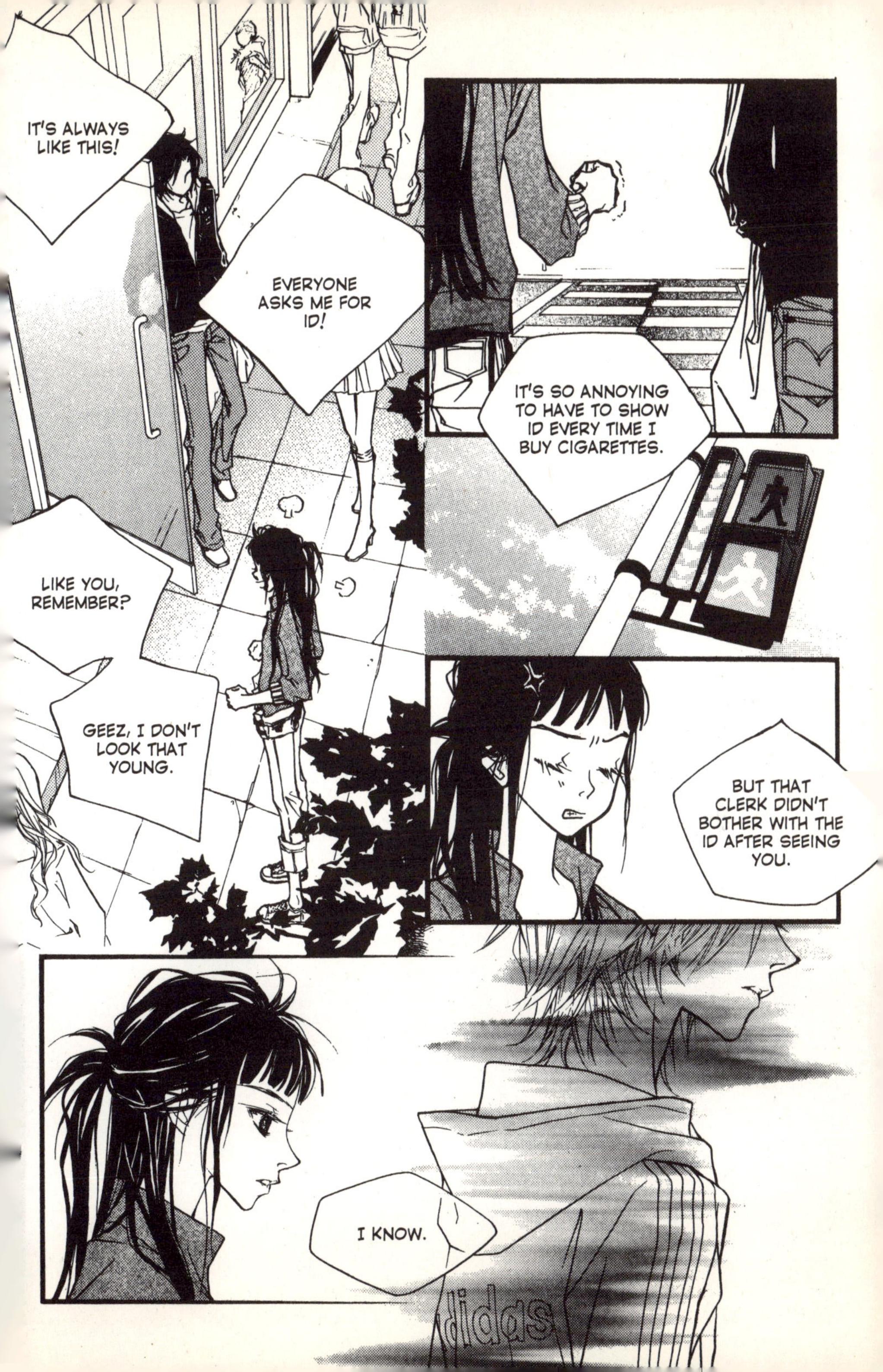
IT'S ALWAYS LIKE THIS!
EVERYONE ASKS ME FOR ID!
LIKE YOU, REMEMBER?
GEEZ, I DON'T LOOK THAT YOUNG.
IT'S SO ANNOYING TO HAVE TO SHOW ID EVERY TIME I BUY CIGARETTES.
BUT THAT CLERK DIDN'T BOTHER WITH THE ID AFTER SEEING YOU.
I KNOW.
idas

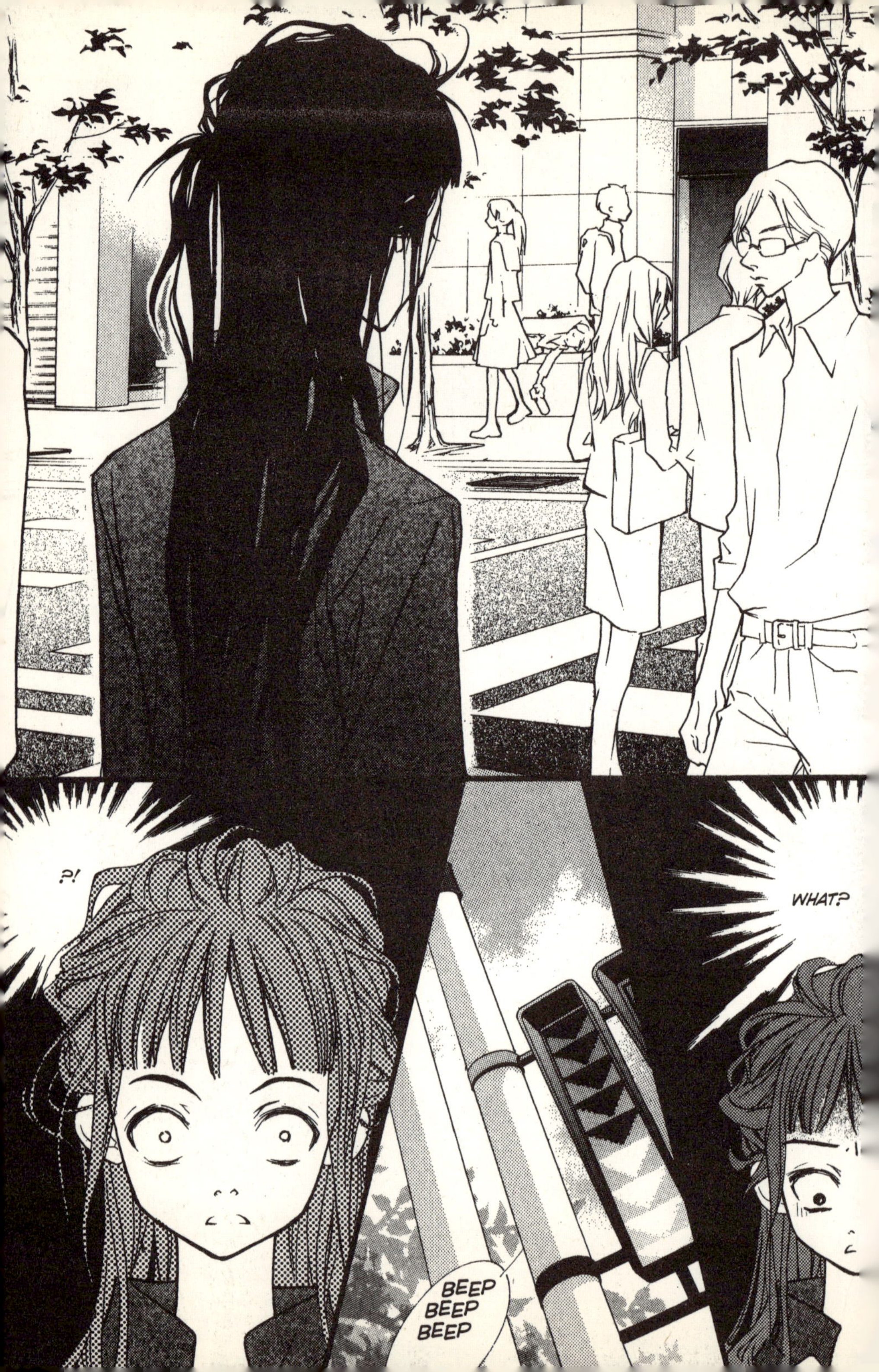
WHAT?
?!
BEEP
BEEP
BEEP

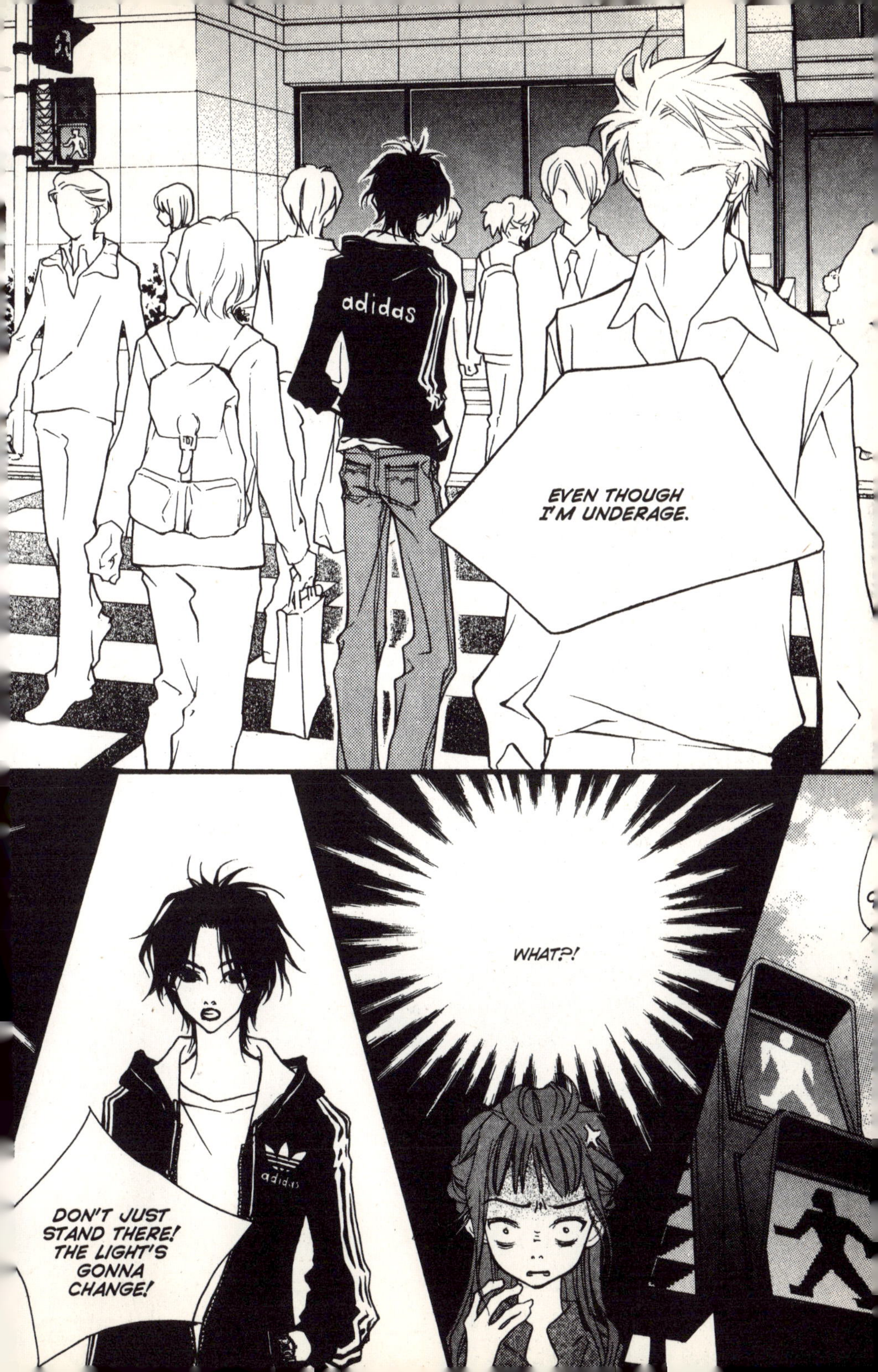
EVEN THOUGH I'M UNDERAGE.
WHAT?!
DON'T JUST STAND THERE! THE LIGHT'S GONNA CHANGE!

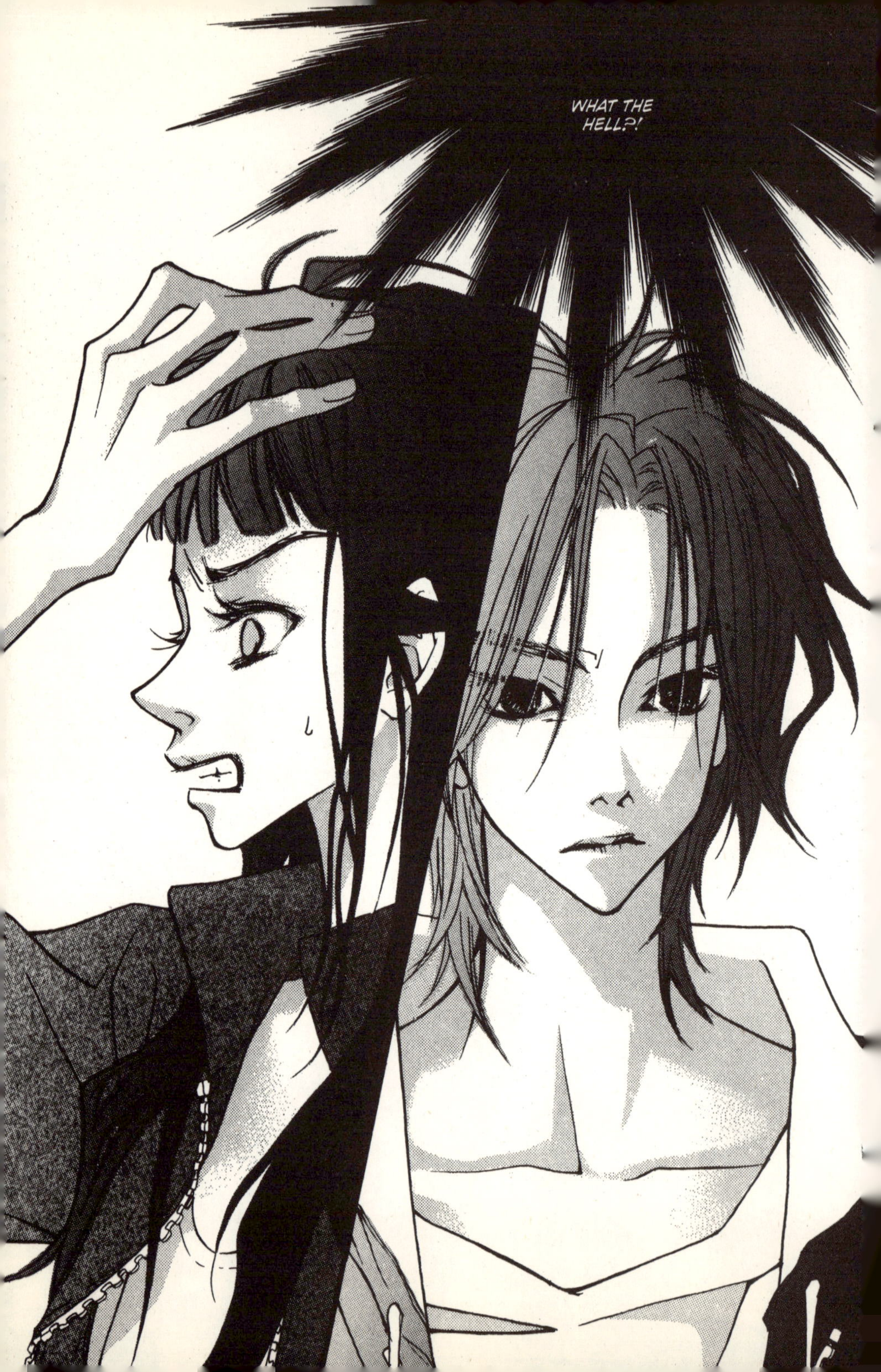
WHAT THE HELL?!

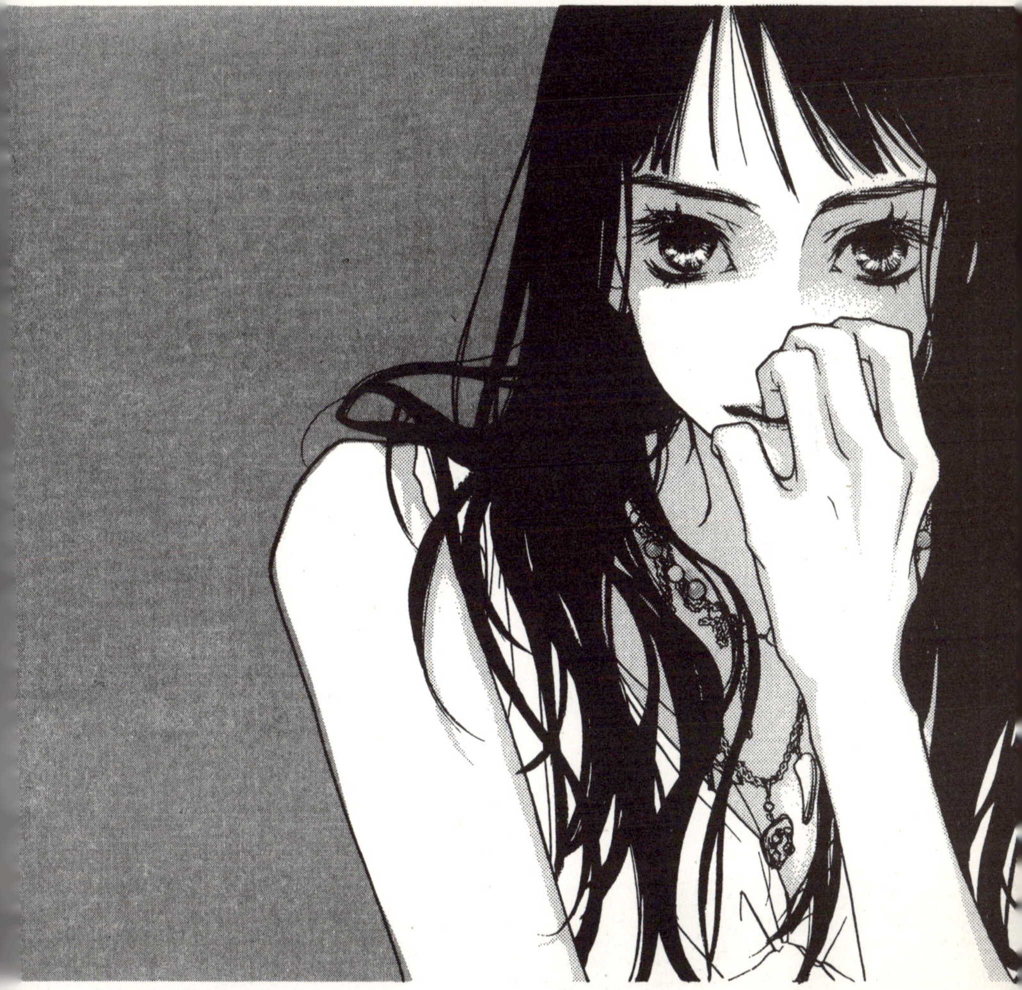

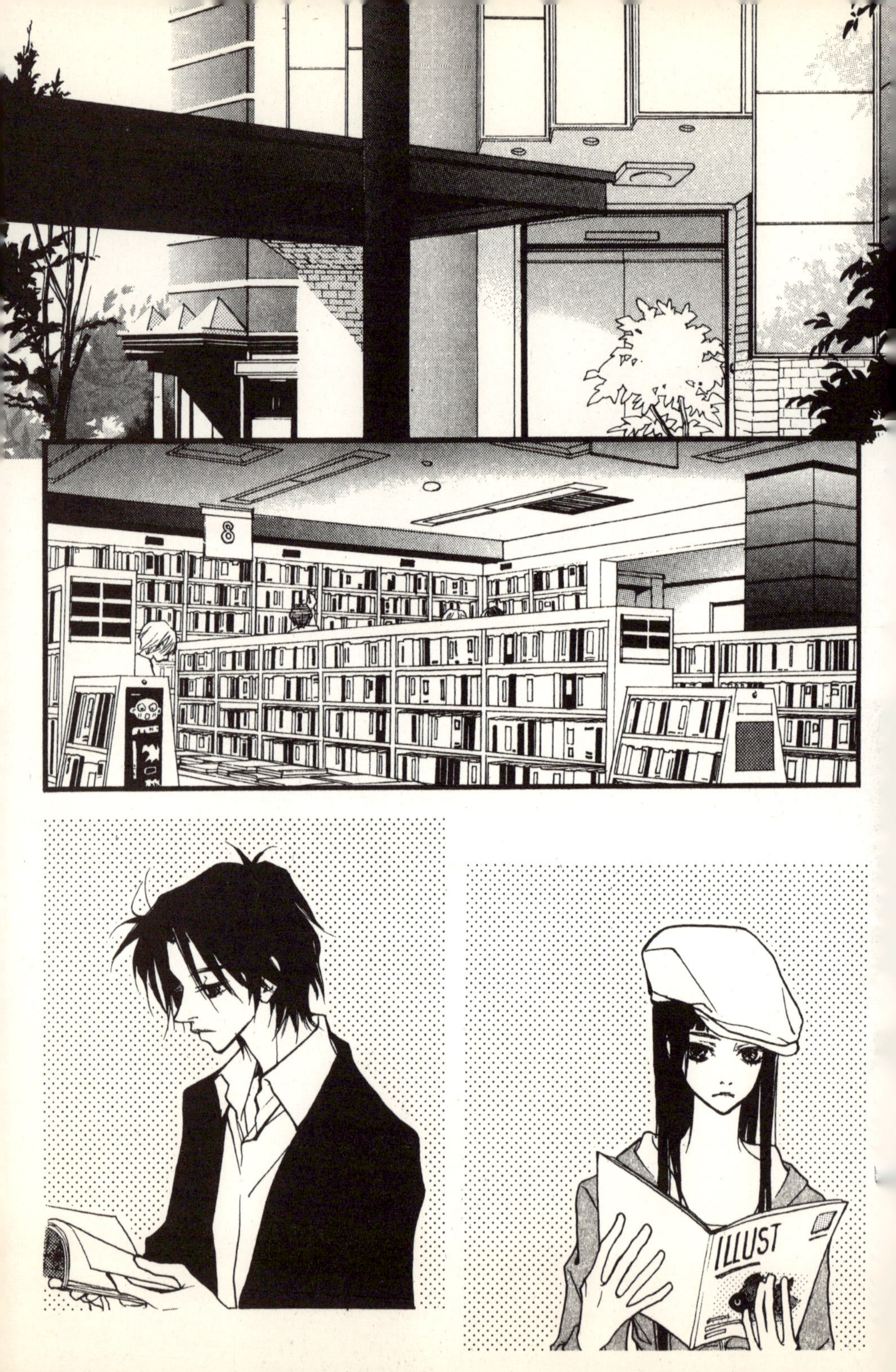
8
ILLUST

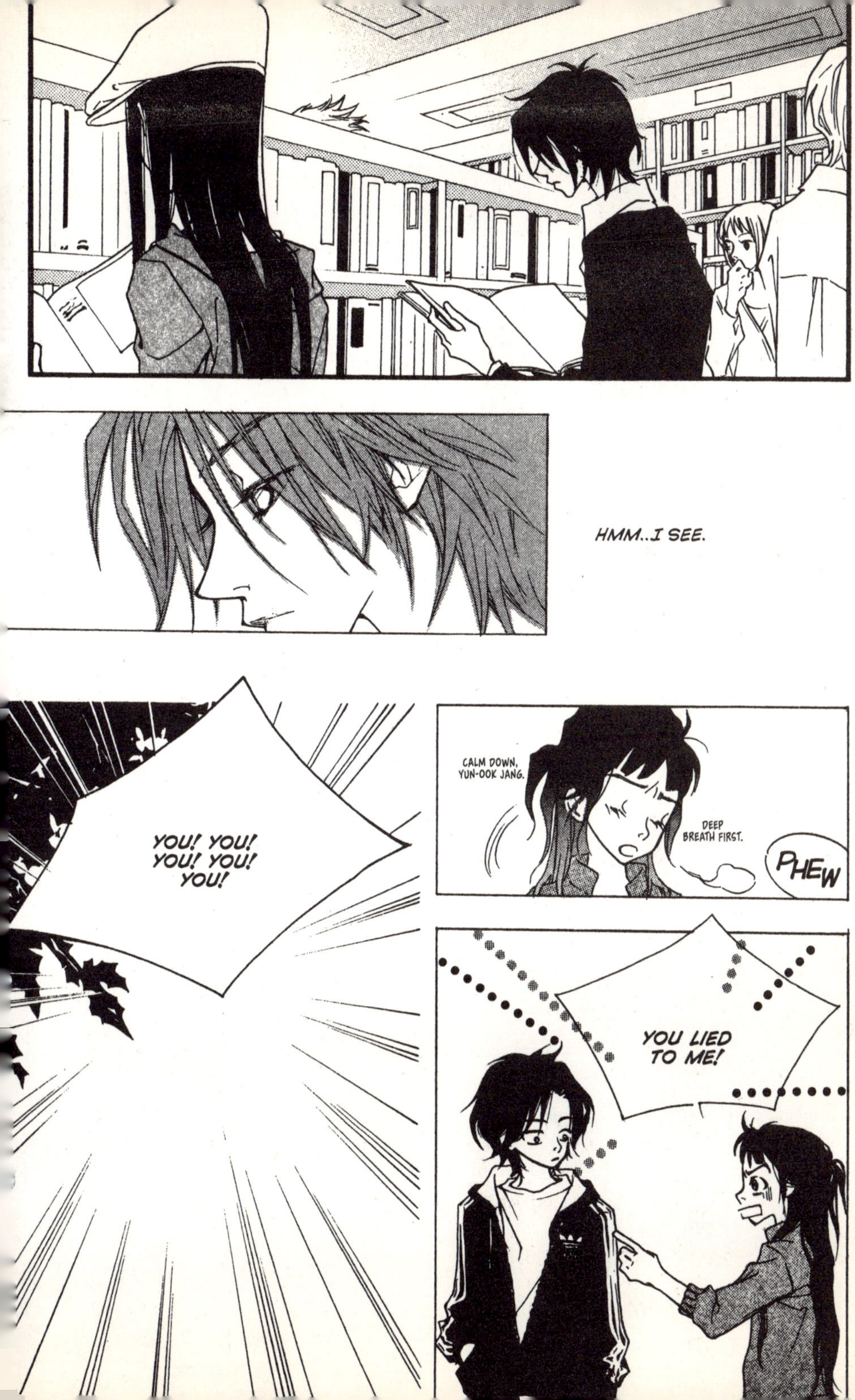
HMM..I SEE.
YOU! YOU! YOU! YOU! YOU!
CALM DOWN, YUN-OOK JANG.
DEEP BREATH FIRST.
PHEW
YOU LIED TO ME!

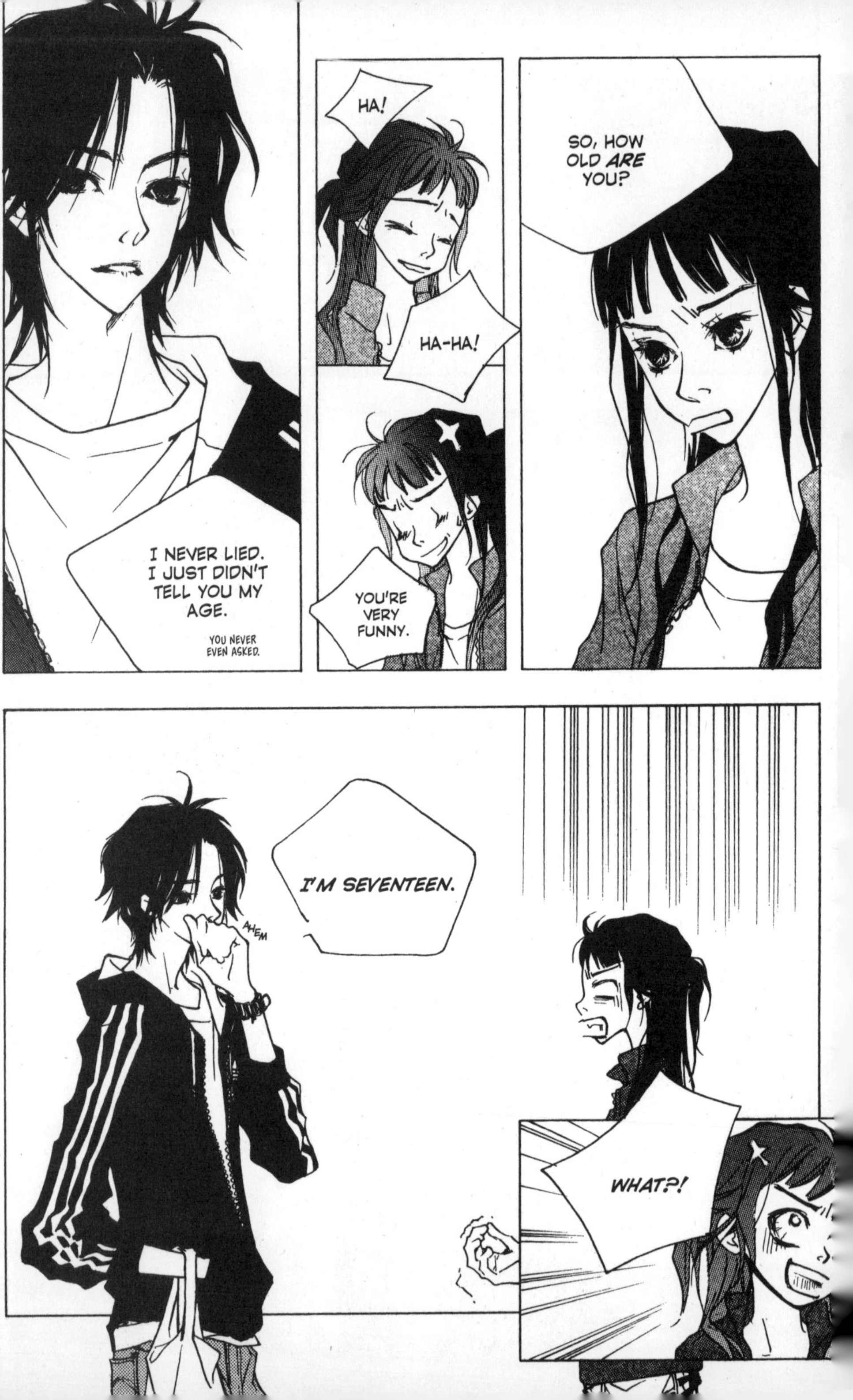
So, how old are you?
Ha!
Ha-ha!
I never lied. I just didn't tell you my age.
You never even asked.
You're very funny.
I'm seventeen.
Ahem
What?!

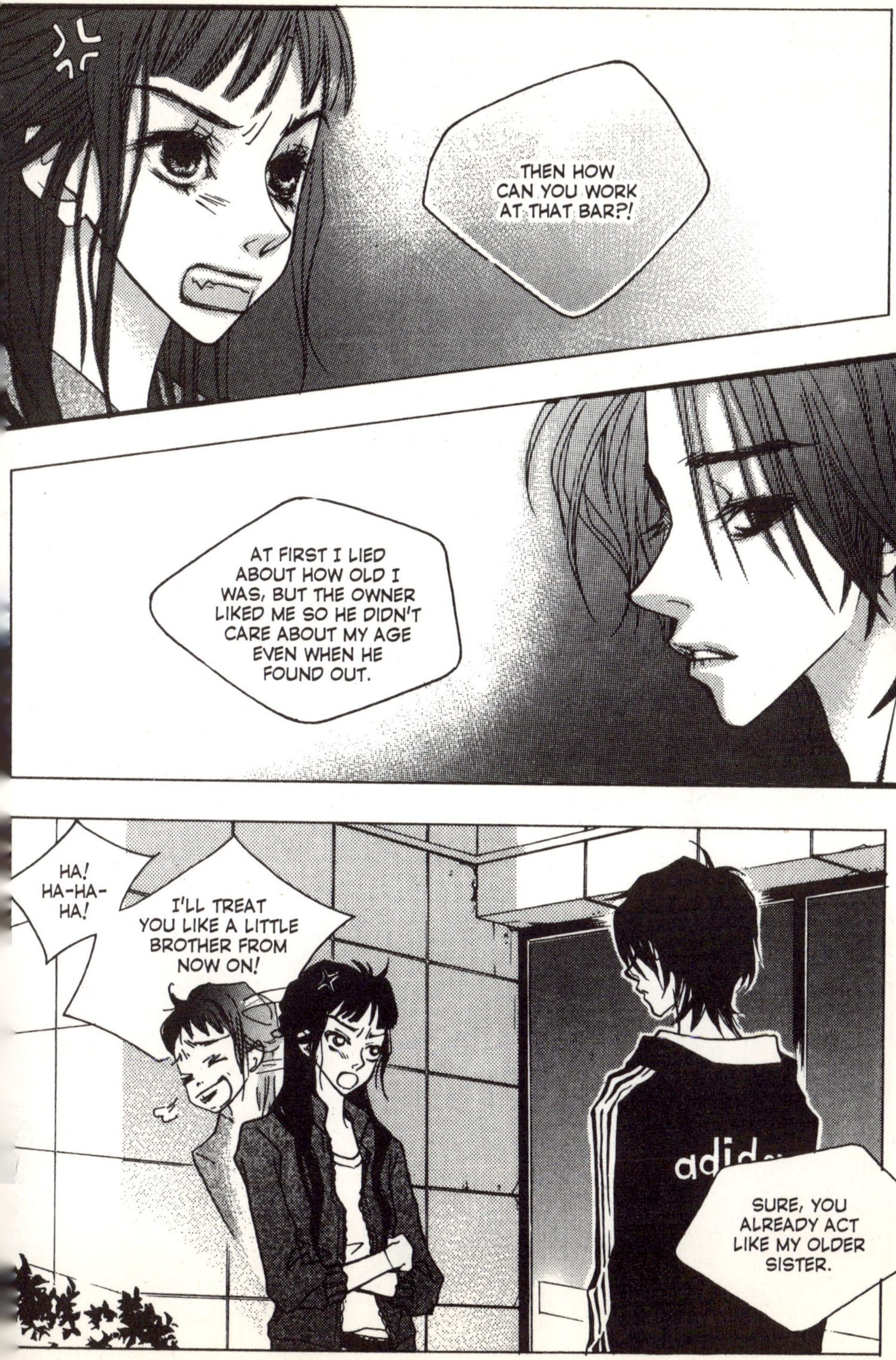
THEN HOW CAN YOU WORK AT THAT BAR?!
AT FIRST I LIED ABOUT HOW OLD I WAS, BUT THE OWNER LIKED ME SO HE DIDN'T CARE ABOUT MY AGE EVEN WHEN HE FOUND OUT.
HA! HA-HA-HA!
I'LL TREAT YOU LIKE A LITTLE BROTHER FROM NOW ON!
SURE, YOU ALREADY ACT LIKE MY OLDER SISTER.
adid

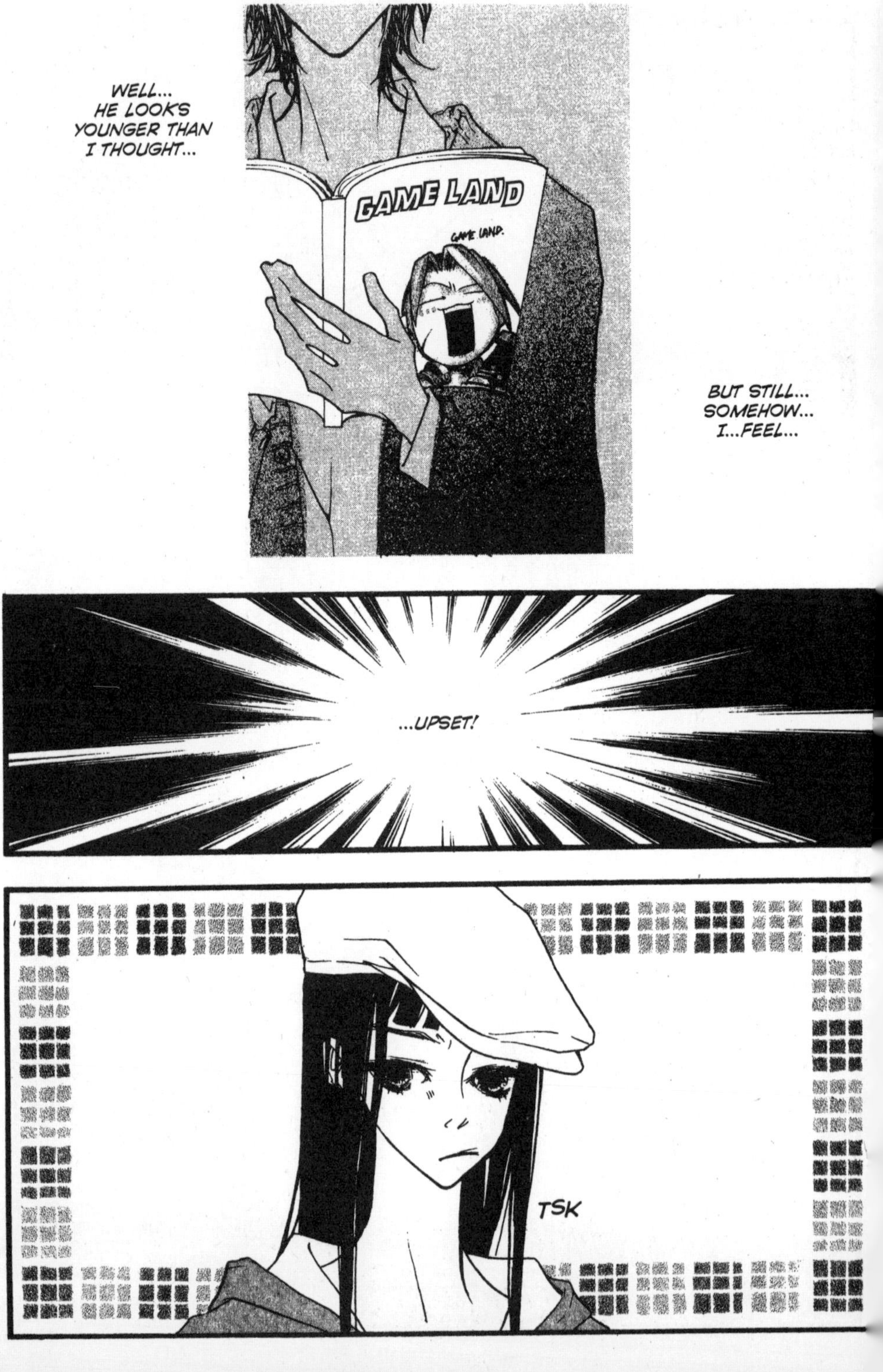
WELL... HE LOOKS YOUNGER THAN I THOUGHT...
GAME LAND
GAME LAND.
BUT STILL... SOMEHOW... I...FEEL...
...UPSET!
TSK

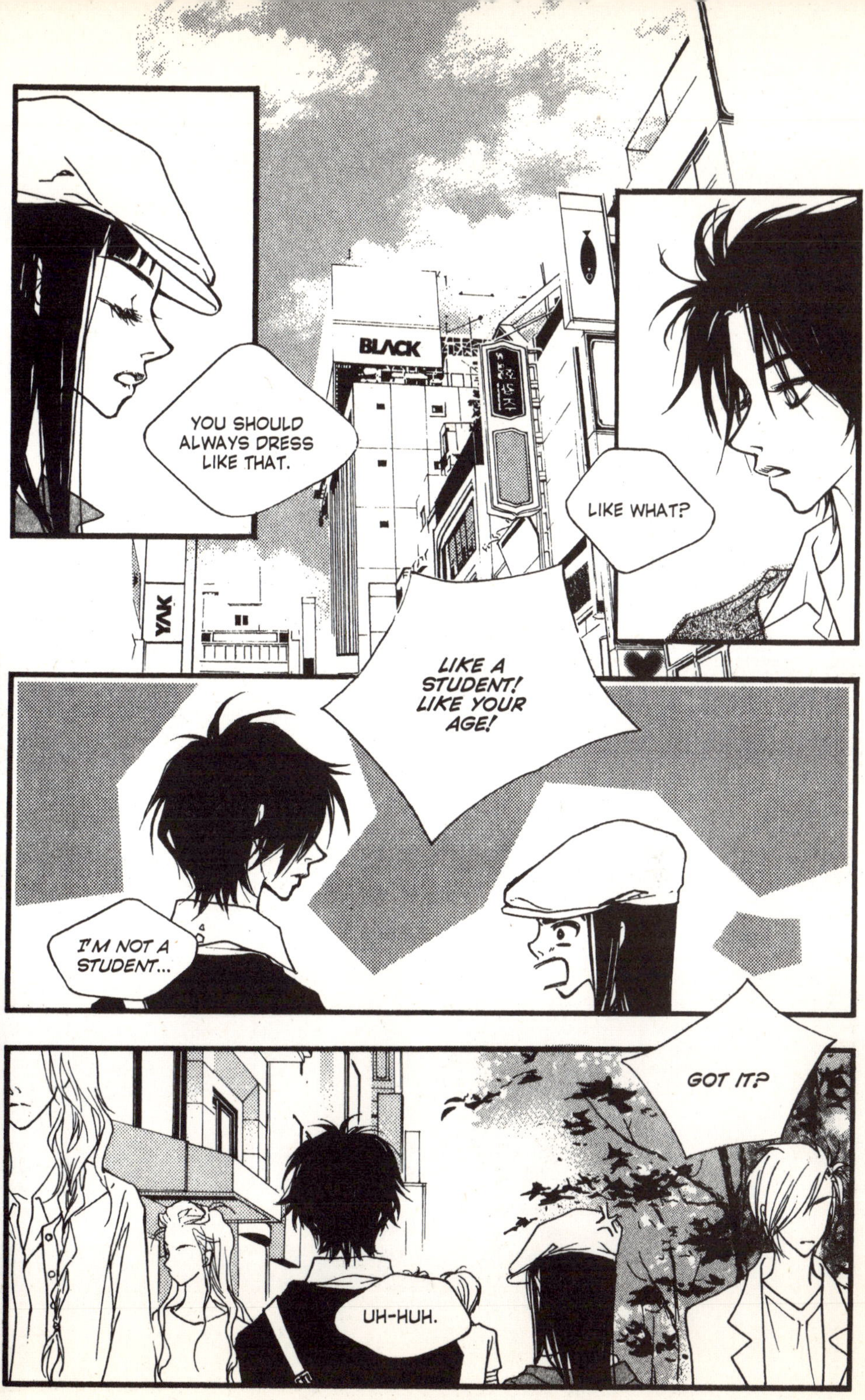
YOU SHOULD ALWAYS DRESS LIKE THAT.
BLACK
YAK
LIKE WHAT?
LIKE A STUDENT! LIKE YOUR AGE!
I'M NOT A STUDENT...
GOT IT?
UH-HUH.

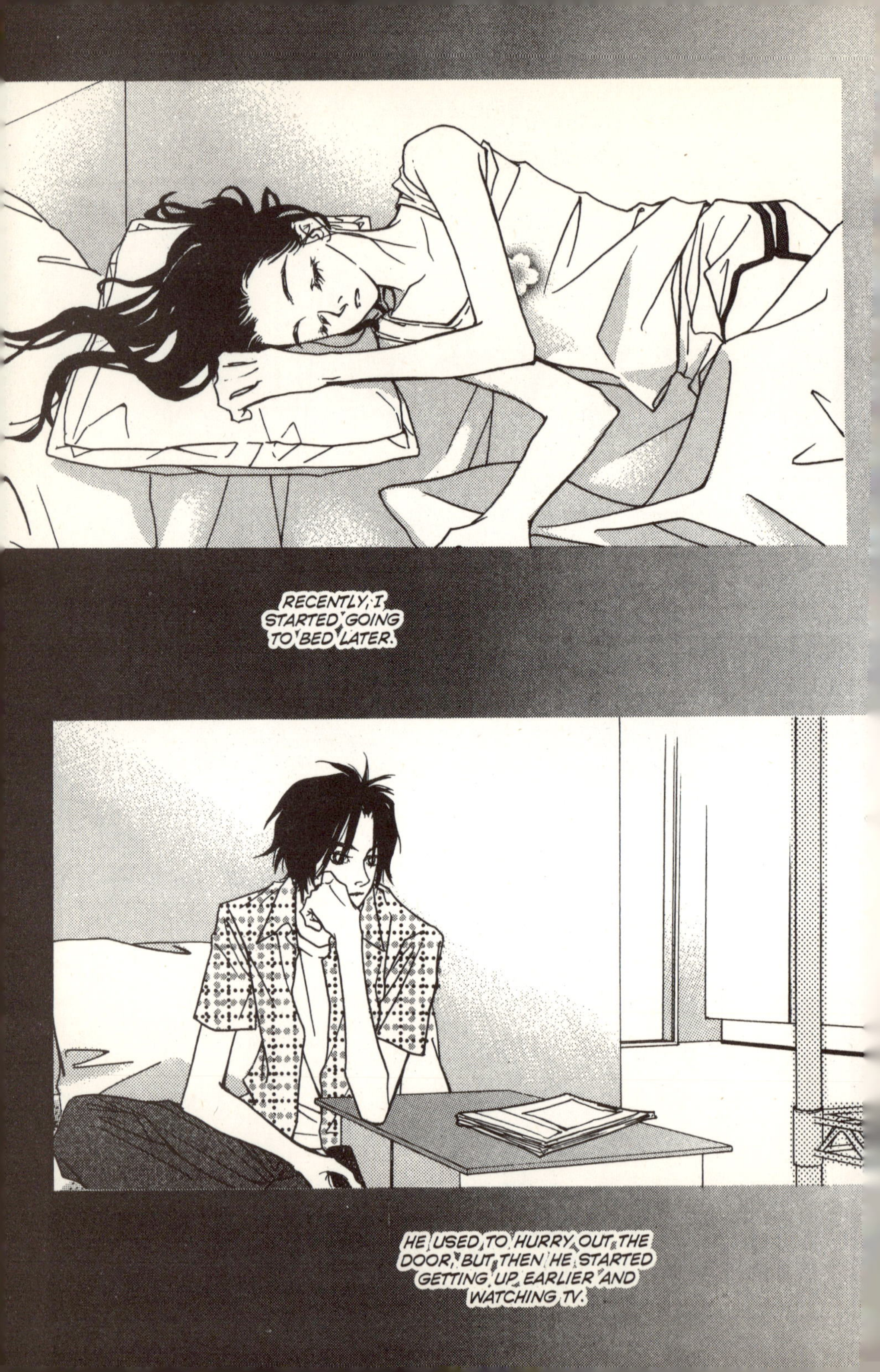
RECENTLY, I STARTED GOING TO BED LATER.
HE USED TO HURRY OUT THE DOOR, BUT THEN HE STARTED GETTING UP EARLIER AND WATCHING TV.

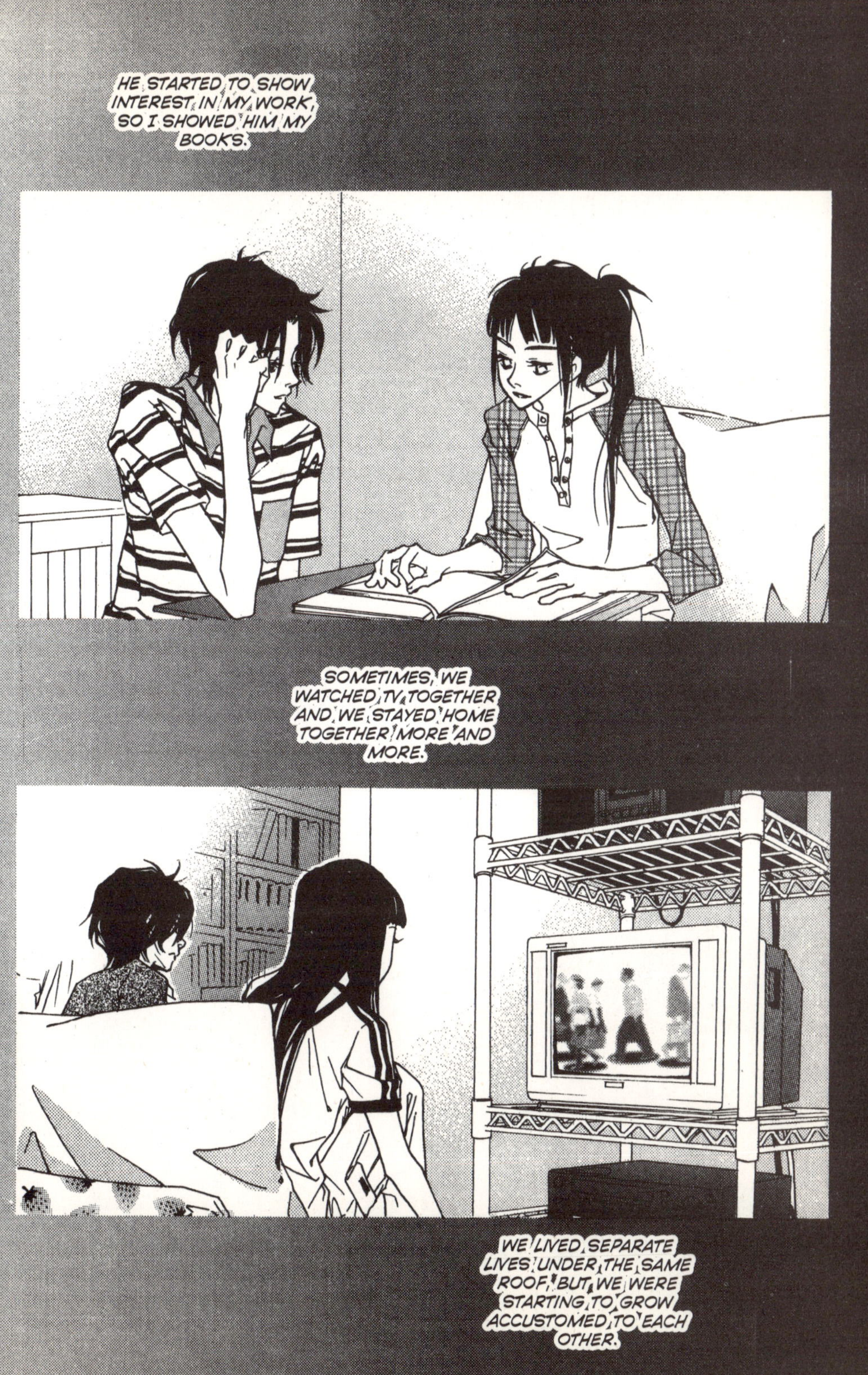
HE STARTED TO SHOW INTEREST IN MY WORK, SO I SHOWED HIM MY BOOKS.
SOMETIMES, WE WATCHED TV TOGETHER AND WE STAYED HOME TOGETHER MORE AND MORE.
WE LIVED SEPARATE LIVES UNDER THE SAME ROOF, BUT WE WERE STARTING TO GROW ACCUSTOMED TO EACH OTHER.

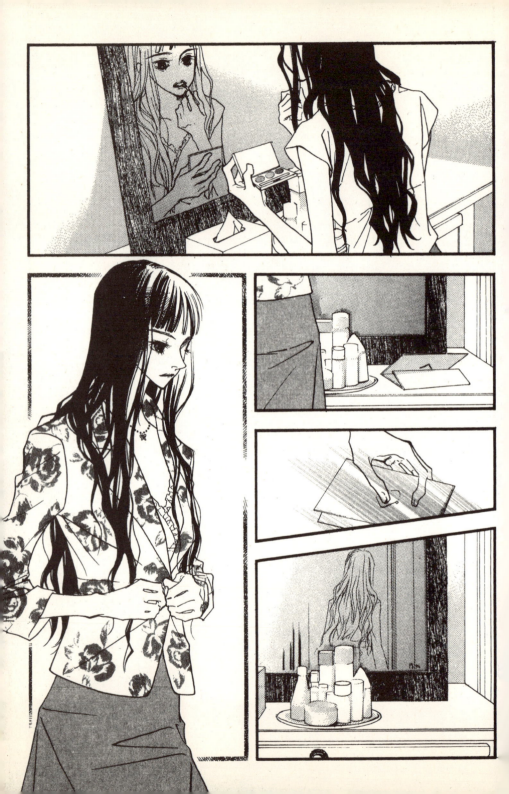

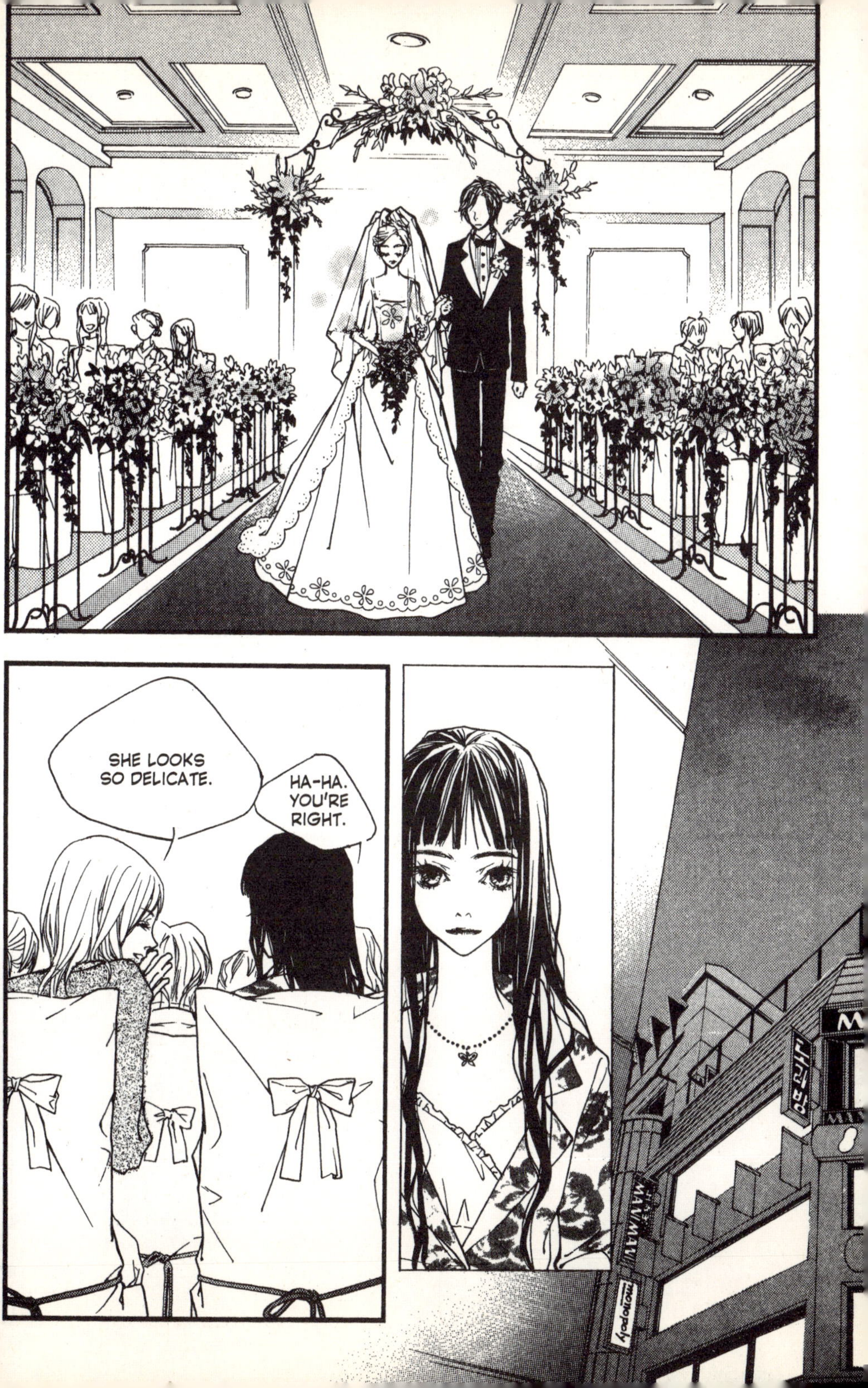
SHE LOOKS SO DELICATE.
HA-HA. YOU'RE RIGHT.
MAVMAV
monopoly

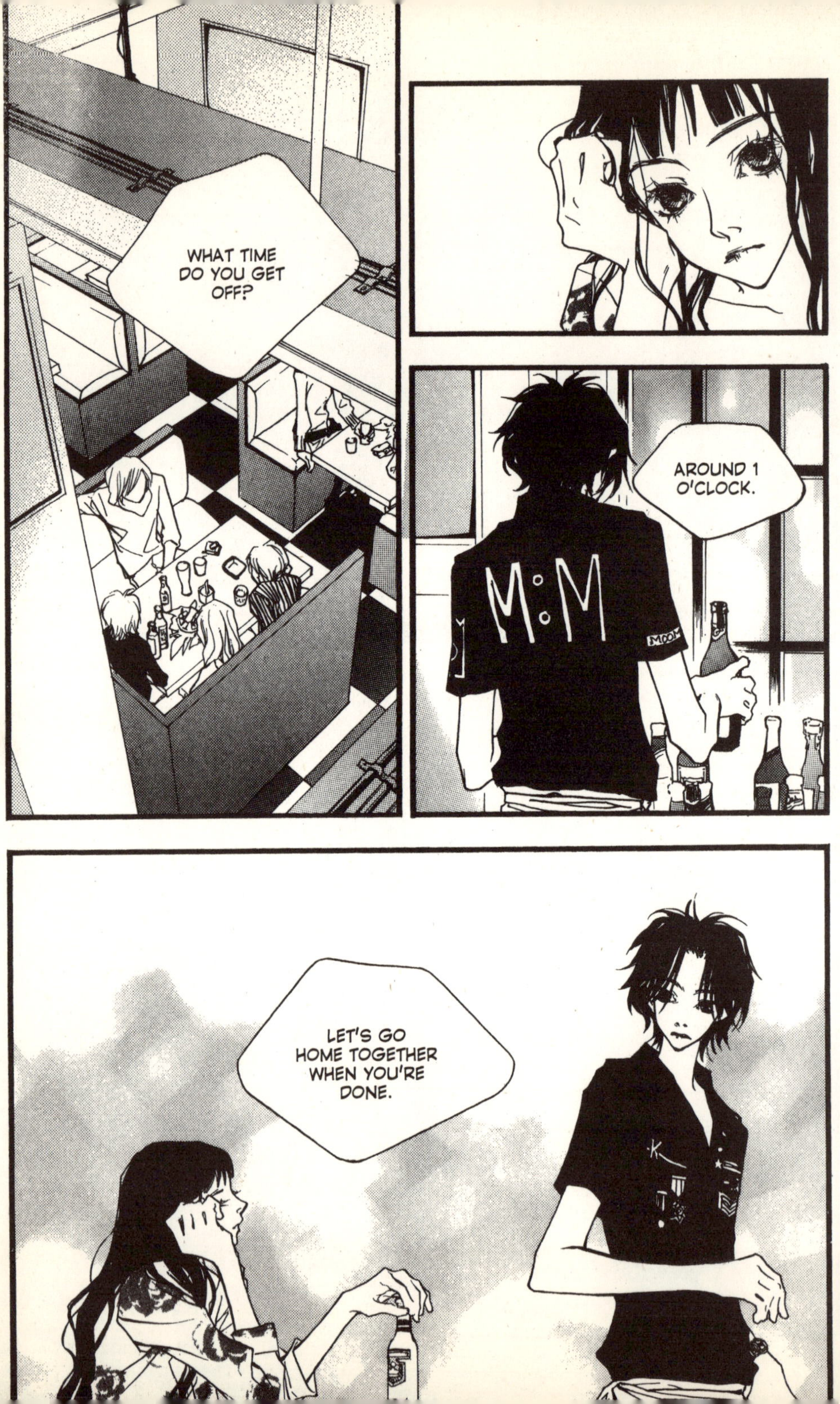
WHAT TIME DO YOU GET OFF?
AROUND 1 O'CLOCK.
M:M
LET'S GO HOME TOGETHER WHEN YOU'RE DONE.

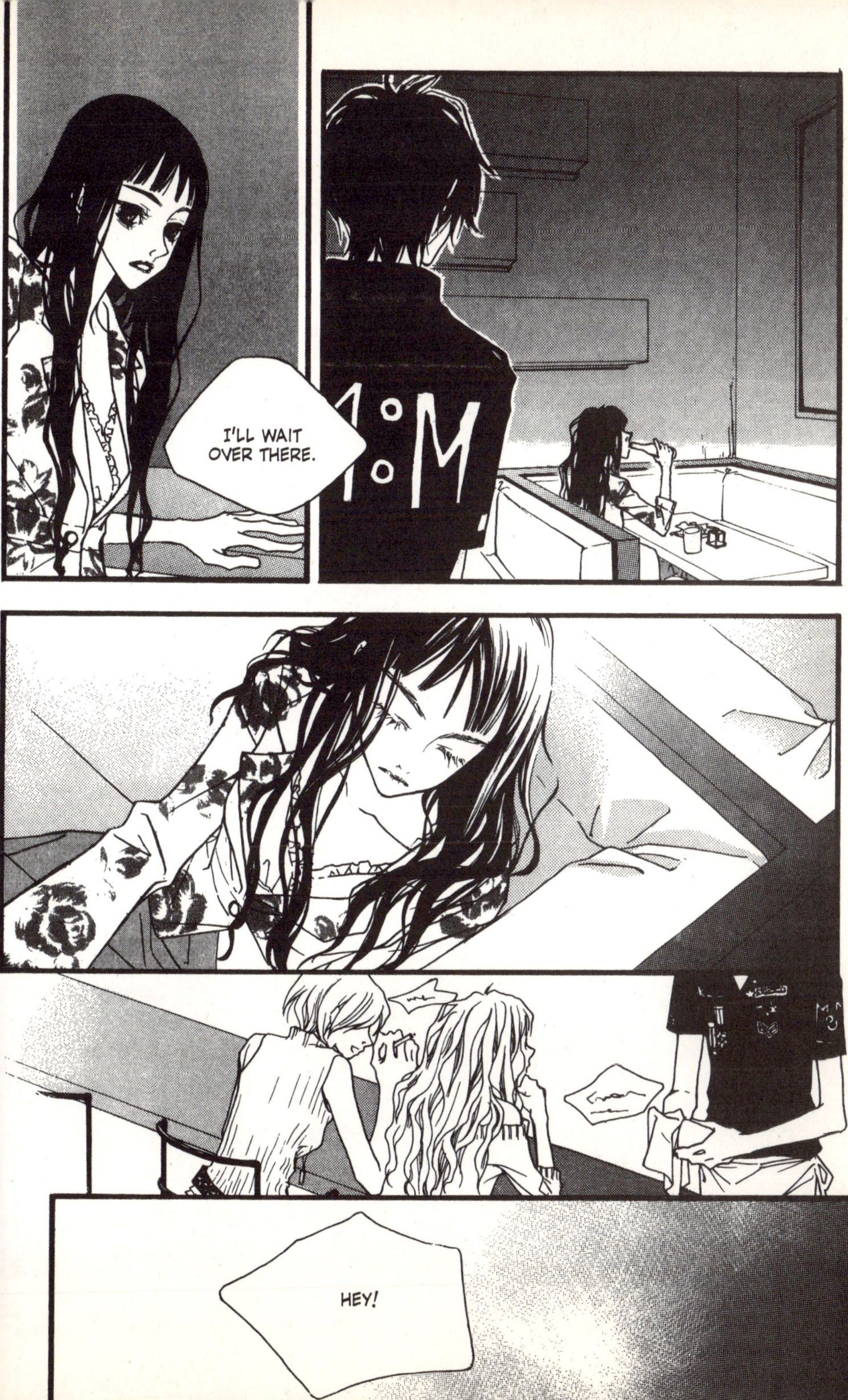
I'LL WAIT OVER THERE.
HEY!

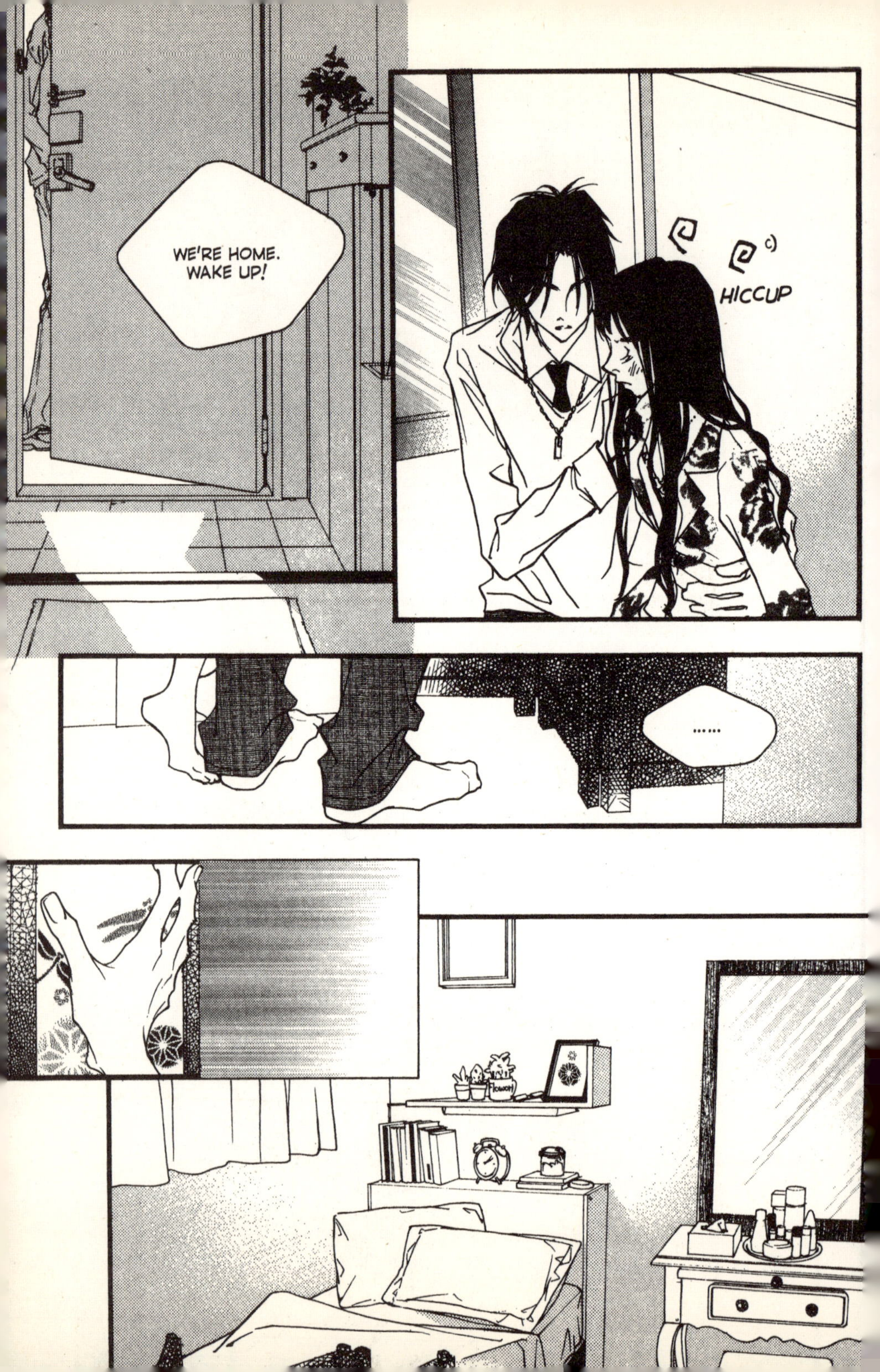
WE'RE HOME. WAKE UP!
HICCUP
......

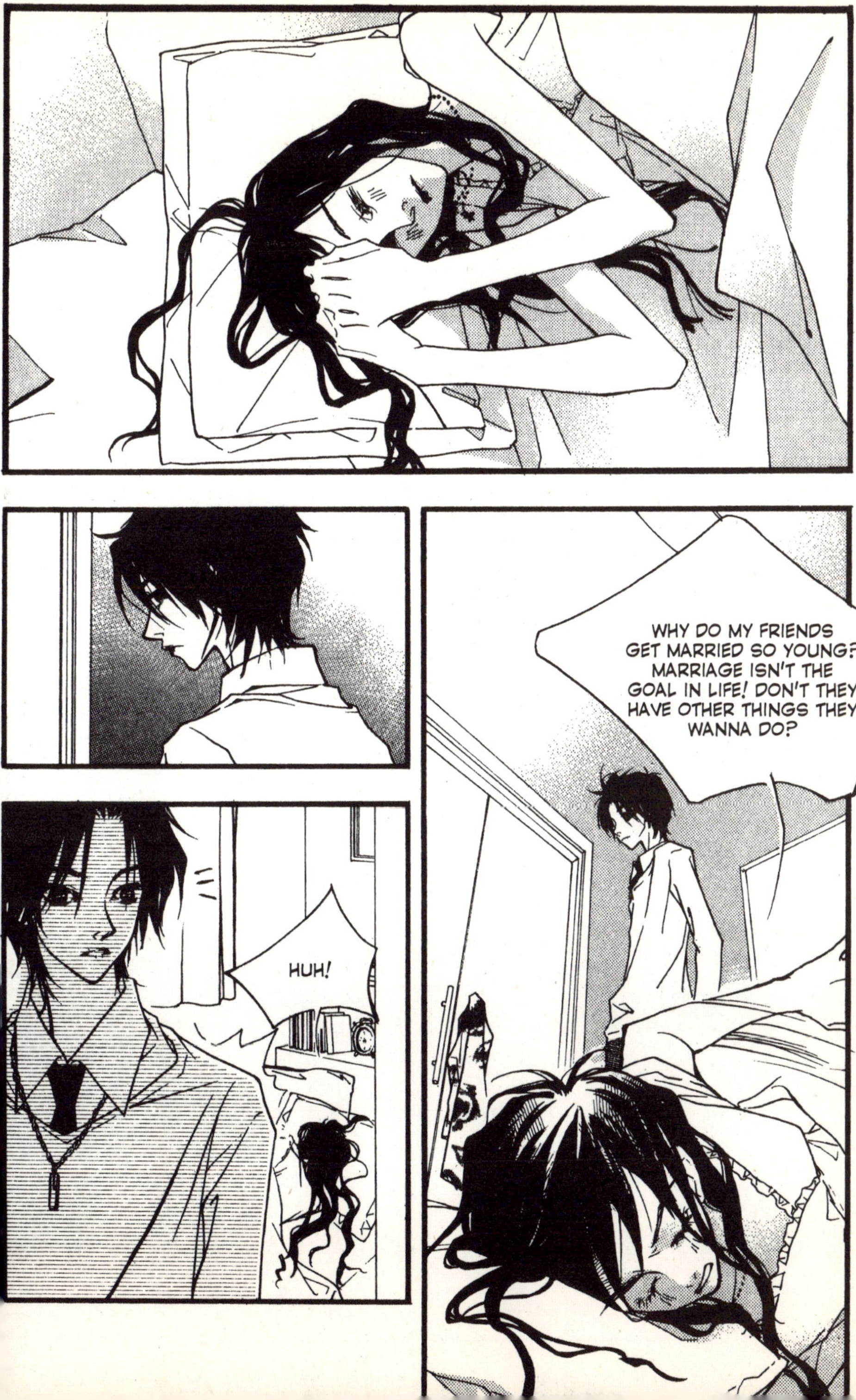
WHY DO MY FRIENDS GET MARRIED SO YOUNG? MARRIAGE ISN'T THE GOAL IN LIFE! DON'T THEY HAVE OTHER THINGS THEY WANNA DO?
HUH!

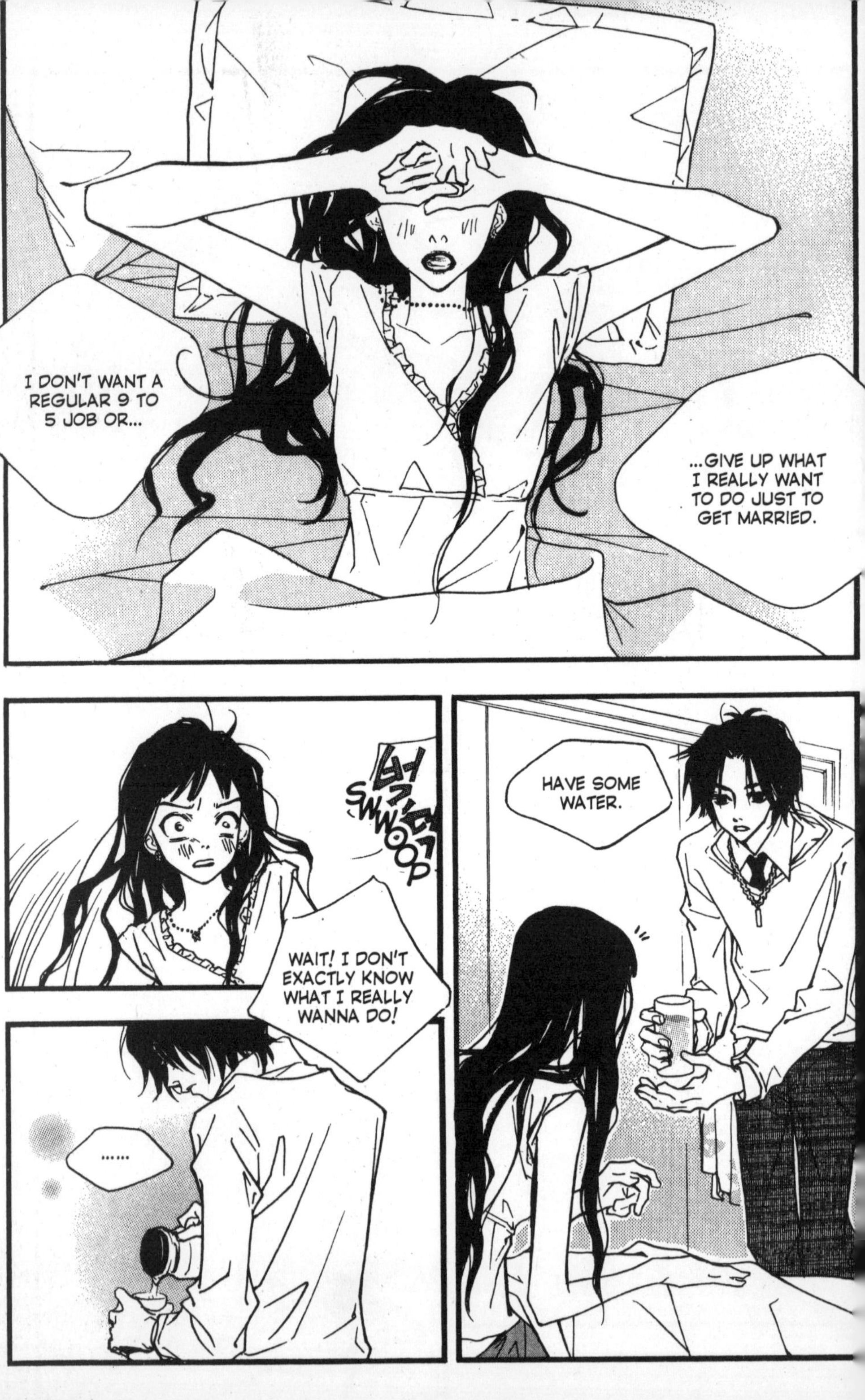
I DON'T WANT A REGULAR 9 TO 5 JOB OR...
...GIVE UP WHAT I REALLY WANT TO DO JUST TO GET MARRIED.
SWWOOP
HAVE SOME WATER.
WAIT! I DON'T EXACTLY KNOW WHAT I REALLY WANNA DO!
......

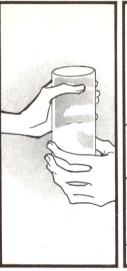

I WANT A COOL LIFE... WORK ON ONLY WHAT I LIKE...

IF I WERE YOUR AGE, I'D HAVE THE GUTS TO START ALL OVER...

I SO ENVY YOU, MAN.

YOU KNOW MY FRIEND WHO GOT MARRIED TODAY?

SHE SPEAKS JAPANESE... IN HER SLEEP... WHEN SHE'S DRUNK.

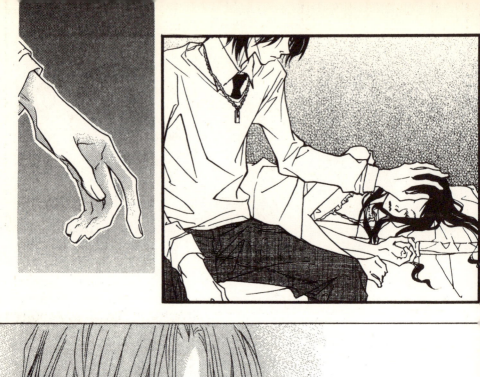

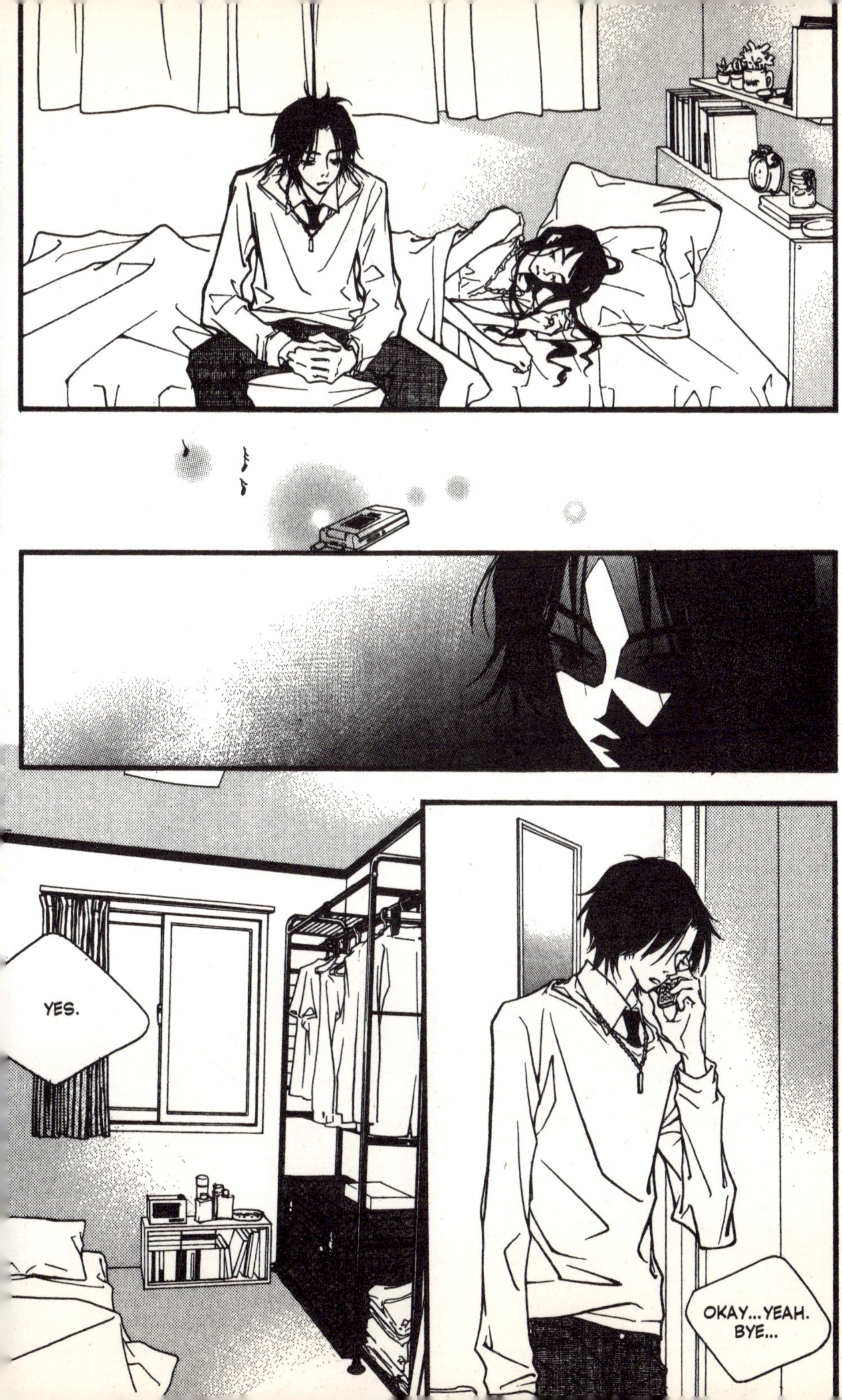
YES.
OKAY...YEAH. BYE...

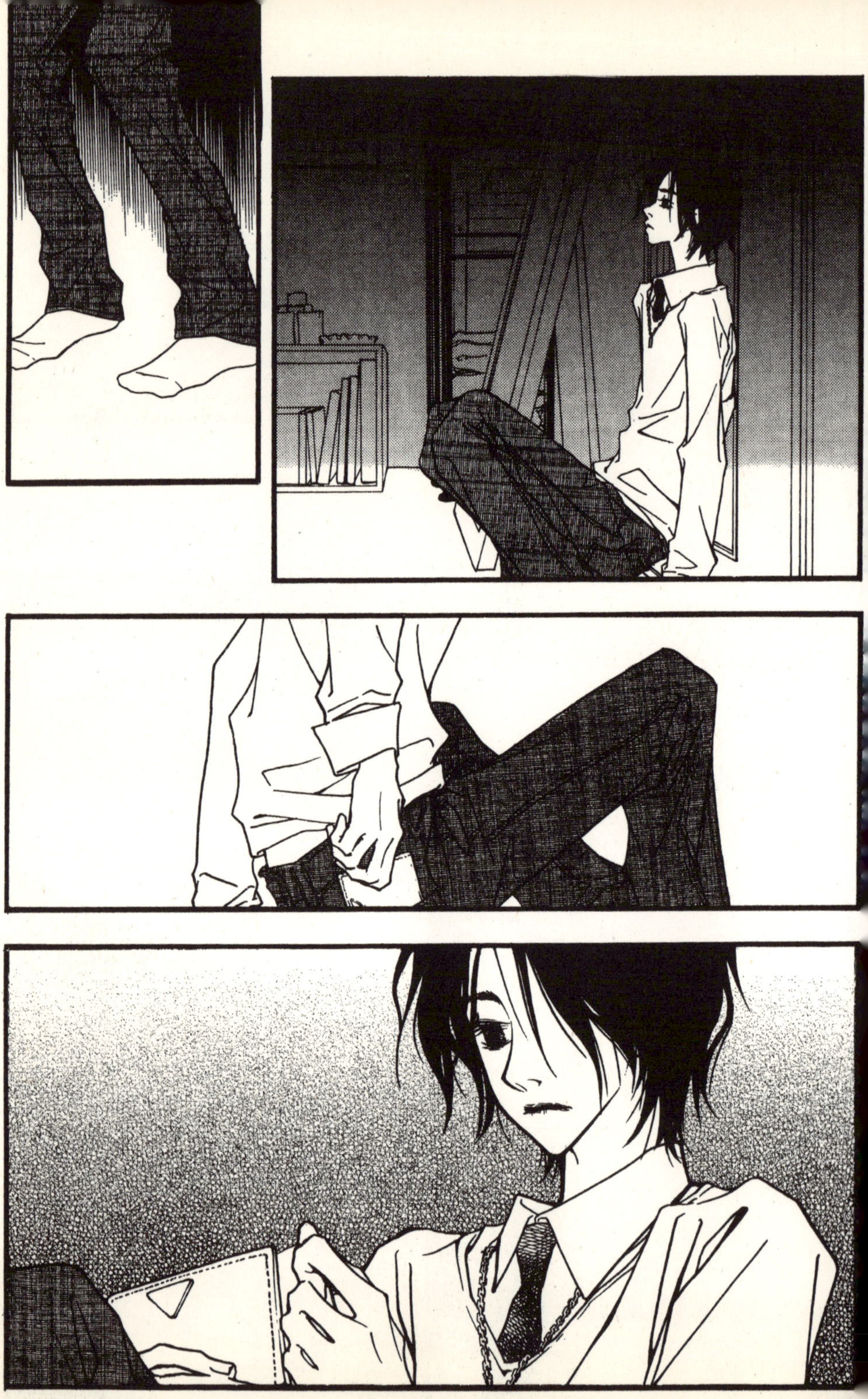

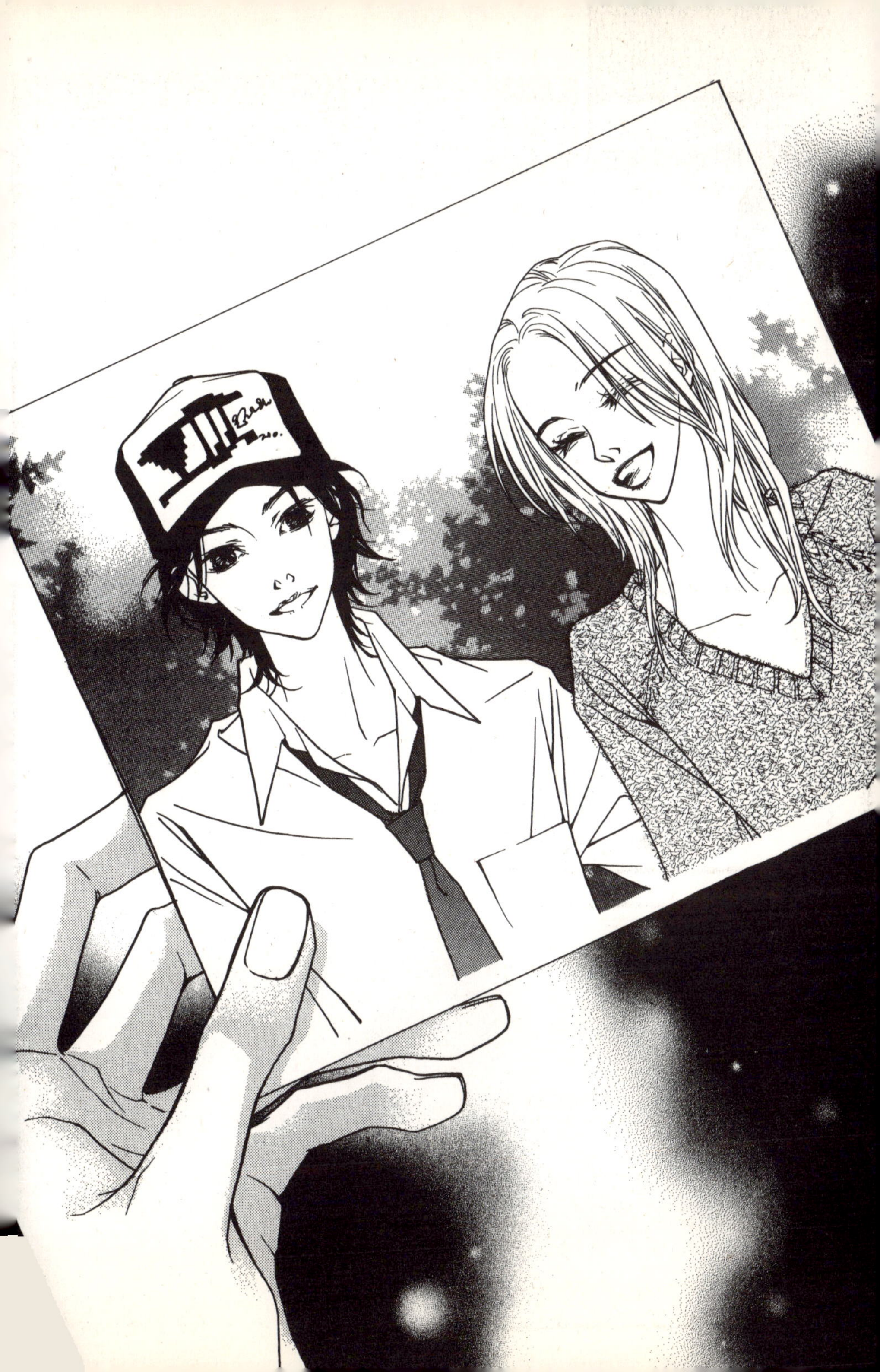

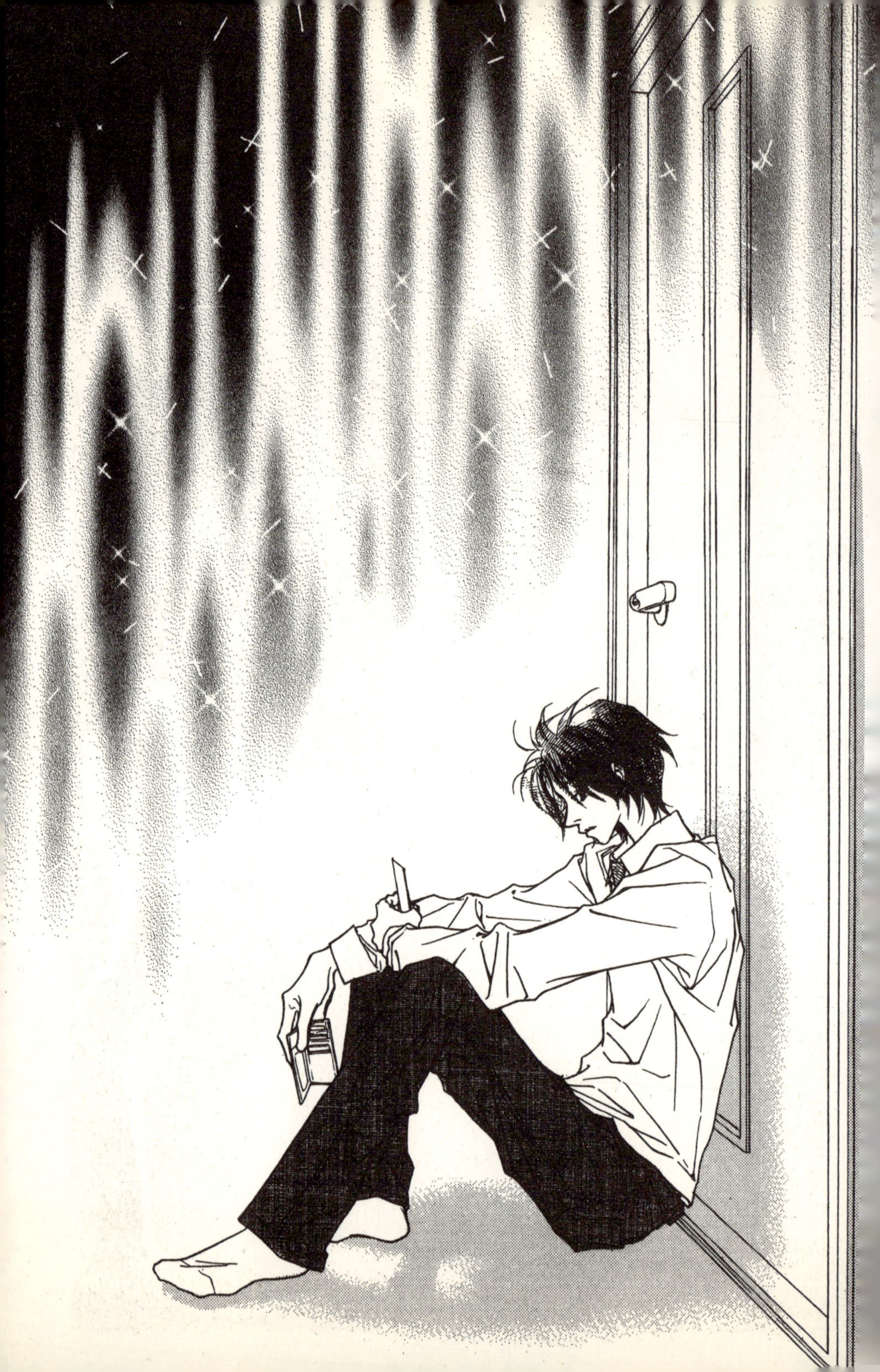

Forest of Gray City

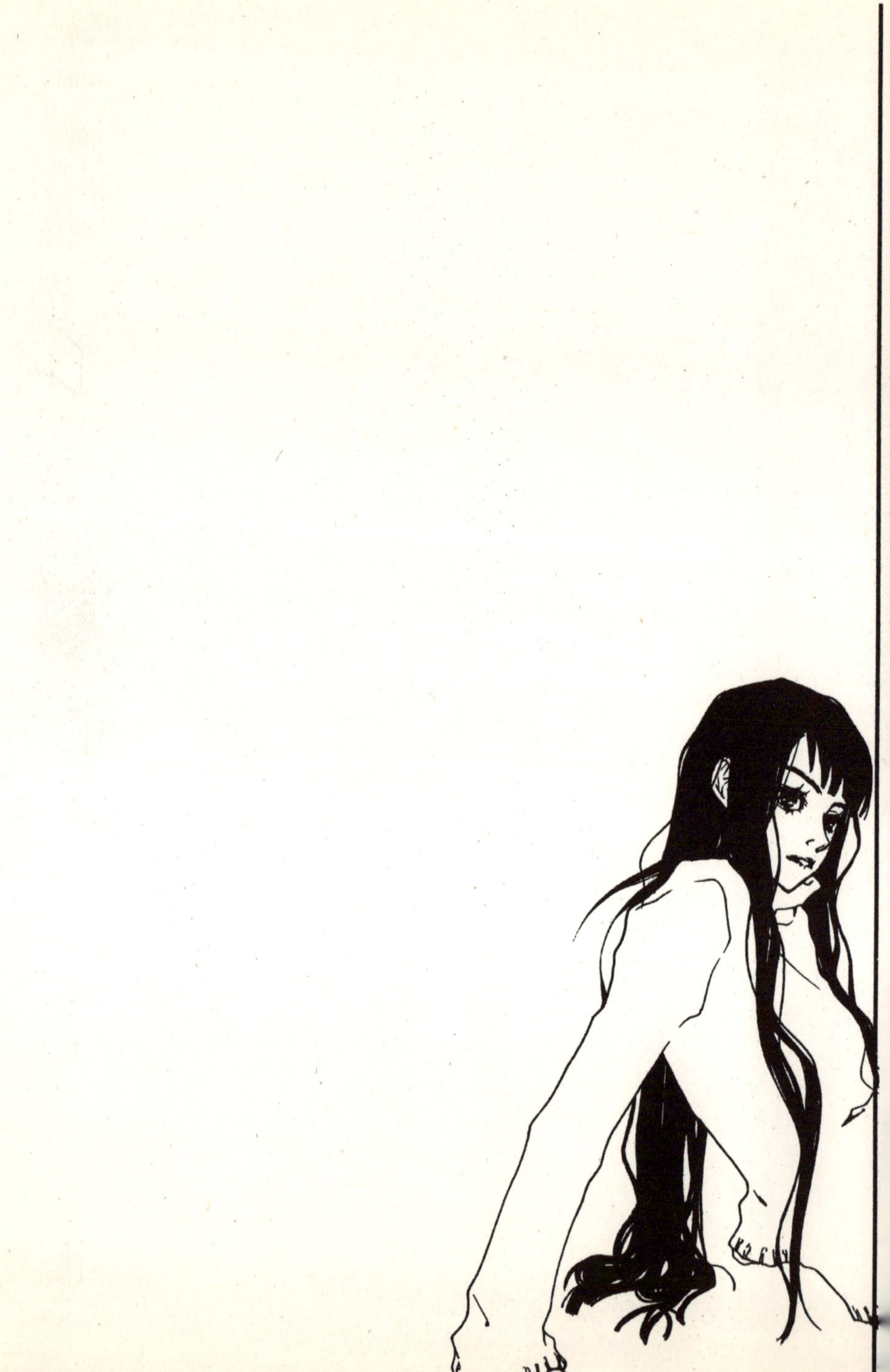

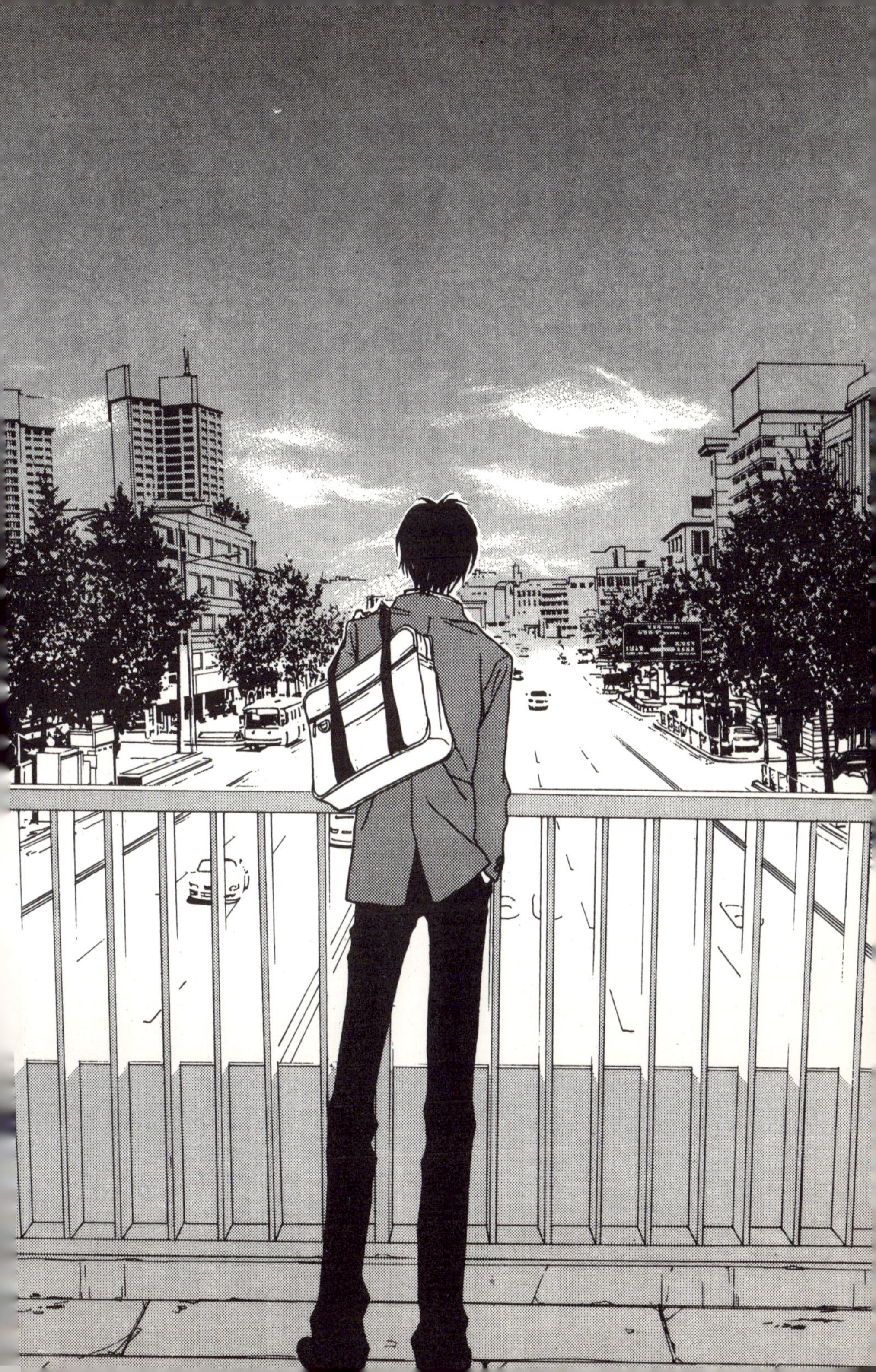

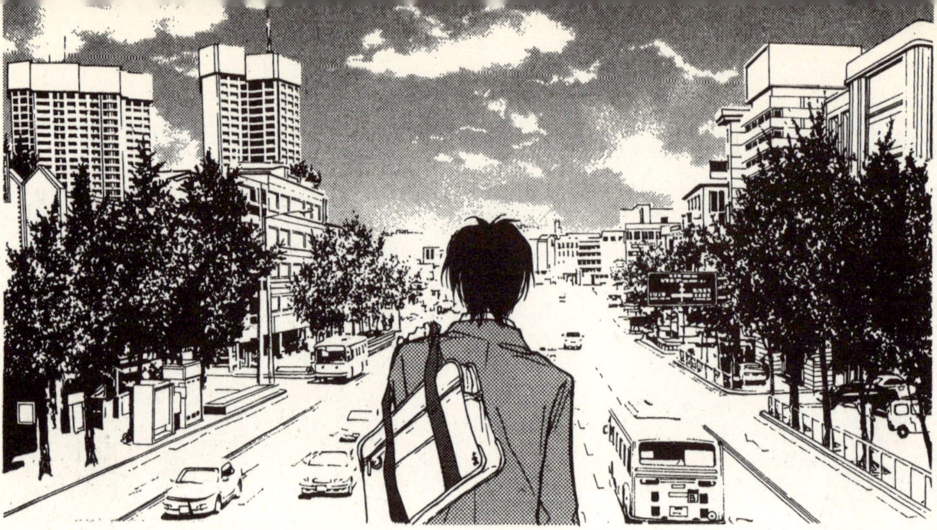

THE SUN RISES.

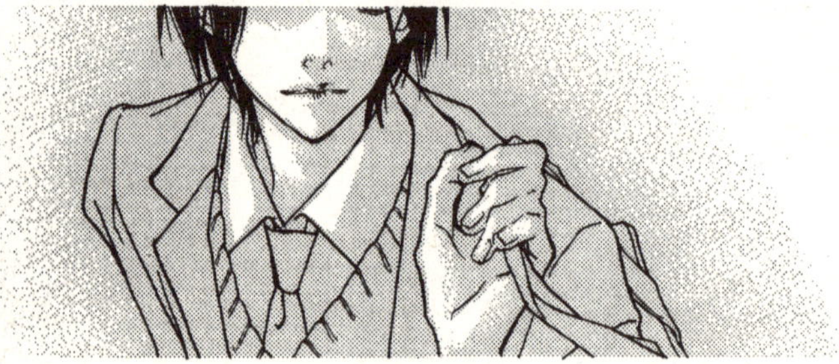

IT'S THE START OF ANOTHER DAY.

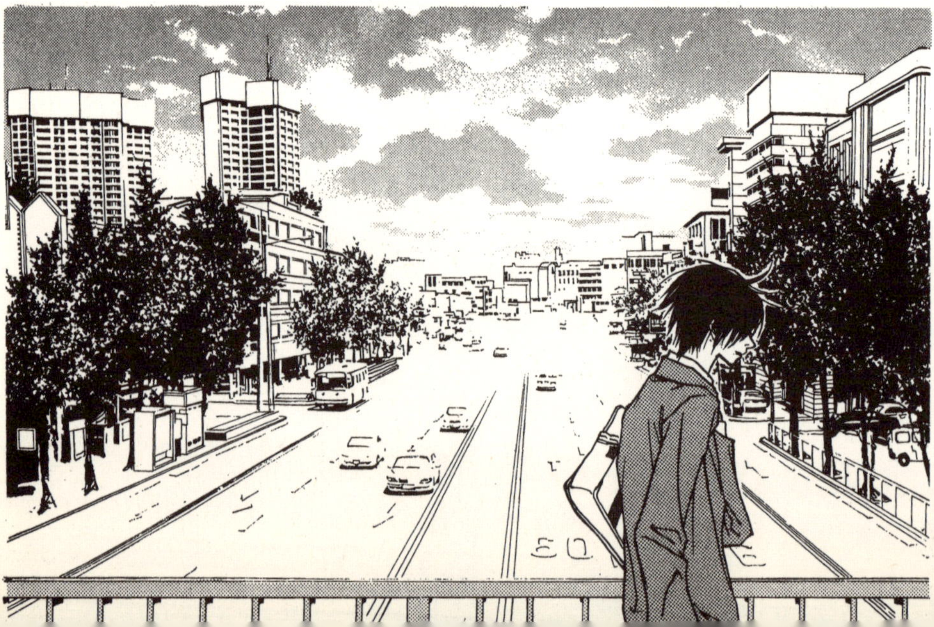

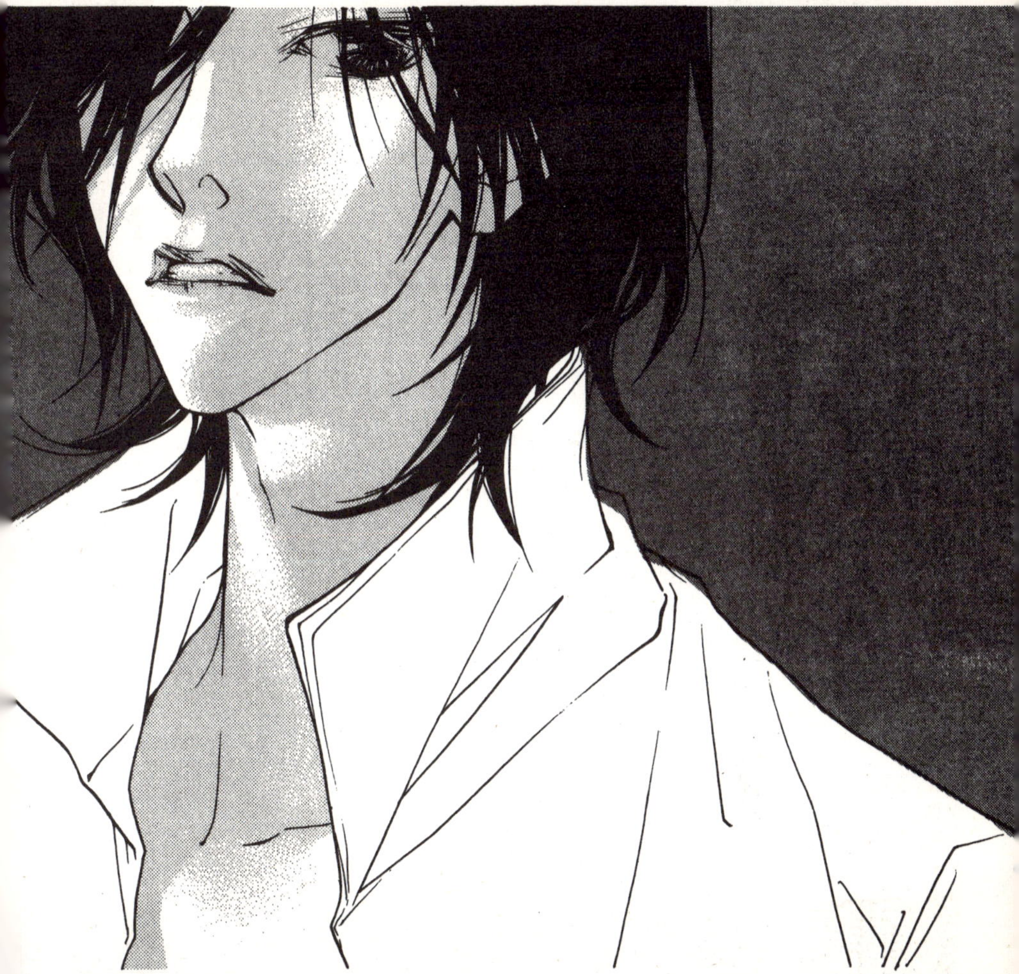

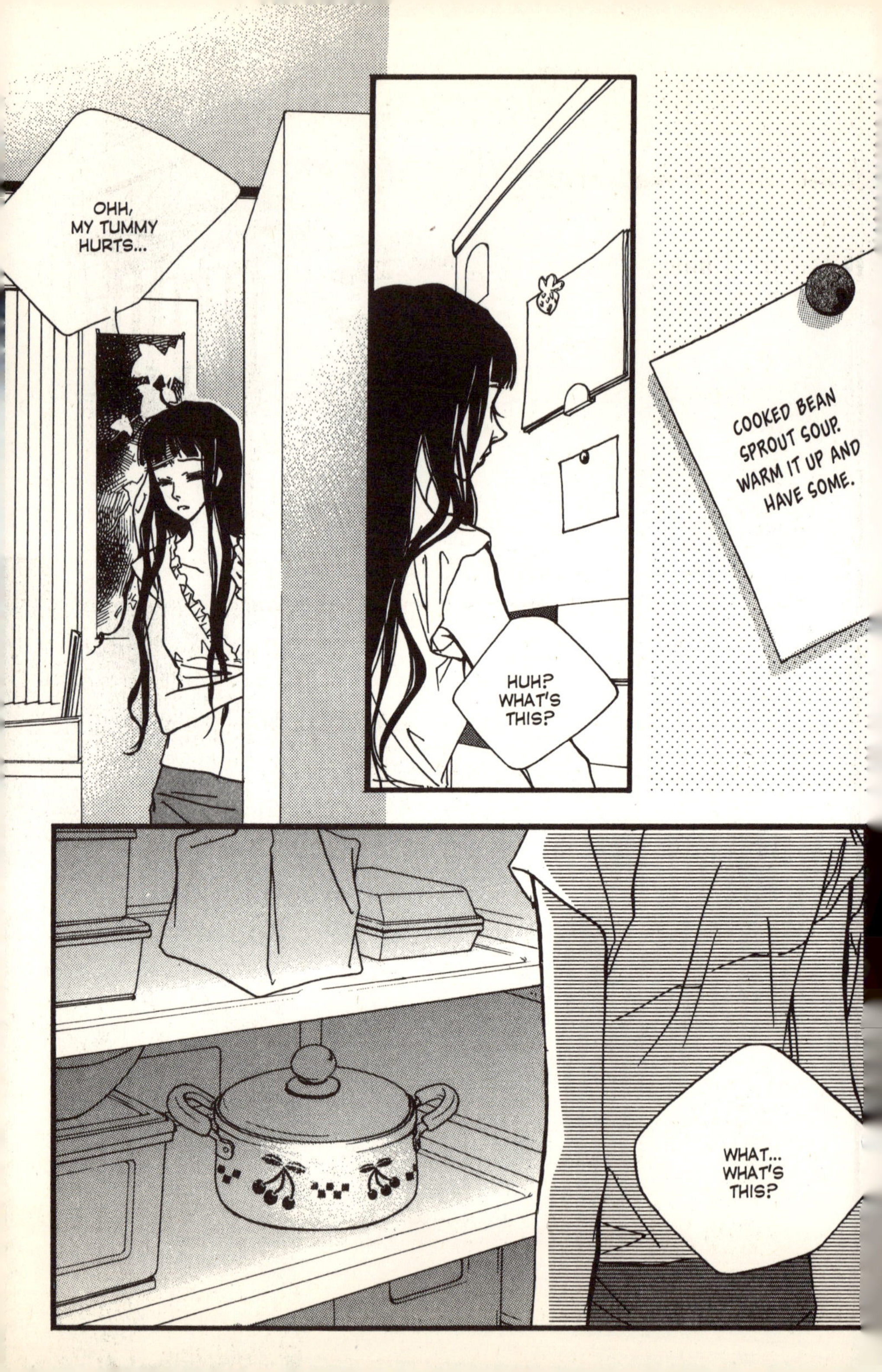
OHH, MY TUMMY HURTS...
COOKED BEAN SPROUT SOUP. WARM IT UP AND HAVE SOME.
HUH? WHAT'S THIS?
WHAT... WHAT'S THIS?

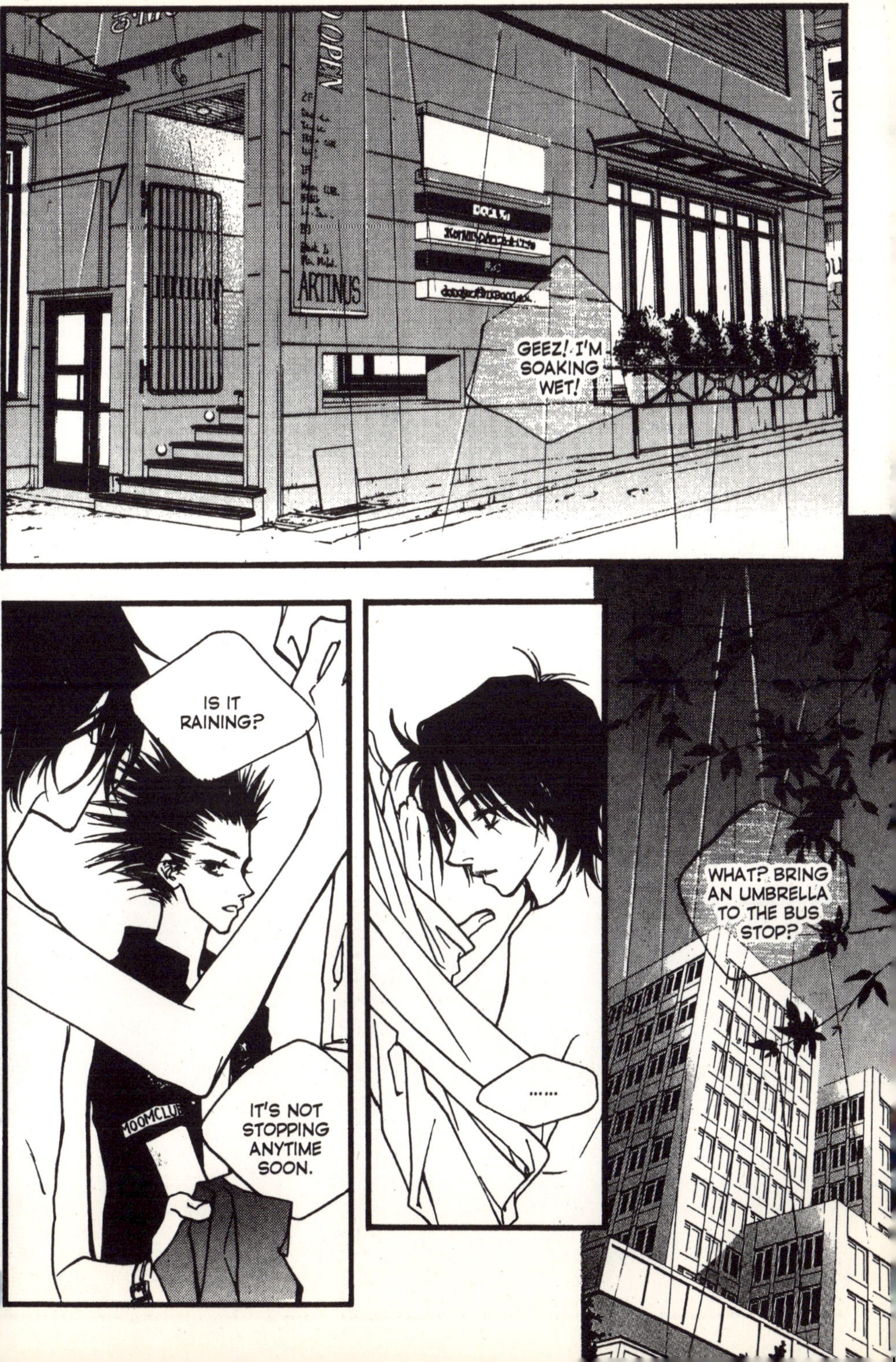
OPEN
ARTINUS
GEEZ! I'M SOAKING WET!
IS IT RAINING?
IT'S NOT STOPPING ANYTIME SOON.
......
WHAT? BRING AN UMBRELLA TO THE BUS STOP?

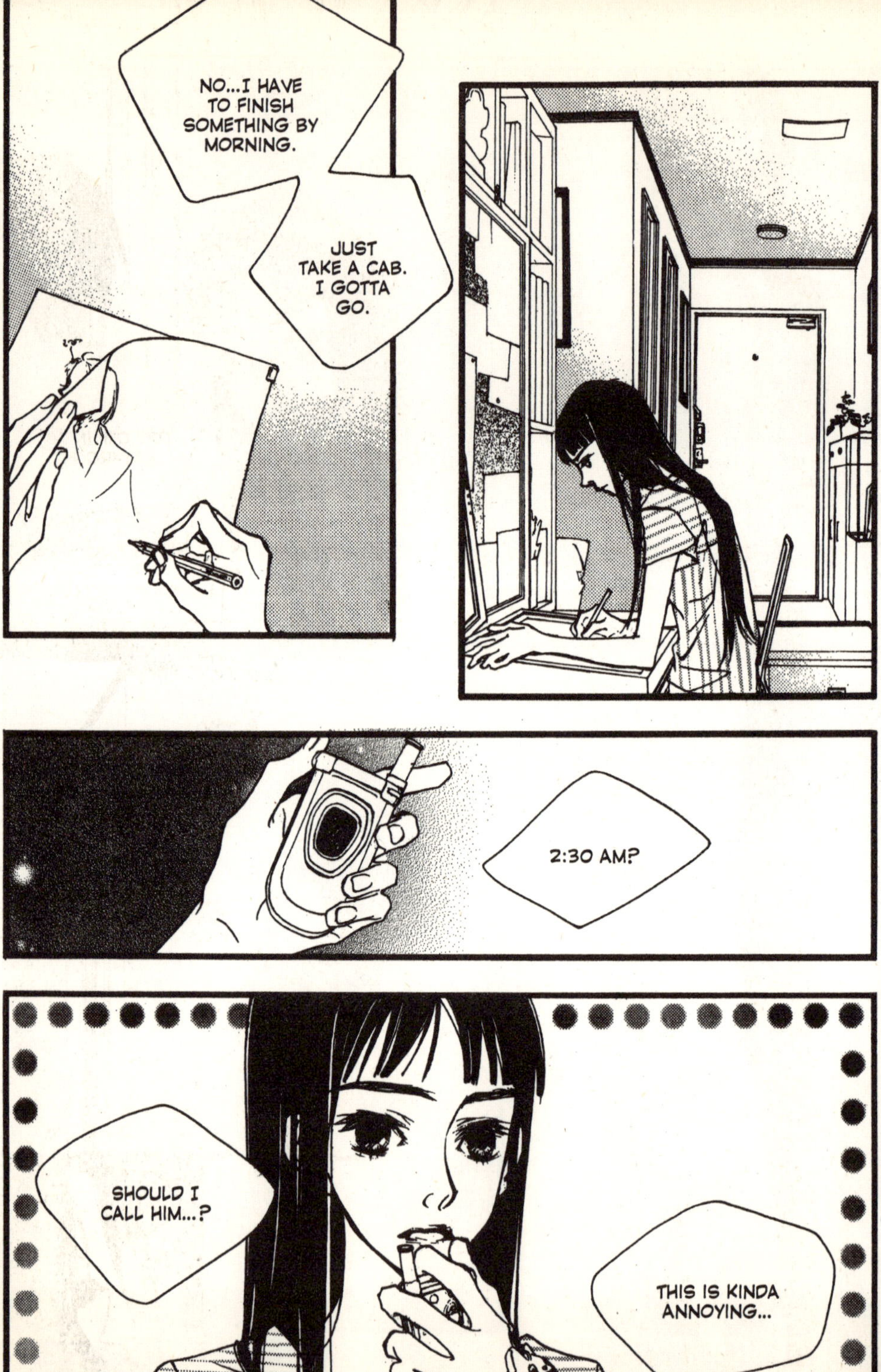
NO...I HAVE TO FINISH SOMETHING BY MORNING.
JUST TAKE A CAB. I GOTTA GO.
2:30 AM?
SHOULD I CALL HIM...?
THIS IS KINDA ANNOYING...

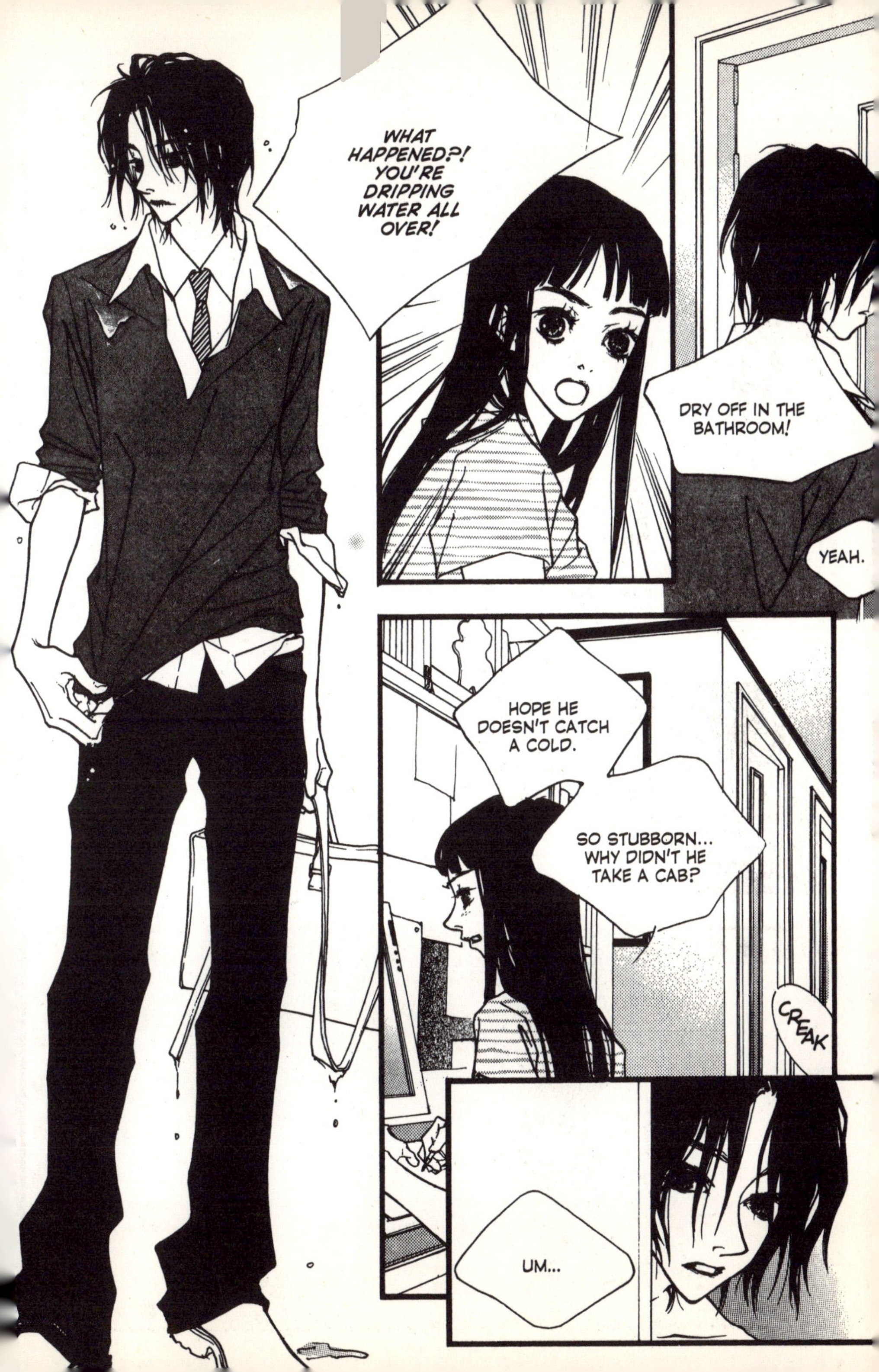
WHAT HAPPENED?! YOU'RE DRIPPING WATER ALL OVER!
DRY OFF IN THE BATHROOM!
YEAH.
HOPE HE DOESN'T CATCH A COLD.
SO STUBBORN... WHY DIDN'T HE TAKE A CAB?
CREAK
UM...

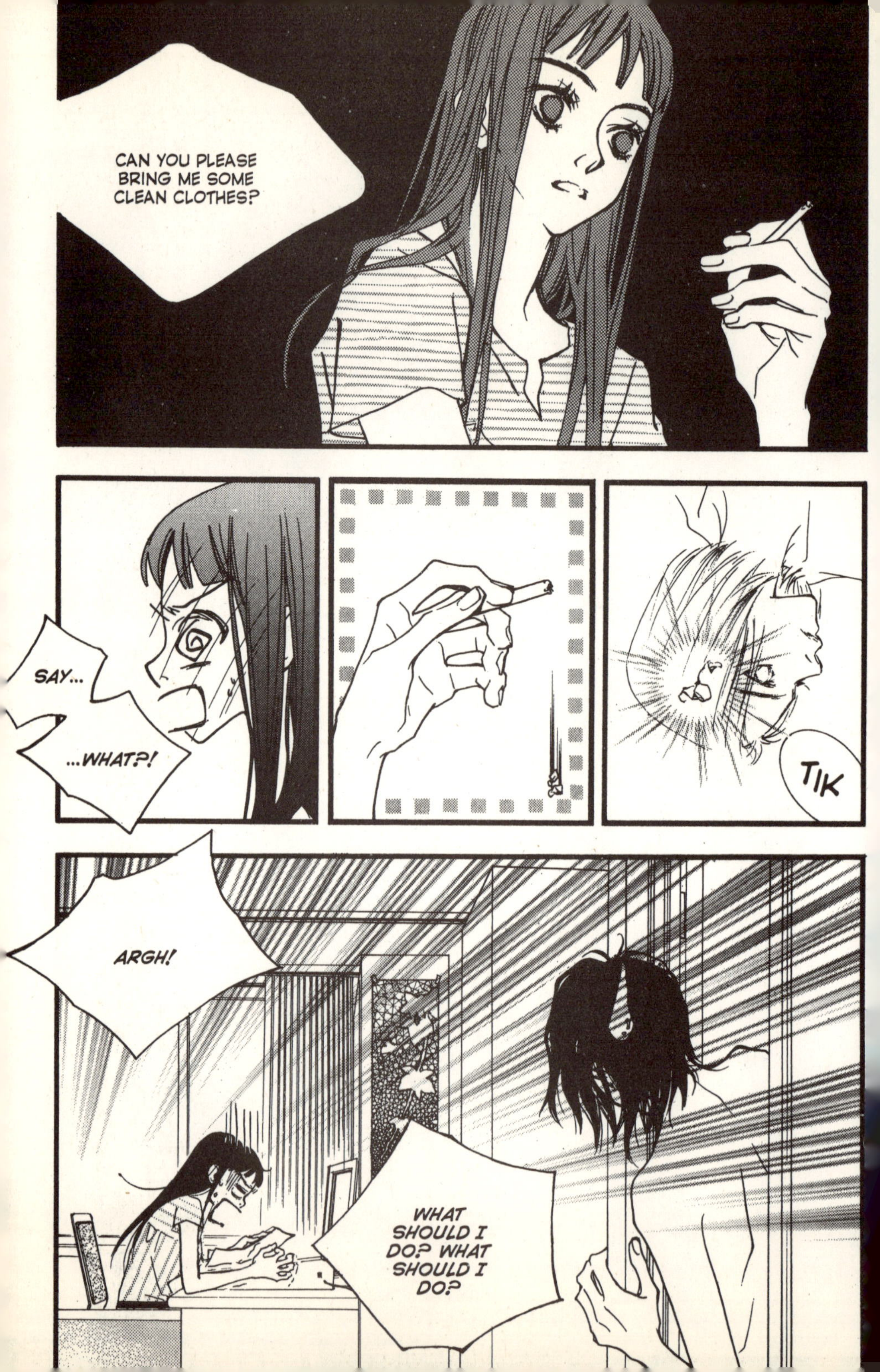
CAN YOU PLEASE BRING ME SOME CLEAN CLOTHES?
TIK
SAY...
...WHAT?!
WHAT SHOULD I DO? WHAT SHOULD I DO?
ARGH!

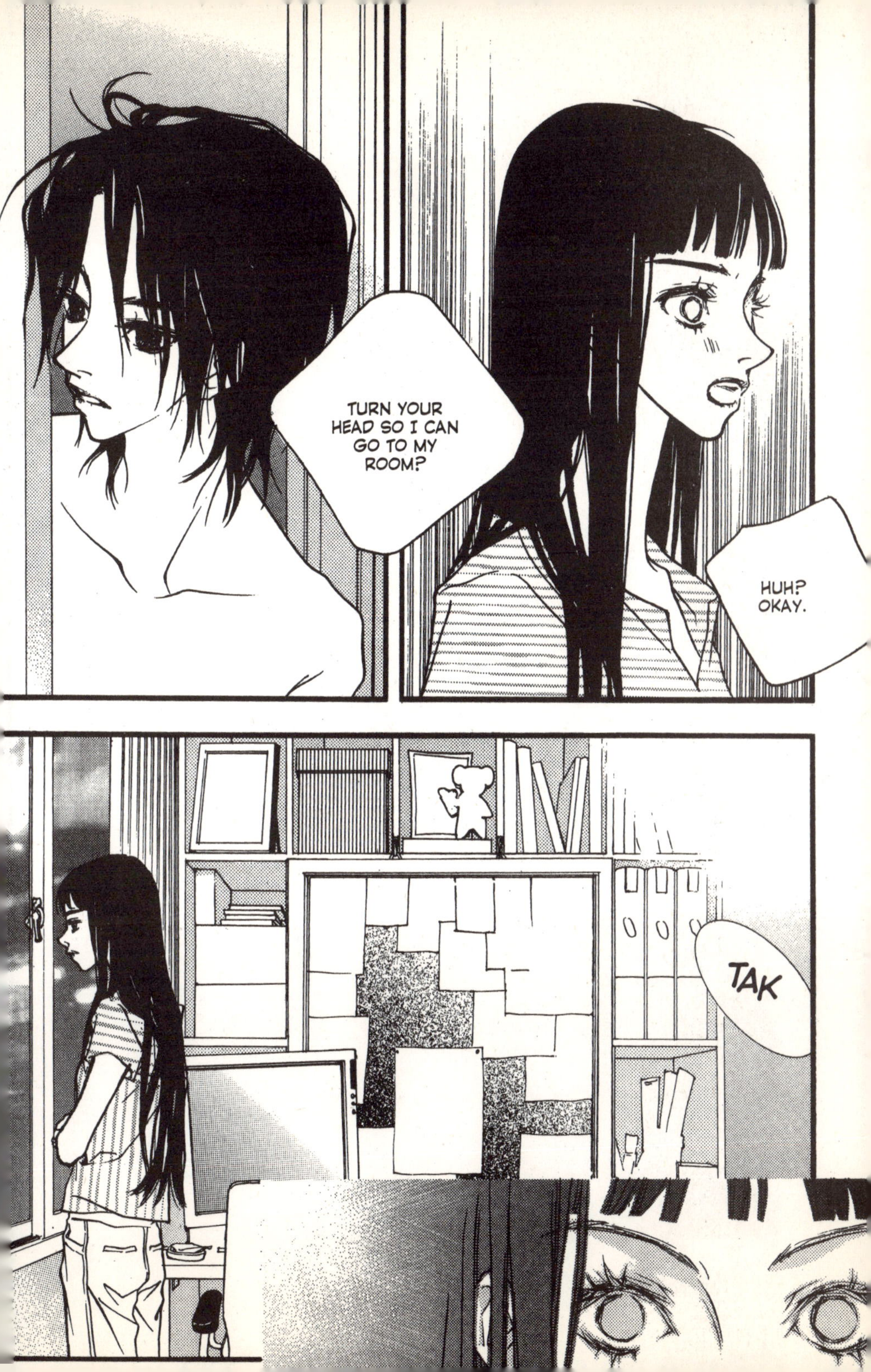
TURN YOUR HEAD SO I CAN GO TO MY ROOM?
HUH? OKAY.
TAK

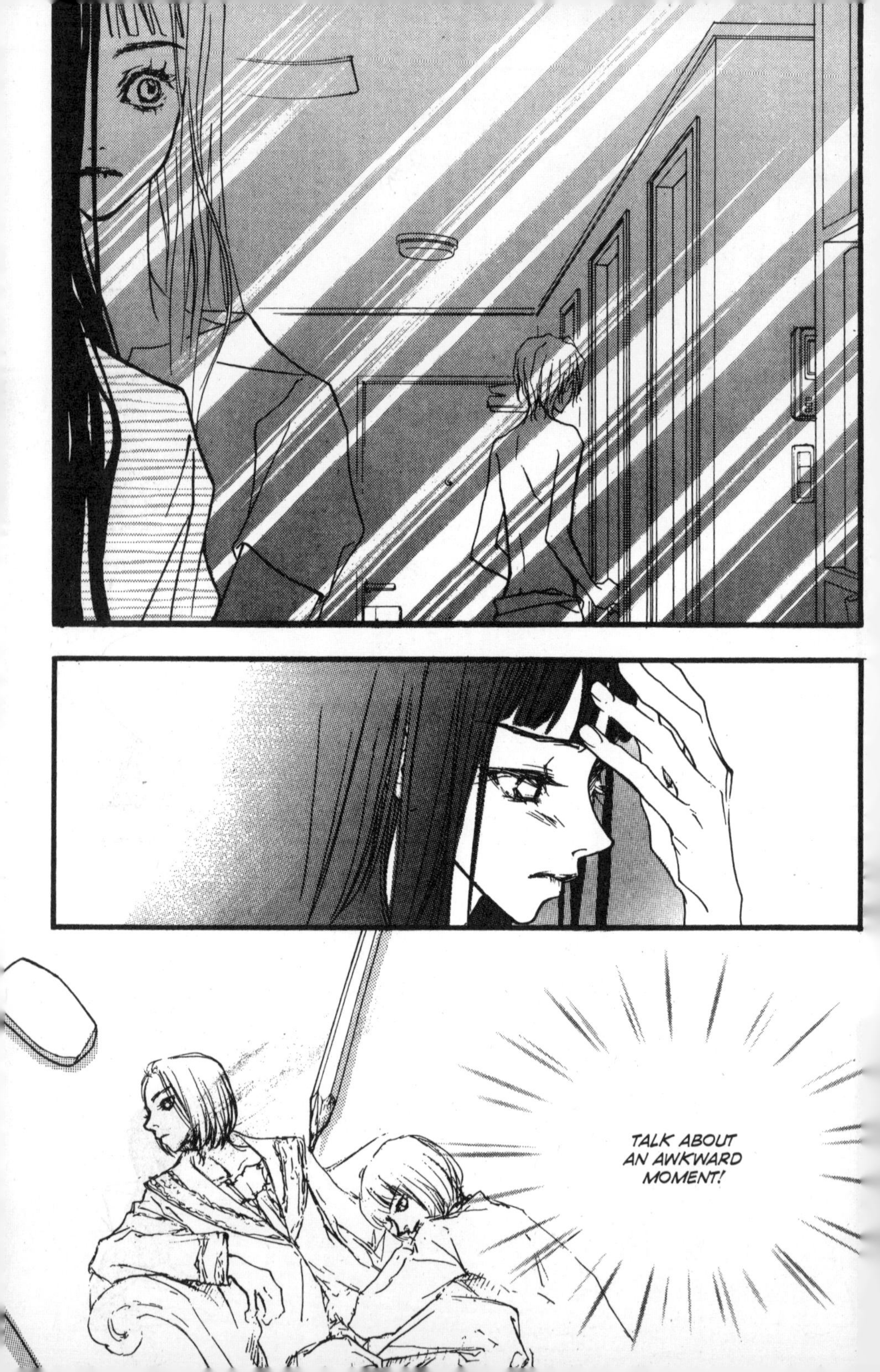
TALK ABOUT AN AWKWARD MOMENT!

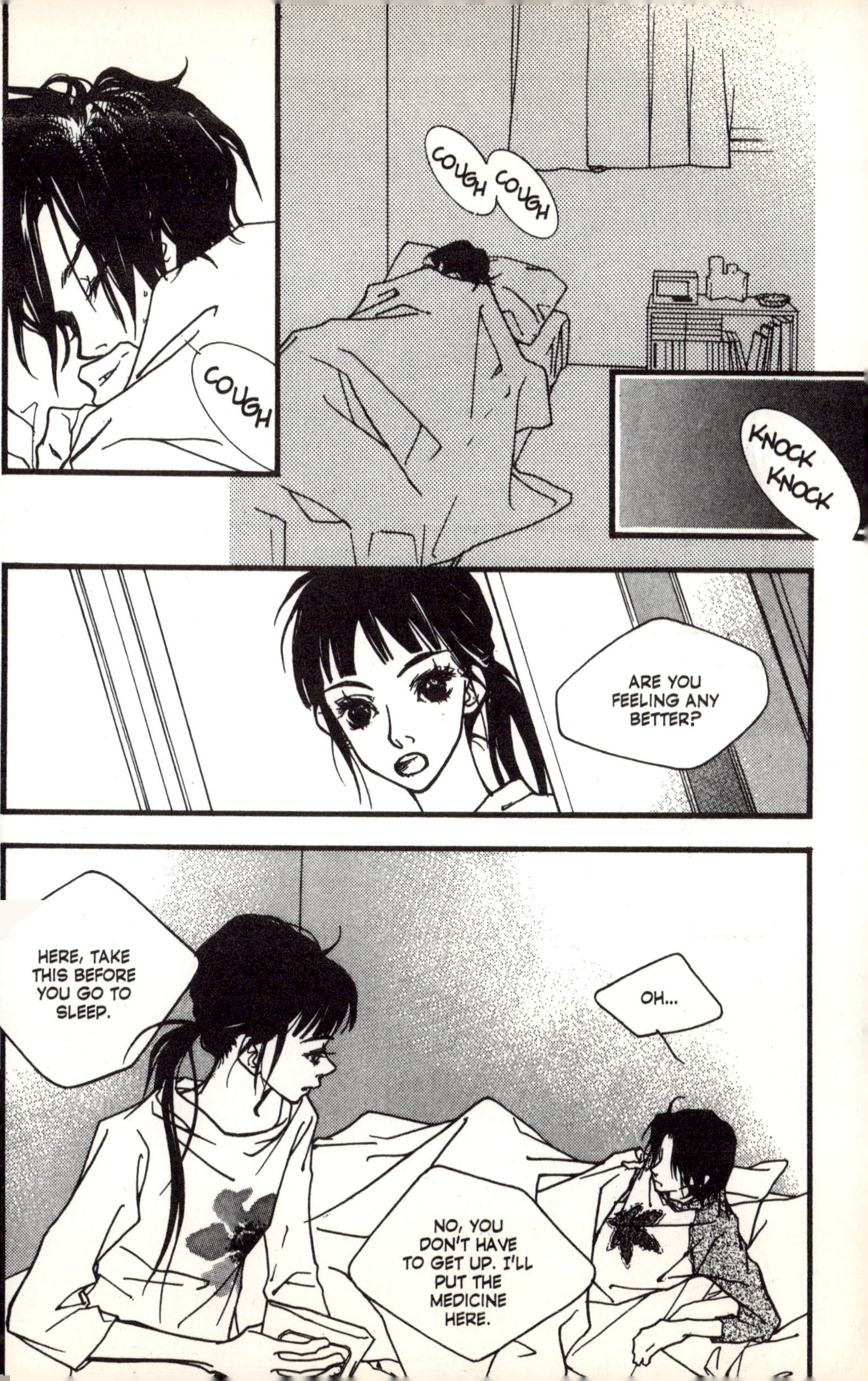
COUGH
COUGH COUGH
KNOCK KNOCK
ARE YOU FEELING ANY BETTER?
HERE, TAKE THIS BEFORE YOU GO TO SLEEP.
OH...
NO, YOU DON'T HAVE TO GET UP. I'LL PUT THE MEDICINE HERE.

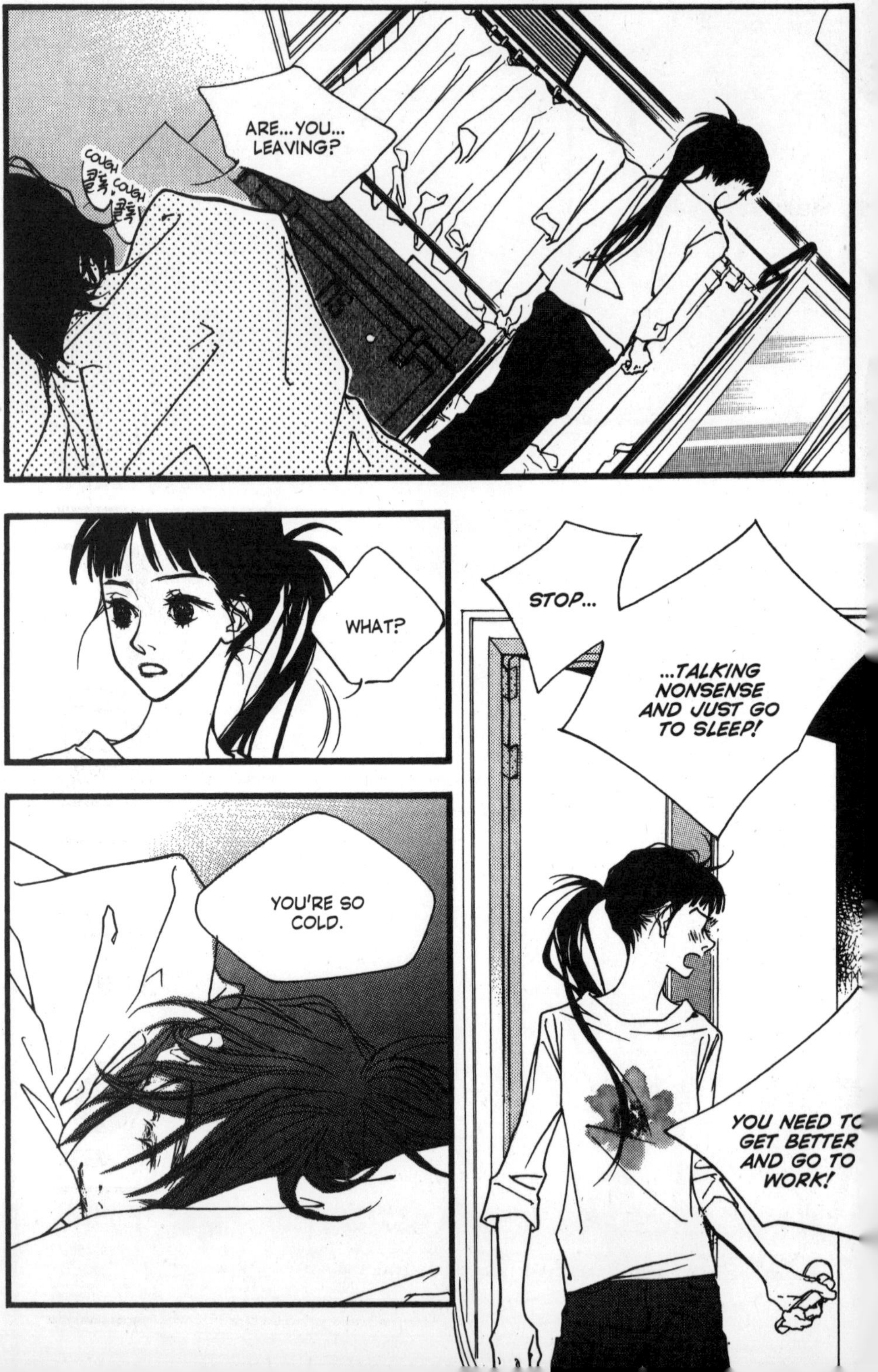
ARE...YOU... LEAVING?
COUGH
콜록,
COUGH
콜록
WHAT?
STOP...
...TALKING NONSENSE AND JUST GO TO SLEEP!
YOU'RE SO COLD.
YOU NEED TO GET BETTER AND GO TO WORK!

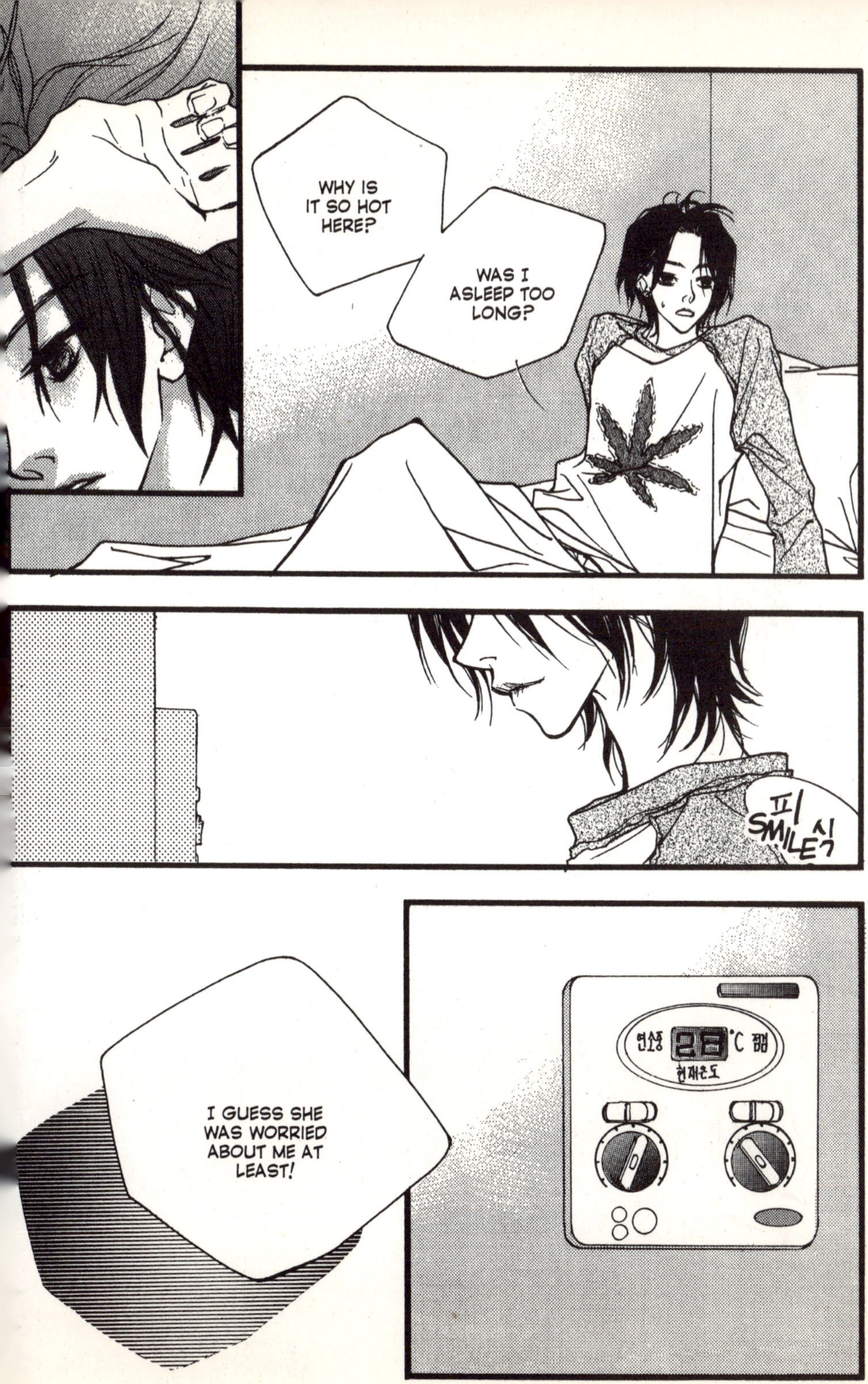
WHY IS IT SO HOT HERE?
WAS I ASLEEP TOO LONG?
피식
SMILE
연소중
28
°C
점검
현재온도
I GUESS SHE WAS WORRIED ABOUT ME AT LEAST!

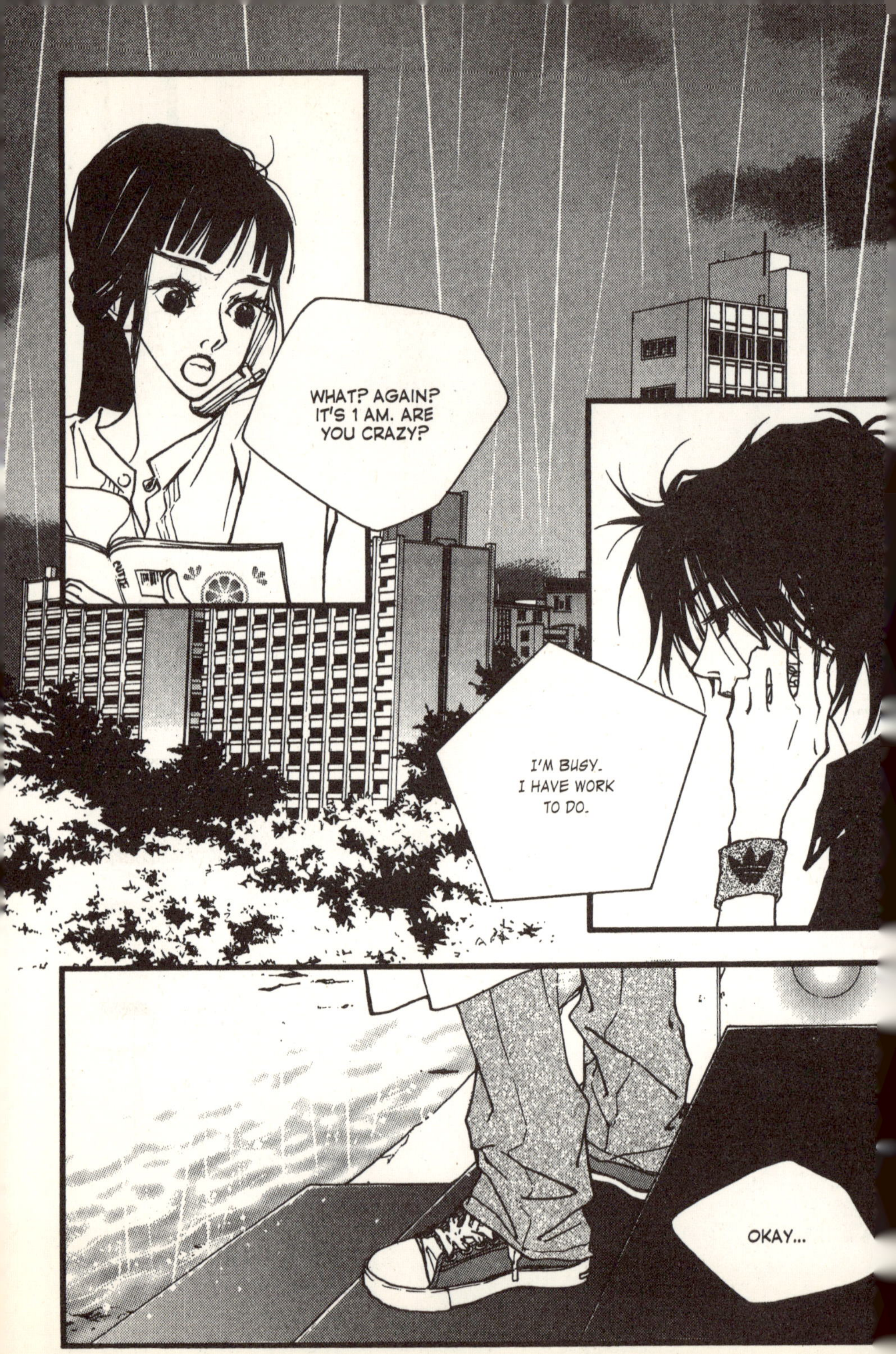
WHAT? AGAIN? IT'S 1 AM. ARE YOU CRAZY?
I'M BUSY. I HAVE WORK TO DO.
OKAY...

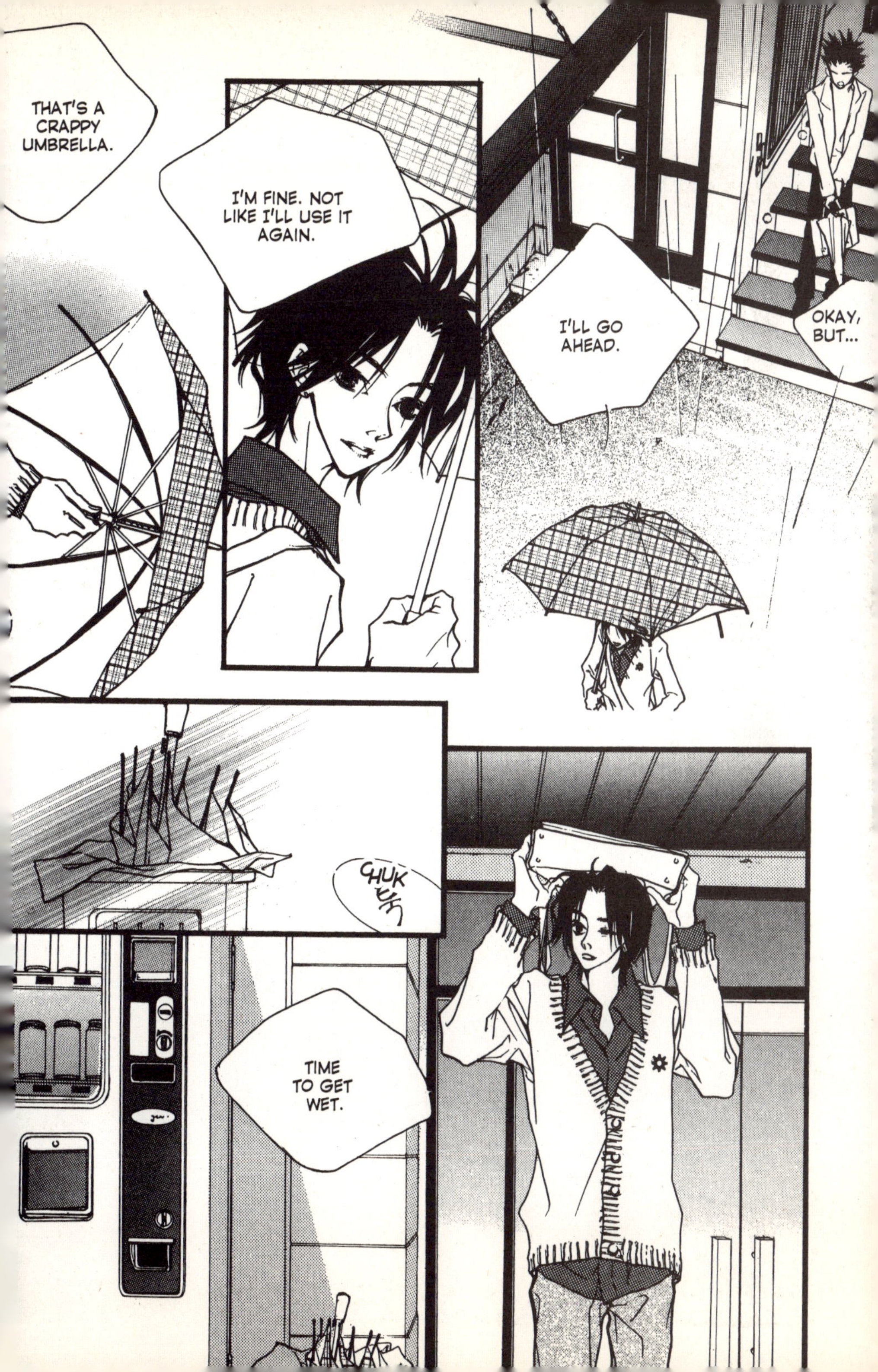
THAT'S A CRAPPY UMBRELLA.
I'M FINE. NOT LIKE I'LL USE IT AGAIN.
I'LL GO AHEAD.
OKAY, BUT...
CHUK
TIME TO GET WET.

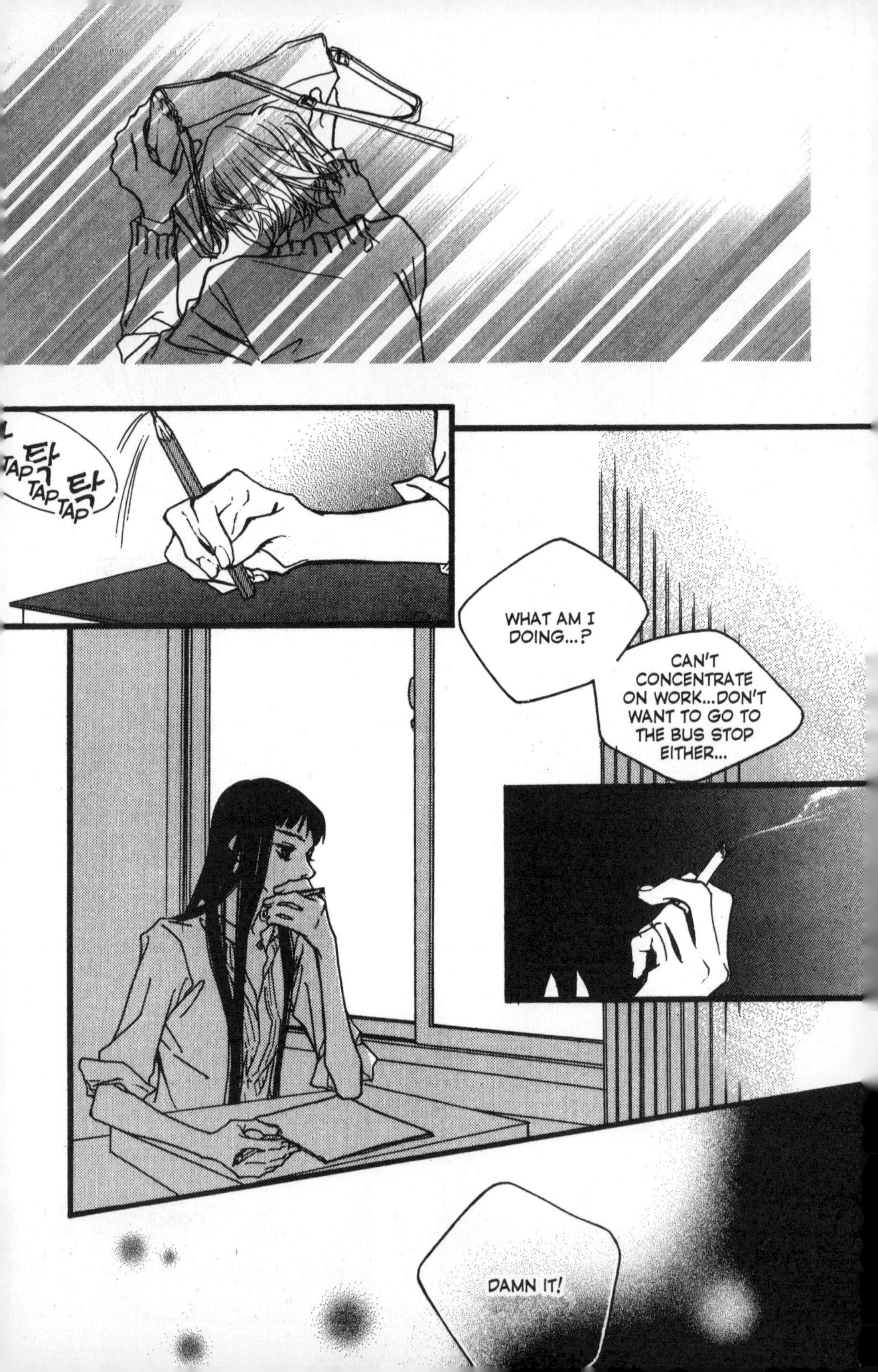
타
타
TAP TAP TAP TAP
WHAT AM I DOING...?
CAN'T CONCENTRATE ON WORK...DON'T WANT TO GO TO THE BUS STOP EITHER...
DAMN IT!

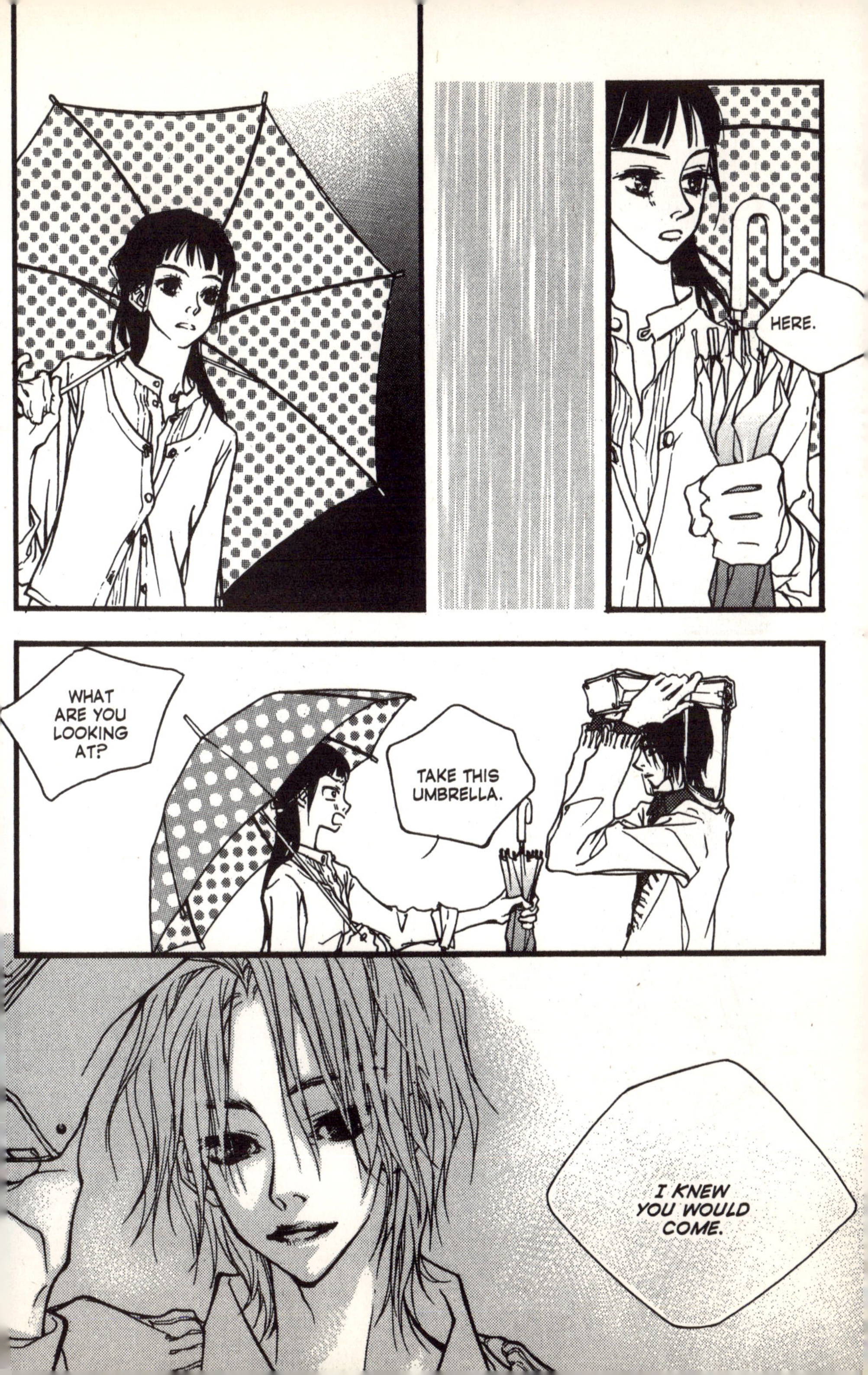
HERE.
WHAT ARE YOU LOOKING AT?
TAKE THIS UMBRELLA.
I KNEW YOU WOULD COME.

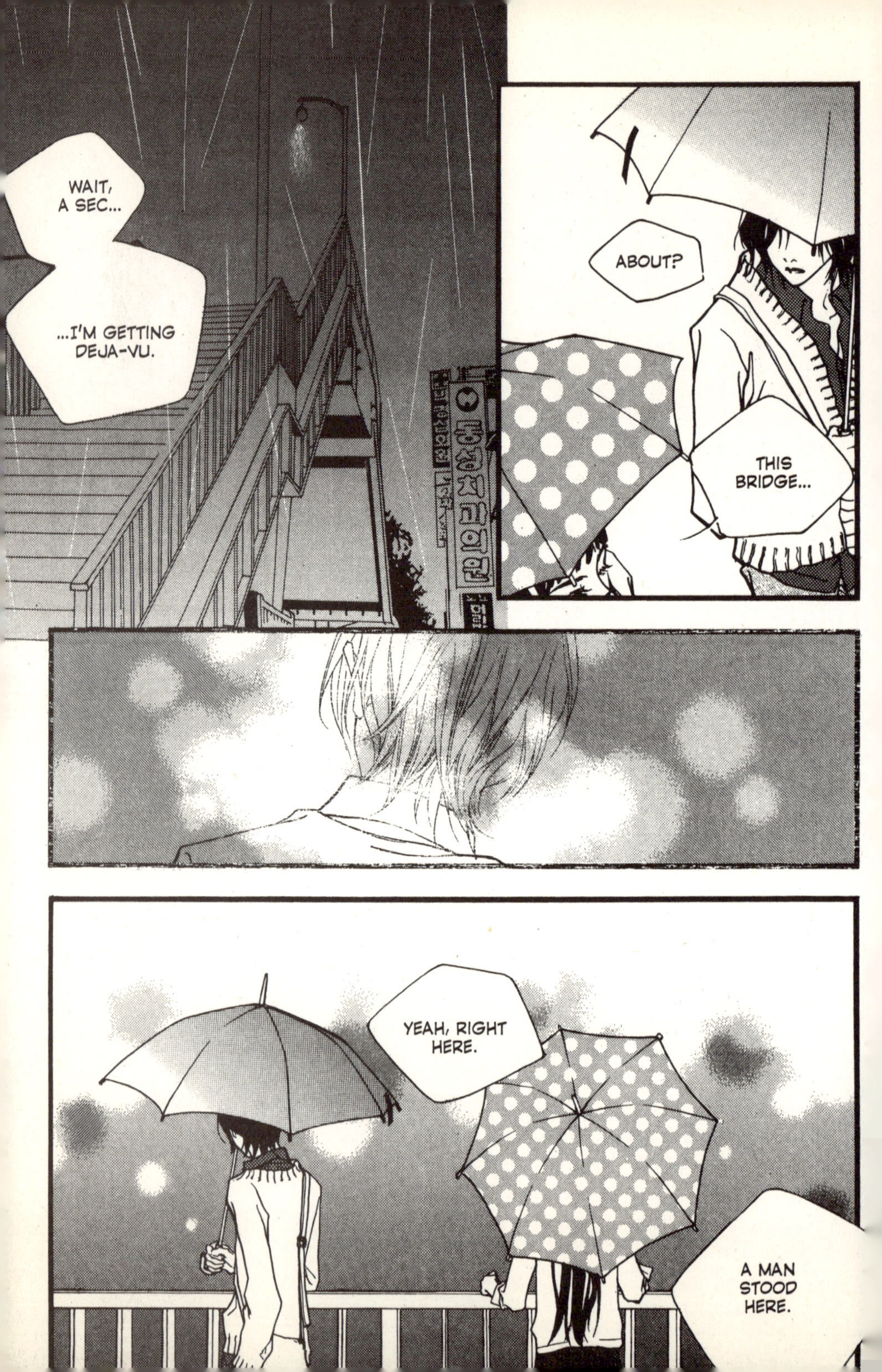
WAIT, A SEC...
...I'M GETTING DEJA-VU.
동성치과의원
ABOUT?
THIS BRIDGE...
YEAH, RIGHT HERE.
A MAN STOOD HERE.

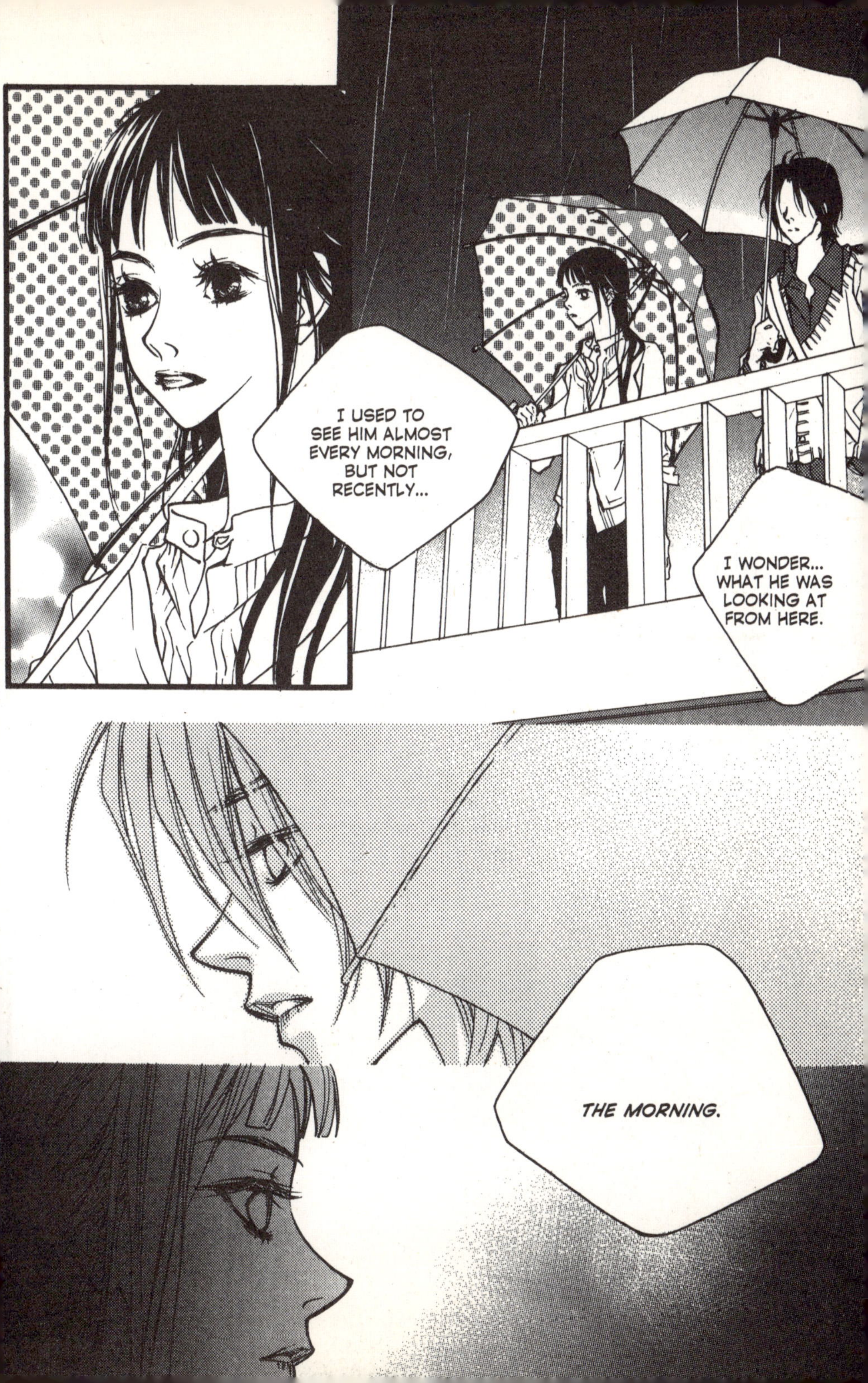
I USED TO SEE HIM ALMOST EVERY MORNING, BUT NOT RECENTLY...
I WONDER... WHAT HE WAS LOOKING AT FROM HERE.
THE MORNING.

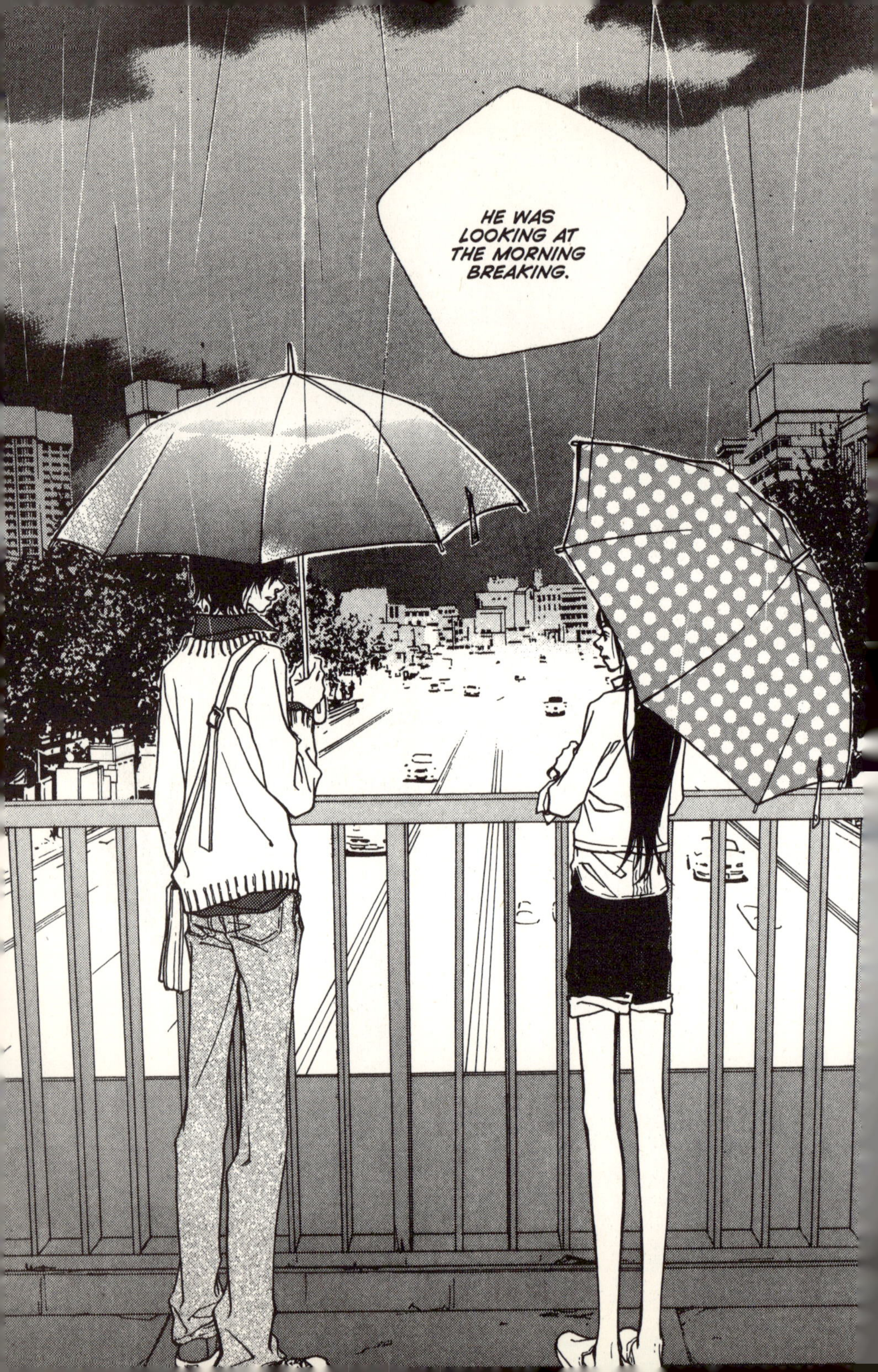
HE WAS LOOKING AT THE MORNING BREAKING.

Forest of Gray City

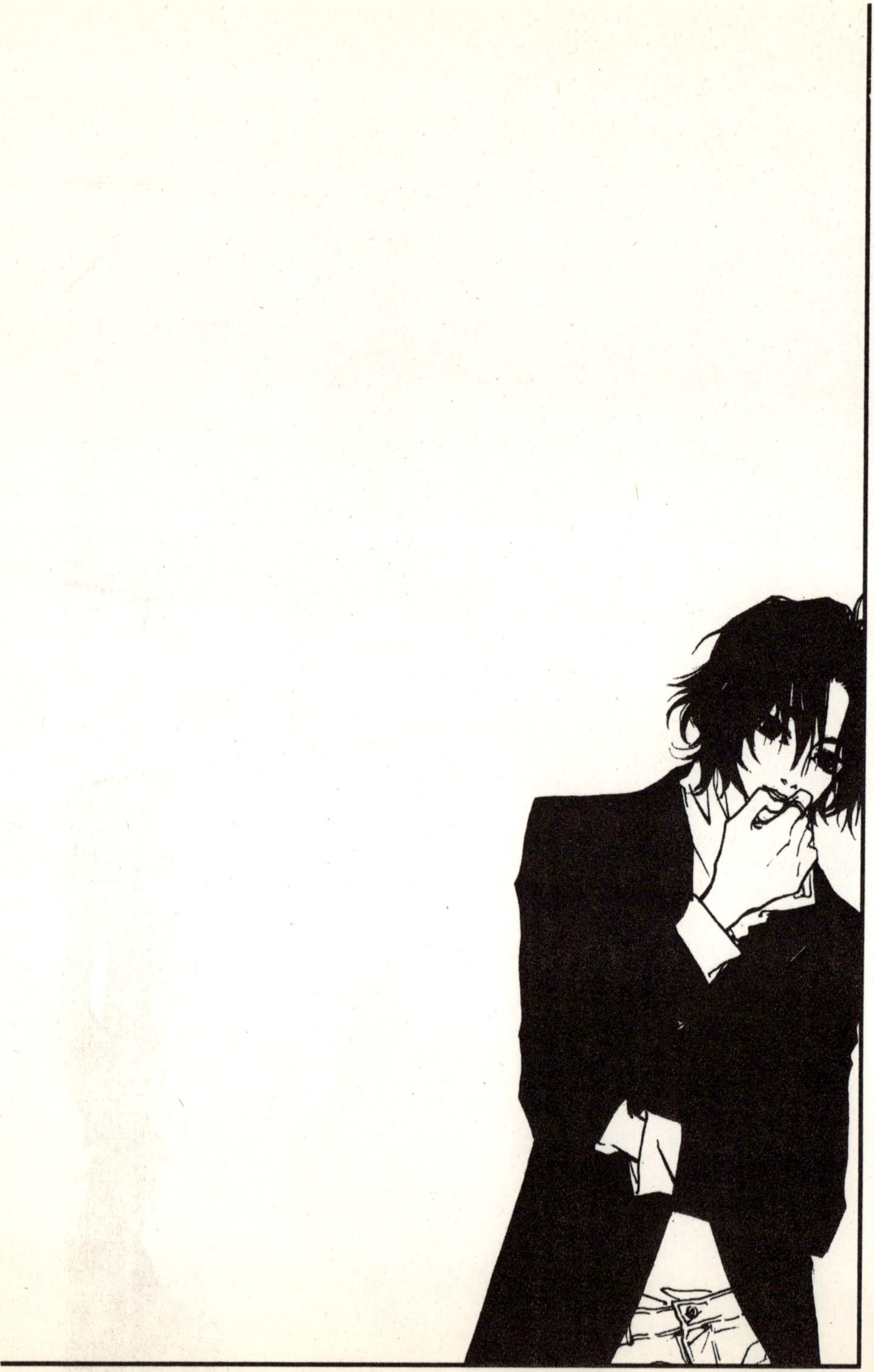

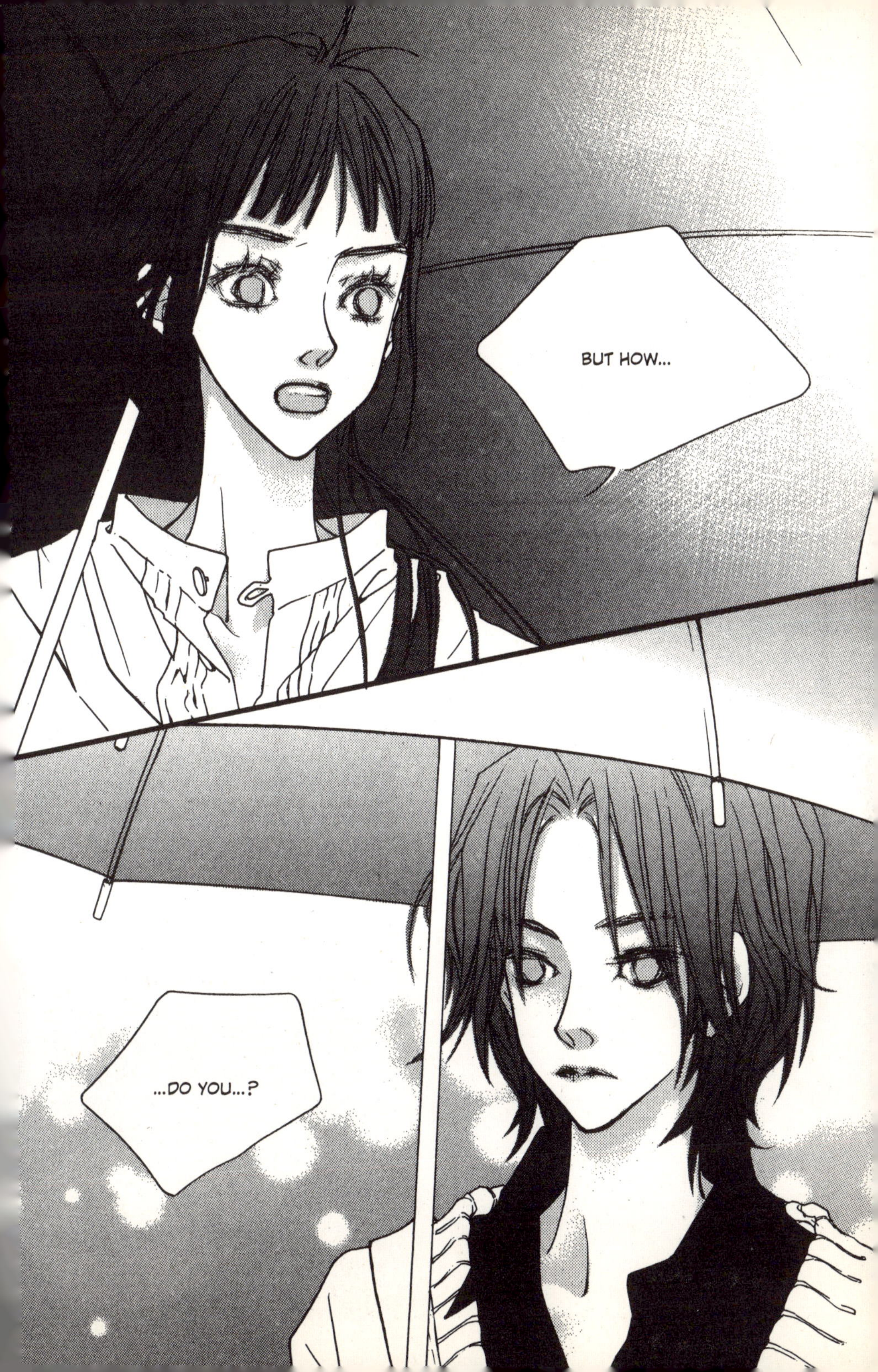
BUT HOW...
...DO YOU...?

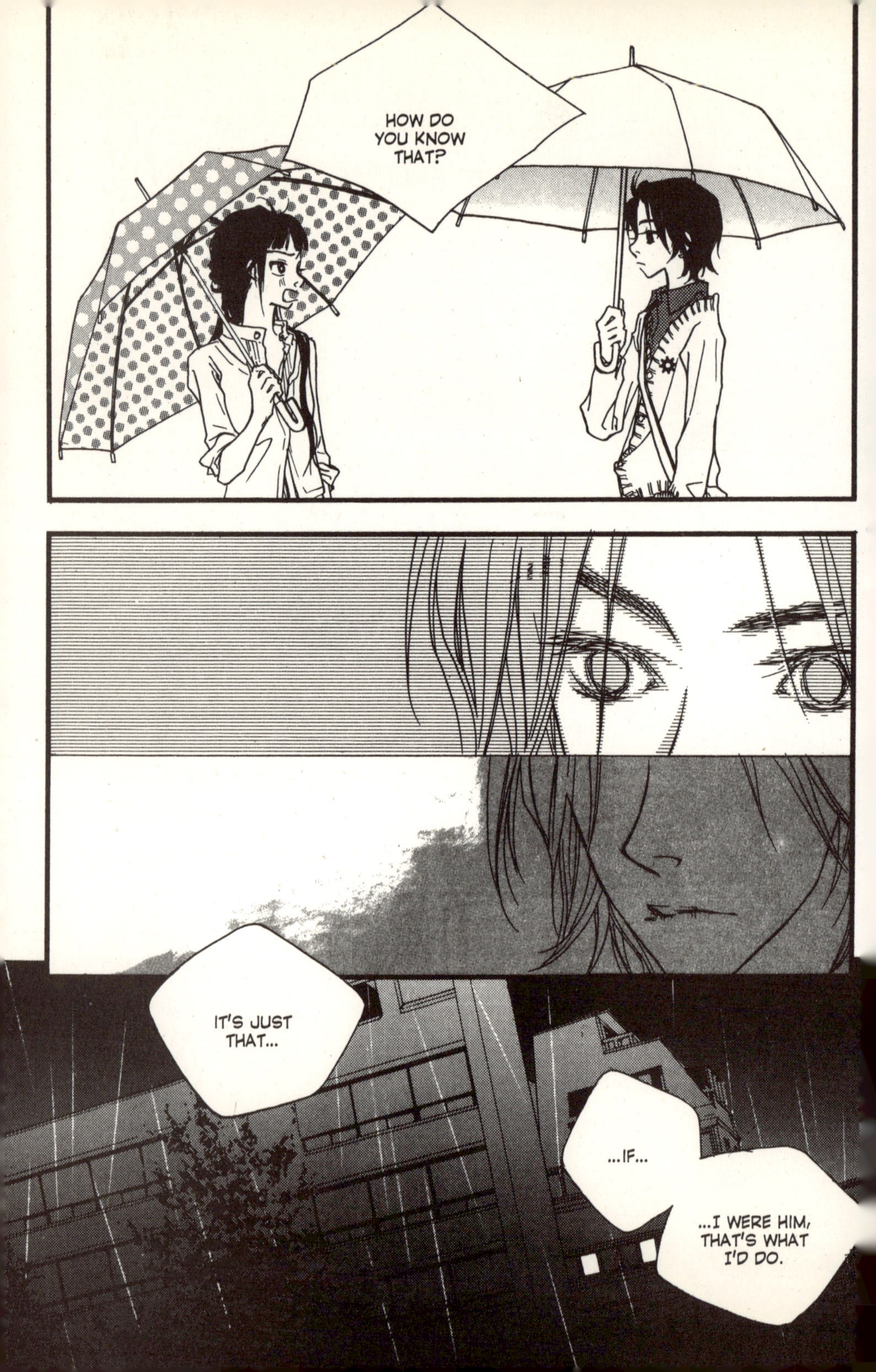
HOW DO YOU KNOW THAT?
IT'S JUST THAT...
...IF...
...I WERE HIM, THAT'S WHAT I'D DO.

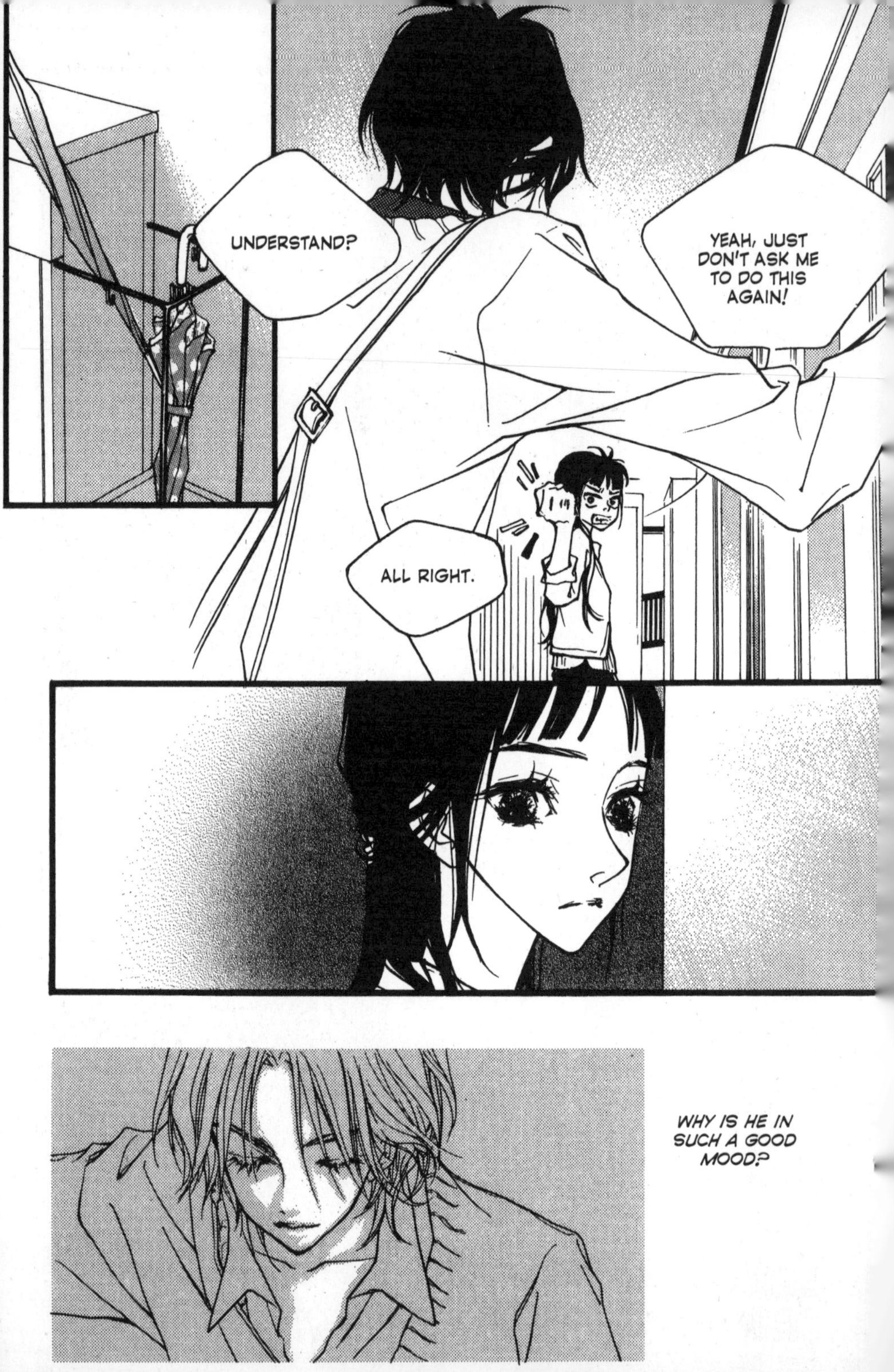
YEAH, JUST DON'T ASK ME TO DO THIS AGAIN!
UNDERSTAND?
ALL RIGHT.
WHY IS HE IN SUCH A GOOD MOOD?

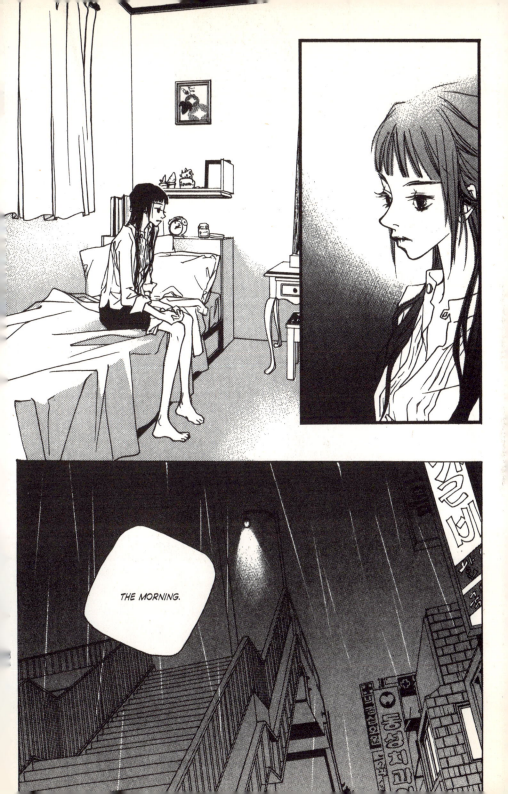

THE MORNING.

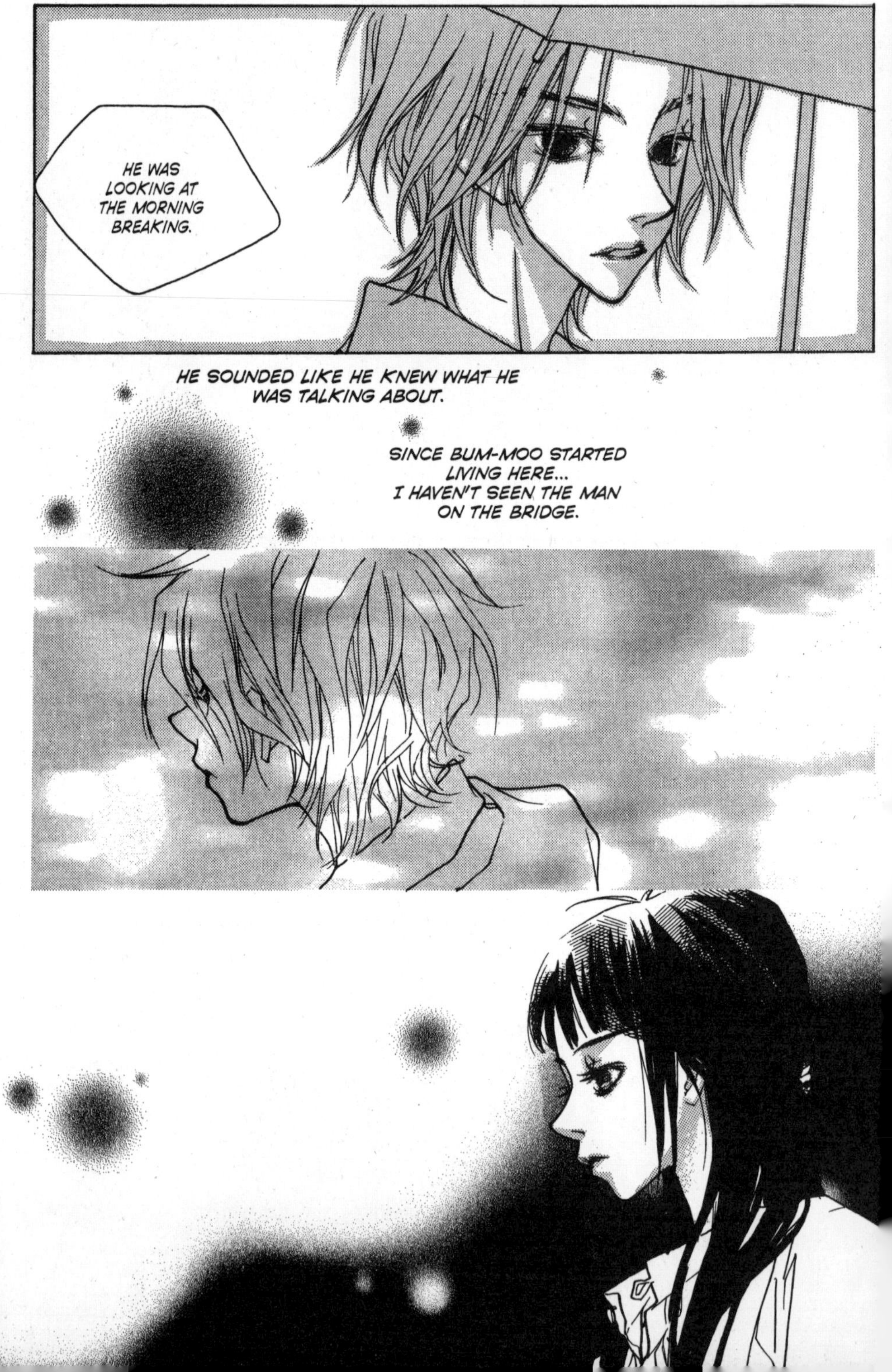
HE WAS LOOKING AT THE MORNING BREAKING.
HE SOUNDED LIKE HE KNEW WHAT HE WAS TALKING ABOUT.
SINCE BUM-MOO STARTED LIVING HERE...
I HAVEN'T SEEN THE MAN ON THE BRIDGE.

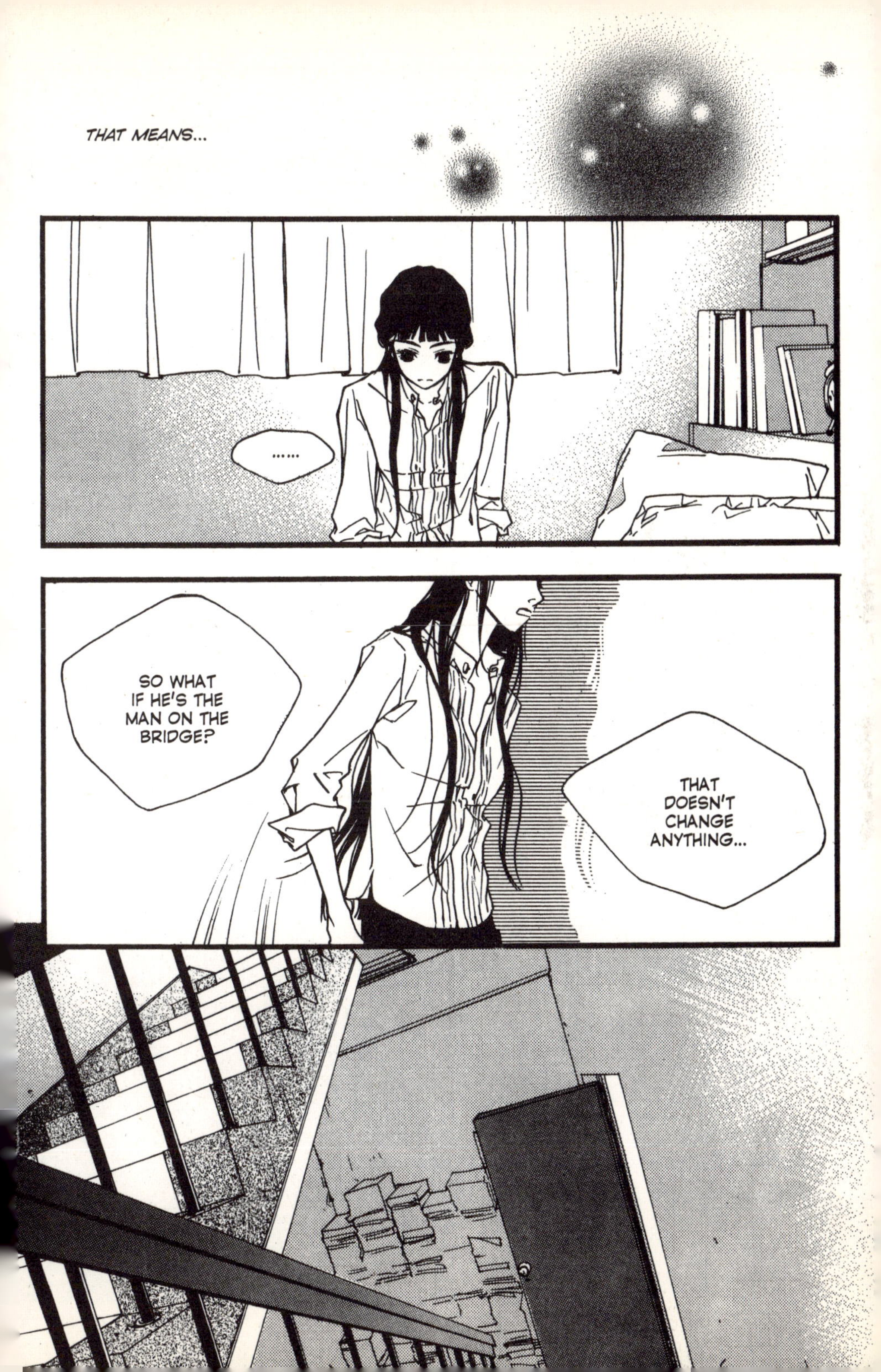
THAT MEANS...
......
SO WHAT IF HE'S THE MAN ON THE BRIDGE?
THAT DOESN'T CHANGE ANYTHING...

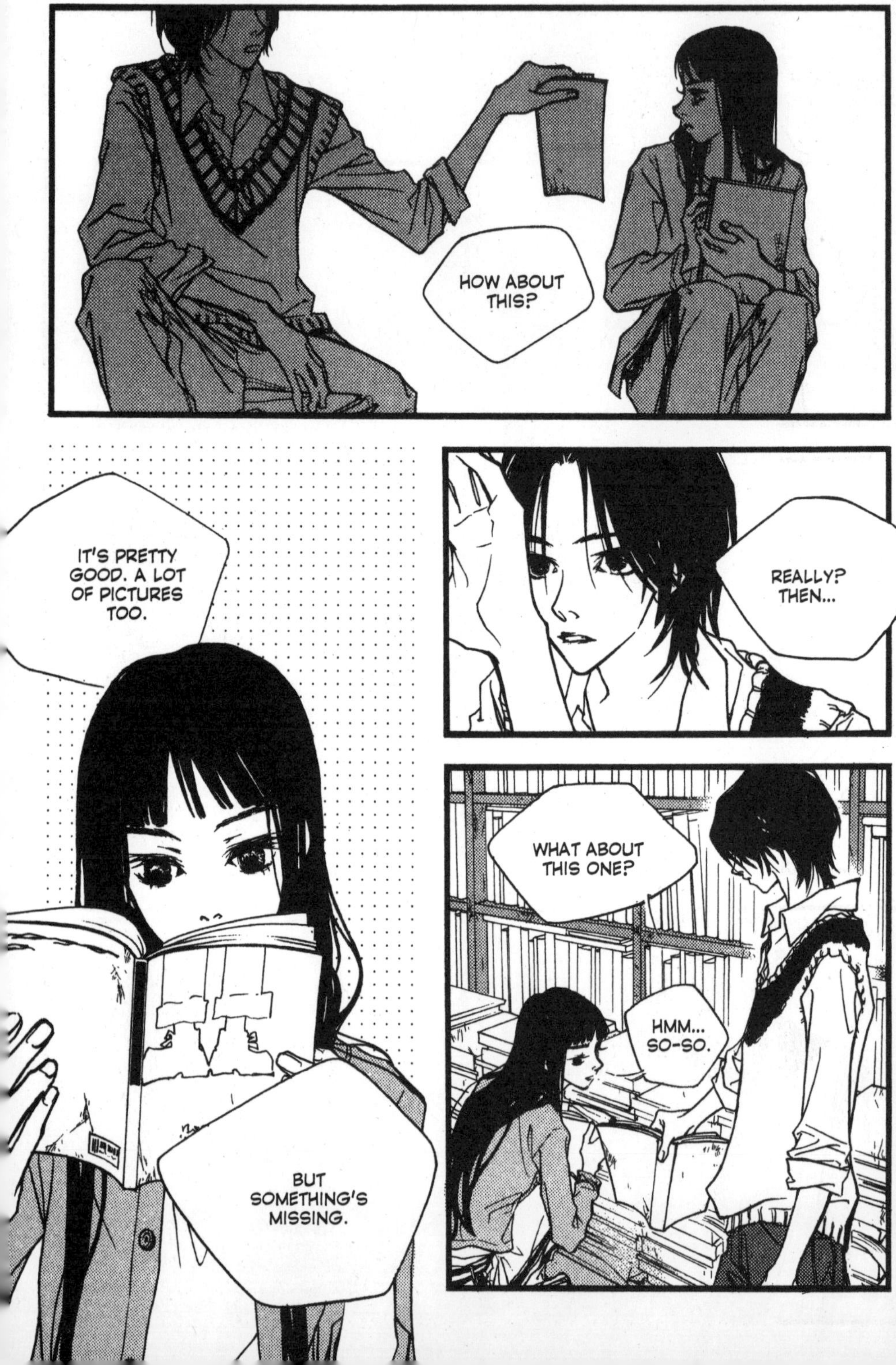
HOW ABOUT THIS?
IT'S PRETTY GOOD. A LOT OF PICTURES TOO.
BUT SOMETHING'S MISSING.
REALLY? THEN...
WHAT ABOUT THIS ONE?
HMM... SO-SO.

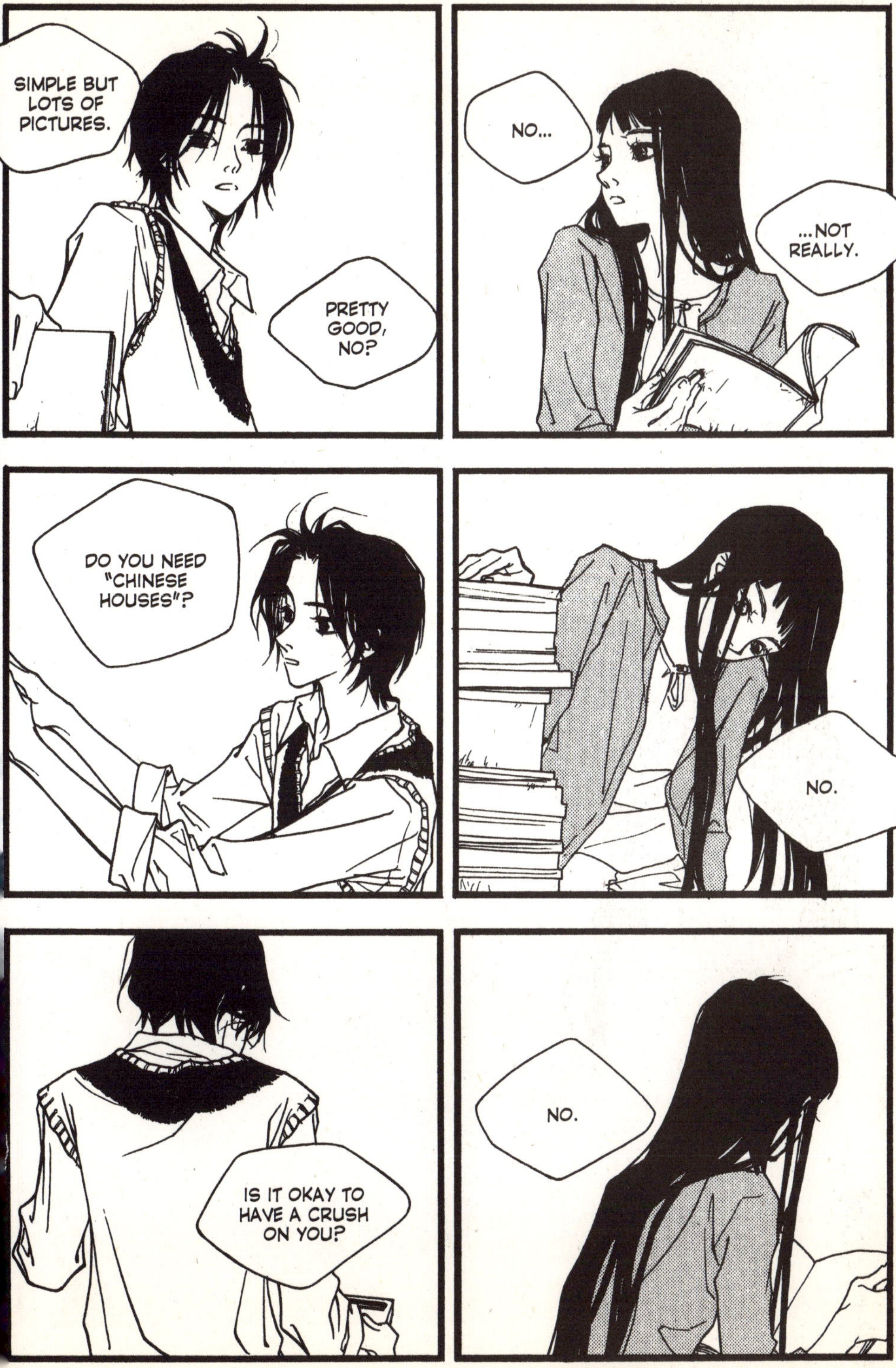
SIMPLE BUT LOTS OF PICTURES.
PRETTY GOOD, NO?
NO...
...NOT REALLY.
DO YOU NEED "CHINESE HOUSES"?
NO.
IS IT OKAY TO HAVE A CRUSH ON YOU?
NO.

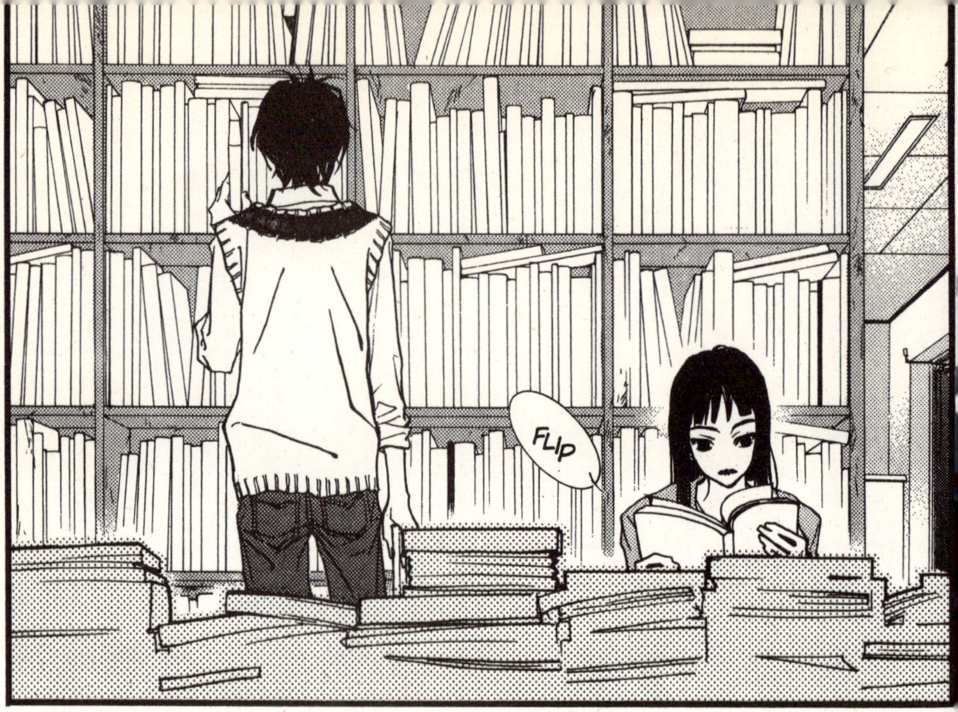
FLIP
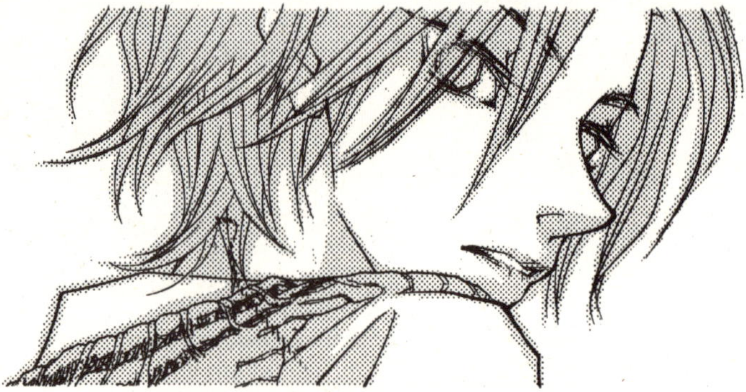
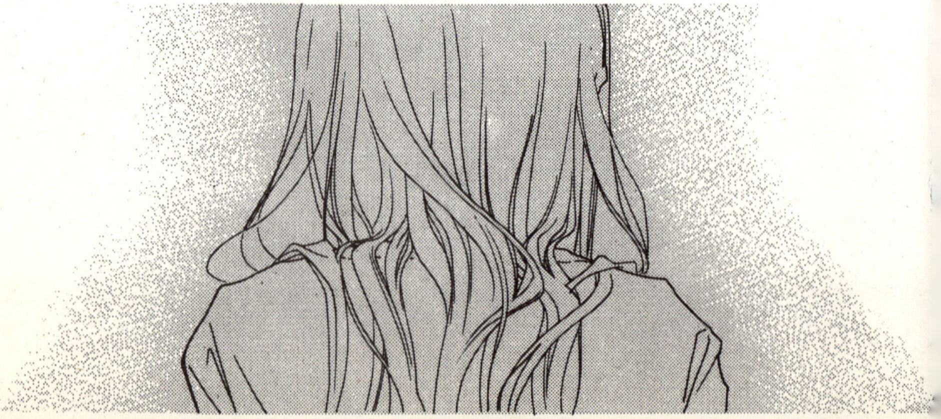

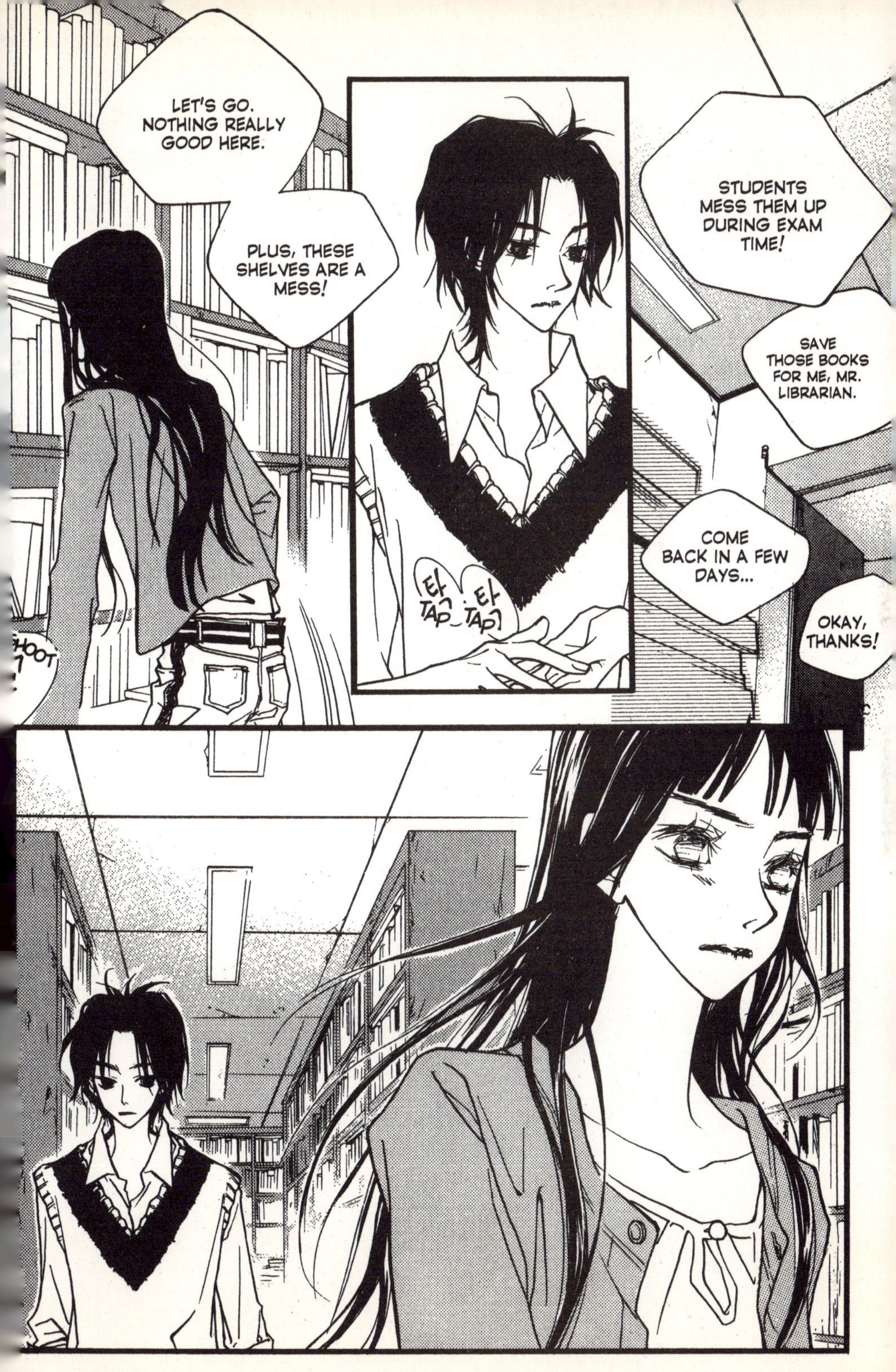
LET'S GO. NOTHING REALLY GOOD HERE.
PLUS, THESE SHELVES ARE A MESS!
STUDENTS MESS THEM UP DURING EXAM TIME!
타 TAP 타 TAP
SAVE THOSE BOOKS FOR ME, MR. LIBRARIAN.
COME BACK IN A FEW DAYS...
OKAY, THANKS!

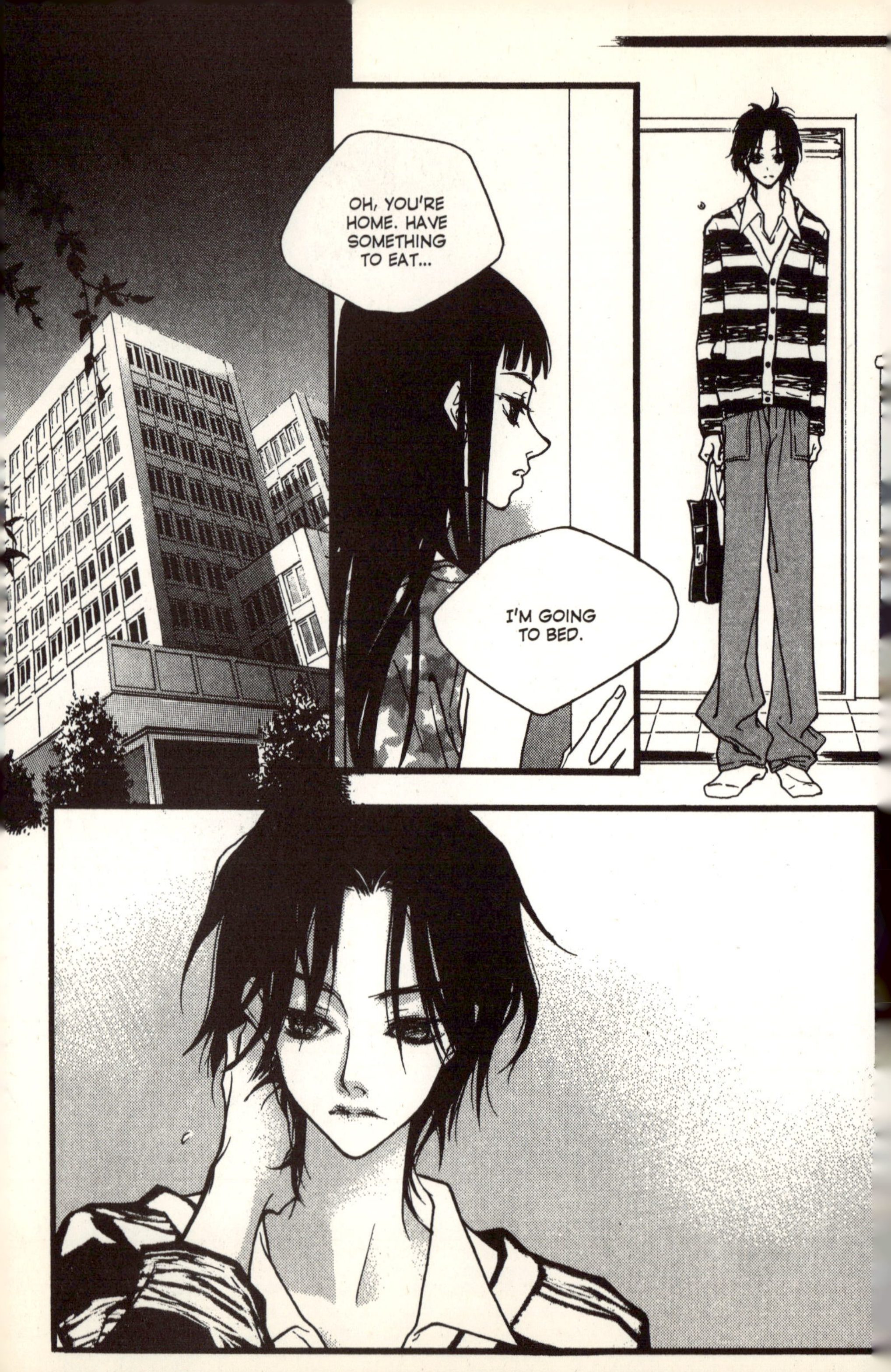
OH, YOU'RE HOME. HAVE SOMETHING TO EAT...
I'M GOING TO BED.

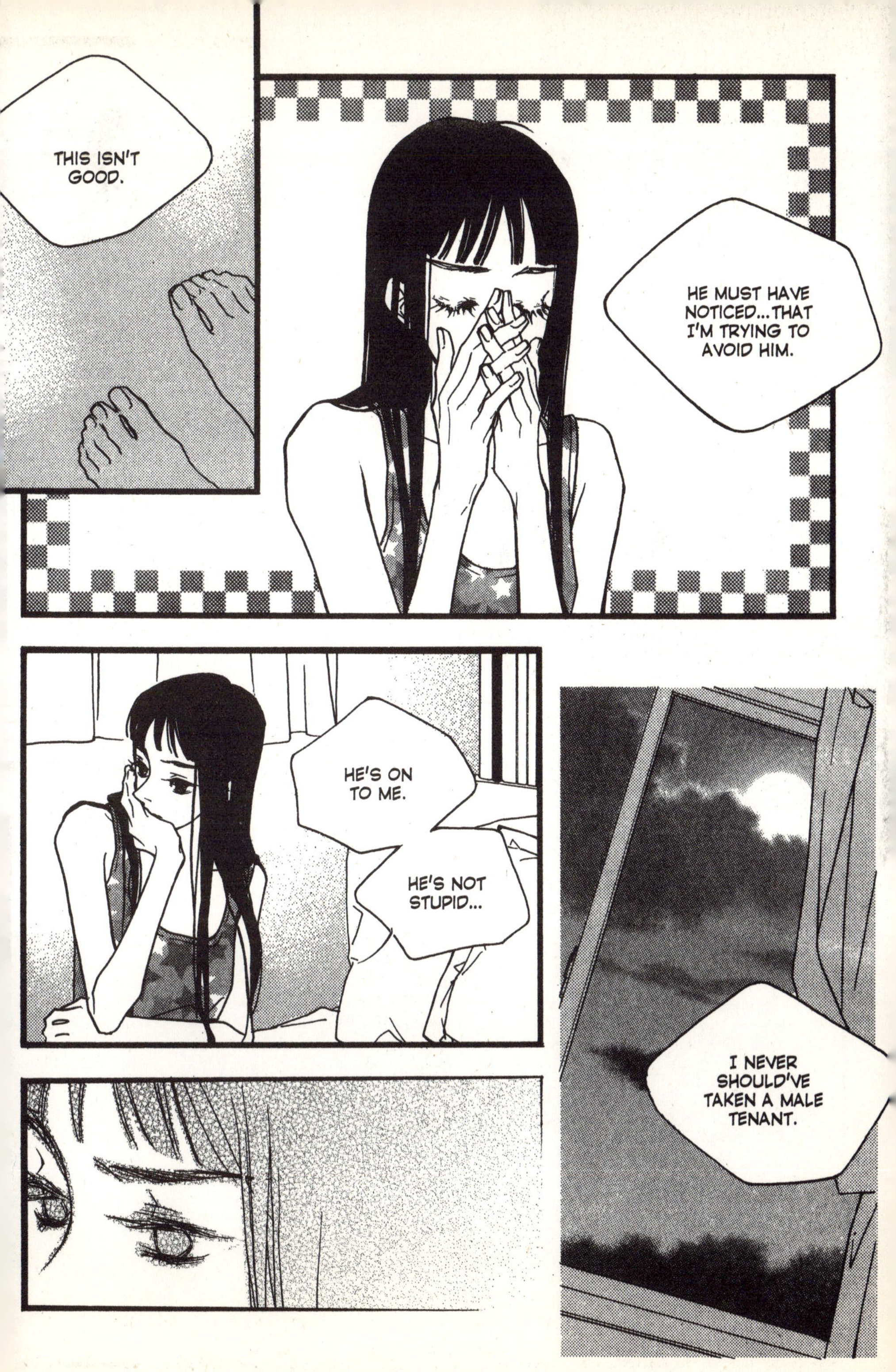
THIS ISN'T GOOD.
HE MUST HAVE NOTICED...THAT I'M TRYING TO AVOID HIM.
HE'S ON TO ME.
HE'S NOT STUPID...
I NEVER SHOULD'VE TAKEN A MALE TENANT.

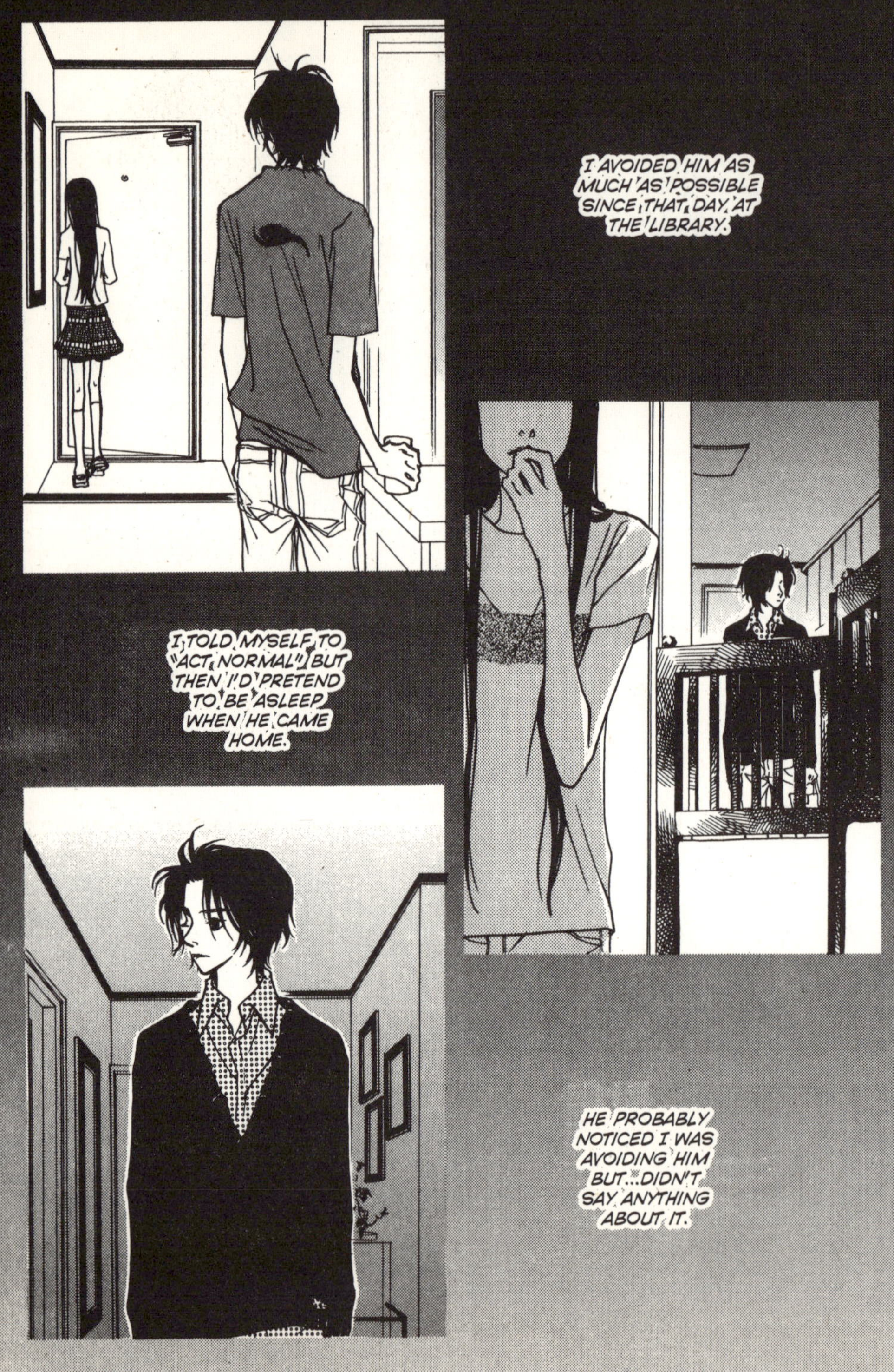
I AVOIDED HIM AS MUCH AS POSSIBLE SINCE THAT DAY, AT THE LIBRARY.
I TOLD MYSELF TO "ACT NORMAL" BUT THEN I'D PRETEND TO BE ASLEEP WHEN HE CAME HOME.
HE PROBABLY NOTICED I WAS AVOIDING HIM BUT...DIDN'T SAY ANYTHING ABOUT IT.

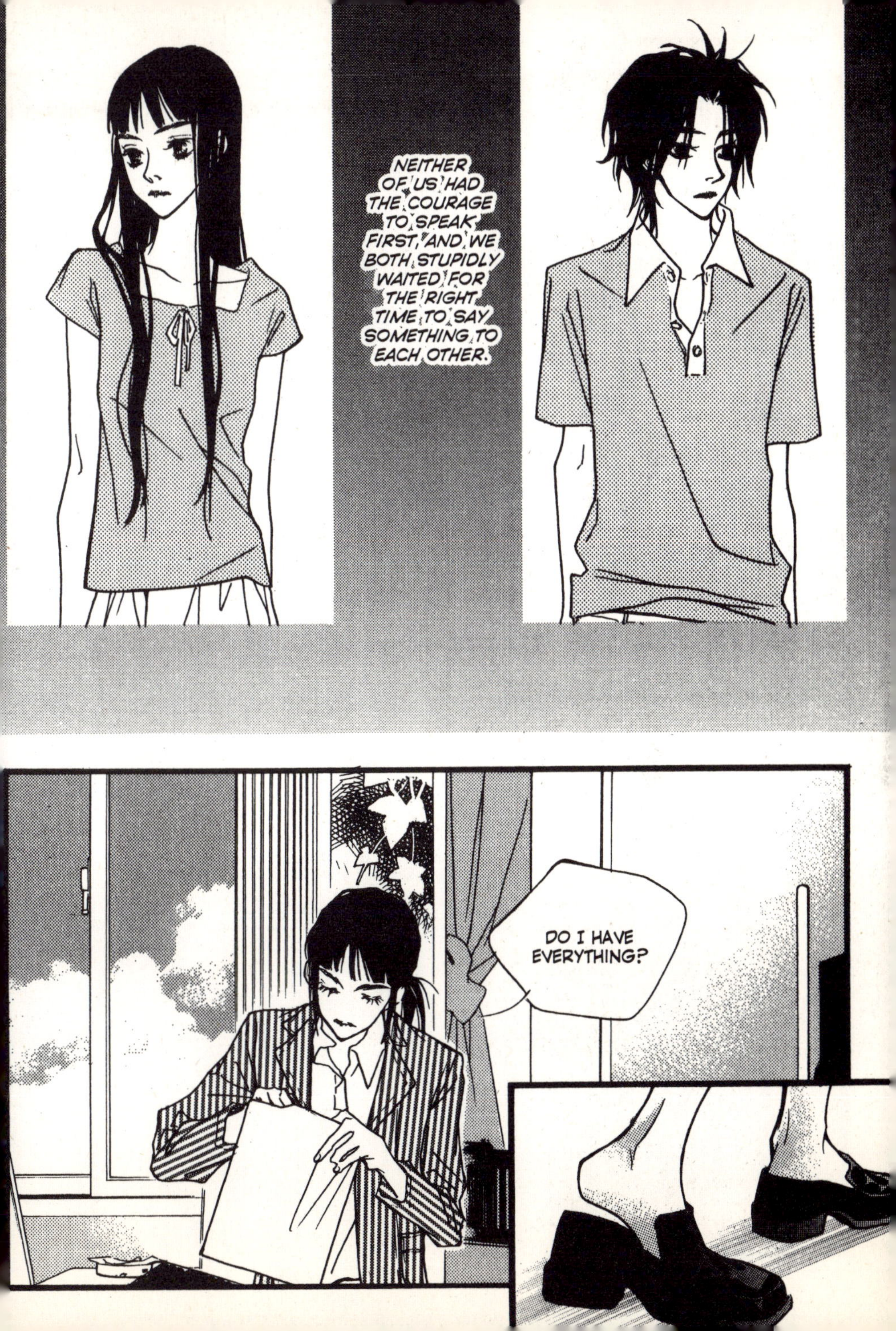
NEITHER OF US HAD THE COURAGE TO SPEAK FIRST, AND WE BOTH STUPIDLY WAITED FOR THE RIGHT TIME TO SAY SOMETHING TO EACH OTHER.
DO I HAVE EVERYTHING?

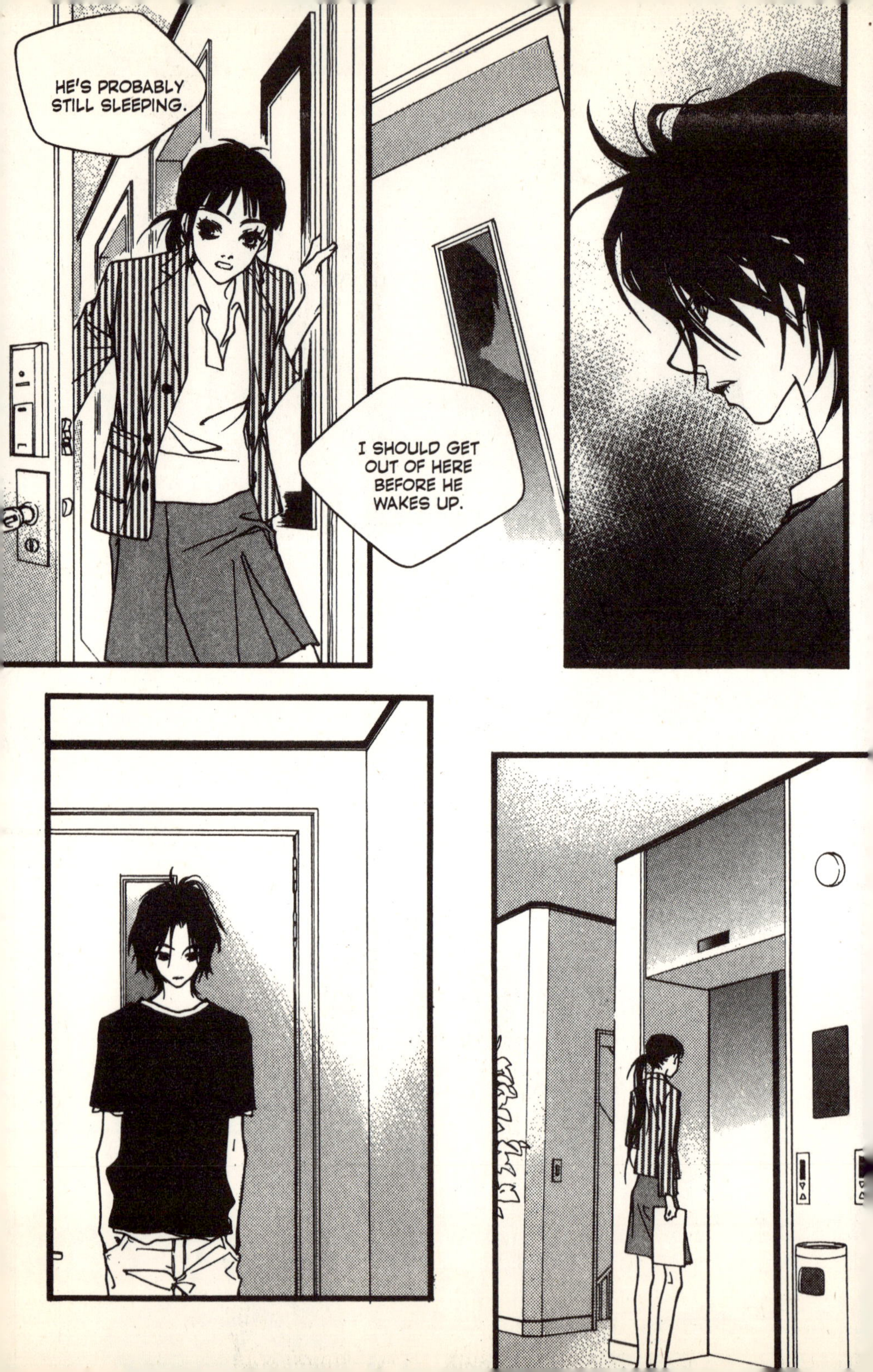
HE'S PROBABLY STILL SLEEPING.
I SHOULD GET OUT OF HERE BEFORE HE WAKES UP.

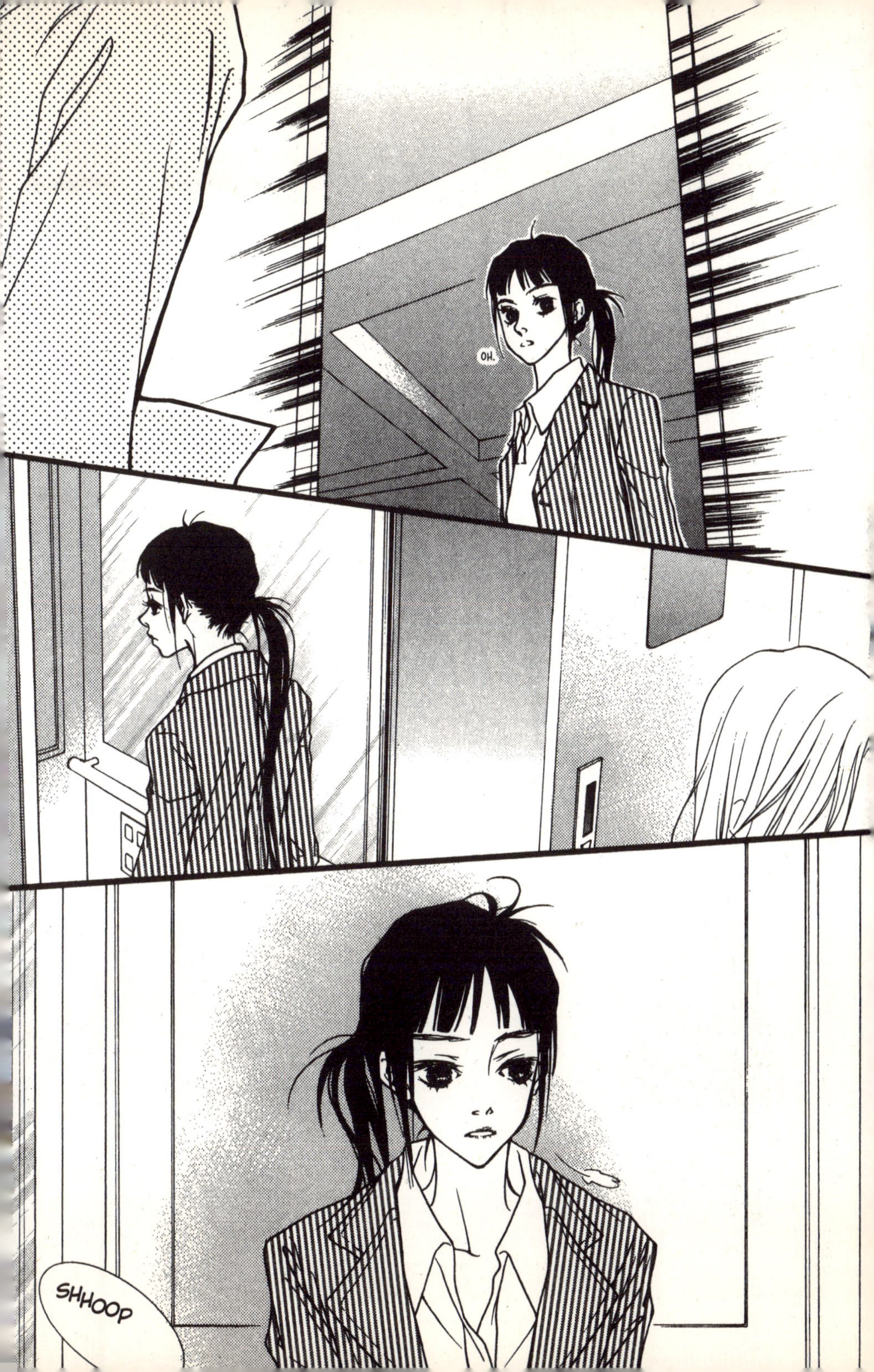
OH.
SHHOOP

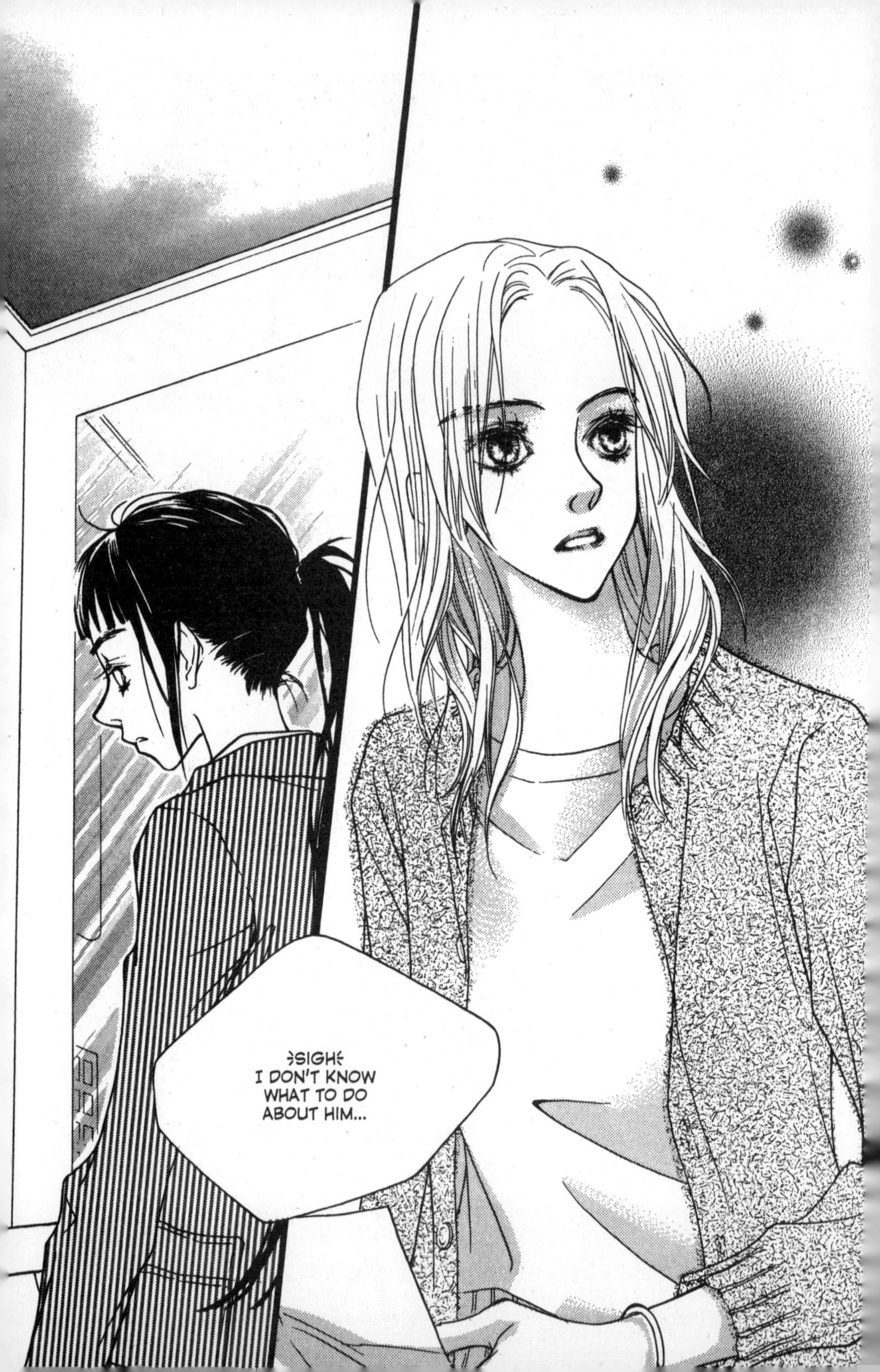

SIGH
I DON'T KNOW WHAT TO DO ABOUT HIM...

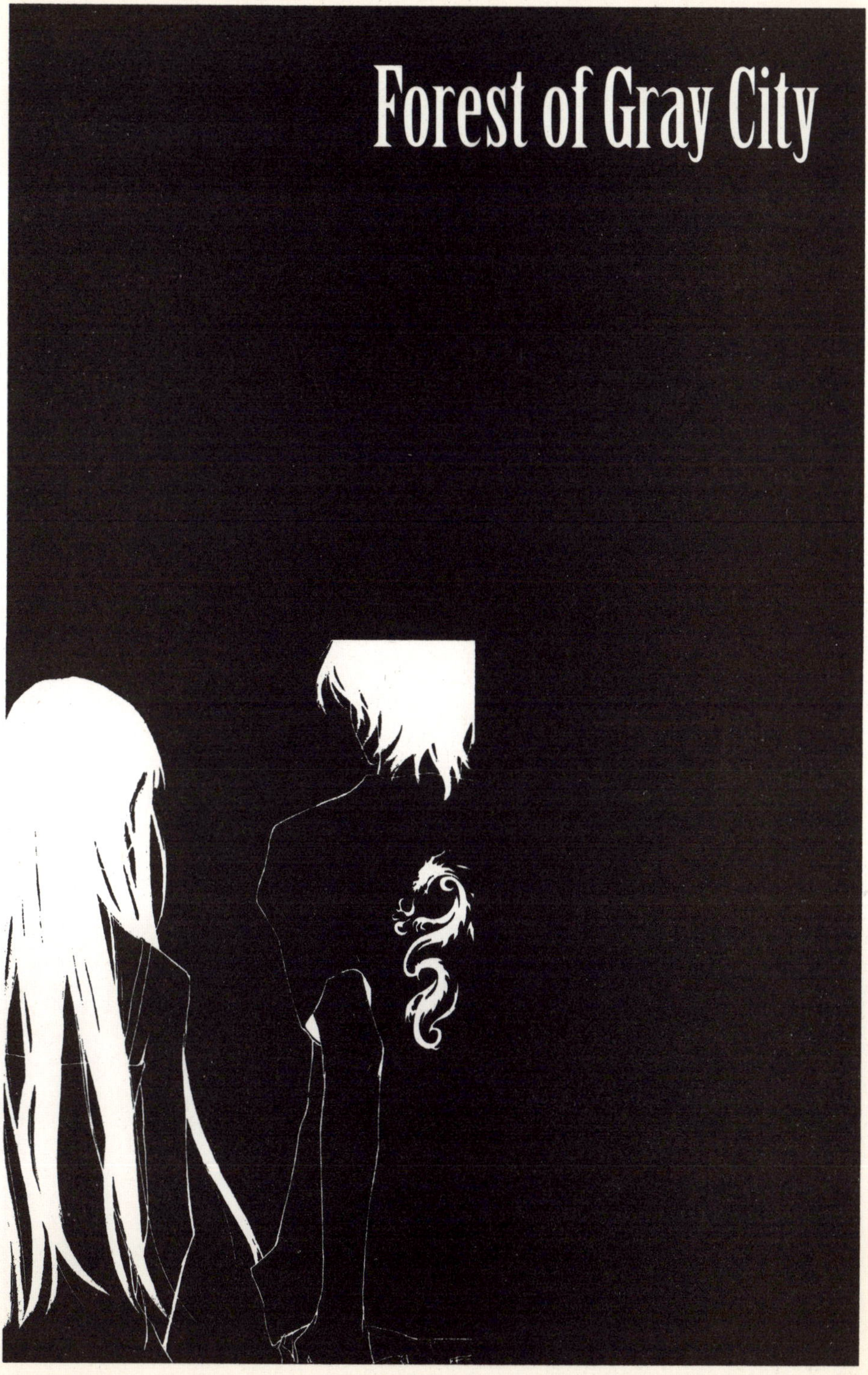
Forest of Gray City

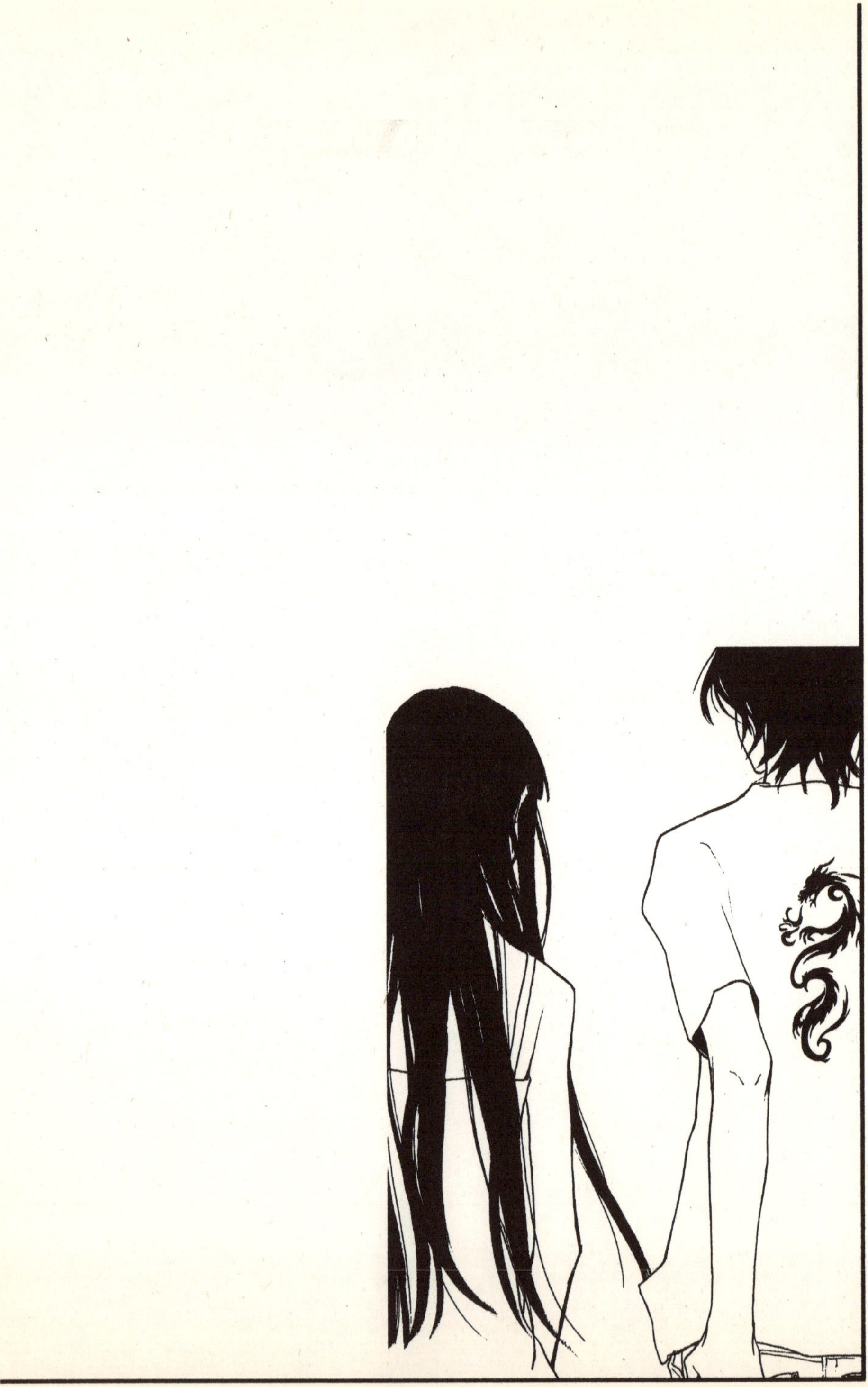

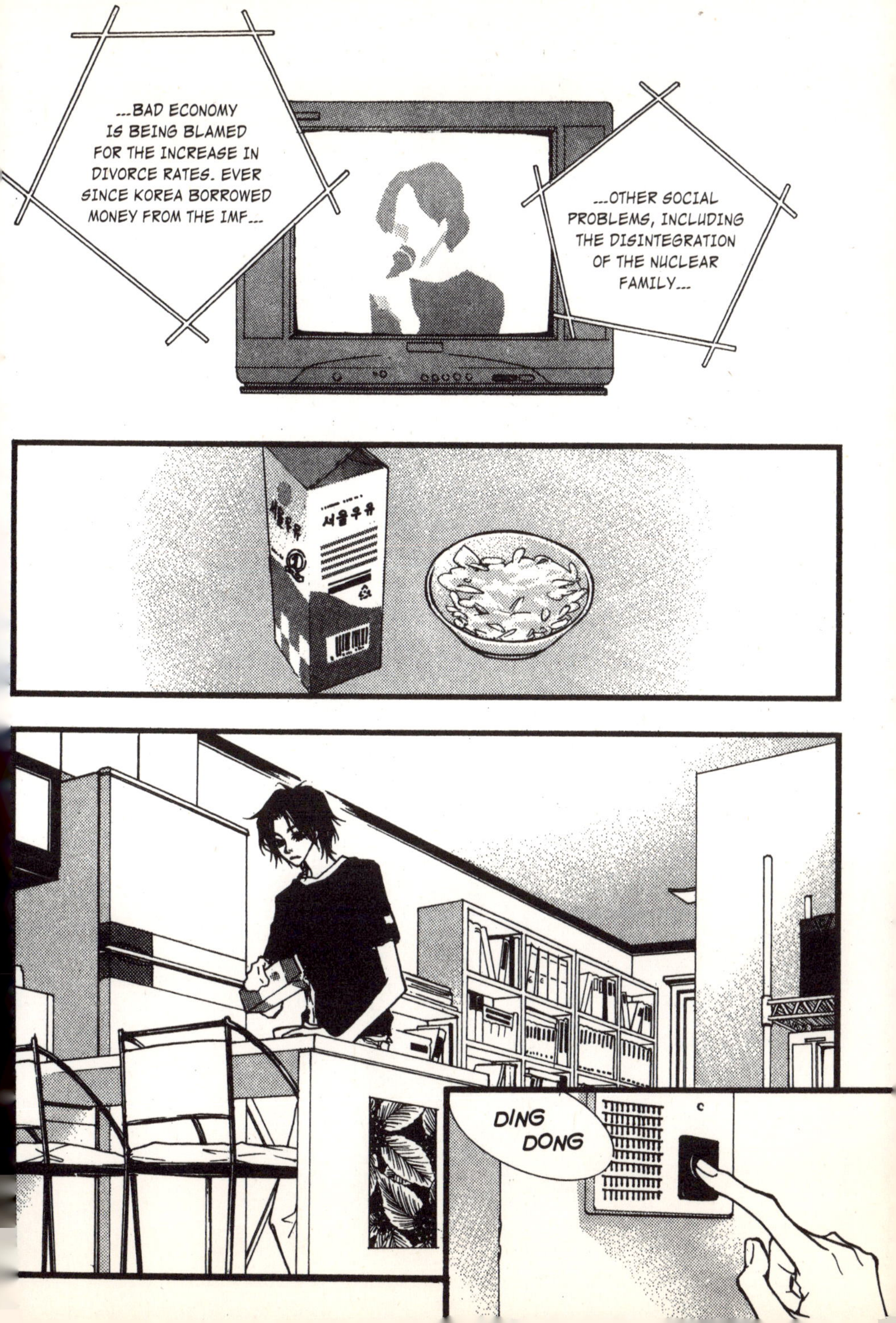
...BAD ECONOMY IS BEING BLAMED FOR THE INCREASE IN DIVORCE RATES. EVER SINCE KOREA BORROWED MONEY FROM THE IMF...
...OTHER SOCIAL PROBLEMS, INCLUDING THE DISINTEGRATION OF THE NUCLEAR FAMILY...
서울우유
DING DONG

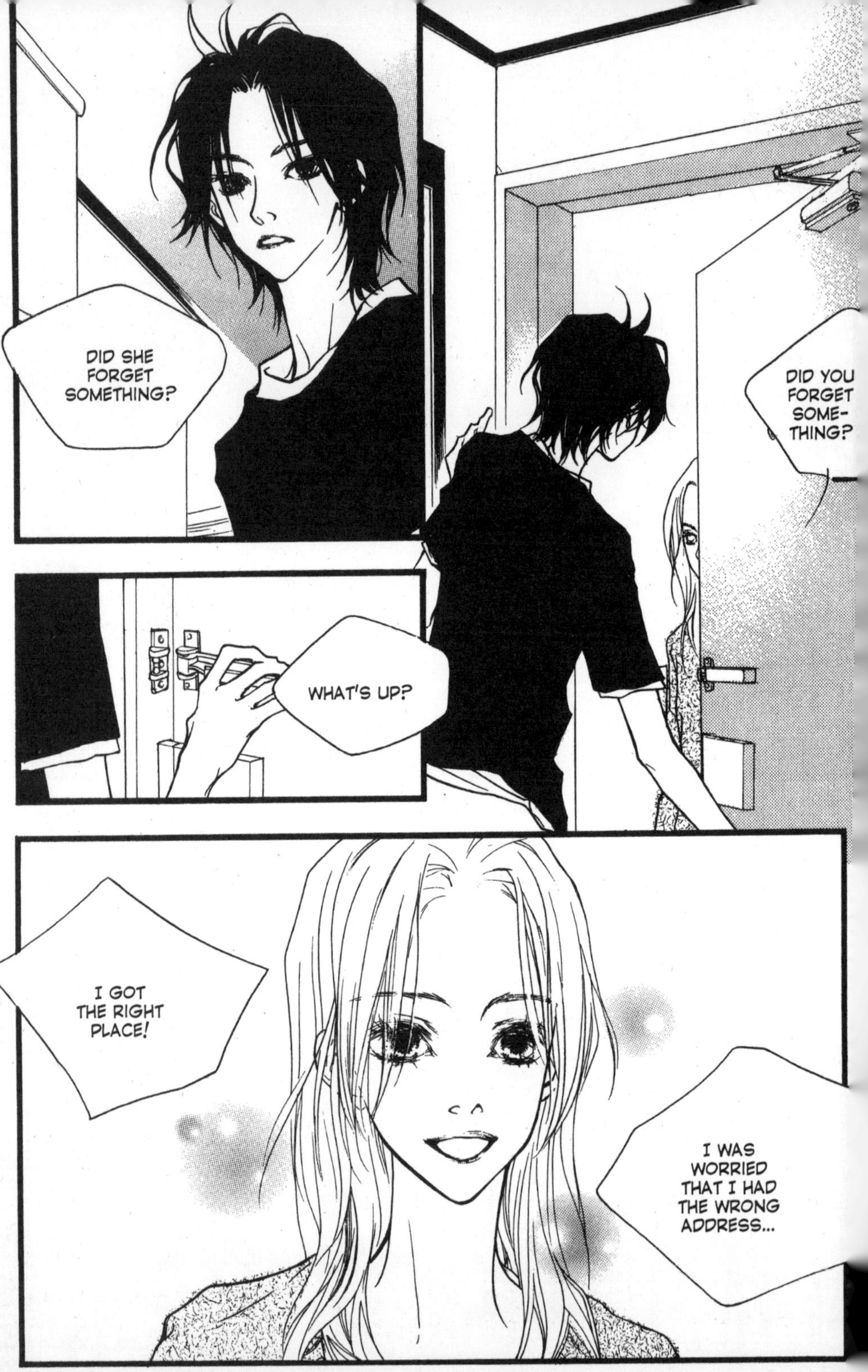
DID YOU FORGET SOME- THING?
DID SHE FORGET SOMETHING?
WHAT'S UP?
I WAS WORRIED THAT I HAD THE WRONG ADDRESS...
I GOT THE RIGHT PLACE!

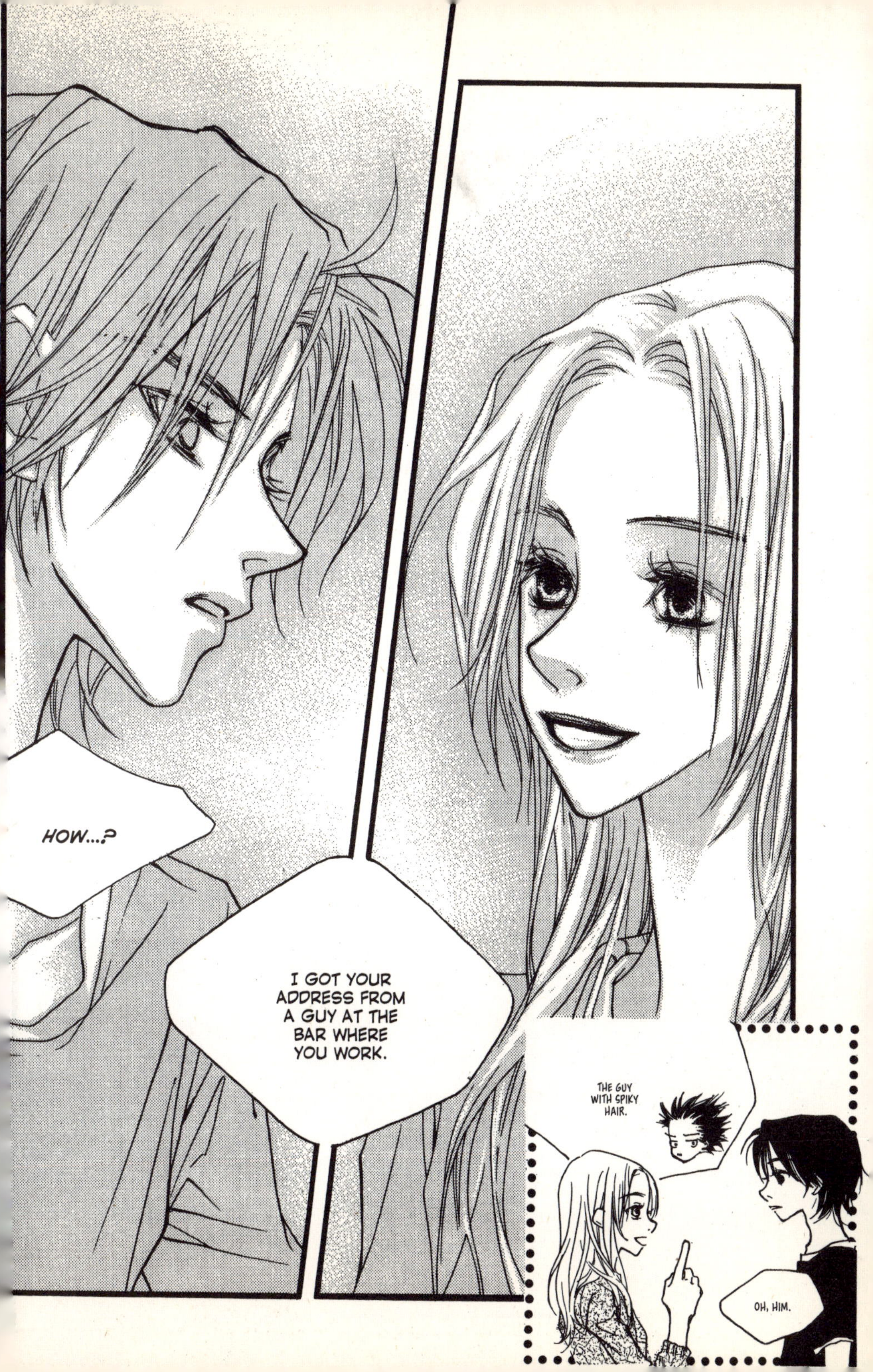
HOW...?
I GOT YOUR ADDRESS FROM A GUY AT THE BAR WHERE YOU WORK.
THE GUY WITH SPIKY HAIR.
OH, HIM.

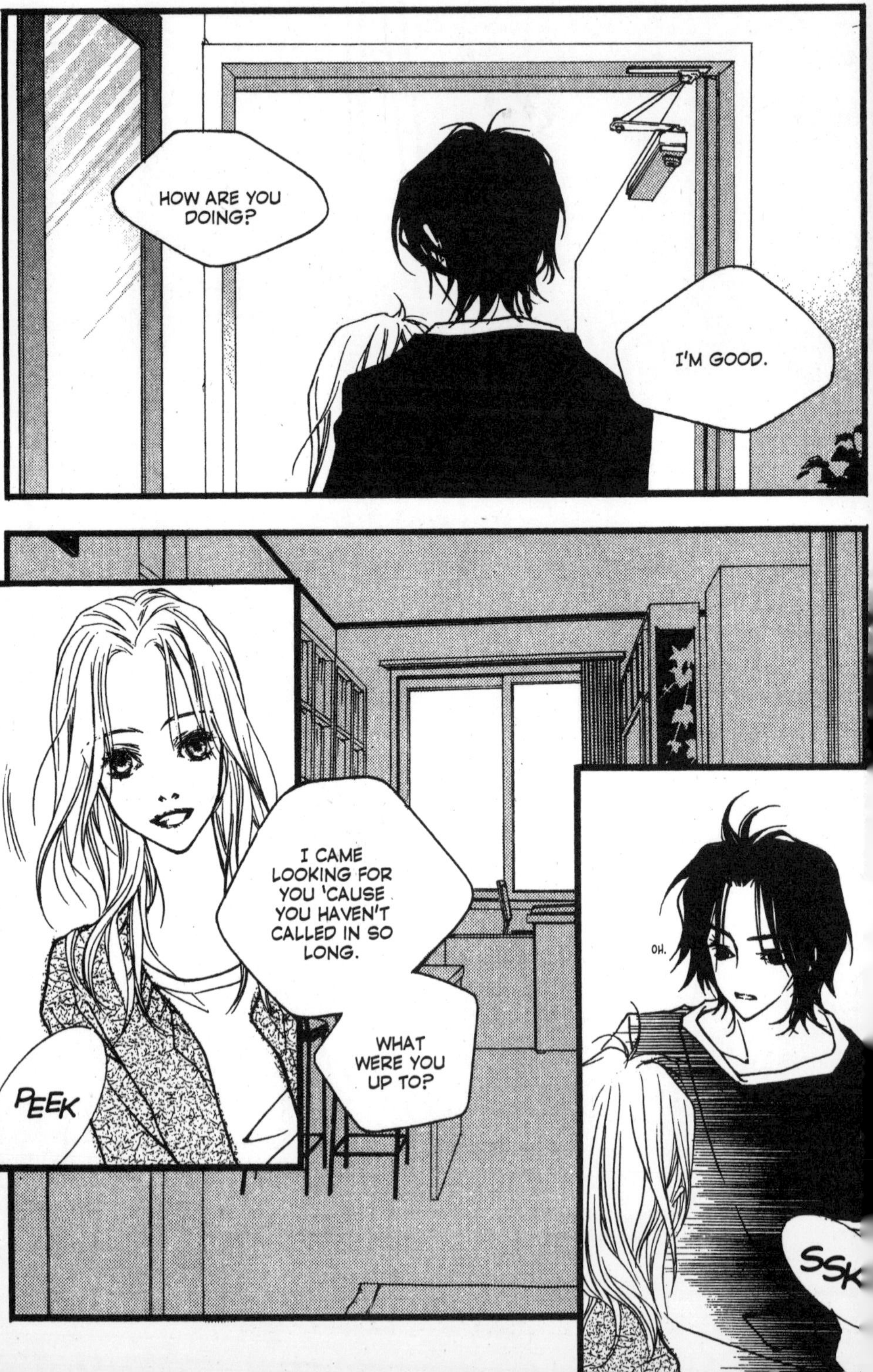
HOW ARE YOU DOING?
I'M GOOD.
I CAME LOOKING FOR YOU 'CAUSE YOU HAVEN'T CALLED IN SO LONG.
WHAT WERE YOU UP TO?
PEEK
OH.
SSK

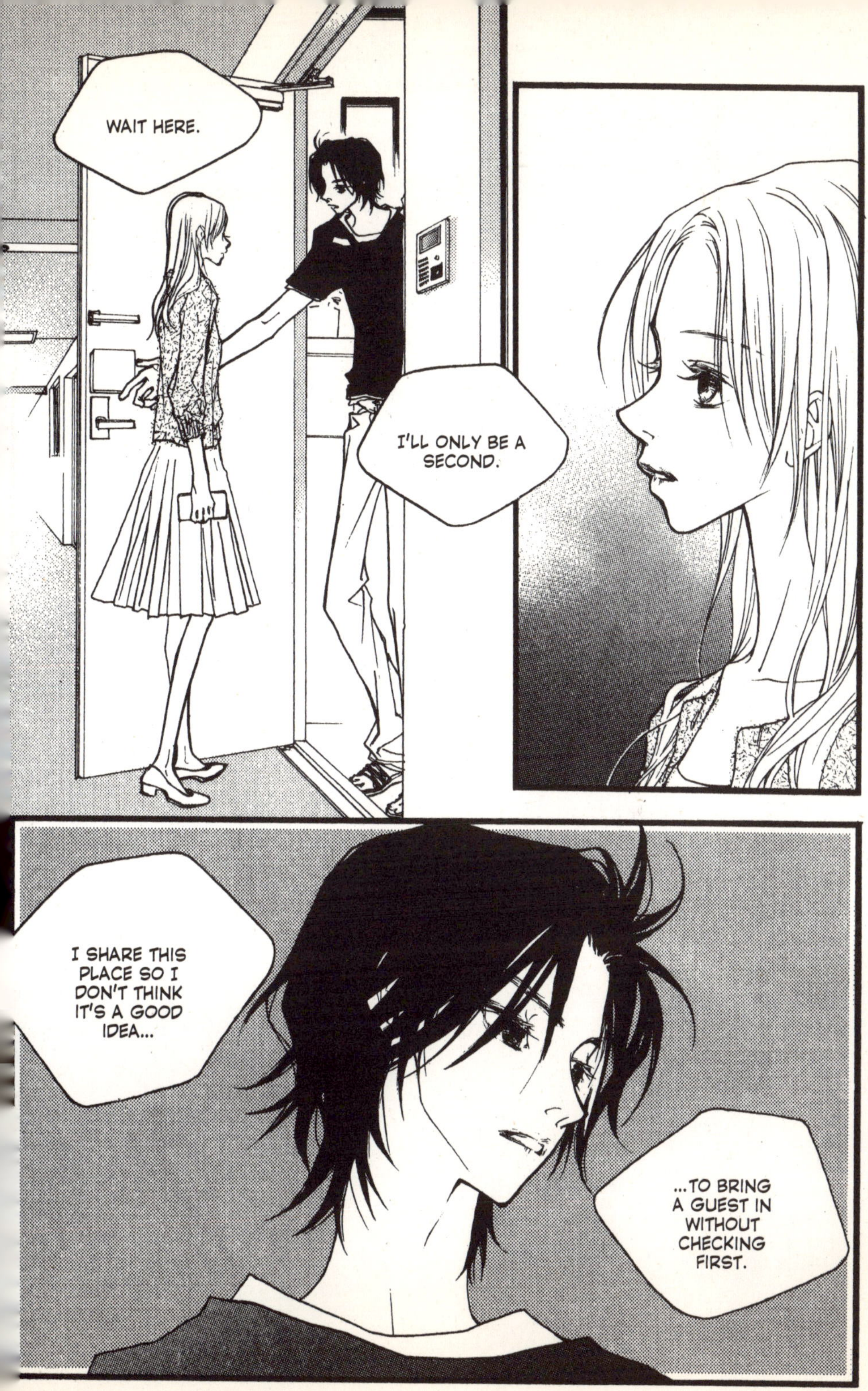
WAIT HERE.
I'LL ONLY BE A SECOND.
I SHARE THIS PLACE SO I DON'T THINK IT'S A GOOD IDEA...
...TO BRING A GUEST IN WITHOUT CHECKING FIRST.

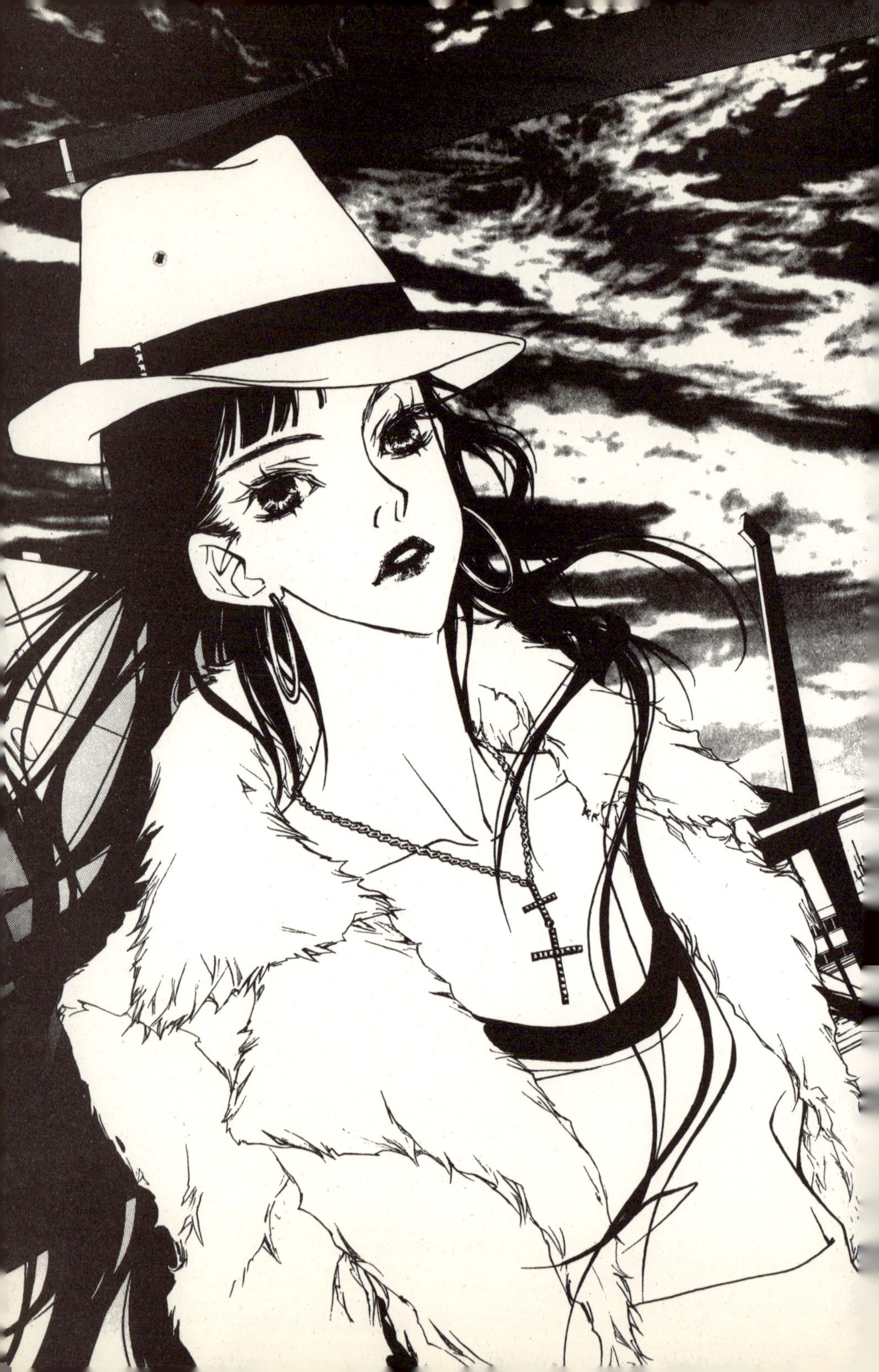

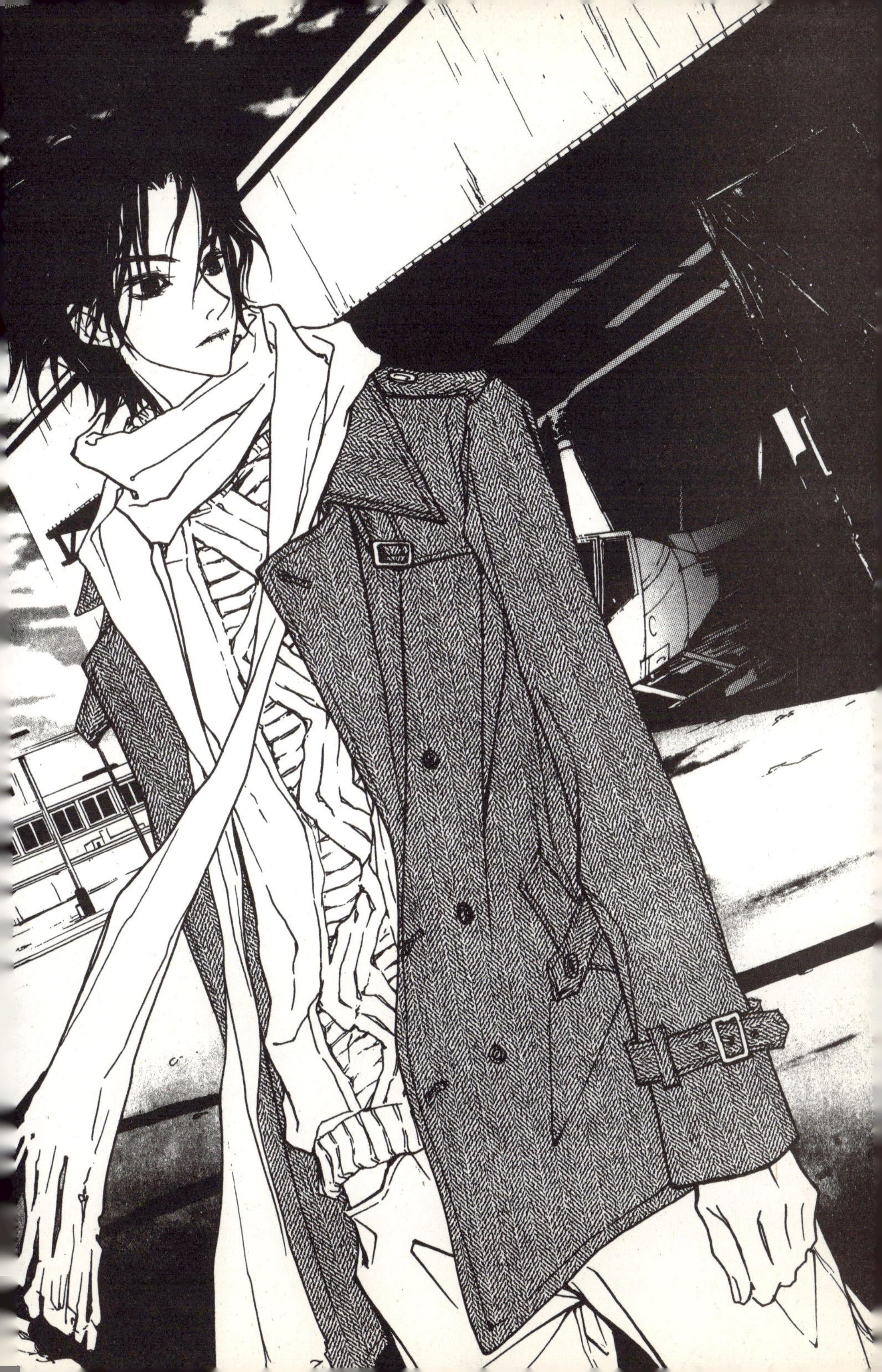

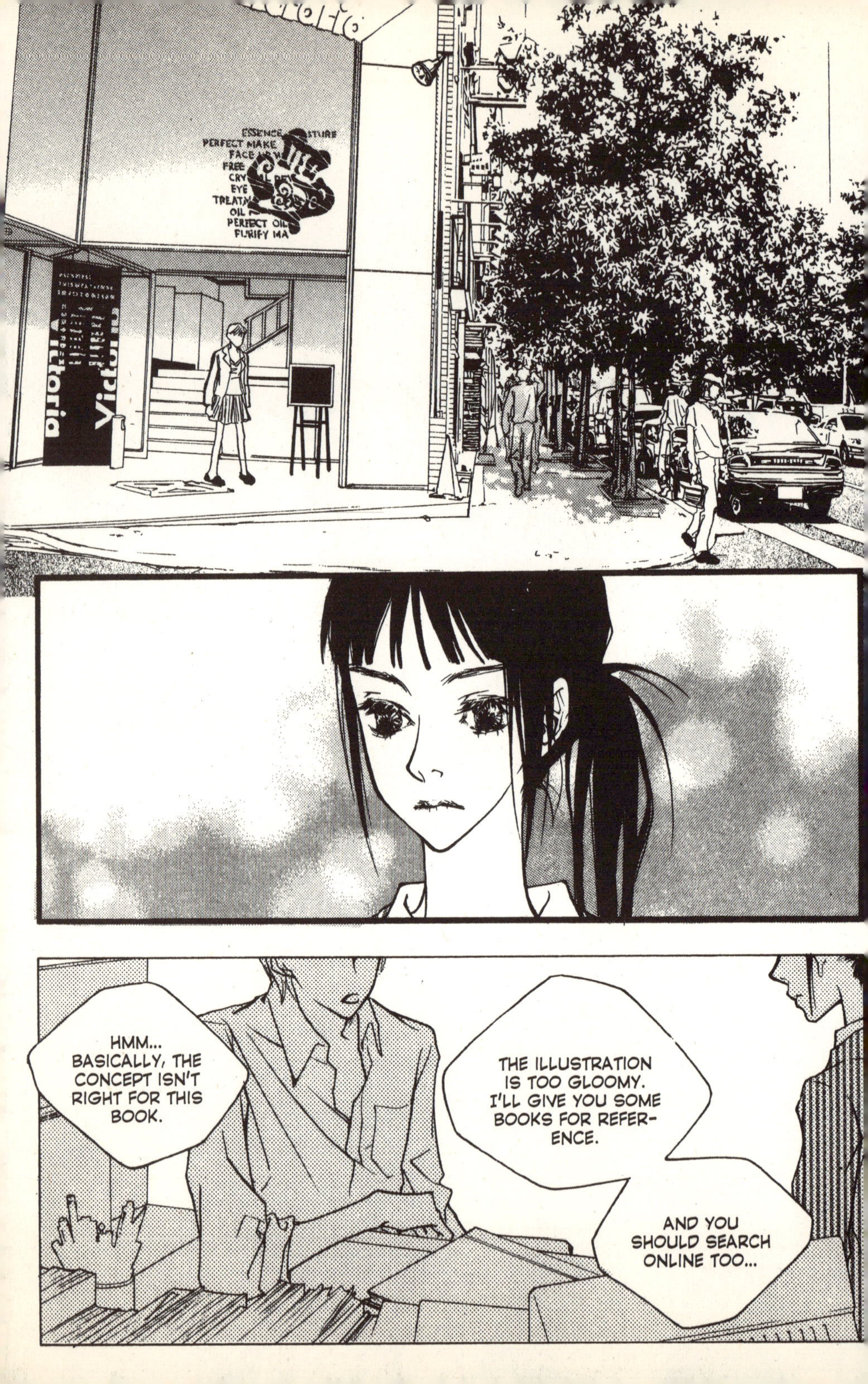
Victoria
HMM... BASICALLY, THE CONCEPT ISN'T RIGHT FOR THIS BOOK.
THE ILLUSTRATION IS TOO GLOOMY. I'LL GIVE YOU SOME BOOKS FOR REFER-ENCE.
AND YOU SHOULD SEARCH ONLINE TOO...

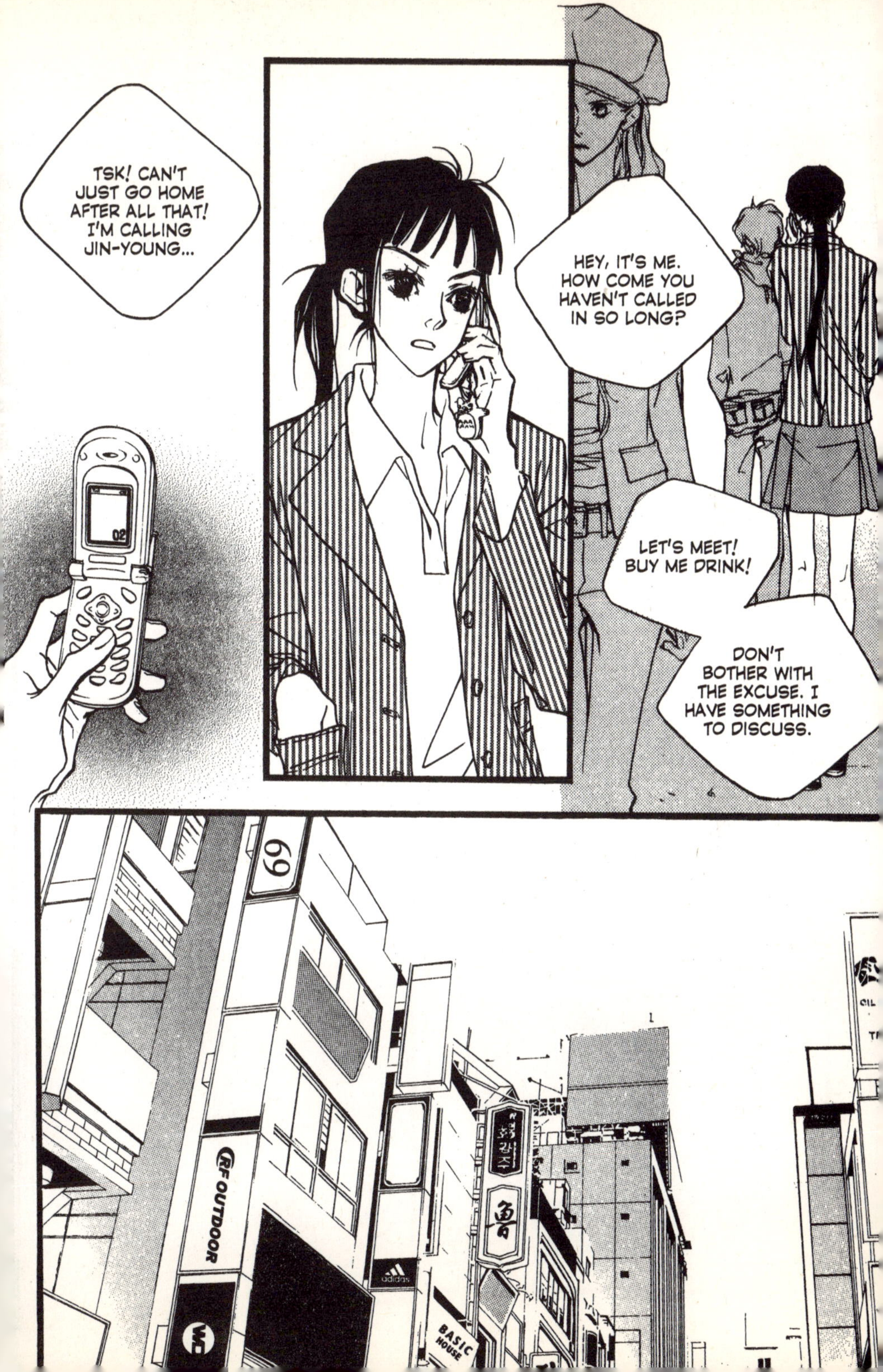
TSK! CAN'T JUST GO HOME AFTER ALL THAT! I'M CALLING JIN-YOUNG...
HEY, IT'S ME. HOW COME YOU HAVEN'T CALLED IN SO LONG?
LET'S MEET! BUY ME DRINK!
DON'T BOTHER WITH THE EXCUSE. I HAVE SOMETHING TO DISCUSS.
69
RF OUTDOOR
adidas
BASIC HOUSE

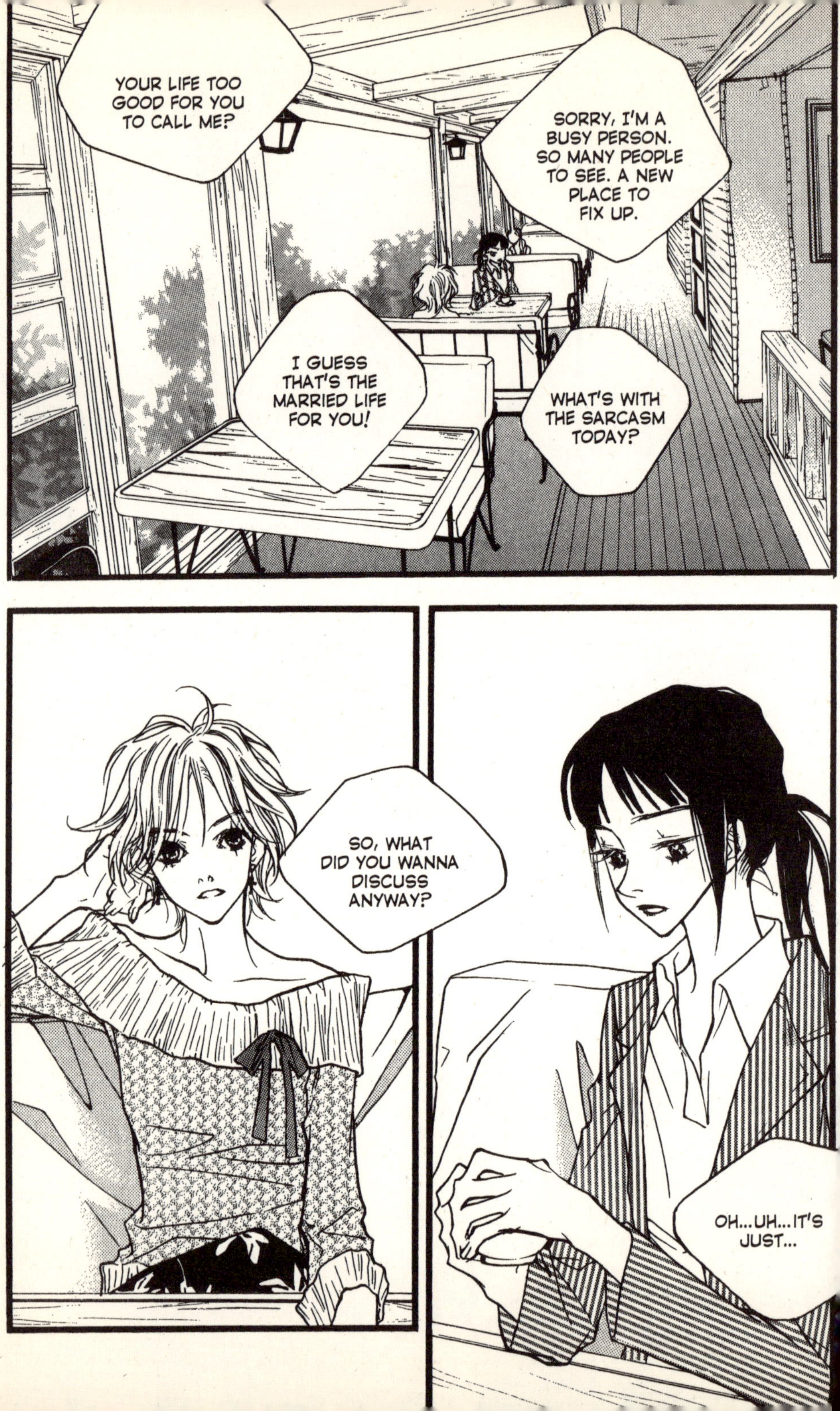
YOUR LIFE TOO GOOD FOR YOU TO CALL ME?
SORRY, I'M A BUSY PERSON. SO MANY PEOPLE TO SEE. A NEW PLACE TO FIX UP.
I GUESS THAT'S THE MARRIED LIFE FOR YOU!
WHAT'S WITH THE SARCASM TODAY?
SO, WHAT DID YOU WANNA DISCUSS ANYWAY?
OH...UH...IT'S JUST...

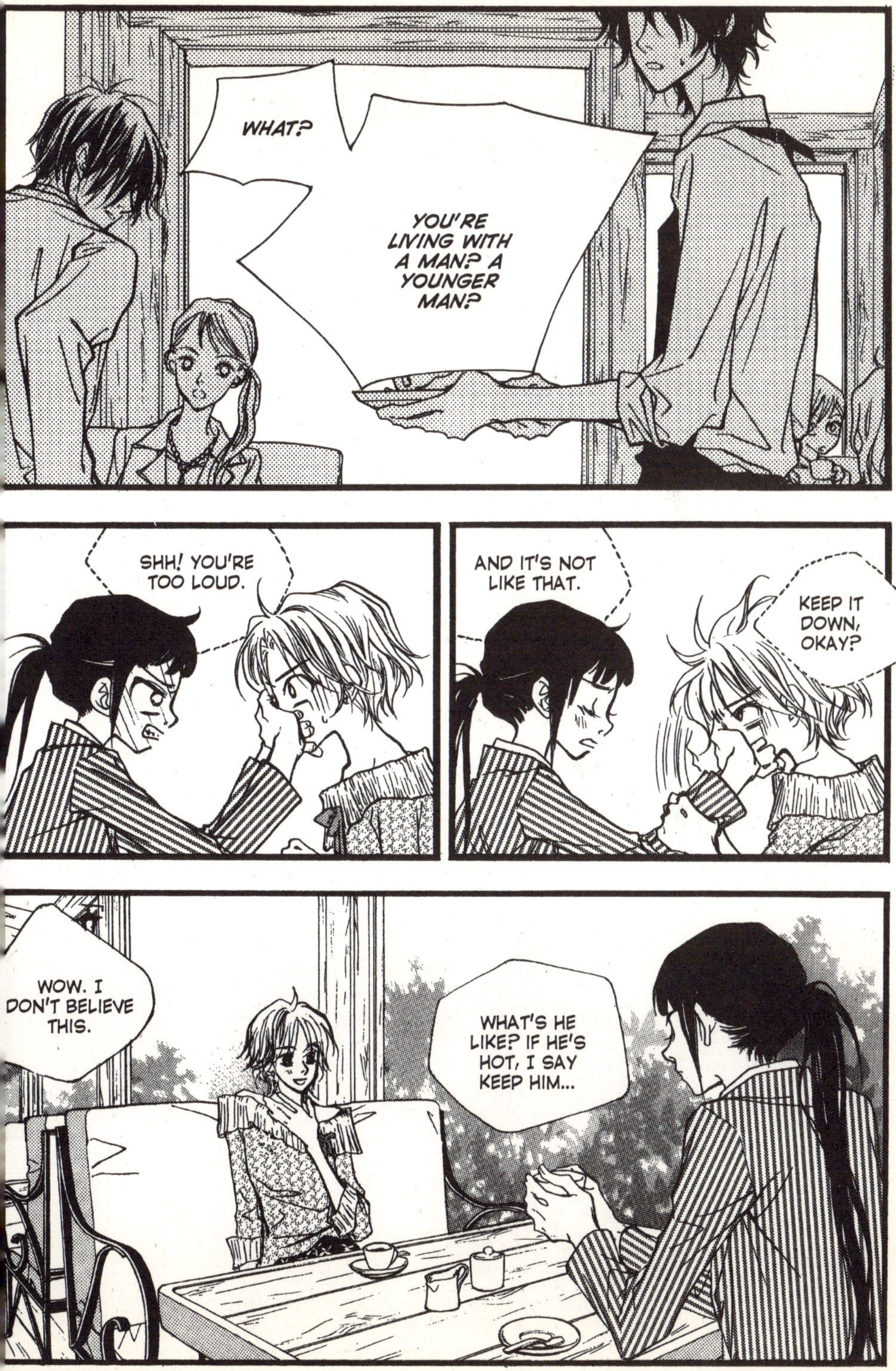
WHAT?
YOU'RE LIVING WITH A MAN? A YOUNGER MAN?
SHH! YOU'RE TOO LOUD.
AND IT'S NOT LIKE THAT.
KEEP IT DOWN, OKAY?
WOW. I DON'T BELIEVE THIS.
WHAT'S HE LIKE? IF HE'S HOT, I SAY KEEP HIM...

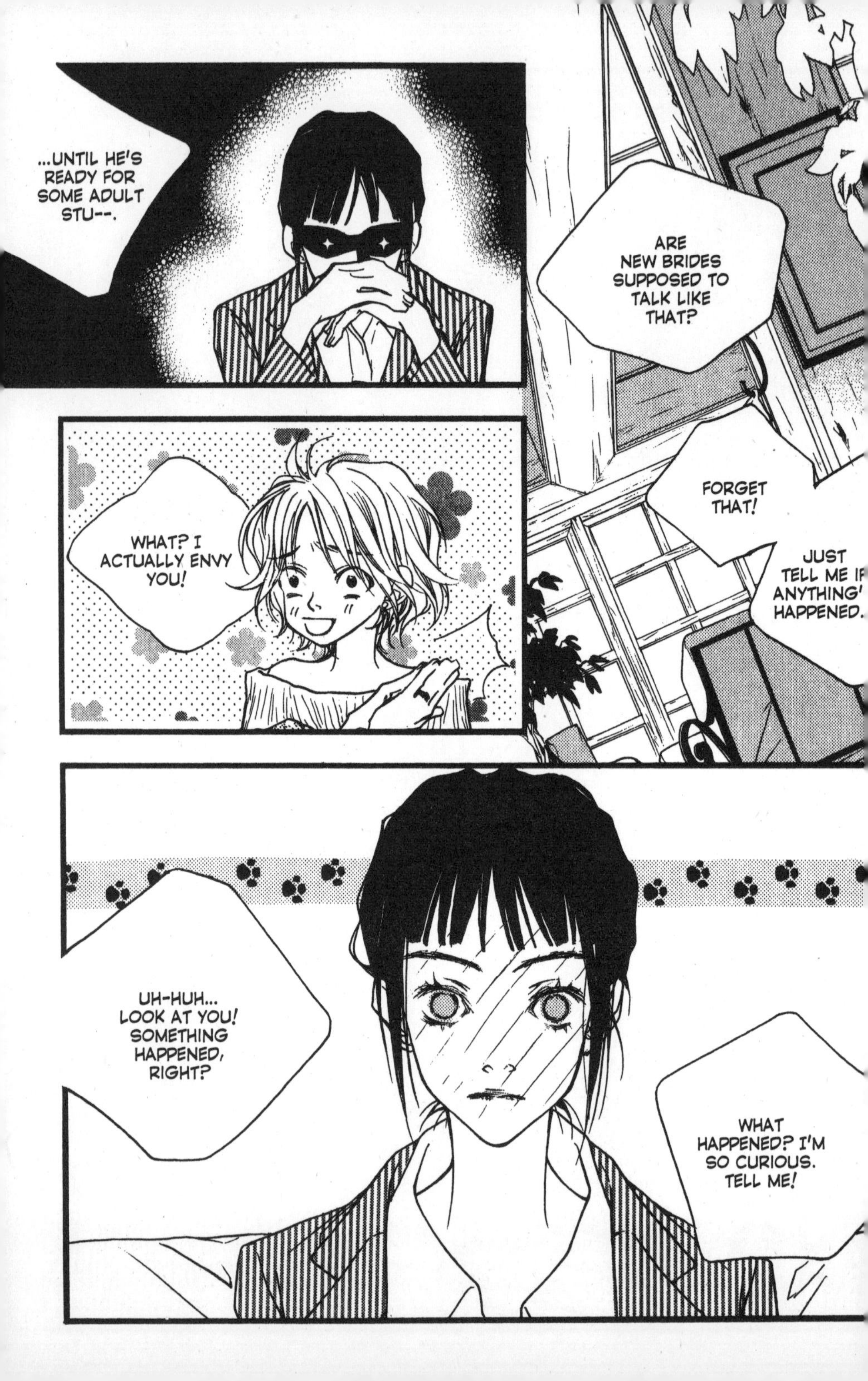
ARE NEW BRIDES SUPPOSED TO TALK LIKE THAT?
...UNTIL HE'S READY FOR SOME ADULT STU--.
FORGET THAT!
JUST TELL ME IF ANYTHING HAPPENED.
WHAT? I ACTUALLY ENVY YOU!
WHAT HAPPENED? I'M SO CURIOUS. TELL ME!
UH-HUH... LOOK AT YOU! SOMETHING HAPPENED, RIGHT?

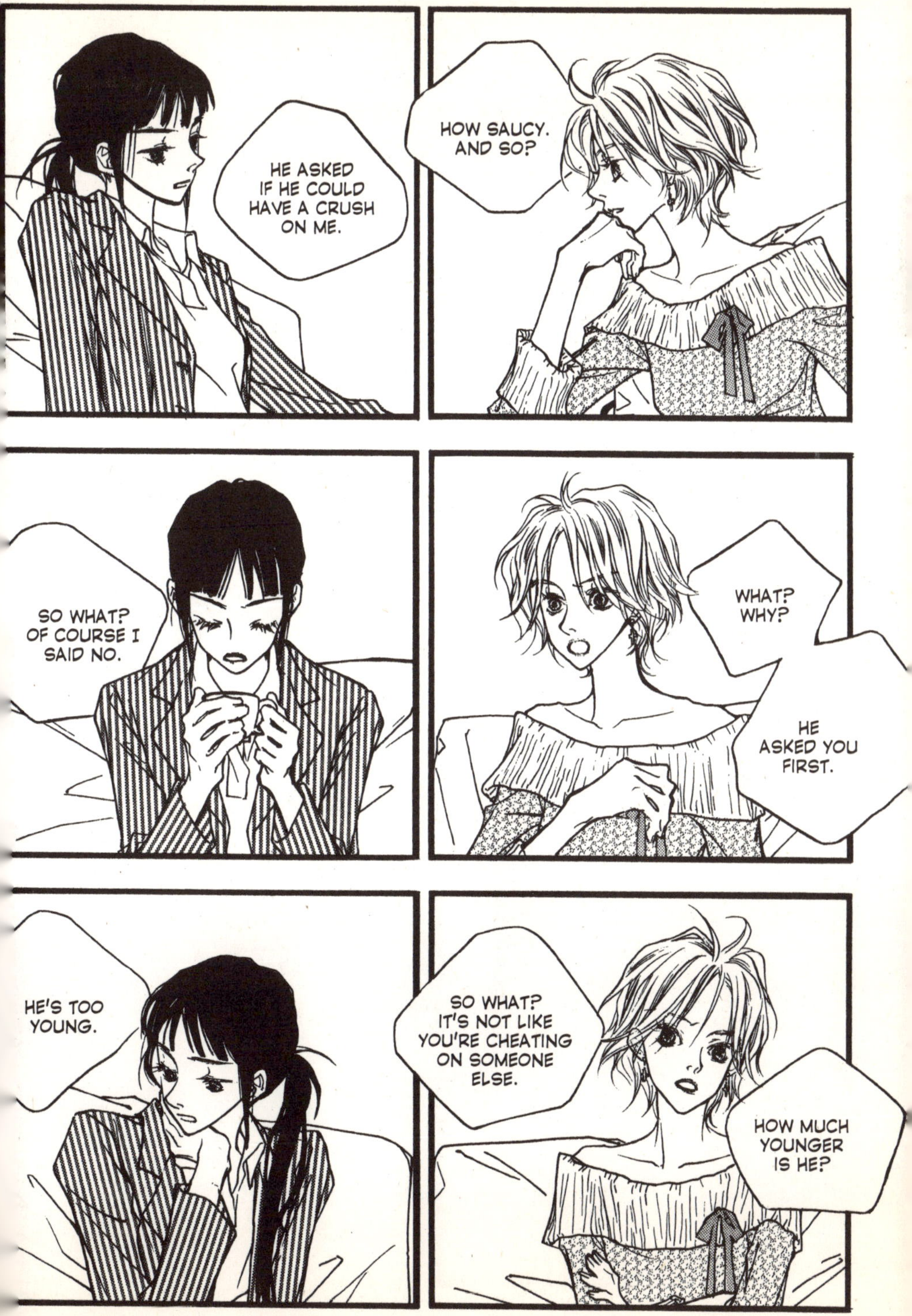
HE ASKED IF HE COULD HAVE A CRUSH ON ME.
HOW SAUCY. AND SO?
SO WHAT? OF COURSE I SAID NO.
WHAT? WHY?
HE ASKED YOU FIRST.
HE'S TOO YOUNG.
SO WHAT? IT'S NOT LIKE YOU'RE CHEATING ON SOMEONE ELSE.
HOW MUCH YOUNGER IS HE?

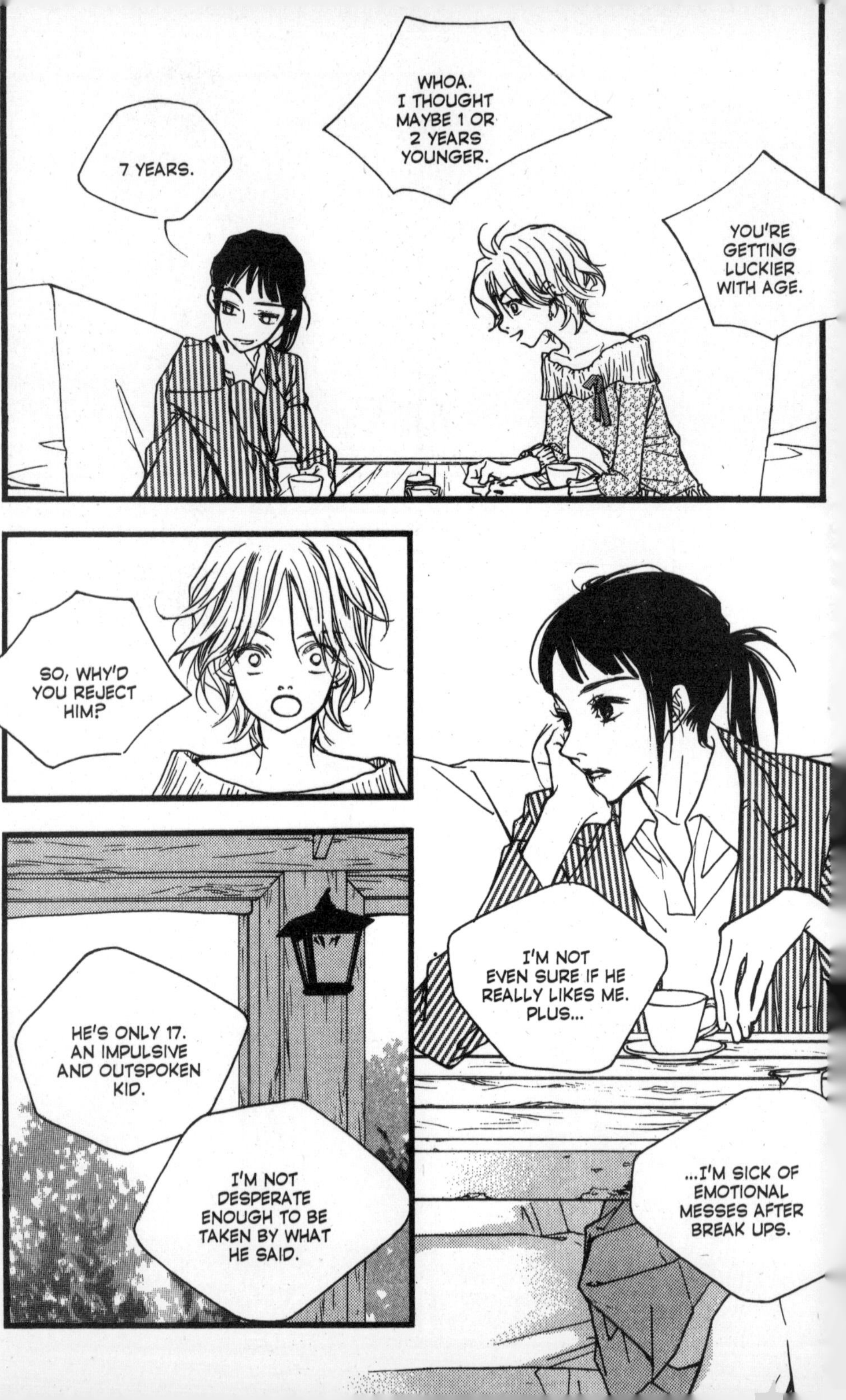
7 YEARS.
WHOA. I THOUGHT MAYBE 1 OR 2 YEARS YOUNGER.
YOU'RE GETTING LUCKIER WITH AGE.
SO, WHY'D YOU REJECT HIM?
I'M NOT EVEN SURE IF HE REALLY LIKES ME. PLUS...
HE'S ONLY 17. AN IMPULSIVE AND OUTSPOKEN KID.
I'M NOT DESPERATE ENOUGH TO BE TAKEN BY WHAT HE SAID.
...I'M SICK OF EMOTIONAL MESSES AFTER BREAK UPS.

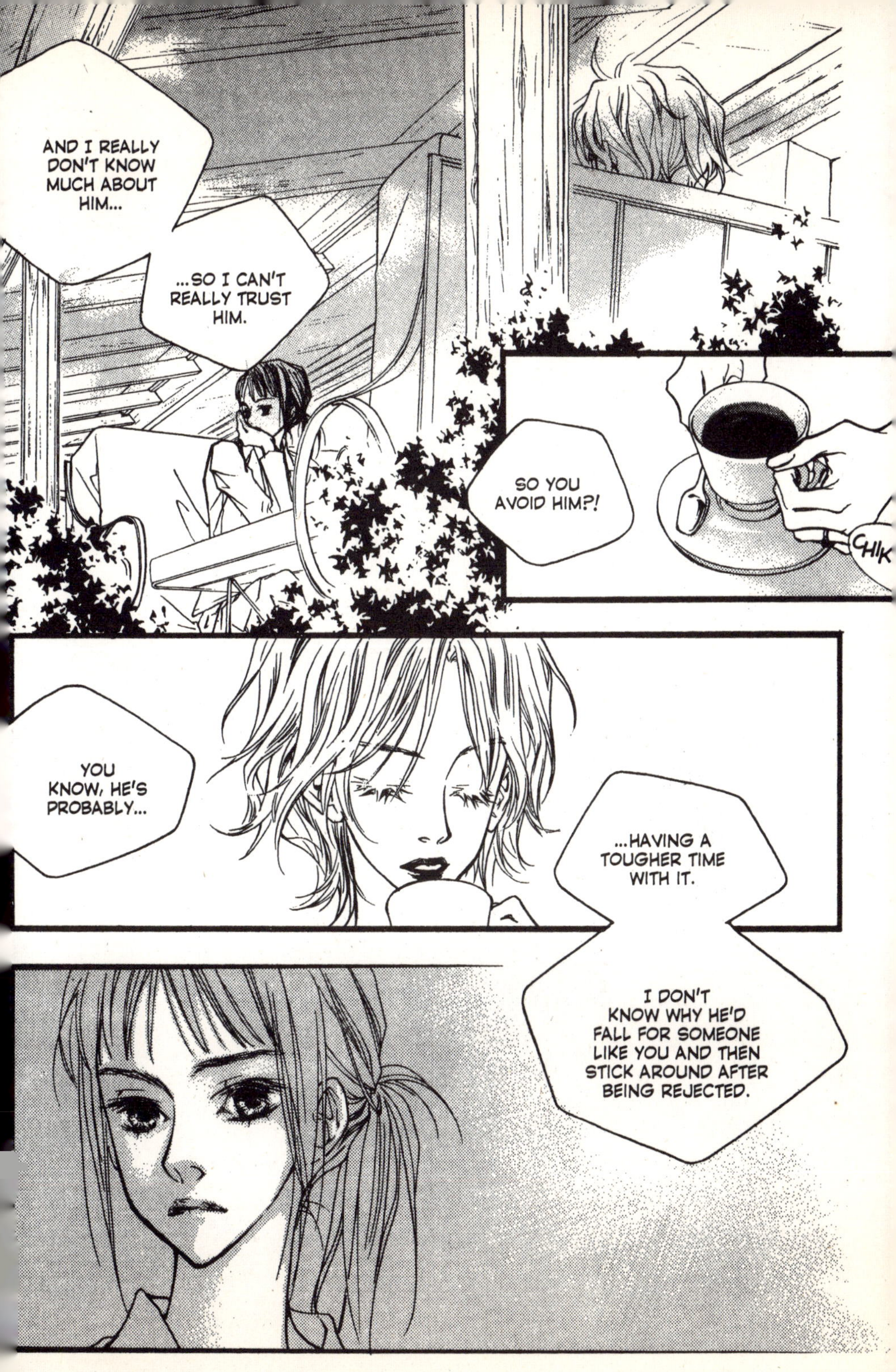
AND I REALLY DON'T KNOW MUCH ABOUT HIM...
...SO I CAN'T REALLY TRUST HIM.
SO YOU AVOID HIM?!
CHIK
YOU KNOW, HE'S PROBABLY...
...HAVING A TOUGHER TIME WITH IT.
I DON'T KNOW WHY HE'D FALL FOR SOMEONE LIKE YOU AND THEN STICK AROUND AFTER BEING REJECTED.

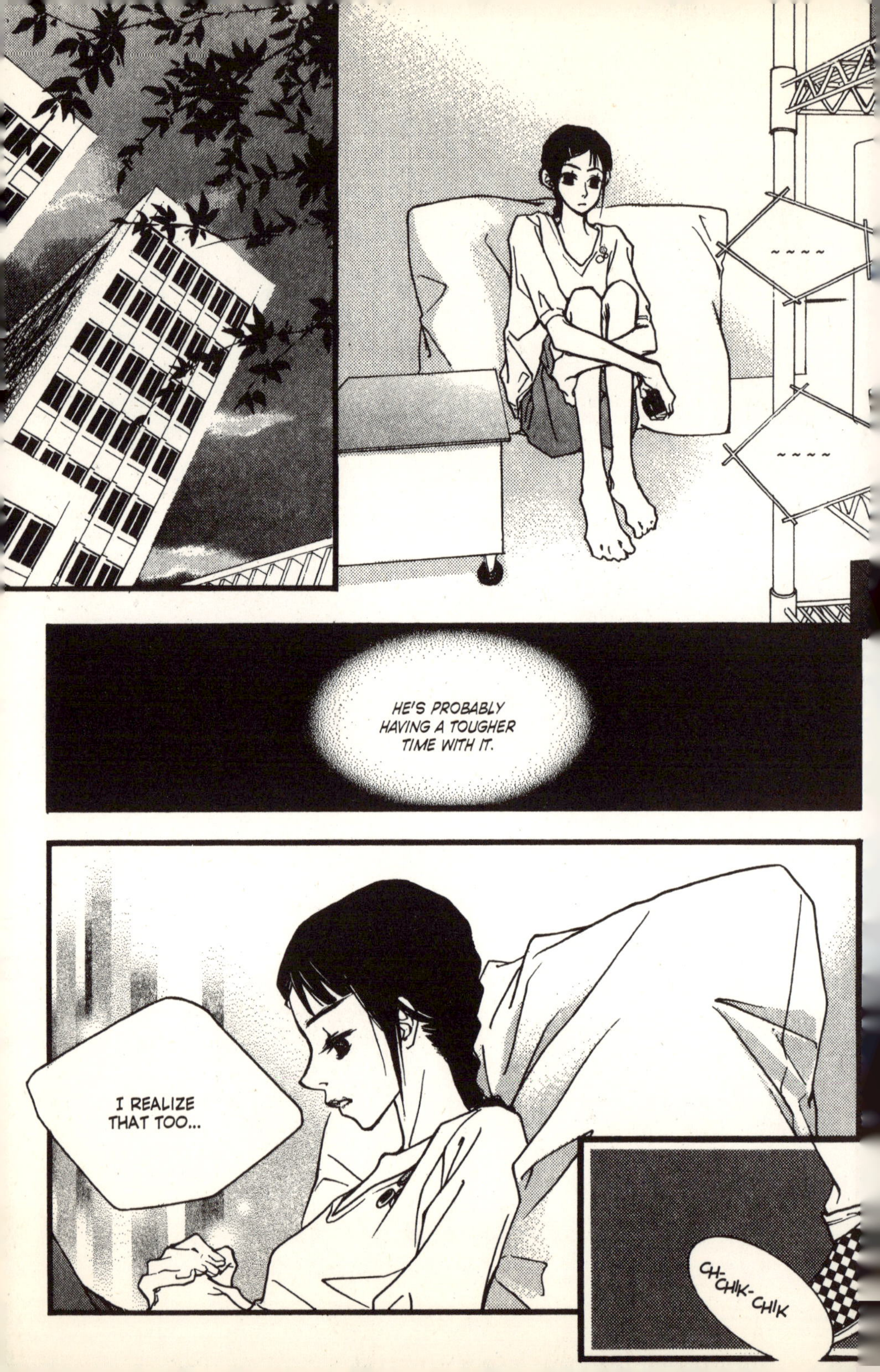
~ ~ ~ ~
~ ~ ~ ~
HE'S PROBABLY HAVING A TOUGHER TIME WITH IT.
I REALIZE THAT TOO...
CH-CHIK-CHIK

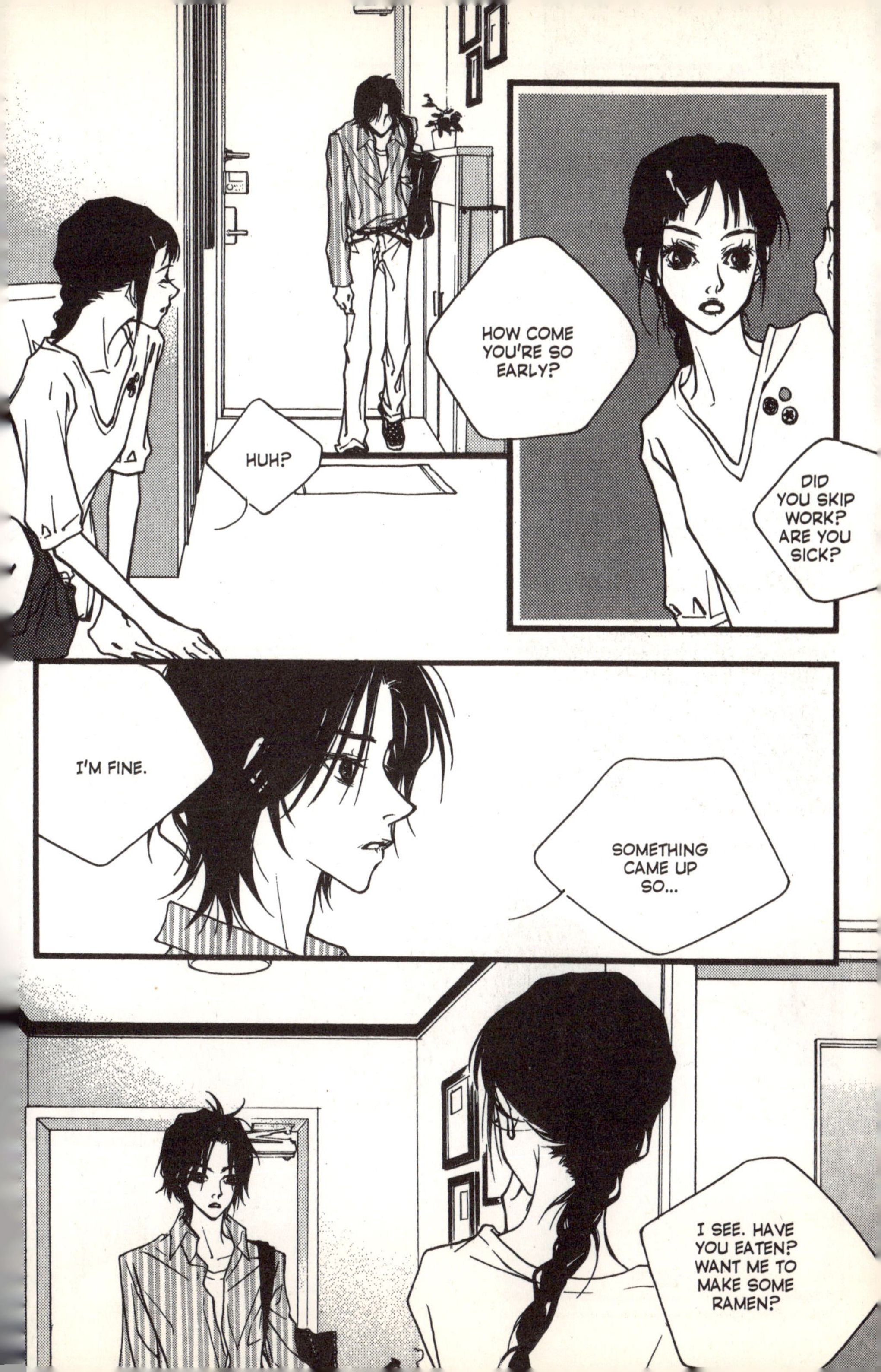
HOW COME YOU'RE SO EARLY?
HUH?
DID YOU SKIP WORK? ARE YOU SICK?
I'M FINE.
SOMETHING CAME UP SO...
I SEE. HAVE YOU EATEN? WANT ME TO MAKE SOME RAMEN?

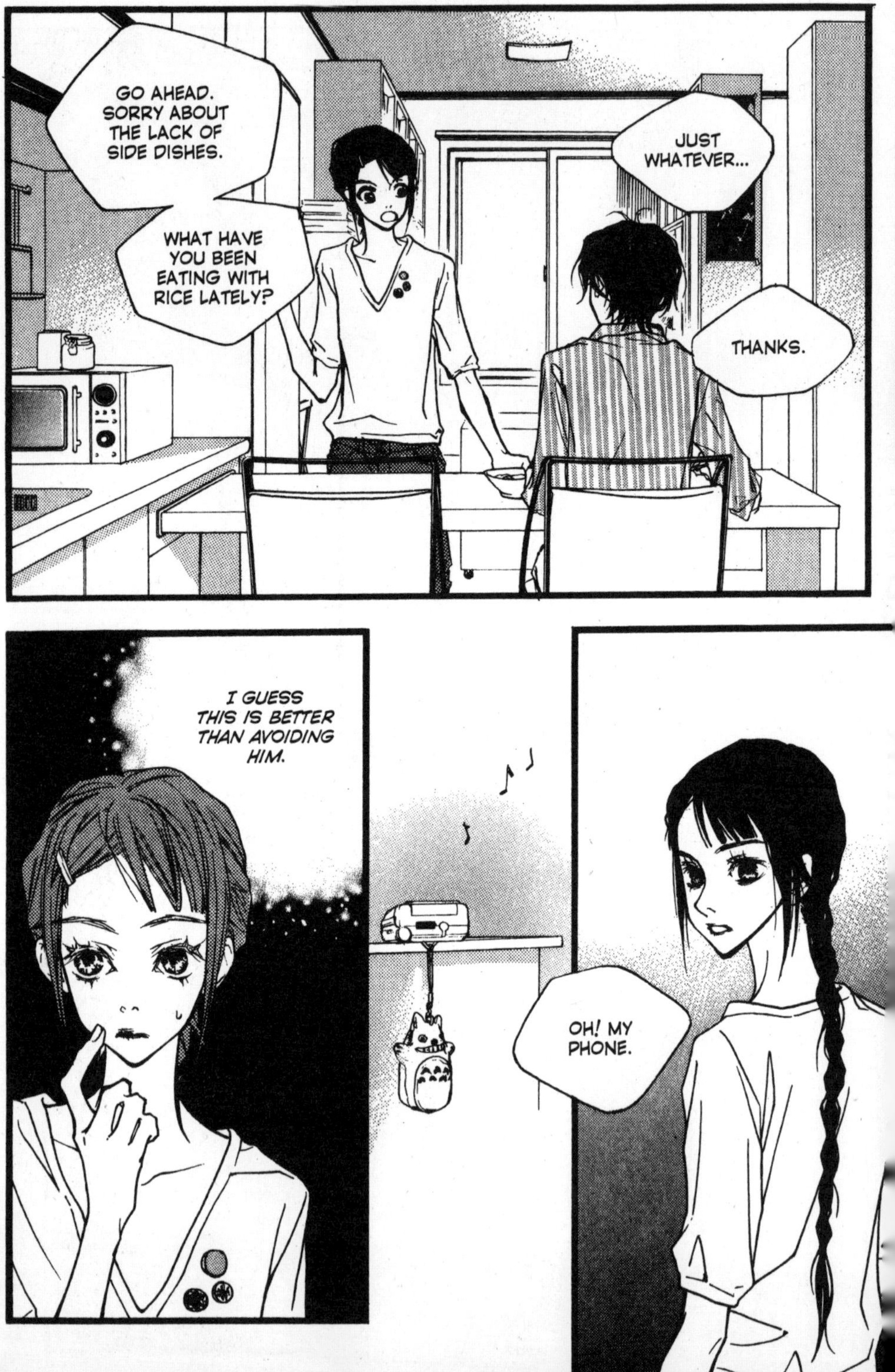
GO AHEAD. SORRY ABOUT THE LACK OF SIDE DISHES.
JUST WHATEVER...
WHAT HAVE YOU BEEN EATING WITH RICE LATELY?
THANKS.
I GUESS THIS IS BETTER THAN AVOIDING HIM.
OH! MY PHONE.

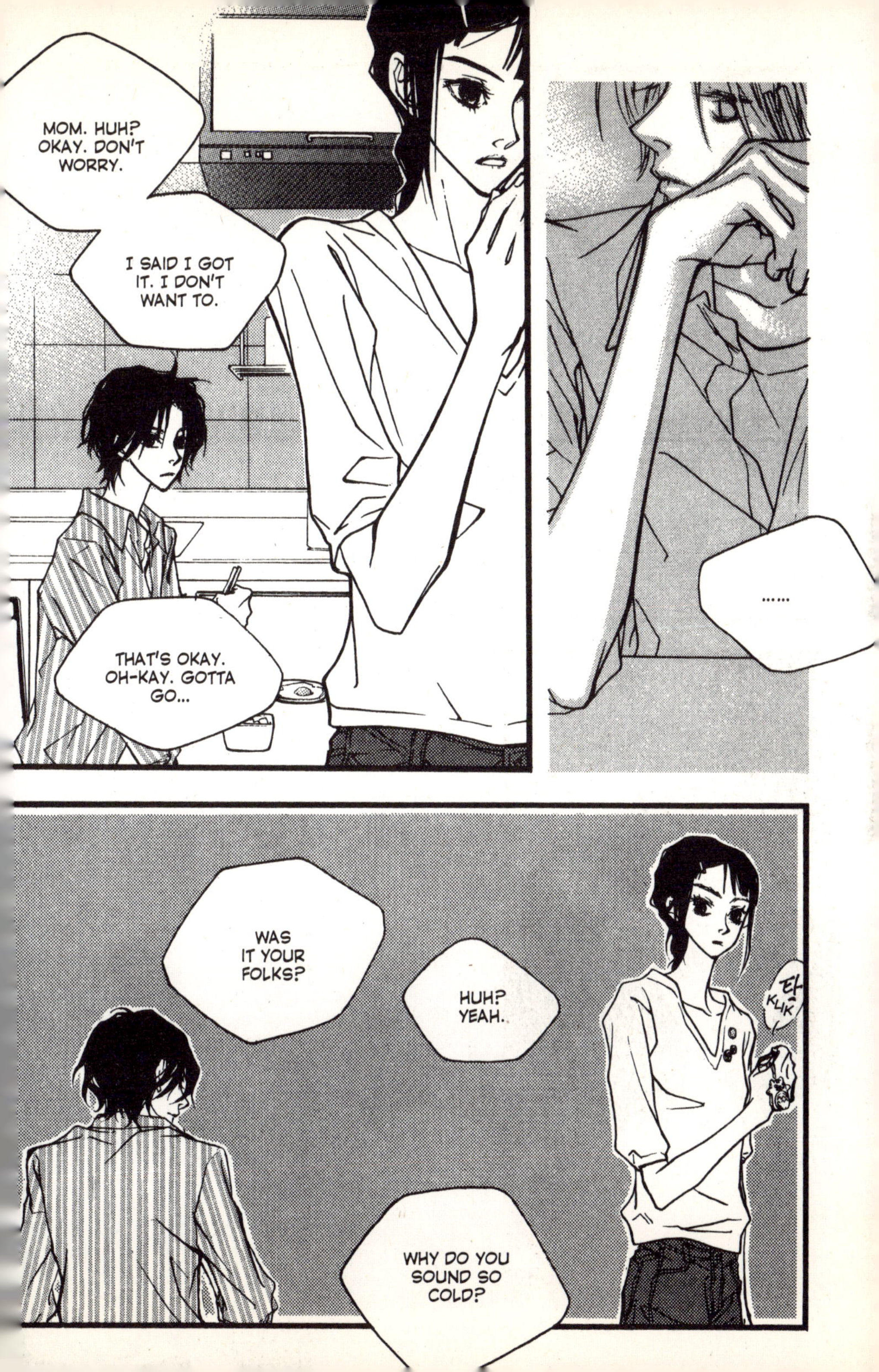
MOM. HUH? OKAY. DON'T WORRY.
I SAID I GOT IT. I DON'T WANT TO.
THAT'S OKAY. OH-KAY. GOTTA GO...
......
WAS IT YOUR FOLKS?
HUH? YEAH.
탁 KLIK
WHY DO YOU SOUND SO COLD?

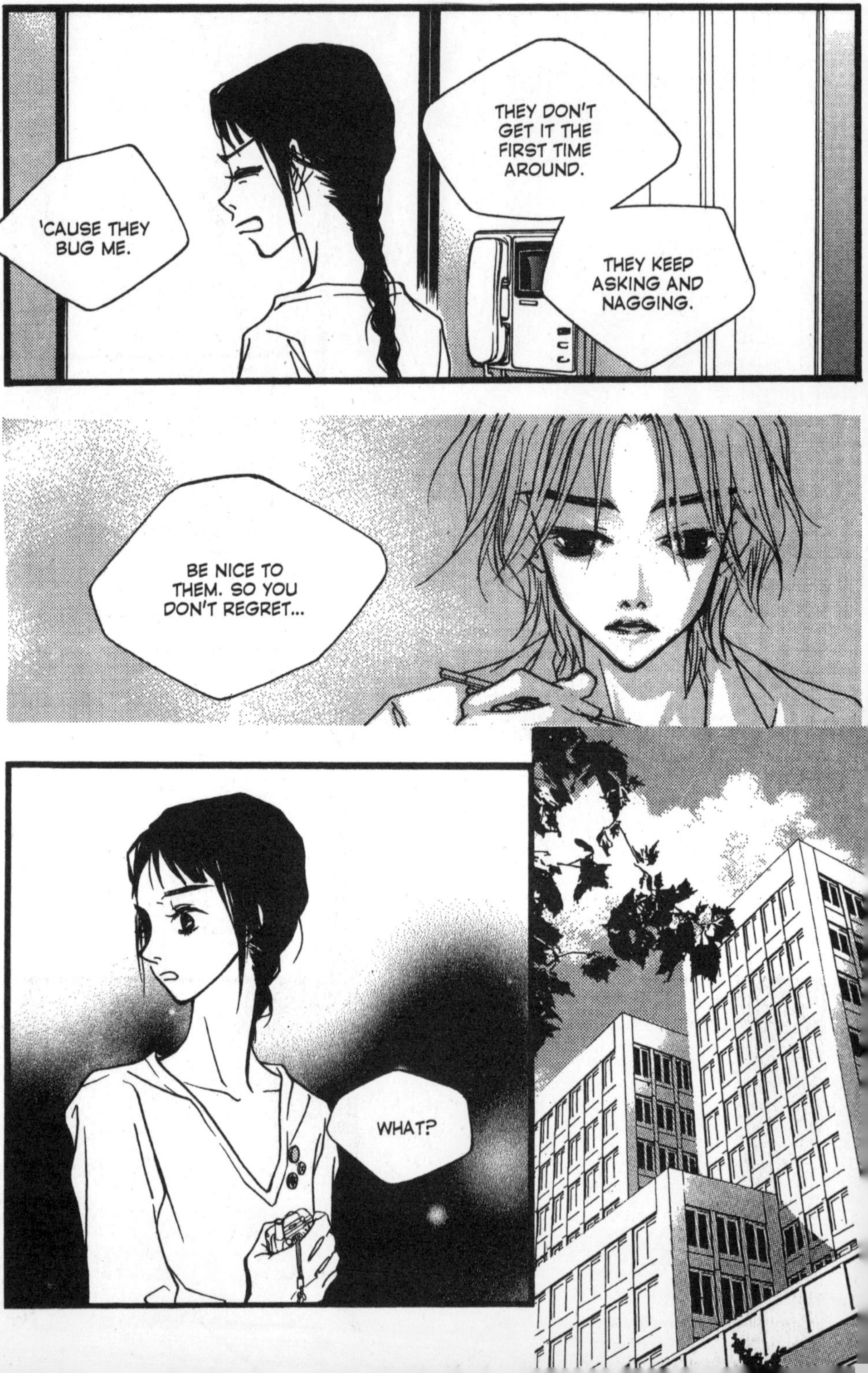
THEY DON'T GET IT THE FIRST TIME AROUND.
'CAUSE THEY BUG ME.
THEY KEEP ASKING AND NAGGING.
BE NICE TO THEM. SO YOU DON'T REGRET...
WHAT?

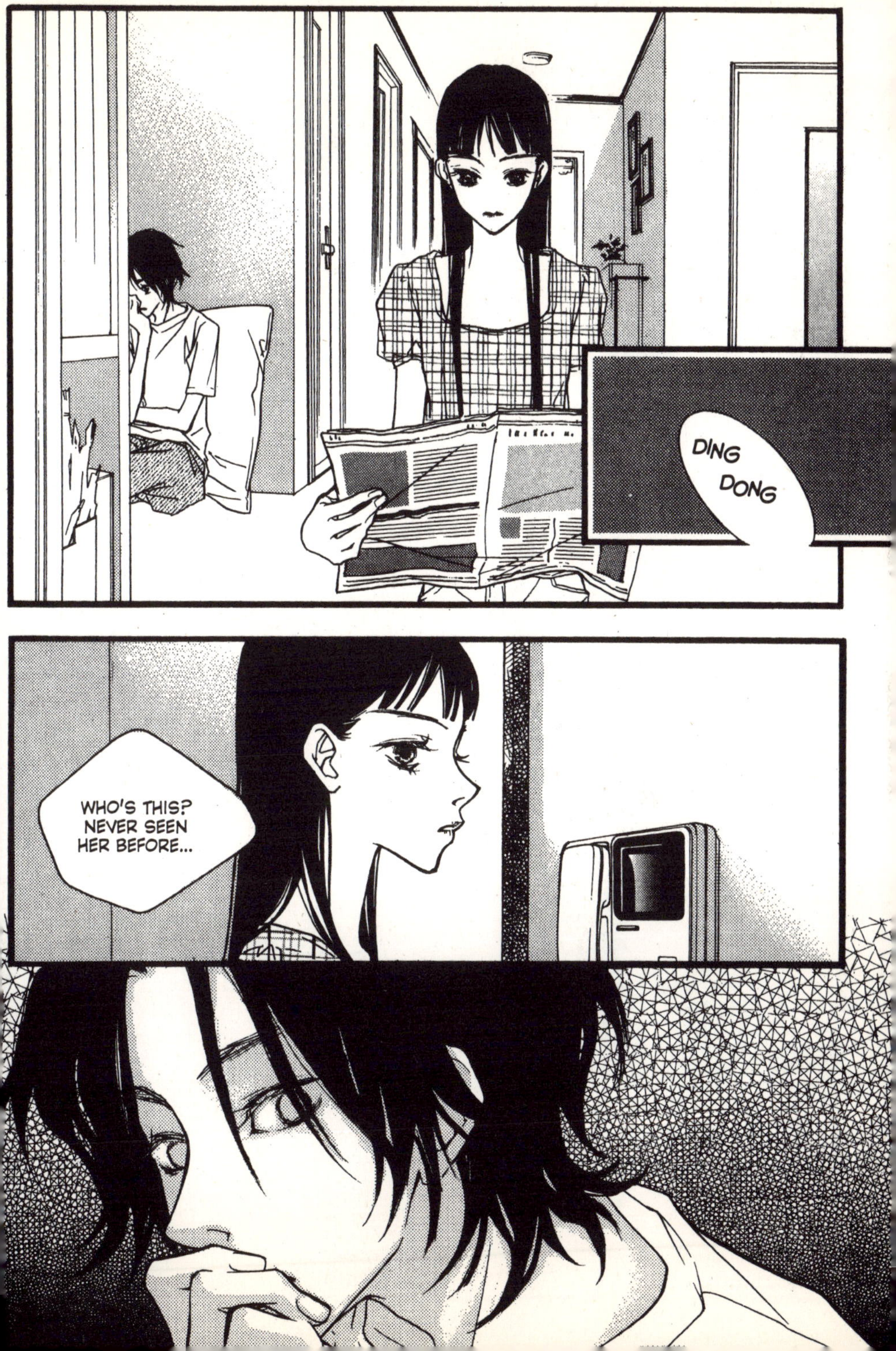
DING DONG
WHO'S THIS? NEVER SEEN HER BEFORE...

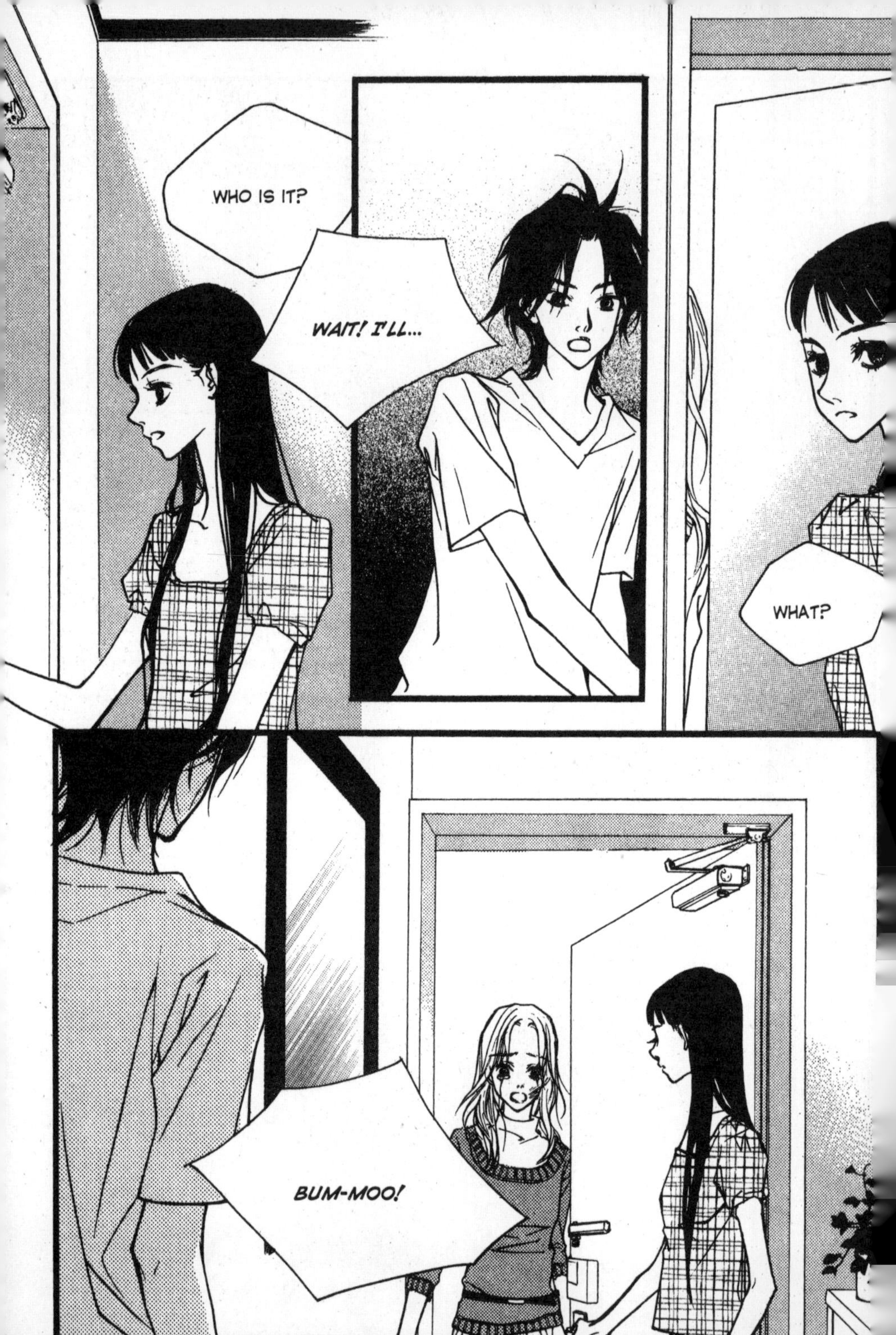
WHAT?
WAIT! I'LL...
WHO IS IT?
BUM-MOO!

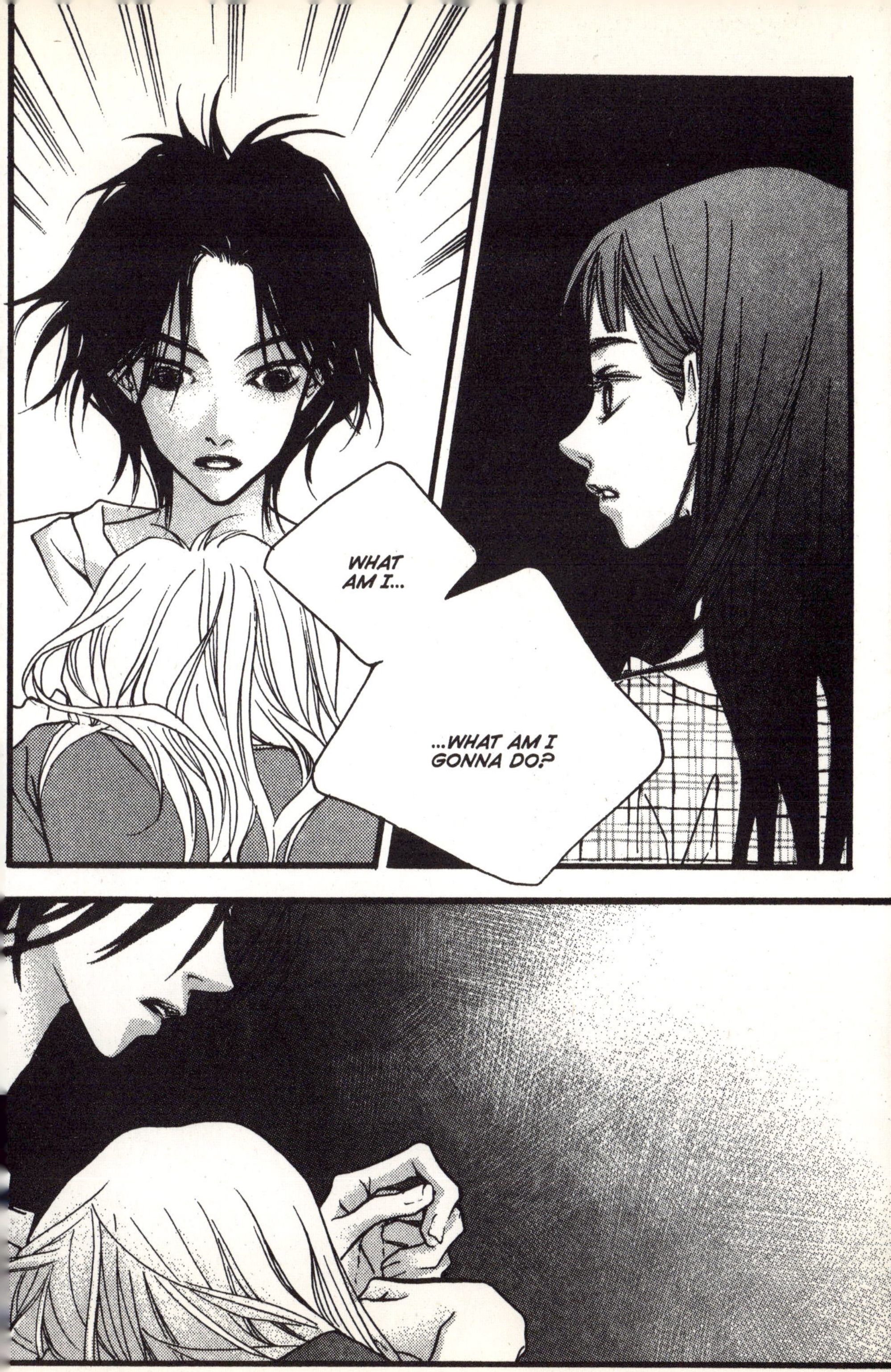
WHAT AM I...
...WHAT AM I GONNA DO?

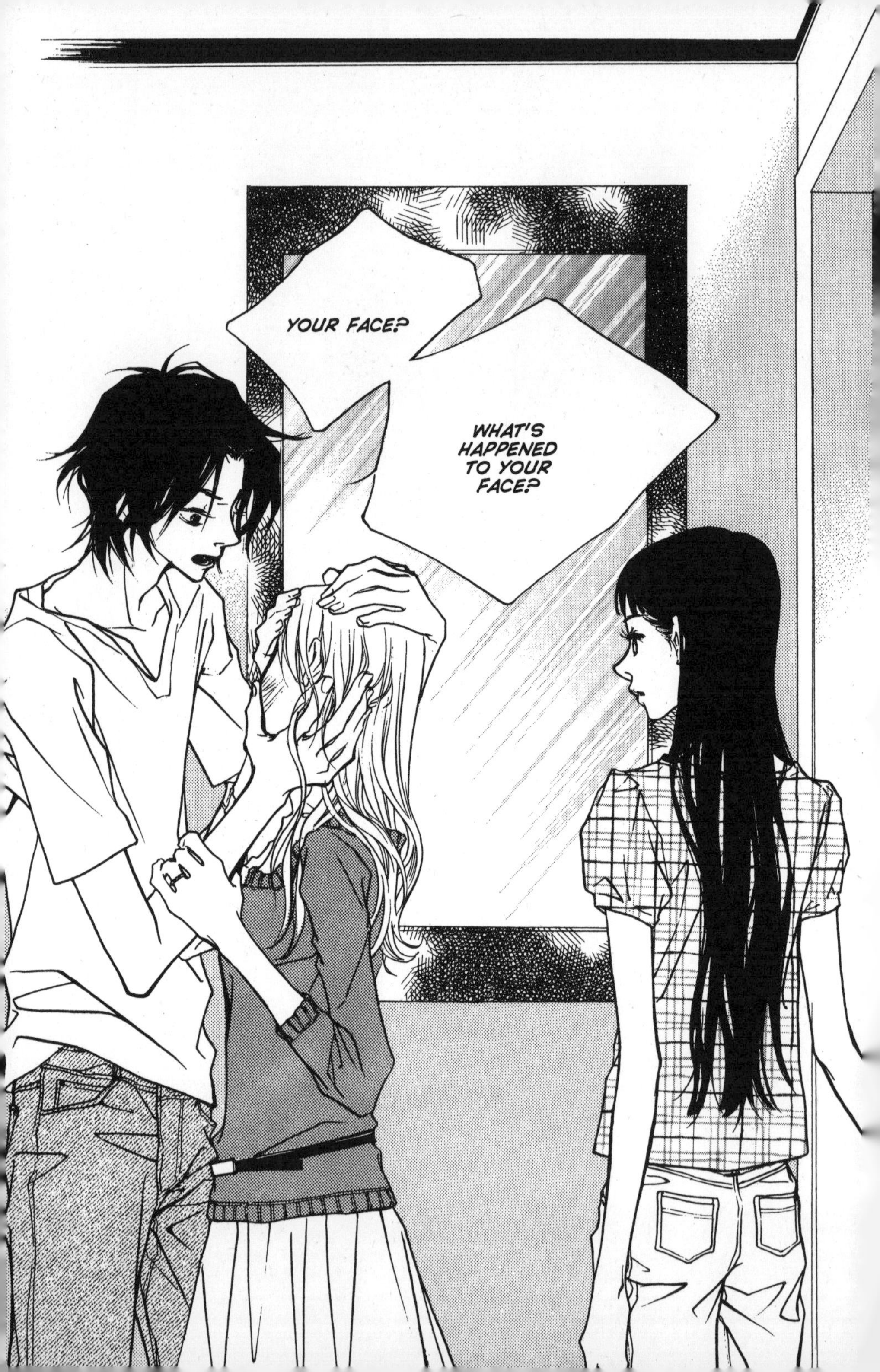
YOUR FACE?
WHAT'S HAPPENED TO YOUR FACE?

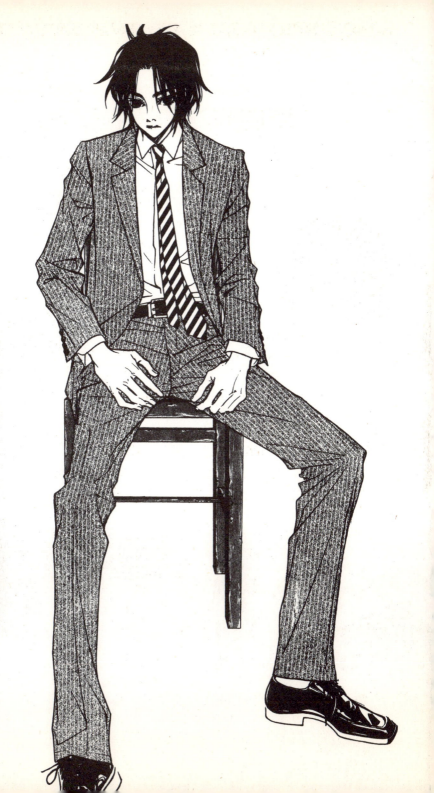

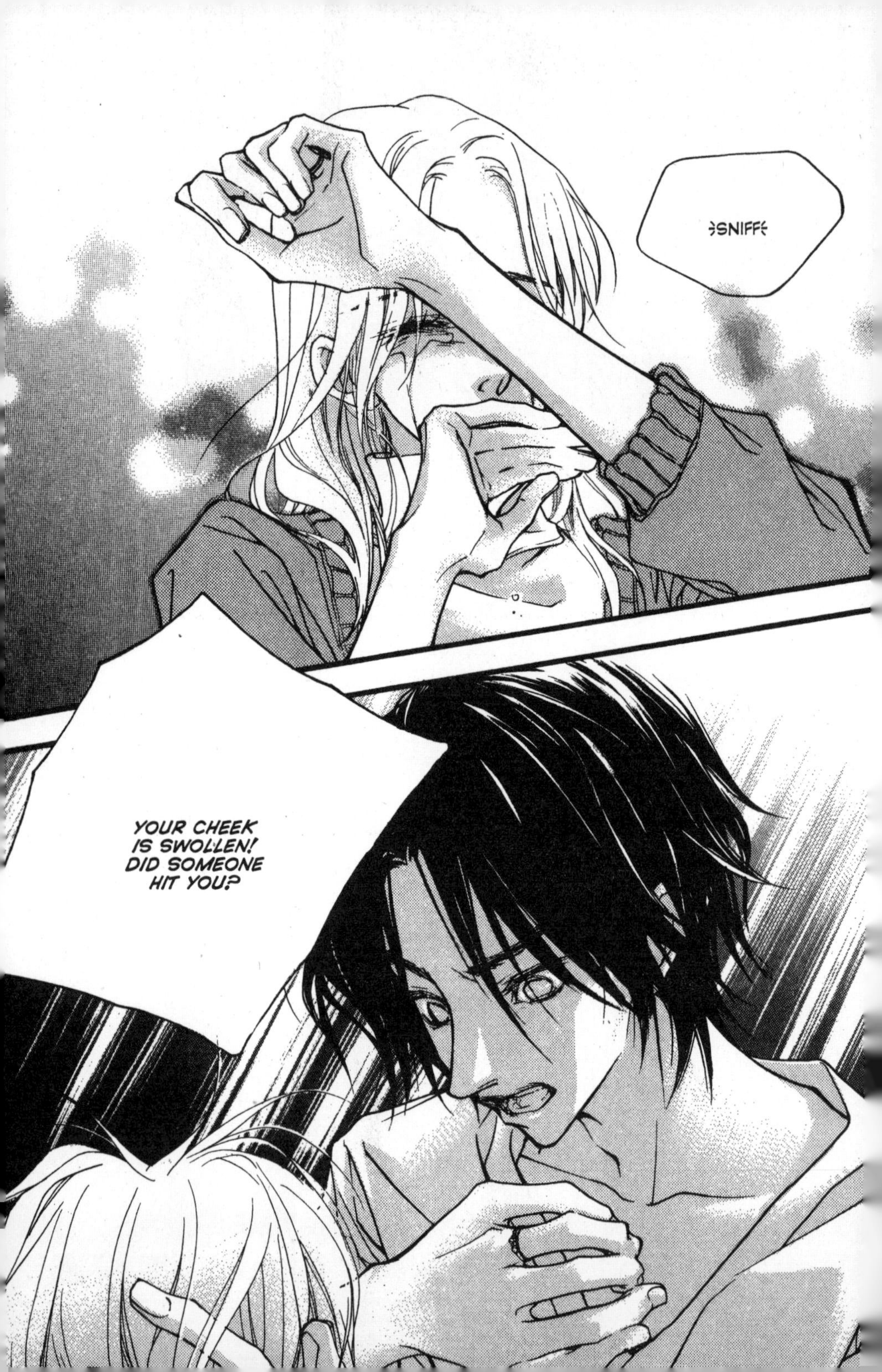

SNIFF
YOUR CHEEK IS SWOLLEN! DID SOMEONE HIT YOU?

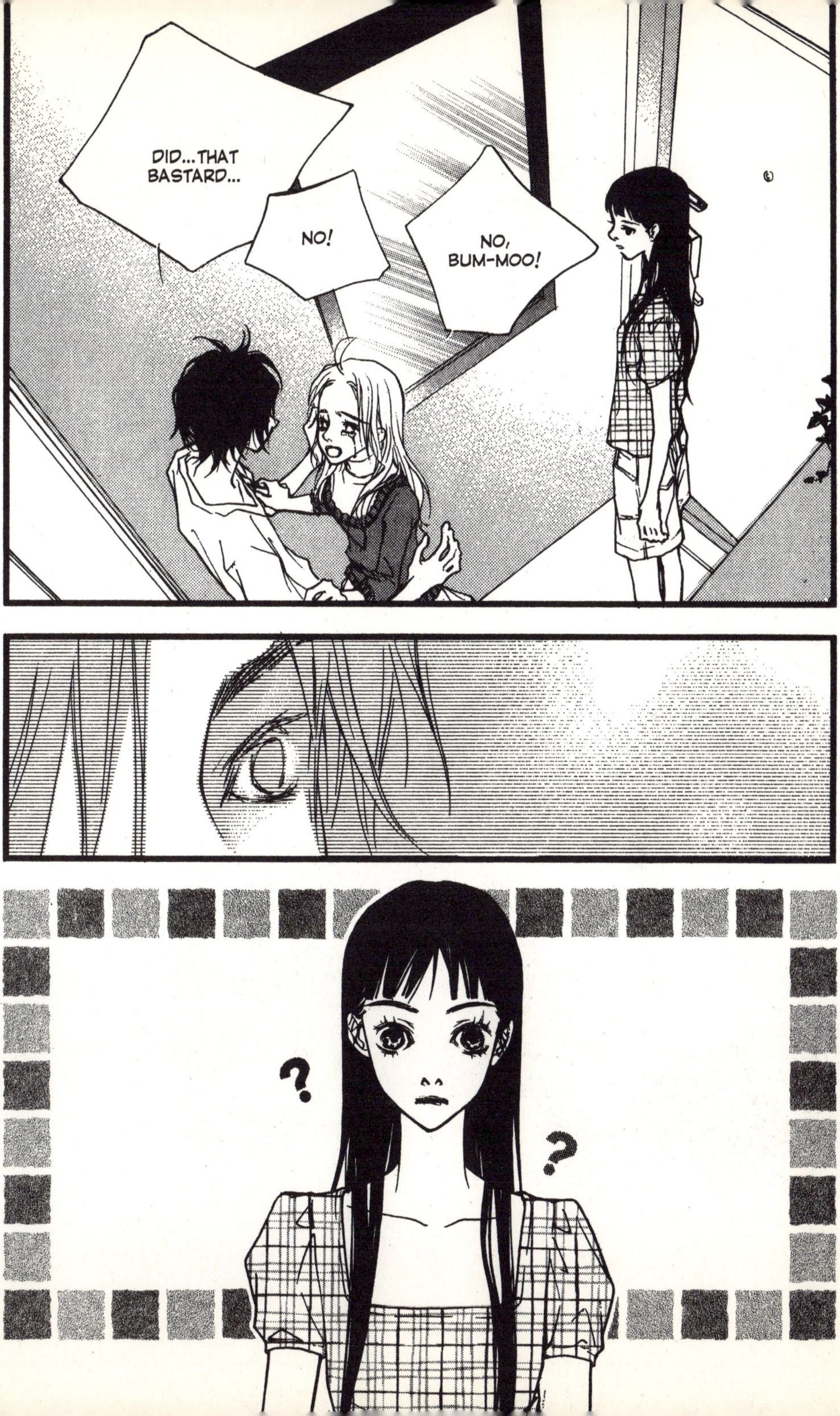
DID...THAT BASTARD...
NO!
NO, BUM-MOO!
?
?

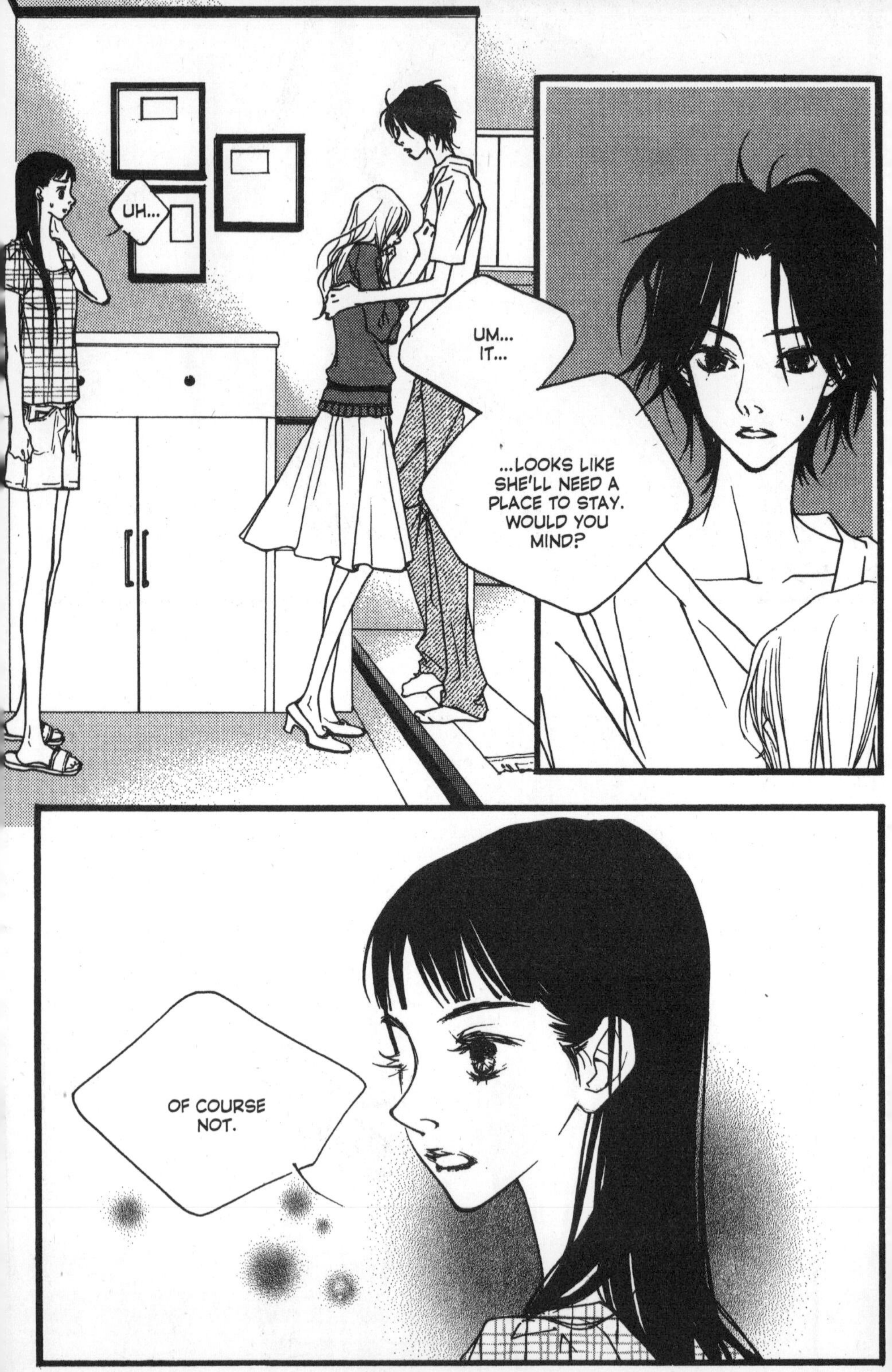
UH...
UM... IT...
...LOOKS LIKE SHE'LL NEED A PLACE TO STAY. WOULD YOU MIND?
OF COURSE NOT.

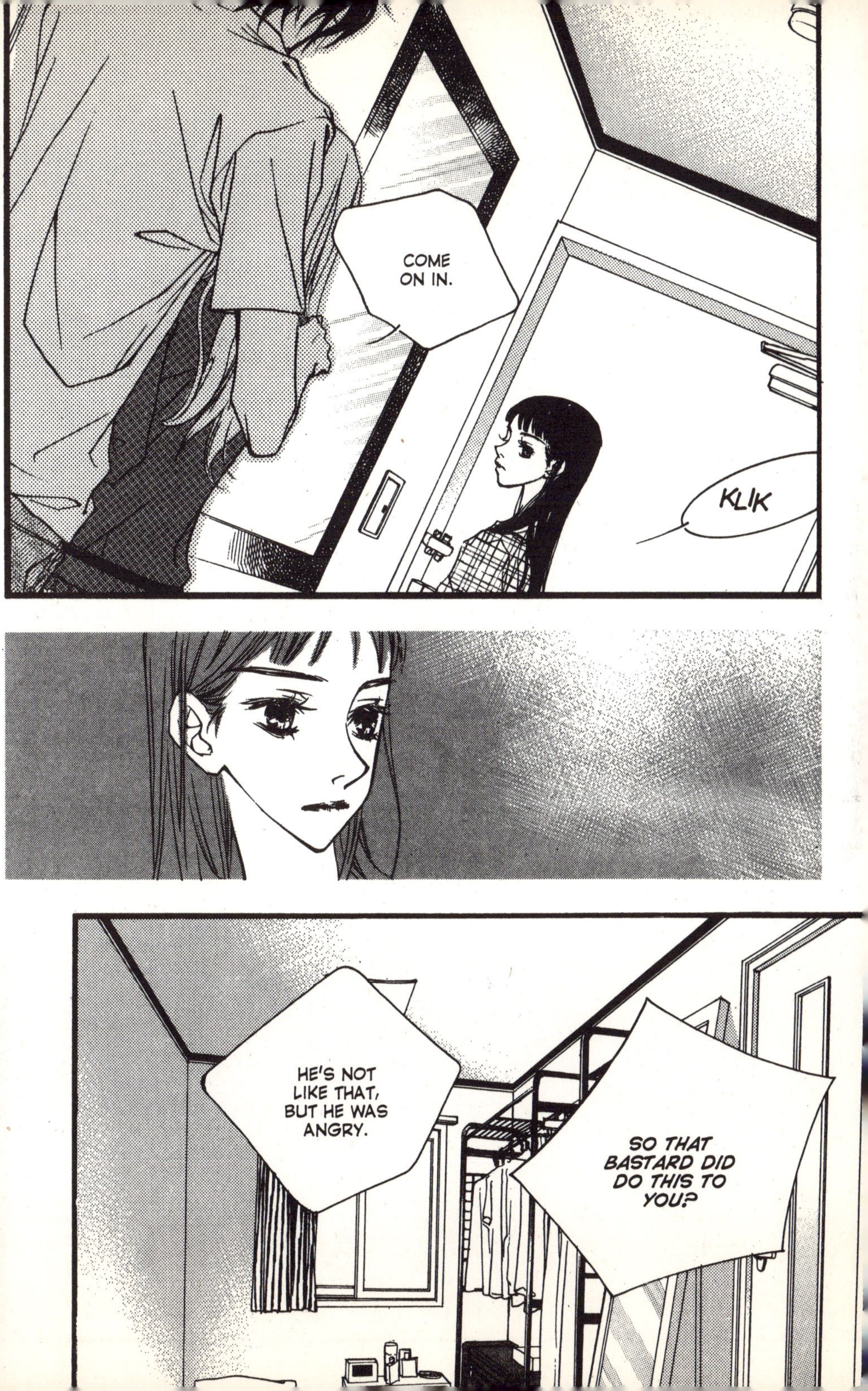
COME ON IN.
KLIK
HE'S NOT LIKE THAT, BUT HE WAS ANGRY.
SO THAT BASTARD DID DO THIS TO YOU?

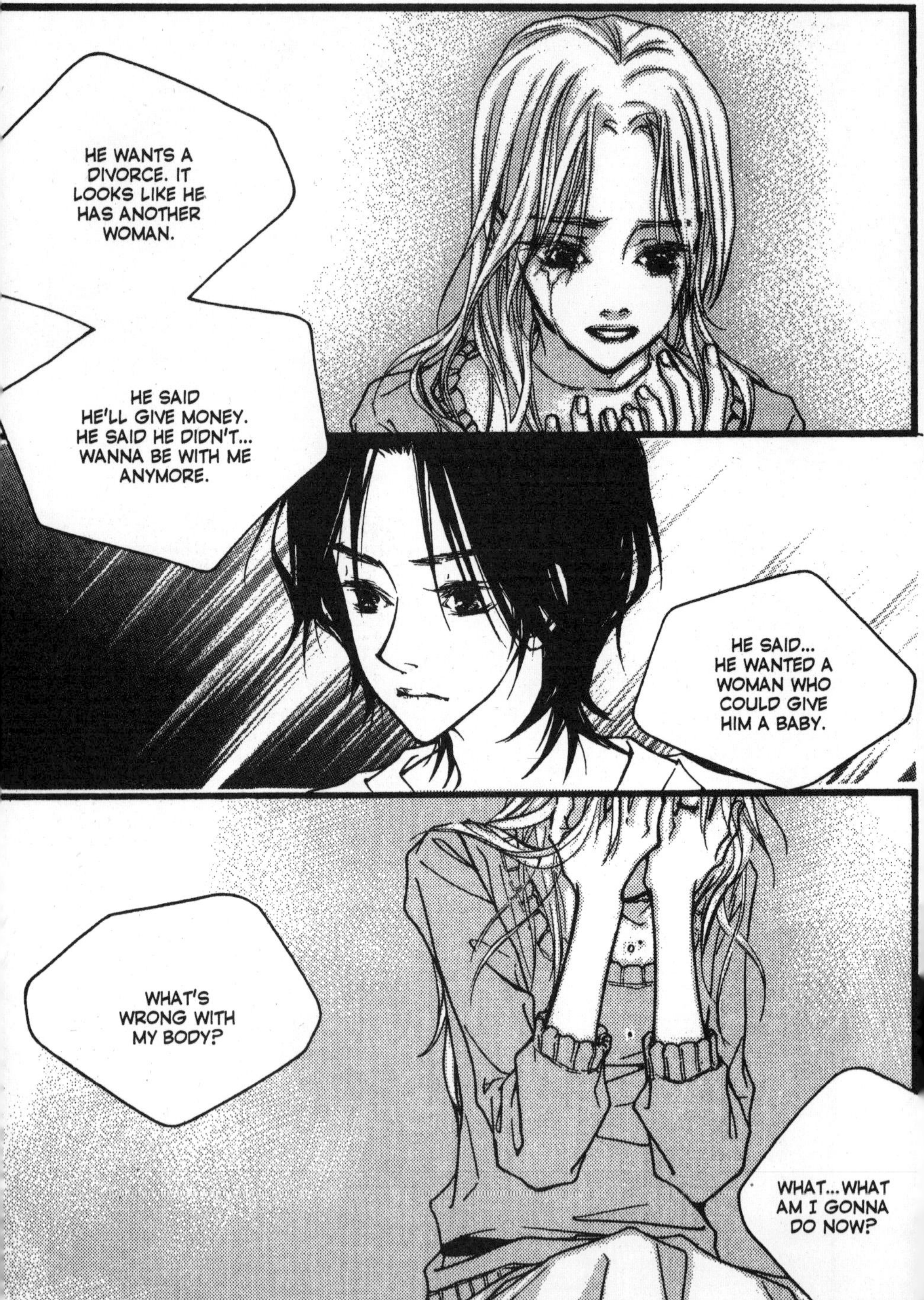
HE WANTS A DIVORCE. IT LOOKS LIKE HE HAS ANOTHER WOMAN.
HE SAID HE'LL GIVE MONEY. HE SAID HE DIDN'T... WANNA BE WITH ME ANYMORE.
HE SAID... HE WANTED A WOMAN WHO COULD GIVE HIM A BABY.
WHAT'S WRONG WITH MY BODY?
WHAT...WHAT AM I GONNA DO NOW?

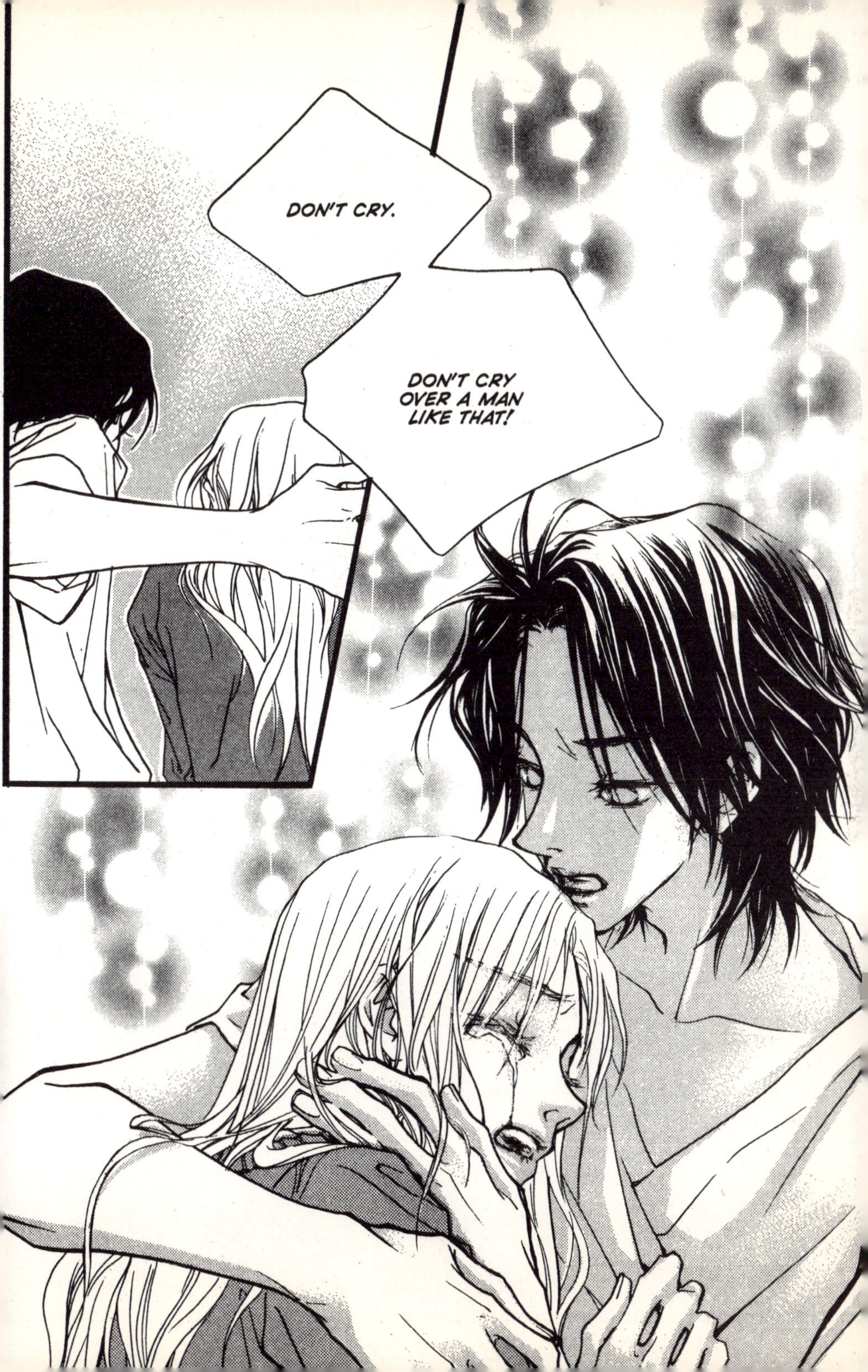
DON'T CRY.
DON'T CRY OVER A MAN LIKE THAT!

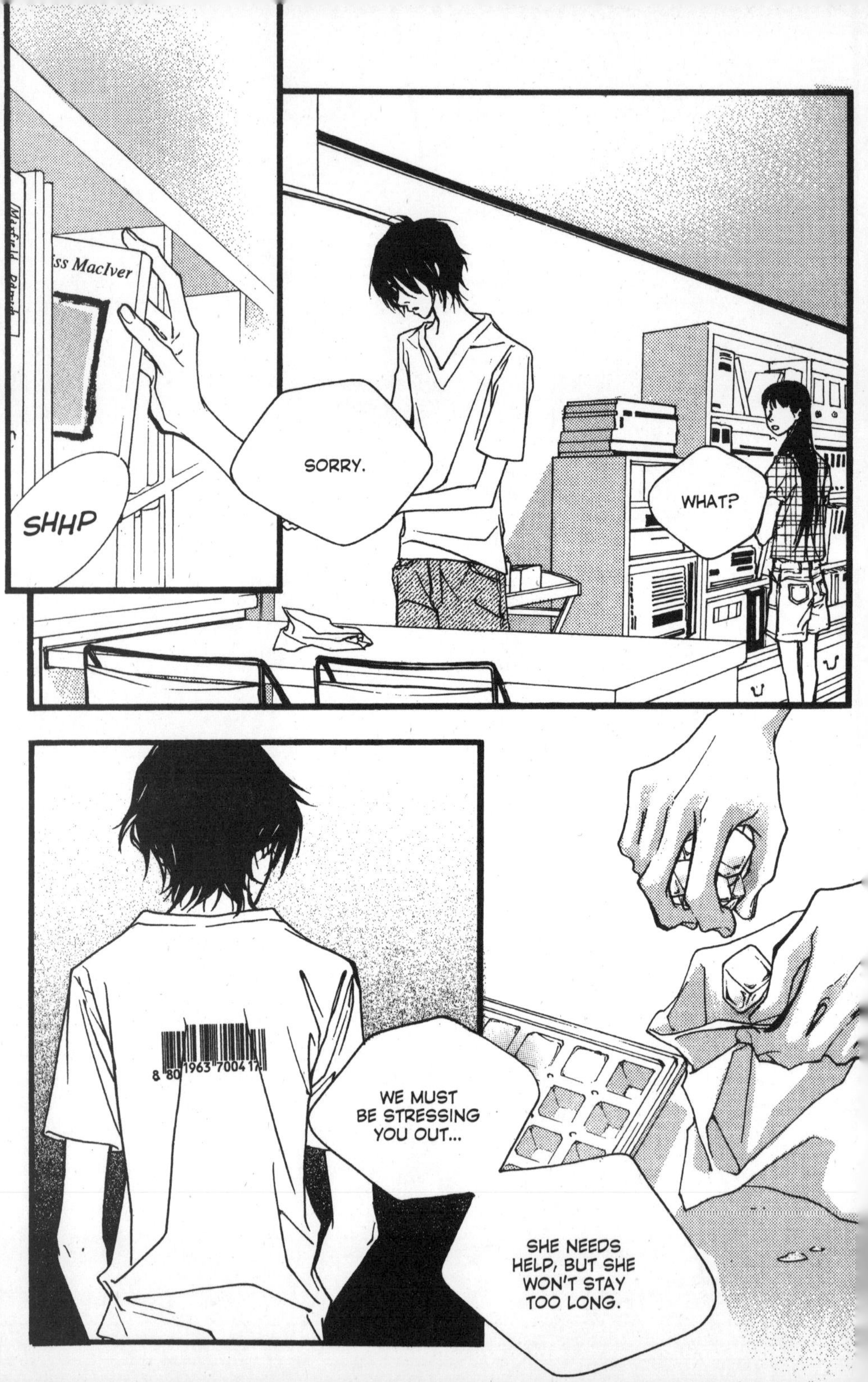
iss MacIver
SHHP
SORRY.
WHAT?
WE MUST BE STRESSING YOU OUT...
SHE NEEDS HELP, BUT SHE WON'T STAY TOO LONG.

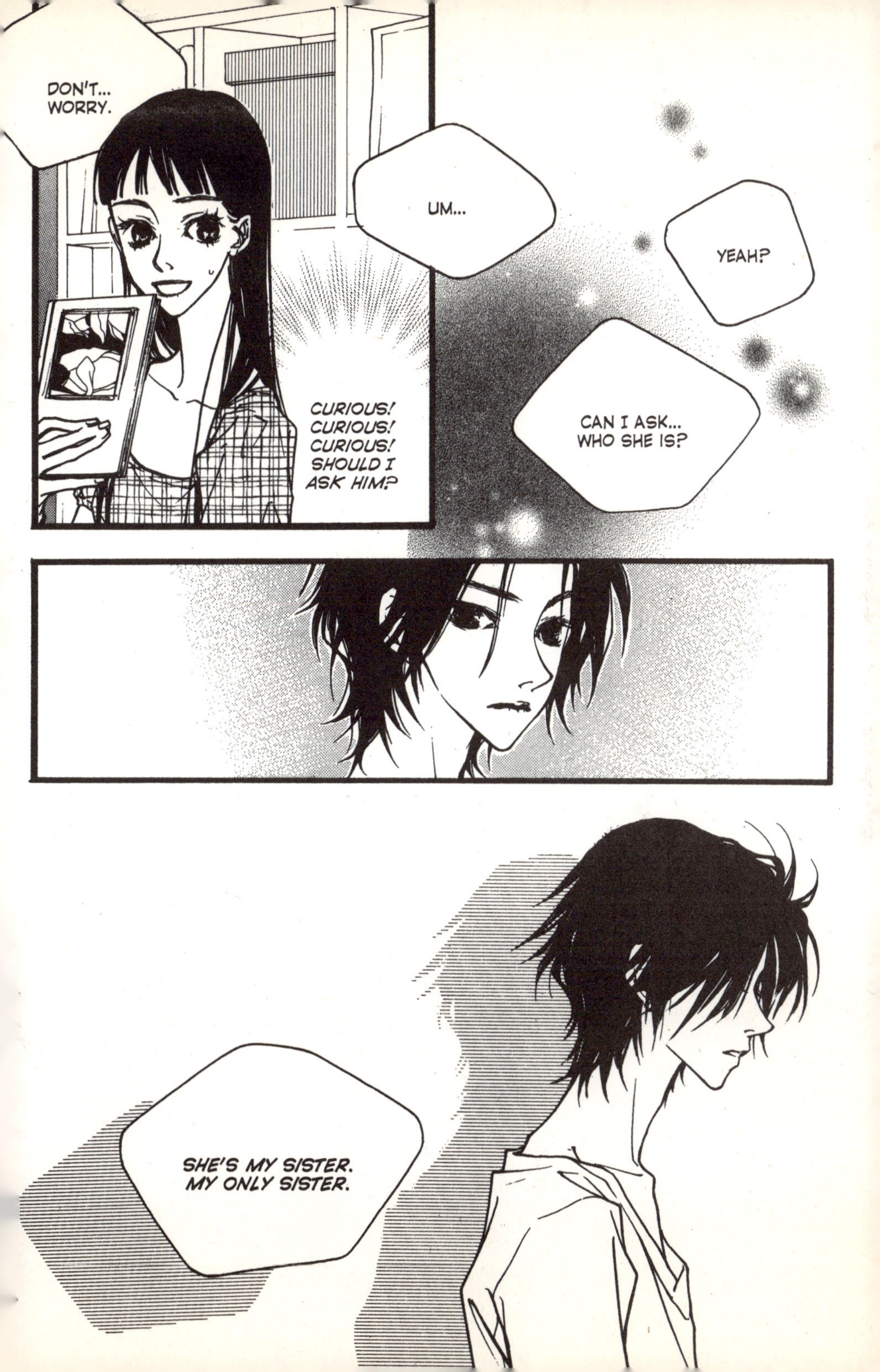
DON'T... WORRY.
UM...
YEAH?
CURIOUS! CURIOUS! CURIOUS! SHOULD I ASK HIM?
CAN I ASK... WHO SHE IS?
SHE'S MY SISTER. MY ONLY SISTER.

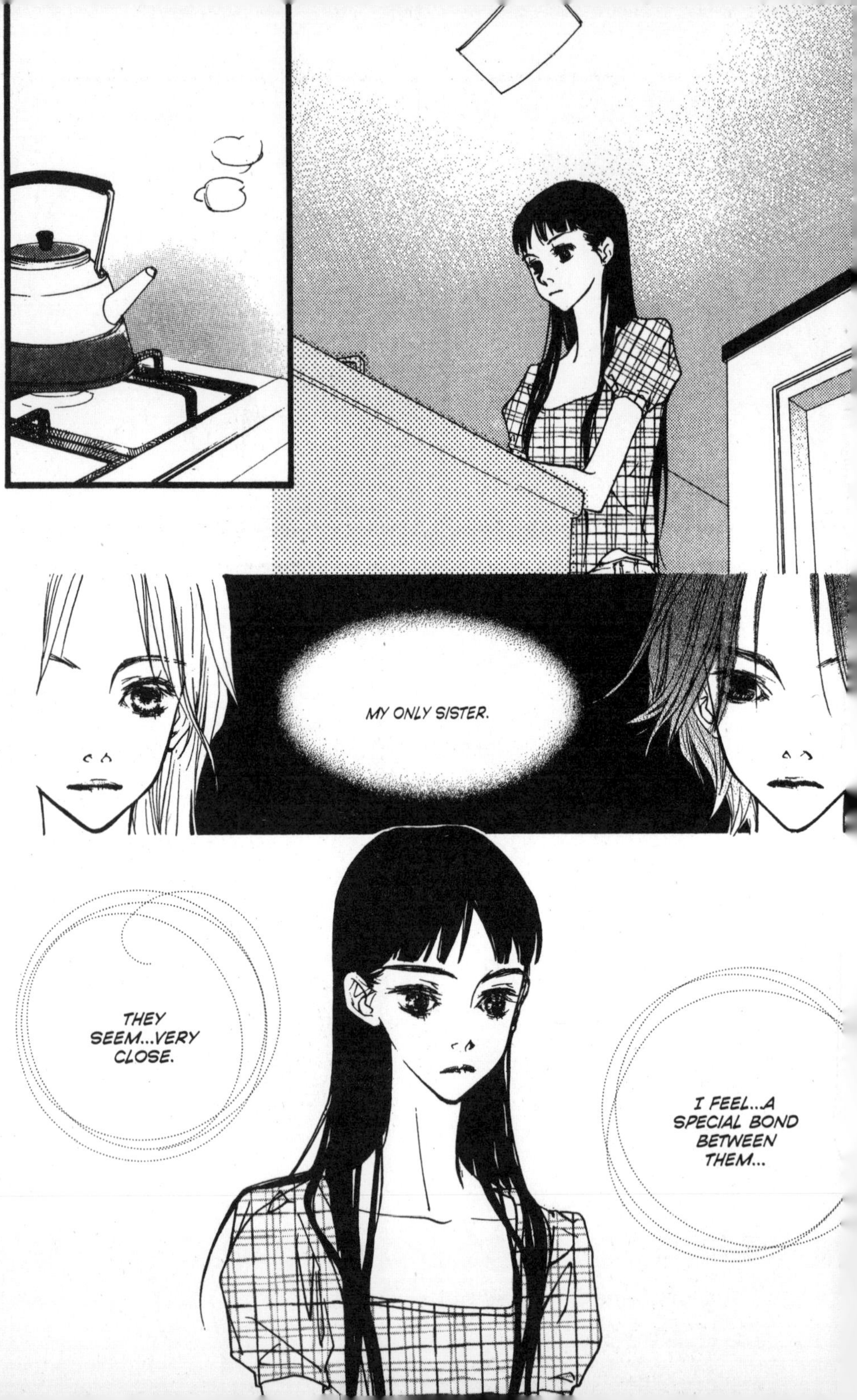
MY ONLY SISTER.
I FEEL...A SPECIAL BOND BETWEEN THEM...
THEY SEEM...VERY CLOSE.

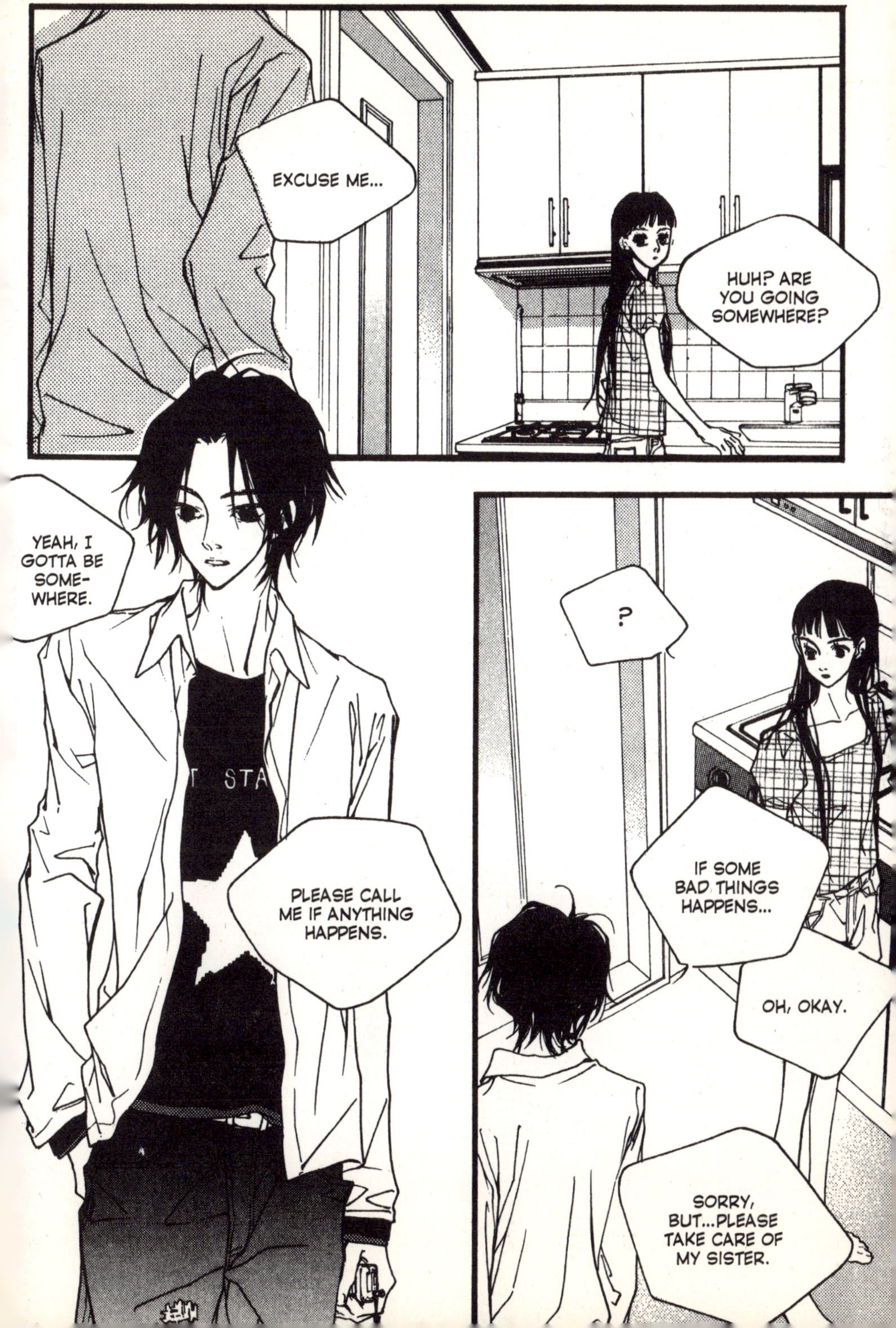
EXCUSE ME...
HUH? ARE YOU GOING SOMEWHERE?
YEAH, I GOTTA BE SOME-WHERE.
PLEASE CALL ME IF ANYTHING HAPPENS.
?
IF SOME BAD THINGS HAPPENS...
OH, OKAY.
SORRY, BUT...PLEASE TAKE CARE OF MY SISTER.

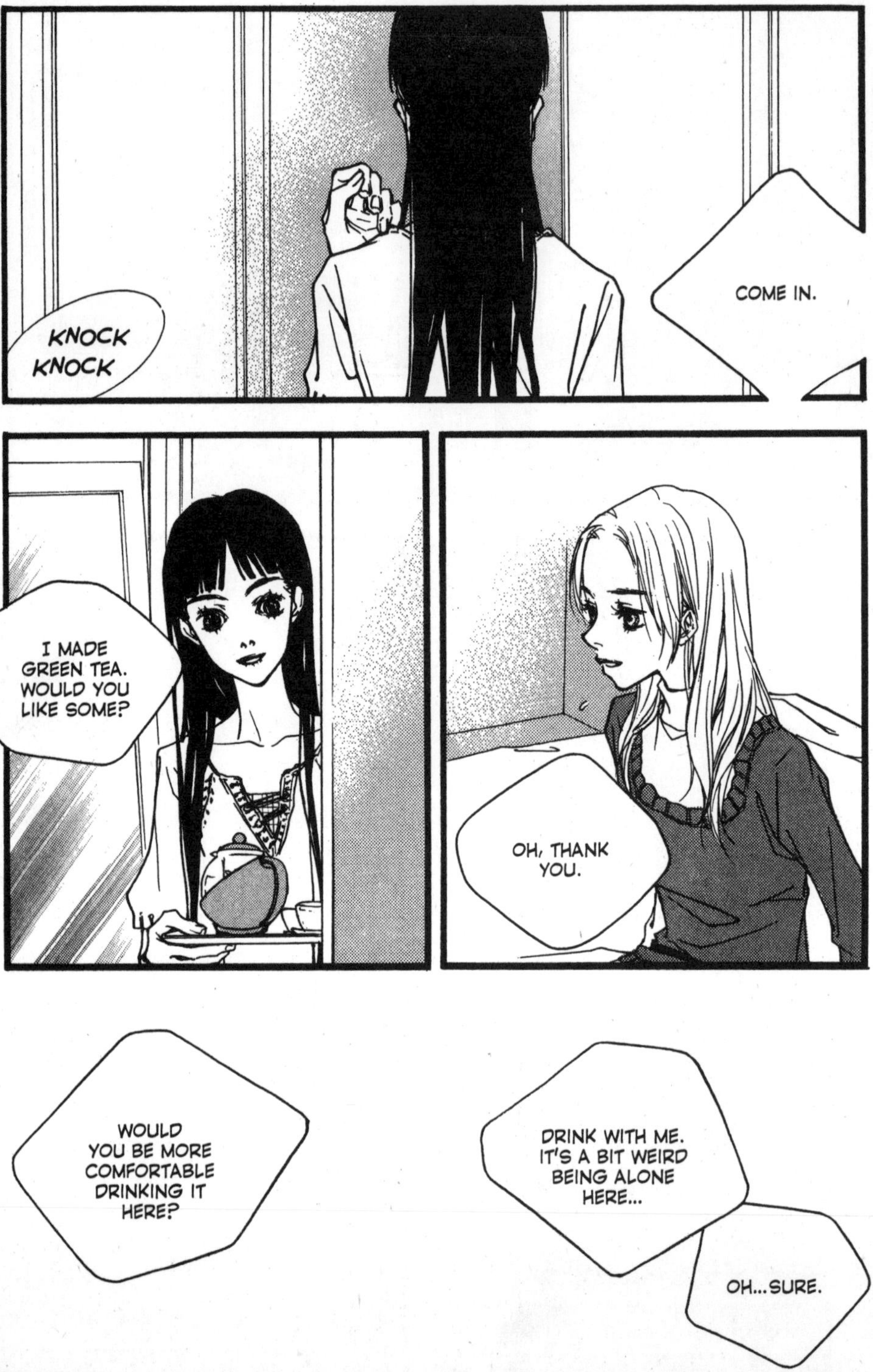
KNOCK KNOCK
COME IN.
I MADE GREEN TEA. WOULD YOU LIKE SOME?
OH, THANK YOU.
WOULD YOU BE MORE COMFORTABLE DRINKING IT HERE?
DRINK WITH ME. IT'S A BIT WEIRD BEING ALONE HERE...
OH...SURE.

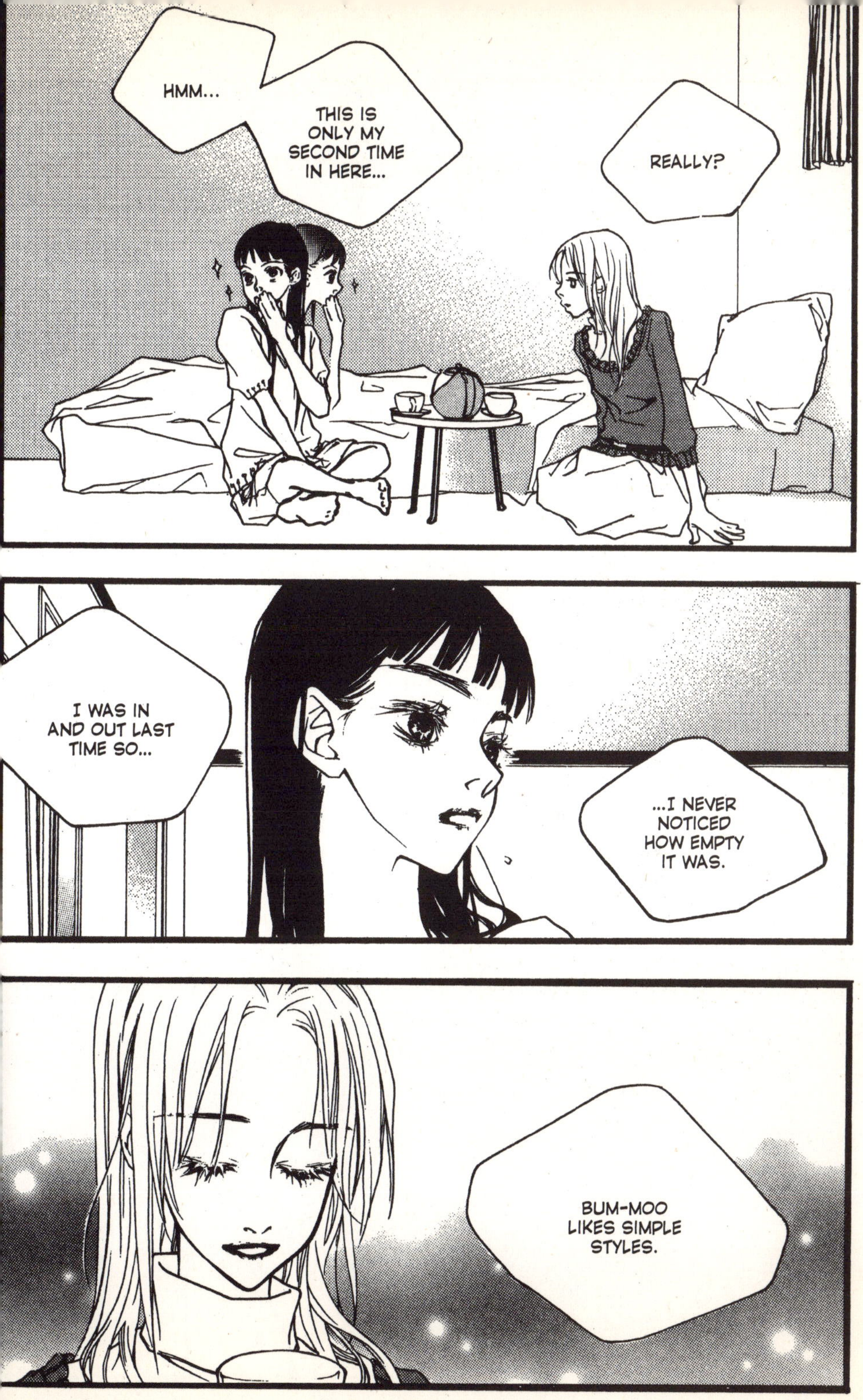
HMM...
THIS IS ONLY MY SECOND TIME IN HERE...
REALLY?
I WAS IN AND OUT LAST TIME SO...
...I NEVER NOTICED HOW EMPTY IT WAS.
BUM-MOO LIKES SIMPLE STYLES.

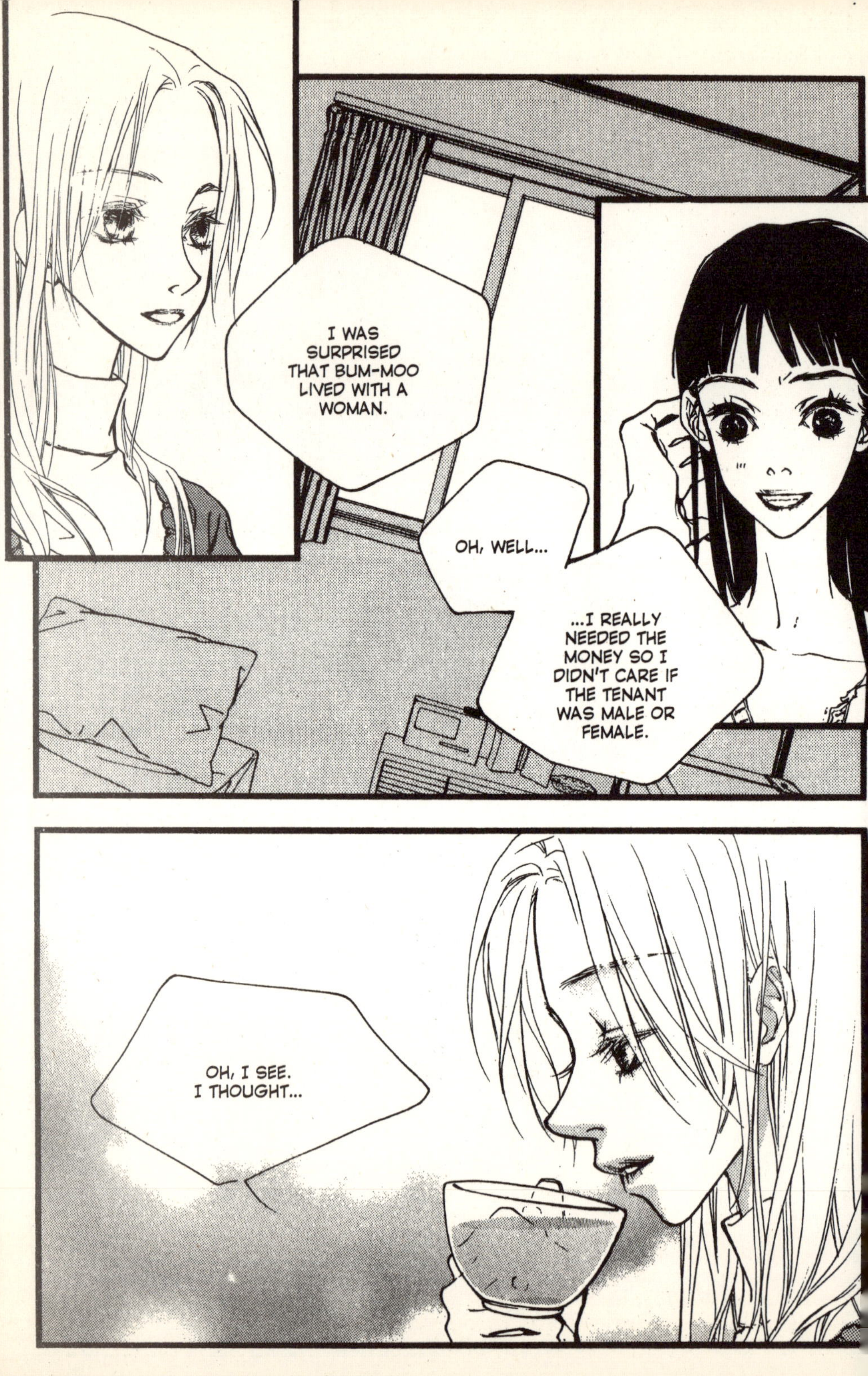
I WAS SURPRISED THAT BUM-MOO LIVED WITH A WOMAN.
OH, WELL...
...I REALLY NEEDED THE MONEY SO I DIDN'T CARE IF THE TENANT WAS MALE OR FEMALE.
OH, I SEE. I THOUGHT...

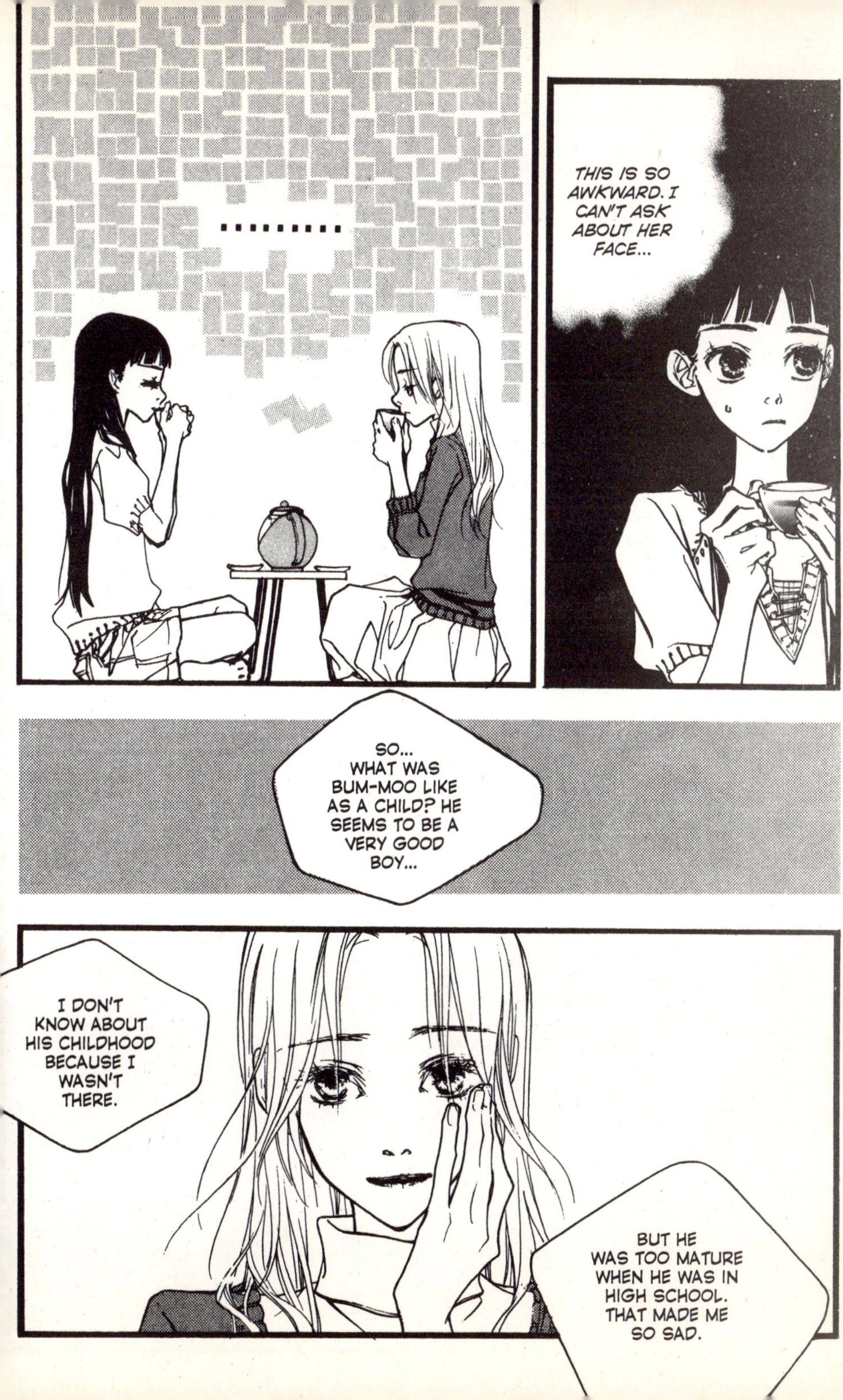
....
THIS IS SO AWKWARD. I CAN'T ASK ABOUT HER FACE...
SO... WHAT WAS BUM-MOO LIKE AS A CHILD? HE SEEMS TO BE A VERY GOOD BOY...
I DON'T KNOW ABOUT HIS CHILDHOOD BECAUSE I WASN'T THERE.
BUT HE WAS TOO MATURE WHEN HE WAS IN HIGH SCHOOL. THAT MADE ME SO SAD.

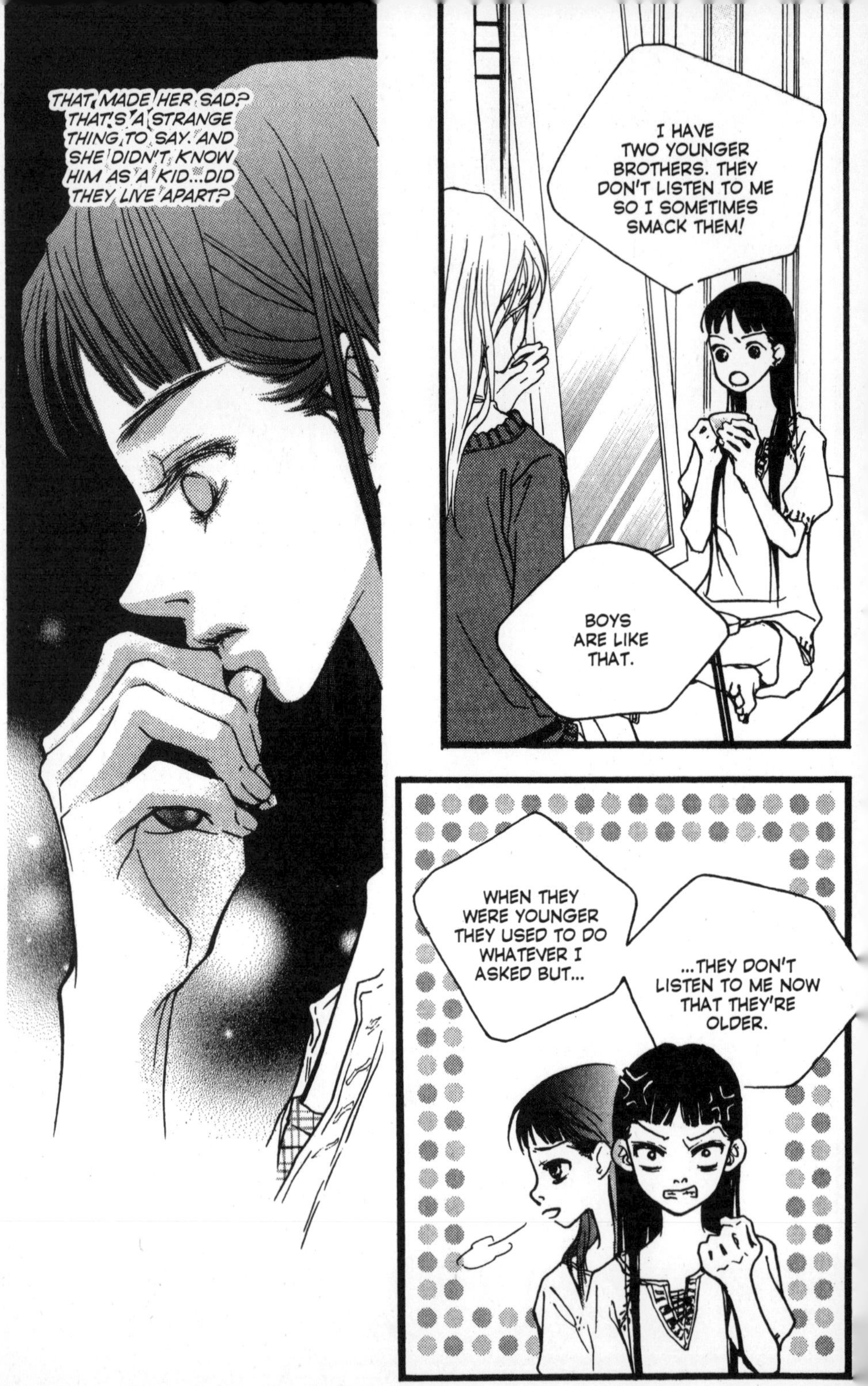
I HAVE TWO YOUNGER BROTHERS. THEY DON'T LISTEN TO ME SO I SOMETIMES SMACK THEM!
BOYS ARE LIKE THAT.
WHEN THEY WERE YOUNGER THEY USED TO DO WHATEVER I ASKED BUT...
...THEY DON'T LISTEN TO ME NOW THAT THEY'RE OLDER.
THAT MADE HER SAD? THAT'S A STRANGE THING TO SAY. AND SHE DIDN'T KNOW HIM AS A KID...DID THEY LIVE APART?

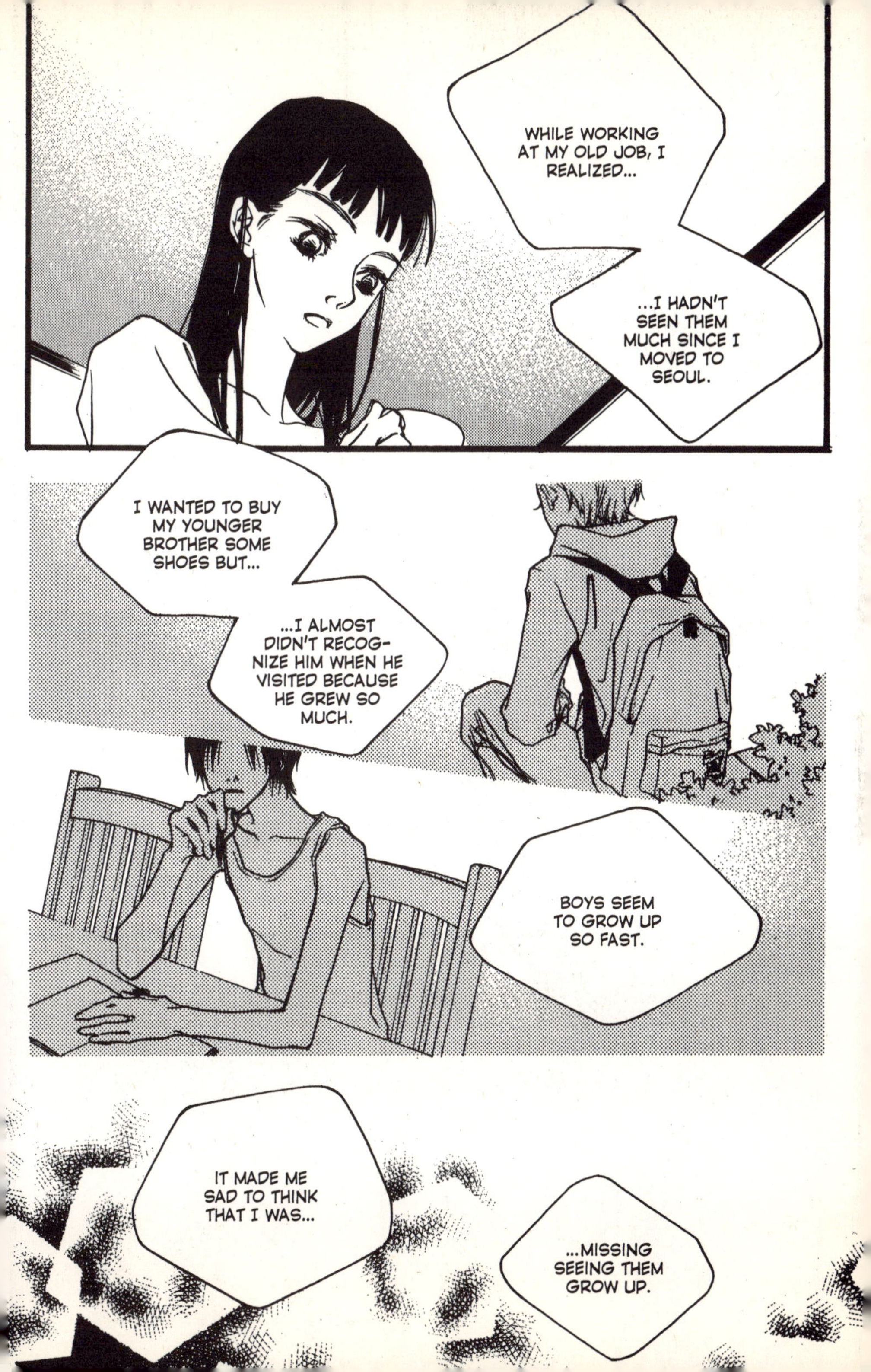
WHILE WORKING AT MY OLD JOB, I REALIZED...
...I HADN'T SEEN THEM MUCH SINCE I MOVED TO SEOUL.
I WANTED TO BUY MY YOUNGER BROTHER SOME SHOES BUT...
...I ALMOST DIDN'T RECOG-NIZE HIM WHEN HE VISITED BECAUSE HE GREW SO MUCH.
BOYS SEEM TO GROW UP SO FAST.
IT MADE ME SAD TO THINK THAT I WAS...
...MISSING SEEING THEM GROW UP.

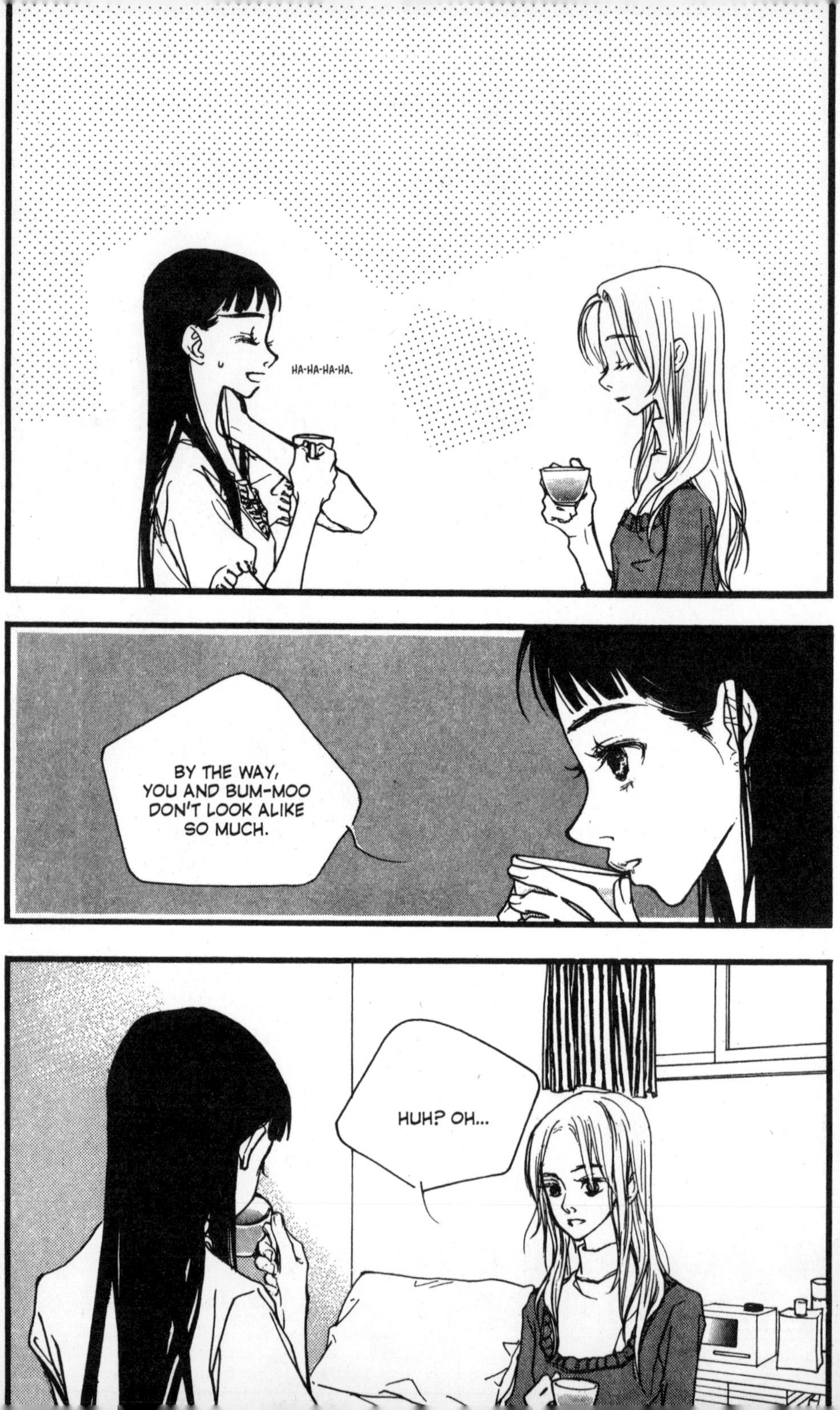
HA-HA-HA-HA.
BY THE WAY, YOU AND BUM-MOO DON'T LOOK ALIKE SO MUCH.
HUH? OH...

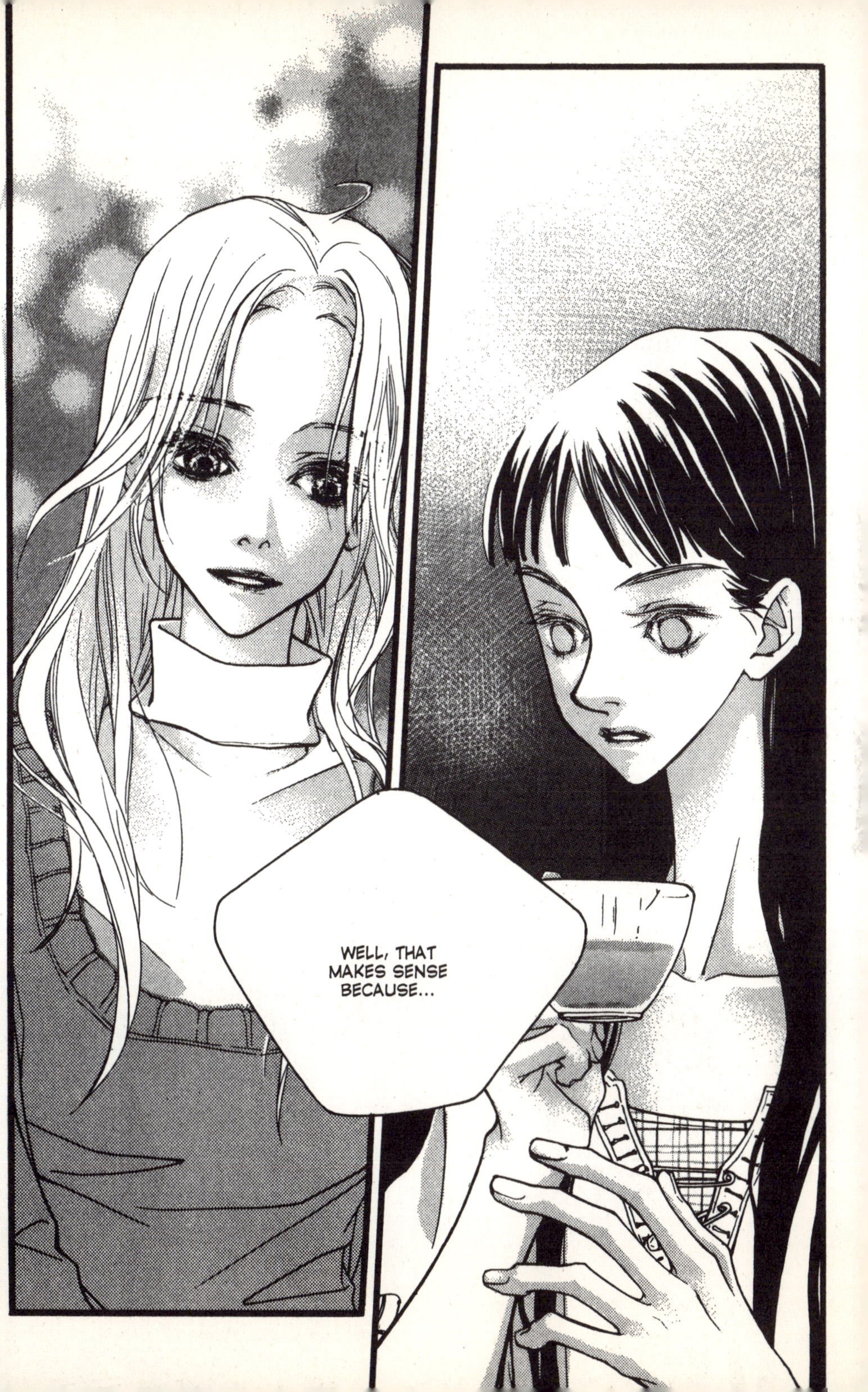
WELL, THAT MAKES SENSE BECAUSE...

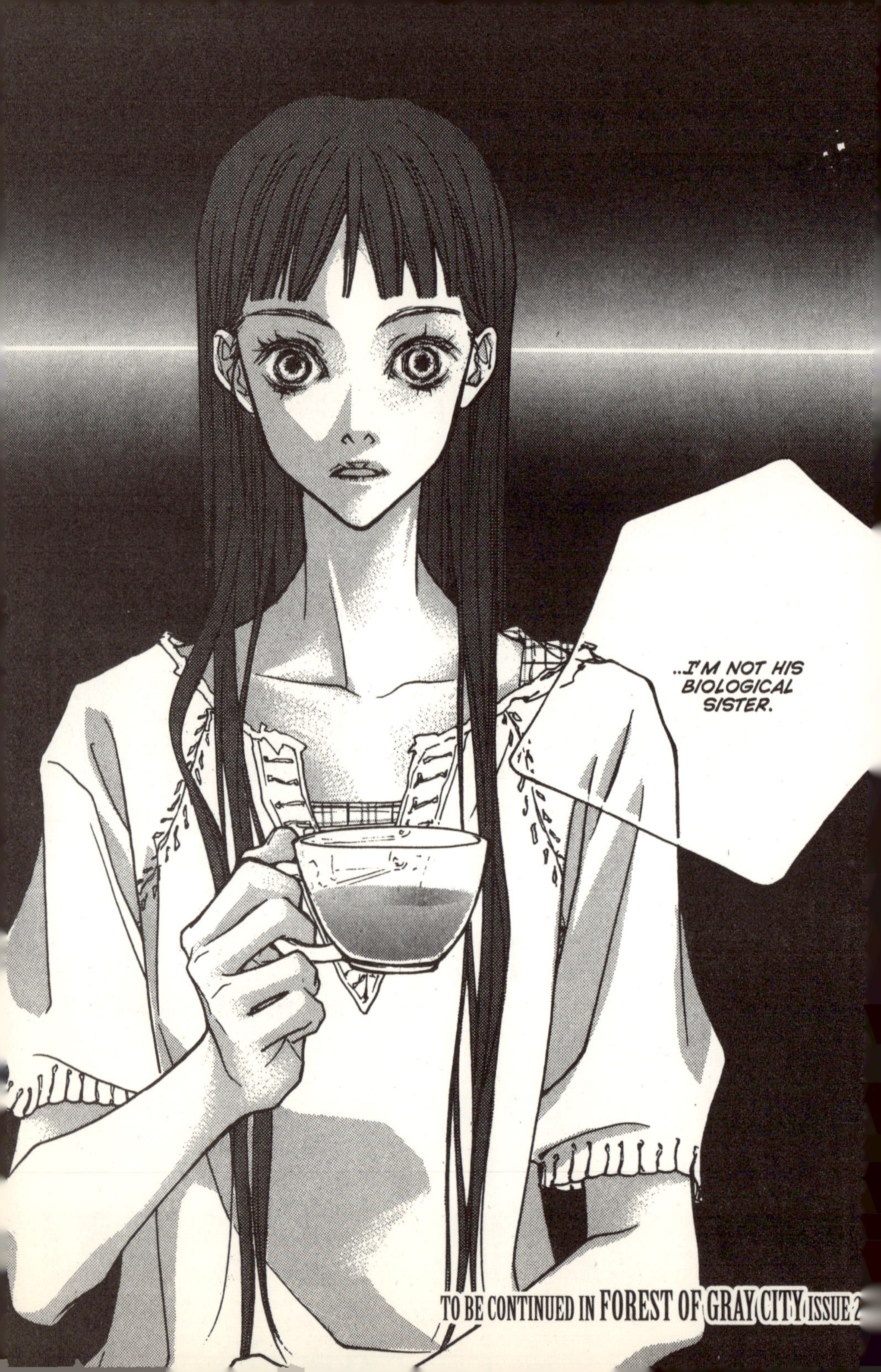
...I'M NOT HIS BIOLOGICAL SISTER.
TO BE CONTINUED IN FOREST OF GRAY CITY ISSUE 2

SPECIAL
THANKS TO...

GOD, MY FAMILY, SE-RA, EUN-MI, AND
EVERYONE WHO HELPED ME GET THIS
BOOK PUBLISHED. THANK YOU SO MUCH
TO ALL THE FANS ENJOYING THIS BOOK.
HA-HA...I ALSO HAVE TO THANK THE
EDITORS I GAVE SUCH A HARD TIME.
LASTLY, I SEND A SPECIAL SMILE OUT
TO GYO-JOO-NIM AND SOOK EVEN
THOUGH THEY MIGHT REJECT IT.

Danbi Original

Forest of Gray City vol.1

Story and art by JungHyun Uhm

Translation HyeYoung Im
English Adaptation J. Torres
Touch-up and Lettering Terri Delgado · Marshall Dillon
Graphic Design EunKyung Kim

ICE Kunion

English Adaptation Editor HyeYoung Im · J. Torres
Managing Editor Marshall Dillon
Assistant Editor SoYeon Kim
Senior Editor JuYoun Lee
Editorial Director DongEun Lee
Managing Director Jackie Lee
Publisher and C.E.O. JaeKook Chun

Forest of Gray City © 2007 JungHyun Uhm
First published in Korea in 2005 by SEOUL CULTURAL PUBLISHERS, Inc.
English text translation rights arranged by SEOUL CULTURAL PUBLISHERS, Inc.
English text © 2007 ICE KUNION

Published by ICE Kunion.
SIGONGSA 2F Yeil Bldg. 1619-4, Seocho-dong, Seocho-gu, Seoul, 137-878, Korea

ISBN : 978-89-527-4623-8

First printing, January 2007
10 9 8 7 6 5 4 3 2 1
Printed in Canada

www.icekunion.com/www.koreanmanhwa.com